Acts of Theft

Acts
of
Theft

Arthur A. Cohen

The University of Chicago Press
Chicago and London

Acts of Theft was originally published as "A Helen and Kurt Wolff Book" by Harcourt Brace Jovanovich.

The University of Chicago Press, Chicago 60637
The University of Chicago Press, Ltd., London

97 96 95 94 93 92 91 90 89 88   5 4 3 2 1

Library of Congress Cataloging in Publication Data

Cohen, Arthur Allen, 1928–
    Acts of theft / Arthur A. Cohen.

    p.   cm.   —   (Phoenix fiction)
    I. Title.   II. Series.
    [PS3553.0418A65   1988]   87-26365
    813′.54—dc19   CIP
    ISBN 0-226-11250-0 (pbk.)

FOR

Tamar Judith Cohen

MAXIMS OF CONSTANTIN BRANCUSI

"Direct carving is the true road to sculpture, but also the most dangerous for those who don't know how to walk."

"Don't look for obscure formulas or mysteries. I give you pure joy. Look at the sculptures until you see them. Those nearest to God have seen them."

"Simplicity is not an end in art, but one arrives at simplicity in spite of oneself, in approaching the real sense of things. Simplicity is complexity itself and one has to be nourished by its essence in order to understand its value."

"There is an aim in all things. In order to attain it one must be detached from oneself."

"Create like a God. Command like a King. Work like a slave."

"Nothing grows in the shadow of big trees."

"Fame mocks us when we pursue her. But when we turn our back on her, then she pursues us."

"I am no longer in this world, no longer attached to my person; I am distant from myself, among essential things."

Acts of Theft

Prologue:
Mauger's Theft

A century, perhaps more. Perhaps four centuries, or longer even, the island was lost or rather, more accurately, when seen from the beach, it was construed as a hump in the waves, or mistaken by the uninformed for a giant fish or a tremor in the distant seascape, particularly when heat, cascading from radiant blue-white skies, blurred the unshielded eyes of bathers and fishermen staring into the green waters of the Gulf.

The island was lost—dropped from sight and memory—for not less than four centuries. Once a cenobite shared his hermitage with the island's crawling things, but that was all briefly. A year, more, who knows? He died unrecorded. Lost like the island, he was rediscovered by fishermen, a skeleton with cross and scapular, miraculously intact but moldy with moss. The island was otherwise uninhabited for these several centuries, except for the dead.

It was lost and forgotten, this bit of two-mile island, until fishermen rediscovered it and, in the mood of a different

3

century, what had been buried with their skeletons (legs broken and drawn up to conserve space), the ceramic effigies glazed blue, rose, yellow, came to be prized, and like tombs in other times and civilizations, the skeletons were left behind, despoiled like fallen soldiers, and the armor of their death, the effigies (by means of which their introductions to the gods of the underworld were made), turned up and were sold in the bars of principal towns in Yucatan, Tabasco, and Campeche. These effigies brought as much as a hundred pesos, more than a day's catch of shrimp and tuna. It is no wonder the fishermen scavenged the island's shallows for figurines.

All this, however, was three decades ago, perhaps four, but not longer. It is different now.

Shortly after the hour of six o'clock, the motor launch left the secluded beach four kilometers beyond the Lerma and moved into the west, pushing back the unresisting darkness from a gentle sea. The old launch, freshly painted with naval gray, was commanded by a middle-aged officer in crumpled uniform. He seemed nervous, guiding the vessel with one hand on the wheel while the other slapped against his thigh in time to a softly hummed melody. Behind him, seated on benches along the gunwales, six soldiers smoked and talked quietly, their words gusting and subsiding like the morning breeze that lifted from the Gulf and blew salty and warm from the expanse of ocean beyond. The officer, El Capitán, as the soldiers called him, had recruited his detail from the police constabulary the day before; they had met up only a half hour before the launch departed from the appointed meeting place. Stefan Mauger, hidden in the shadows at the edge of the savanna that burgeoned almost to the water's edge, briefed the Captain for the last time, handed over the initial sum of money, and wished him good luck.

4

The launch cut through the water, slowly at first, hugging the coast, taking advantage of the concealing darkness. The trip would take two hours, a bit less if they caught a tail wind, but Stefan Mauger had cautioned the Captain to proceed slowly near the shore, since opening the throttle caused the old vessel to groan and shudder, risking the attention of fishermen mending nets at dawn on the stretch of beach at the Lerma.

Just south of Campeche—they had been traveling about twenty minutes—the Captain turned the launch sharply and they were quickly away from land, cutting in a northwesterly direction toward the island. Captain Gutiérrez had visited the island only once, three weeks before, to check certain details that Stefan Mauger had described to him, but that day he had not been in uniform. He had come as a *campesino*, asking for work at the digs, wearing baggy white trousers, a dull and undistinguished serape hanging over his left shoulder covering a torn cotton shirt. He didn't look like much, spoke little, smoked constantly, coughed occasionally, and, failing to inspire confidence in either the Professor or the overseer in charge of the crew of workmen, he was refused. It suited him. He wandered among the idling workmen who stayed six days at a time, sleeping in tents beyond the sacred precincts, circled the shed that served as the Professor's office, storerooms, communications center—a single trunk line that went through Campeche to Mexico City was all—and, satisfied that nothing could be easier, he returned on the late afternoon boat to the mainland.

"Estará muy fácil, Capitán," Stefan Mauger repeated as he described the operation. Stefan Mauger always addressed Jaime Santiago Gutiérrez as "Capitán." He was an El Capitán. A faded officer in his late fifties who had risen through the ranks of the Rurales, Jaime Santiago had been born in a jungle village near Campeche, had once spent a

week in the capital during the twenties, had even seen the Pacific, but now he ran the little constabulary in Campeche, with a score of policemen under his command, whom he ordered about like a landowner, and a dozen more he could conscript for guard duty when an emergency arose. It was from these that he had selected his soldiers, securing for them the odd bits of uniform and insignia that transformed them from unkempt policemen into disheveled soldiers. No point describing his morals. If he was corrupt, his corruption was no more than a natural phenomenon like thick mud, which seasonally covers the Mexican earth, ugly and indifferent.

Stefan Mauger called on Captain Gutiérrez from time to time when there was an important delivery or a shipment that required special assistance, a proper pass, a rubber stamp, information about officialdom down the line to Mexico City or up the line across the border into the United States. El Capitán earned from Stefan Mauger a few hundred dollars every year, but for this operation he had been offered much more, employing his own men whom he paid himself (for they never met Stefan Mauger or had, for that matter, any particular interest in the source of their special duty), who relied upon their Captain's generosity and doubled their loyalty to his authority when he told them that each man would receive two hundred pesos when they assembled before dawn, another two hundred when they returned, and a final three hundred a week later, after silence and forgetfulness had slid back over the city of Campeche. El Capitán Jaime Santiago, for his services, would receive six hundred pesos before, six hundred after, and another thousand when the significant week had passed. In all, a very great deal of money, Gutiérrez thought, interrupting his tune. It was approaching Easter, and everyone in Jaime Santiago's company was desperate for something extra,

Jaime Santiago even more than the rest. His youngest son, a boy of seventeen who had been working on a chicle plantation inland from the town, had had a desperate accident six weeks before, almost severing his right leg when he tripped on a concealed root and his machete tore through his thigh. He had been sewn up and the wound was mending, but he wouldn't work outdoors again. The extra money would help him. He was married, and already a second baby was coming. Jaime Santiago had reason to be anxious that the expedition go well.

The launch slicked through the speeding water, the Gulf current hitting the boat at its back and pushing it fast against the dawn. The island was in view, three miles away. Not a big island, but big enough; not very distant from the mainland, but distant enough. The sun was rising and for an instant the island—an interruption in the webbing of water, a solid expanse that rose like a reclining body from the horizon—was bathed in morning light, the sun dazzling the flatness of the island that the ancient ancestors of Jaime Santiago and his company had once imagined was the entranceway to the underworld beneath the sea where the unhappy living came at last to rest.

The island of Jaina became sometime in the ninth century, it is guessed, the burial site favored by the dwellers of the mainland. It was conjectured by some that once the island had been part of the mainland, eroded over centuries by the biting sea; others, however, thought it possible that a causeway had joined the island to the mainland or that a ceremonial road had been fashioned along which to conduct the dead, linking the coast to the island in the west. Whatever the case, Jaina sank into desuetude only to be rediscovered in this century. The island that remains (smaller than its original scale suggests, for many gravesites have been uncovered along its sandy coastline) was a giant mortuary, a cemetery of astonishing complexity, in which every personage from the ruling aristocracy, the priesthood, the great family of Mayan royalty, and their satraps of soldiers, peasantry, and merchants were buried, whole families having made their final journey to this coastal appendage to demonstrate to the watchful and suspicious gods that they were cooperating with the design of the universe to ease the passage of the dead through Jaina's trapdoor into the caverns of blessedness.

The prow of the launch eased up to the makeshift dock, which heaved and quaked in the morning wind. There wasn't another sound. The island seemed deserted. "Be on the ready. Come to attention, now," El Capitán hissed. The men drew themselves up, slung their carbines over their shoulders, and climbed out of the launch. Jaime Santiago made fast the vessel, lifting a length of rope and making a loop over the pilings that quivered alongside the dock. He followed after the soldiers, his hand gripping a begrimed leather briefcase in which he habitually kept a bar of chocolate, an extra pack of cigarettes, and a torn photograph of his wife, Asunción, taken in Merida on their wedding day. The squad of troopers, marching by twos, climbed up the gentle slope past a swamp that stank of rot, and taking a path beside the Zacpool, a tumble of gravesites and monuments, marched toward the main plaza of the burial town. The few stone buildings, crumbled and overgrown, that remained alongside the soldiers' path may have contained the workshops of the morticians and liturgists of ancient times, where the bodies were broken and prepared for burial, the pottery accouterments fired and sold, and the effigy figurines modeled and baked.

Jaina was given over to the industry of burial, one of the

largest, most prosperous industries of the Mayan Empire. Clearly, to have been an accomplished artisan—to have been able to work in stone, ceramic, gems, and precious metals, to have known how to incise the glyphs and to tell the stories of the great gods and their fatal ministrations upon any surface—was an immense good fortune. In the hierarchy of that civilization, artisans were at the very summit of occupation; being poorer than merchants, but more protected from spoliation and royal extortion than they, the artisans were the protégés of the priests. Without such astonishing craftsmen, it may be doubted whether the civilization could have endured as long and mightily as it did. The priests developed a grammarian's language for their pantheon, and the artists executed it, doing to order what was needed, even making molds from which thousands of identical votives could be fashioned (these turning up as far south as the Andes, where traders had carried them before the destruction of the capitol), supplying the poor with ready-made viaticums for their journey to that uncharted country where tame jaguars and sun-sodden serpents lay still in gardens filled with ripe maize plants and sweet potatoes, where pulque flowed from the maguey plant, and the flesh of tiny pigs and dogs was cured in the cool air, their succulent meat laid out on leaves for the delectation of new arrivals. But to reach that place, through the caverns of the earth, passing through trials which none of us can imagine, requires that first their bodies be smashed and folded into a mound that is the scale of a fist to a full stomach, that the watery innards be fired into the air, and that in their place figures be modeled by the burial artisans of Jaina, effigies of their brief time of endurance upon this difficult earth.

The sculptures of the Isla Jaina were intended by their purchasers not to recollect the dead, but rather to introduce the dead to the guardians of the hereafter, to introduce them, so to speak, by the accouterments of their station— jaguar headdress, pomegranate wand, warrior axe, grotesque face and face wrinkled and submissive with the age of long service, clothed in capes or clothed in layered bird feathers. Each of the dead received the consecration of an effigy that described his person, his tribe, his station, in a species of shorthand that summarized his qualities—to the ageless, durable arcana of the ancient race of Mexican mankind.

Just beyond the Zacpool, a turkey buzzard that had watched the troop of soldiers making their way through the empty and silent village cried suddenly and Captain Gutiérrez, startled, put his hand to his holster. The trooper behind him, Angelito, smiled, red lips parting over his white teeth, the only feature perfect in a face notched by pox scars. The men were silent. They thought it strange that no one had observed their passage through the town. But the town was, after all, a vast mortuary.

The soldiers entered the small plaza before the temple ruins, beyond which could be seen scores of tombs, each open and empty, their contents tagged and classified in the wooden shed that stood near the eastern wall of the temple where archaeologists gathered annually for several weeks in the fall to review the findings of the diggers. The excavation had been inaugurated more than a decade earlier, but work had begun in earnest only five years before. Six hundred tombs had been opened, principally those nearest to the temple, on the assumption that they had been reserved for the aristocracy of the living and that the accouterments of their death would be more distinguished, rich, and revealing.

Captain Gutiérrez signaled his raggle-taggle group to come to order. The troopers had been warned before they left the mainland to maintain military discipline. It was not difficult to impress authority; a loud voice, a curse, an occasional slap or punch to the stomach was all that was needed. Things had changed in the decades since the Captain's enlistment and passage from the mounted troop of the Rurales where he had served his apprenticeship to the virtually permanent sinecure of the constabulary of Campeche. Torture and solitary confinement were no longer used, even in the military, to break the spirit of recruits from the tribes of the peninsula, and now Indians like himself, not only *gachupines* and *ladinos*, commanded the army. Even Jaime Santiago from the Tsoltsil tribe could come to a position of command in these times. Only a signal was needed.

"Stand at ease," the Captain growled, and the message was passed by Angelito down the line to the last of the troopers, who, already leaning, one arm against the rough stone workshop of his ancestors, picked at his scalp. Captain Gutiérrez advanced to the entrance of the shed that sheltered the command post of the archaeologists. Drawing himself to attention, he knocked loudly, but there was no reply. He turned back toward the troopers and smiled. A trooper went around the side of the workshop and cut the phone wires, but it proved an unnecessary precaution. Stefan Mauger had done as he had promised. The island was uninhabited. Captain Gutiérrez turned the handle of the door; it was locked, but he smashed the lock easily with the butt of his revolver, entered, surveyed the interior, and calling to his men, ordered them to bring up the wooden cases that had been stowed beneath the gunwales of the launch. Within a half hour the work of packing the Jaina treasure had commenced.

The Jaina figurines mystified the little army of Captain Gutiérrez, not only that they should be handled with such

11

care, but that they should be considered desirable at all. The men had been told nothing, of course; Captain Gutiérrez had explained only that the treasure was being secretly removed by order of the government and that the extra payment was for their silence and forgetfulness.

These soldiers, descendants of the very stock that had fashioned the clay effigies, must have thought of the long gray faces, incised with designs and scarifications, in some cases with pictographs that narrated the tale of their coming to death, as somehow parodies of themselves, perceiving in the slant of an eye, the elongation of a chin, the tight and gently curved cheeks and flattened noses, a recollection of themselves, their wives, parents, children, glimmerings of the origins of their stock that descended out of Asiatic folk who had made their way in the mists of the Tertiary Age over the Straits of Bering and down the coast of western America to the plains, deserts, jungles of Mexico.

The soldiers mocked the figures as they gently lifted them from the shelves in the workshop and placed them in the wooden boxes, each cushioned with layers of palm fronds. *"Mire la putana,"* one said, holding up the figure of a young woman, her ears pendulous from the weight of ceramic plugs. *"¡La putana santa!"* another exclaimed, shaking with laughter as he admired, suspiciously and with not a little fear, the clay portrait of what he recognized might be his wife. Captain Gutiérrez despised her no less than they, but cautioned the soldier that she be laid to one side and packed separately. It was that very piece, her foot marked by a chalk cross, which Stefan Mauger required for his own collection.

The operation had been a success, as completely successful, efficient, uncomplicated as Stefan Mauger had promised.

"¡Estaba muy fácil. Verdad!" Gutiérrez reflected, as he

guided the launch farther out into the Gulf, having left the men to wade ashore at a point where a sandbar extended a quarter mile into the ocean from the very beach they had departed before dawn. The sun was high in the sky, but it was still cool and fresh. Several hours later he made contact with the trim and powerful fishing ship out of Brownsville, Texas, and the transfer took place. Turning about his vessel, he returned at a more leisurely speed toward the Lerma. By late afternoon—it was nearly five o'clock—he was back in his little office in the guardroom of the police station of Campeche. One by one the six men who had composed his squad made their way to his office and received their second payment. It was done. He would report to Stefan Mauger later that night as arranged.

1

The Young Count

In the early hours of the morning of this century, Stefan Friedrich Martin von Mauger, the first son of Count Peter Nickolaus von Mauger, was born prematurely while his family was passing the Christmas holidays at the ancestral lodge in the great forest of southern Silesia. The Viennese doctor whom the Countess had visited the day before the family's departure had warned that such an elaborate travel schedule was unwise given the profuse bleeding that had followed the birth of her second daughter two years earlier, but she insisted imperiously, disregarding the authority of the bits of ribbon that the doctor wore in his lapel. ("My dear Countess, if the Emperor sees fit to do me these honors, the least you can do is listen to me.") It was not that she was indifferent to the dangers. It was only that she knew quite well how unhappy her husband would be if she were absent from the lodge. He counted upon the gathering of the family at Christmas time as a form of sanction and confirmation of his titular control of its members, which numbered more than a score of immediate brothers, sisters, nephews, and nieces. Moreover, since it was planned in any event that the child would be born at the end of January, the preceding weeks would be filled with a gaiety that would all but evaporate if the bearer of that Magian gift were herself absent. Those years were extremely intimate, one might even say happy were it not for the dubiety with which such simple-minded bestowals are usually received. If, however, happiness consists of the certain knowledge that one's existence is fully confirmed by another, that one's well-being, pleasure, enterprise, and preoccupation are not only supported but gratefully espoused by another, it could be said that the Count and Countess were exceptionally and fortunately happy. The times of their marriage—they were joined at the beginning of the nineties—were generally peaceful throughout Europe, certainly in that narrow cut of Europe that might be described as not quite Middle Europe, no longer Western, but most assuredly not Eastern.

Spring and fall were passed in Vienna, winter months from November until the first thaw at the Silesian lodge, and summer at one or another Czechoslovakian, Swiss, or German spa. The daughters were born, Anna Liselotte and Theresa Franziska; the lands were rich, the timber trade prospered, the mines continued to produce. But more than all these bounties was the humane affection with which Count and Countess attended to each other, he succumbing to her enthusiasm for the English game of bridge, just then beginning to sweep Vienna, and she to his passion for music, even tolerating the generous support he gave to young composers and performers, scheduling musicales in which a succession of ensembles would play on the same evening to a splendid array of Vienna society, the festivities concluding with the award of an extra bursary to the quartet or soloist whose interpretation was voted with unconventional democracy to be the most spirited or profound. Delicious years, savored to the last, like fingers licked surreptitiously long after the feast of cakes has disappeared.

It is understandable, therefore, that the collapse of the large and otherwise formidable carriage that bore the Countess and her daughters through the forest on the last stage of their journey to the family estate would be regarded as an omen, particularly after the advice of the doctor had been so egregiously ignored. Fortunately, the accident occurred only three kilometers from the lodge and the Countess was soon installed in her bedroom overlooking the gardens, reduced at that time of year to row upon row of snow-capped pine trees interspersed with naked rosebushes. The accident had not been serious by any means—the snapping of an axle was all—but the suddenness with which it had occurred, combined with the natural superstition with which the Countess received it, set in motion a train of events that culminated eleven days later in the birth of a son, several minutes into the new year of the twentieth century. The infant was pitifully small, just over four pounds in weight, his face covered with a mysterious tissue of placenta, word of whose appearance went through the wings and back stairs with an alacrity almost greater than the actual birth itself, for the peasants regarded such eccentricities of birth as being marks of special favor. It was not long before the birth of the child, swathed in the caul of marvel, should be elaborated by the sighting of falling stars and meteors, unseasonable stillnesses in the wood reported by some, mysterious zephyrs by others.

The "young Count," as he was called immediately by everyone including his father, was tenacious, and after several weeks during which his life was in the balance, his breathing strengthened, he slept soundly, and the expert wet nurse into whose charge he had been given succeeded in turning him resolutely toward health and growth. It was then, the danger past, that Count Peter Nickolaus undertook a ritual of initiation required for no other reason than his own delight and gratification. Late one March night, wearing the orders and decorations of his title, he removed the infant from the nursery and carried him into the reception hall, where he installed him upon the ancestral chair onto whose back the coat of arms of the Von Maugers had been stitched, and there he put upon the thumb of the infant a ring he had received in succession from the first Count— an oriental star sapphire of exquisite color and depth set in a gold bezel of no less magnificent workmanship. The eye of the child was transfixed by the floating image of the star, rising and receding as the lights of the candelabrum flickered, burned bright, and withdrew. Quietly attentive, a bunched fist beneath his chin, the baby lay back upon the cushions, appearing to listen as the Count interpreted in a fluent voice—pausing occasionally to make certain that the child was attentive—the litany of the processional lintel that had been installed above the massive fireplace. Proceeding from incident to incident with flourishes consonant with the neoclassical exaggeration of the panels, the Count interpreted the narration of the marble relief, recalling the history of the Mauger line from its marauder origins in the seventeenth century through its ennoblement by the courts of Poland and Prussia, to the time of his great-grandfather, a genial eminence who, after extending the Mauger fortune more by imprudence than by cunning, had ended the ravages of a brain tumor with a bullet, leaving his wealth and estates to a charming heir who built the lodge, commemorated the founders with the lintel, and proceeded to spend a good deal of his inheritance in cultivated recreation and entertainment. A charmed history; the baby gurgled at the last and his father, concluding that the story was done, pass-

17

ing out of marble into life, told the boy of his great good fortune in being a son to such a house, and Count to be.

The young Count was certainly special; it was to the regimen of a special youth that he was delivered. The mystery of the caul was interpreted variously, by the peasants as a certain mark of prodigy, by his parents, more pragmatic than they, as a notice given of some precarious physic, a discharge that accompanied premature birth and a sign therefore that the young Count be watched more closely than other children who—gestated in the full term of a three-quarter year and come to the world rosy, full, and unshrouded—might be allowed to scamper and play from the earliest age. Of course, to the perplexity of the caul must be added the no less ponderous consideration that the young Count would one day inherit the title and the estates, accounts, treasures that came with it. On this, at least, both Count and Countess agreed without reservation—the boy would remain at home to be educated, at home in the company of Anna Liselotte and Theresa Franziska, his older sisters, at home under the supervisory eye of their tutor, a pallid Englishman in his early thirties whom the family had secured through an advertisement in the *Zürcher Zeitung* the previous fall.

Sefton Richards was an Englishman of no family distinction, but evident breeding. He knew how to peel fruit at the table, to play bridge, to muffle coughs in handkerchiefs, as well as to teach Greek, Latin, German, and French, to manage sums and lower mathematics, to organize a presentable history of Europe that was egalitarian without being radical and authoritarian without being Napoleonic. He was, in a word, an ideal tutor and, when occasion demanded it, he could throw a ball, play a passable game of lawn tennis, and ride. Mr. Richards came by this remarkable variety of aptitudes quite honorably, for his father had been, until his dismissal, the vicar of a prosperous parish in Dorset. It was unfortunate that during the second year of his studies at the University of Zurich the old vicar was surprised accommodating a wealthy parishioner to an un-religious vocation and dismissed. With his dismissal went any hope of supplying his son with the stipend he required to survive in Zurich, and hence it was no surprise that he answered the advertisement of Count Peter Nickolaus von Mauger and after several exchanges of letters agreed to come to Vienna to take up his duties.

The day of Mr. Richards's arrival by train from Zurich and his presentation to the children at tea took a rather different course than anticipated. The Countess thought it a sufficient introduction for Mr. Richards to be present when the children were offered daily by their nurse along with the tea sandwiches for their parents' delectation. After the greetings, curtsies and bows, brief chats, the selection of cookies and chocolates, the children would disappear again and Mr. Richards would remain for further consultation before being allowed to withdraw to his quarters on the top floor of the house, down the hall from the rooms of the children. It happened, however, that no sooner had the children entered the room than the young Count, by then a child of six years, caught sight of a remarkable stone glinting from the small finger ring that Mr. Richards wore on his left hand. He cried out: "Sir, would you tell me how you come to wear my father's ring?" Until that moment, the Count, who had been whispering to his Aunt Sophia, had not turned to greet the young tutor, nor could he have noticed the gold-set mauve stone shining with a fragile star. The first reaction of the Count was an astonished, "It *is* like mine, isn't it? But Stefan, you've never seen that ring. How could you possibly know of its existence? I lost it six years ago when you were just an infant."

"What is it, Peter? You're absolutely white. What's the matter?"

"But don't you see? The child's amazing! He's never seen my star sapphire; I wore it last at the winter lodge when he was born. The ring's been gone for years. I wear only this signet ring now," he said, lifting his hand and indicating the gold ring that hugged his index finger. The young Count was, of course, delighted. He laughed with amusement, not at all disturbed by the discovery of his unusual percipience. Mr. Richards, less amused, was somewhat ill at ease. He didn't enjoy having his personal effects discussed at tea.

After both children and tutor had retired, leaving the Count and Countess alone with Aunt Sophia, there was a pall of silence interrupted only by the clucking disbelief of the Count, who recollected only too well the occasion on which the young Count had seen the star sapphire. He felt, however, an obscure guilt which prevented him from telling the story of that night. It seemed to him at the time and now vaguely obscene that he should have made the infant a man, decked him in the robes and signs of his posterity in order to celebrate his own paternity. The memory of the child, however fragmentary, was utterly deep as though he were of the circle of those rare persons to whom any sight, any word, any impression, however transitory, is registered like a stamp in wax, clear and distinct.

Stefan Friedrich was, indeed, a gifted student; anything that passed before his eyes was fixed instantly upon his brain. His mother, no less astonished by his intellectual gifts, invented a brilliant conceit to interpret for him his occasional upset stomachs. "Think, dear boy, that your stomach is filled with shelves on which everything you learn and everything you eat is arranged alphabetically from

Aesop and apricot jam to Zeno and zucchini. Now if you read too fast or eat too quickly (as you did this evening at supper), everything falls down from the shelves and the little librarian in your tummy doesn't have time to organize the shelves correctly. Mixing up makes you ill." A delicious conceit and one that Stefan Friedrich adored, asking his mother to tell it to him again and again, going so far as to invent stomach aches to hear her tell of the librarian in his tummy. When he was small—the time of this telling—he would even open a new book or sit down to supper with an admonition, never overheard, "Get yourself ready, old man, you're going to work now."

Mr. Richards, a patient and inventive pedant who managed to make his own enthusiasms vivid, awakened in Stefan Friedrich a passion for the ancient world, which compassed all the disciplines in which he was obliged to instruct the young man. His grounding in Greek and Latin, which by the time Stefan was eleven was well advanced, enabled master and pupil not only to read Herodotus and Plutarch, but also to learn geometry from the original of Euclid, rudimentary astronomy from Archimedes, moral philosophy from the *Protagoras*, *Apology*, and *Crito*, supplemented by Marcus Aurelius, and natural philosophy from the miraculous Lucretius. These were further elaborated by turns through the changing exhibitions of the great library of the Emperor and visits to the halls of the Kunsthistorisches Museum, where both original marbles and casts of the ancient world were assembled and on view. It was during the course of their fourth afternoon stroll through the halls of the Imperial Museum that Stefan Friedrich announced to the delighted Englishman, "You know, Mr. Richards, I think I shall begin to draw."

It is of course incomprehensible to adults, forgetting the ways of their own childhood (or perhaps never assaulted by talents made manifest in early years), how it is that children —in this case a boy of eleven—should decide that they would undertake something prodigious. Far too many parents dismiss such announcements as chattering—"stop your chattering, your prattling, your prathering and bathering—always something or other you will or you won't"—and that's the end of it. The child is cut off in the midst of fancy and sent out to walk in the cold rains where so many things end as childish which might have gone on to become glorious. Parents oddly prefer the apple near the tree. Fortunately, Mr. Sefton Richards was not of that world of adults, closer in spirit as he was to this eleven-year-old than was Stefan to his parents, the Count and Countess.

"But of course you will. Let's go off right now and get some paper and tools—some inks and pastels, some brushes and water color. I should tell you, though, that I have a blind eye to art. I convert everything into an idea that I can't see. I won't be any help at all, except as critic."

The young Count smiled and seized his tutor's hand with delight. "It won't matter, Mr. Richards. I shall see for both of us and when I can draw I will be able to tell you what I see better than before. You've taught me so much already. It's my turn to repay you."

It was precisely that way. The young Count passed hours every day in his study room, after the schoolbooks had been cleared away and his afternoon rest was over. There were two hours free before he had to be dressed to accompany his sisters and Mr. Richards on the daily visit to his parents, and those hours were filled at his drawing table. From the very beginning he worked curiously, as if blowing upon embers inside himself to keep alight the small and indistinct flame that sparked the recreation. After a period during which he drew somehow from inside, the pencil moving on the paper without reference to any object, any image, any vista from his window to the milling streets below, the natural hand acquired a kind of knowledge that was implicit. The fingers could hold and move; the pen, the charcoal, the pastel, the brush described a universe of swathes and swirls, shapes and forms, which went beyond the firemen and soldiers of little boys' familiar drawings. Not people but the shapes of arms and legs without the discernment of the natural arm and leg; not orange or apple, but the sensuosity of the circle; not eye or egg but ovular grace —these were the critical months of apprenticeship and many hundreds of hours went to the mastery of this repertoire. Whenever Mr. Richards inquired about some one or another of his drawings, he inevitably asked what it was, rather more traditionally than the innocent Countess who inquired what it meant. But to both questions (and with variation they were asked by everyone in the same way) Stefan Mauger learned to reply, "Now look here, if you look at a man, what do you see? You see only skin. Correct? Of course you know that skin is not a man. Everything that makes a man is underneath the skin. Correct? My work is to make the skin tell you everything that's underneath. That's clear, isn't it?"

The following year, after the family's return from the winter lodge at the beginning of spring the Countess became ill with pleurisy and was obliged to rest, away from visitors and the tasks of her establishment. It was difficult for her but the doctor required it. The young Count visited her every afternoon in her rooms rather than in the *salon de thé* as previously. One day, arriving early, he sat waiting in the little anteroom to her boudoir until the servant would wheel in the tea caddy and his sisters appear for their daily visit. The door was ajar and the anteroom dim; the only light came from the hallway, where little electric bulbs, recently installed, winked insubstantially. Suddenly before him he caught his mother in the inch crack of the doorway examining herself in the floor-length mirror that paneled her sitting room. She was naked but for a flowered hat with a silk veil that covered her face. At first the young Count turned away because it was his mother. But reconsidering, he looked, for his mother was nonetheless a woman and he had never seen before a fully matured woman—to be sure, not that he ever saw her *toute entière*, but only in glances and perspectives, shadows and volumes, which an inch crack allows, a cut of profile down her breasts to a slight swelling of thighs that obscured some darker, tufted region; next a turn revealing angled head and taut neck strained to see her hat in yet another position, a partial buttock, swollen hips tapering to slender legs as if an inverted viola; another buttock and a severe and critical glance of the magnificent profile down the angle of her shoulder; once more her breasts, as though peaches brushed each other in a fruit bowl, one slightly larger than the other, bristling from nudity.

The young Count did not avert his eyes. A minute later it was over. The door opened and the Countess, now robed in gray silk, admitted his sisters, whom she kissed on their cheeks, and he, receiving a kiss upon his forehead, blushed, and pleading that he was ill, asked for permission to be excused.

During the months that followed, Stefan Friedrich, hardly surprisingly, began to draw women. Mr. Richards could not explain the transformation. The abstract drawing that had occupied the boy for nearly two years had given way to an almost voluptuous celebration of the female body. Remarkably, however, not a single drawing portrayed a woman of the Caucasian race. Each was of a black woman, explicit and complex, with shading and articulation to suggest the scaffolding and musculature of the unnamed model. She remained, however, unnamed and unnamable, for there were no black women to be seen at that time in the neighborhood of Vienna where the Von Maugers had their residence, nor in the park where they walked, nor in the forest where they rode; indeed, there were no black women whom the young Count might have been likely to see, much less in their nudity. And yet it was the case that every drawing of the voluptuous woman was in its completion covered with a swathing of black pastel, filling in what had been empty, completing the space that had been outlined. What is curious about this exercise in embarrassment is that it contained the origins of Stefan Mauger's later enthusiasm for sculpture. Had the drawings remained unfilled, the line would have implicated flesh without the requirement of modeling it. In his own black-white woman the young Count had begun to draw for wood and marble.

It is not at all certain when Count Peter Nickolaus first began to behave strangely. Some thought the change in his disposition so gradual they did not bother to account for it in the terms of time, situation, or accident. "Quite simply, he's like his moody *grand'maman*," one said. "She always dipped off into reveries in the midst of her own dinner parties," Aunt Sophia contributed. These and other comparable suggestions were of scant value. The immediate family had as little conception of mental unrest and perturbation as did the general medical community at that time. There were those who pursued a deeper scrutiny of the unconscious, but they were regarded as quacks or in any case as Jews and hence doubly unreliable. Nineteen-twelve was not at all a propitious year to obey the instruction of secret voices, much less to hear them in the first place; to barricade oneself in the study, piling furniture upon the enormous baroque desk that the Count had, with astonishing energy, pushed from its position near the window against the double doors that fronted the sitting room where he sometimes entertained; to break into song in restaurants or into tears at his own musicales. Whatever it was that began to trouble the Count was not discovered at the time. He refused to see a specialist in nervous disorders, contenting himself with taking the potions provided by the family doctor to insure him a few hours sleep each night. There were, of course, periods of comparative calm and tranquillity when the Count was able to attend to the business affairs of his family, to meet with the bailiffs of his estates, to bother with complaints and repairs, the ordering of new glazed tile for the entrance hall of the winter lodge and a hunting outfit for the young Count, who had been promised permission for his thirteenth birthday that he might accompany the Count and his party on the New Year's Day hunt at the winter lodge. The periods of respite were, at the beginning at least, considerably longer than the periods of derangement and, therefore, the latter were regarded more as preoccupations or *idées fixes* or manias than as signs of incipient madness. There is sufficient indication nonetheless that the year 1912 was the pivotal time. Had precautions been taken early enough and the Count restrained, at least the calamity might have been averted that plunged the Count into the despair from which he was unable to return. The derangement had at its center his son, the young Count, Stefan Friedrich. He, it appears, more than any other, focused the ferocity and terror that described the closing period of the Count's life.

Stefan Friedrich was emerging from childhood. He was remarkably handsome, his features sharp but delicate, his coloring fair except for his dark eyes and black lashes; and although his slenderness tended to enforce an impression of fragility, it was belied by a strong and vigorous constitution, muscles well developed and employed, and a body altogether consonant with a fine and high-minded intelligence. In those days of the early twentieth century, parents habitually ignored children who seemed apt, well formed, and without embarrassing blemish. If the body was healthy and the mind alert, nothing more could be wanted from nature. The rest was to be supplied by breeding, education, discipline, and these were conferred in equal measure upon the young Count by wealth and the affectionate Mr. Richards. The young Count, however, maintained an ardent and by no means uncomplicated private life, quite private in fact, since he had no friends and only a few acquaintances, the children of other families of privilege, his sisters, whom he regarded with affectionate indifference, and Mr. Richards, who accompanied him when he went riding in the countryside and occasionally took him on foot into the forest, where they tracked game and watched birds. It was a solitary existence, but one that he enjoyed. He had little free time in all events, what with tutoring in languages, history, and mathematics throughout the morning and drawing every afternoon. The evenings he spent reading a large illustrated encyclopedia of the arts of ancient peoples, books on any and all Indians, those of North America and Canada being his favorites, and historical novels. Sir Walter Scott and Victor Hugo were particularly treasured although he had recently discovered the American, James Fenimore Cooper, who combined the lore of Indians with tales of intrepid and daring frontiersmen. His head spun with the imagining of places other than Vienna, and when the flames of the night fire had begun to die and only embers glowed in the hearth he dreamed himself falling asleep in an encampment of the Iroquois and on the day that would follow going forth with other braves to hunt deer and spear fish in the icy lakes of northern New York.

The first intimation that the young Count was somehow implicated in the erratic behavior of his father occurred during the spring, shortly before the family gathered up to depart the winter lodge before Easter. The house had filled before the last week, guests coming from as far away as Paris and Budapest to be present for the festivities of Carnival, which were celebrated in a rather spontaneous fashion by the Von Mauger household since that particular tradition was more constrained in northern Europe. There must have been thirty house guests present during that last week, and the children, the three Maugers strengthened by the addition of two others, twin boys of ten years, the sons of the Countess's brother, had gone off into the woods the day before the last to spend it by a brilliantly clear pool that filled each spring from thaw waters that poured over a natural dam nearly invisible in the dense forest. The children cut their way through the path, Stefan Friedrich using a steel hunting knife to pare back vines that had not been disturbed since the previous year. After a walk of not more than a mile, during which the young Count had shown his friends how to run in Indian fashion, lifting their feet so that the soles were never long in contact with the matted earth, their arms close to their sides, relying on toes for balance and spring, they came to the clearing, into which they descended from a basalt bluff that jutted out over the site, forming a small covering ledge beneath which the moss and earth, already dried from an uninterrupted four days of sun, was soft and warm. The children spread out a blanket, which Anna Liselotte had carried about her neck, and the other children began to unpack the small hampers in which their lunch had been packed, putting the two thermos bottles of lemonade and white wine into the stream to cool. It was a radiant day, sun glinting through the immense pine trees to the clearing and, beyond, only the suspicion of blue streaked with swiftly moving clouds. "We are in Arcadia at last," Stefan Friedrich shouted, transported by a delight that was both archaic and inappropriate, since he saw himself an Indian, not a settler bound from Europe to the new paradise. None of the other children noticed or cared. They were as delighted as he. His cousins were his admirers, and his sisters, even though older, thought him not a Chief of the Iroquois, but the young Alexander of Macedon. In those days it was quite impossible for Stefan Friedrich to be at fault.

After a leisurely lunch and circuit through the forest that surrounded the clearing, the children returned and fell quiet, tired by their energy, waiting for some suggestion to ignite them again, slipping into reveries, arms over faces shielding them from the sparkling sun that shot like the separate strands of a rainbow through the opening where not even the highest pine trees could obscure it.

It must have been three o'clock when the young Count roused up his braves and called them to play Indians. It was a game Stefan Friedrich adored; he played it often, but mostly by himself, being all in one chief, brave, warrior, and his most cherished role, that of medicine man. But with a whole tribe to hand, it could be a proper round of Indians and he fell to the task with ingenuity. Each of his sisters and cousins was assigned an identity and a task. Anna Liselotte, since she was the oldest, was made chief of the tribe, and for her office the young Count gave her a large feather he had borrowed from his mother, which she pushed through the winding of her braid; Theresa Franziska was appointed scout and was obliged to run barefoot in her black wool stockings, her feather carried in her hand like a relay baton; and the two cousins, being the youngest, were braves, each receiving a simple turkey feather that they inserted in the buttonholes of their loden jackets. The young Count set them first to making bows and arrows, cutting sapling branches and notching them for the thick bolt of twine he had in his pocket, the scout was sent off to report on the distance of the British soldiers in the wood, the others to hunt for game, each being required to bring back to the medicine man a living offering for the gods. A half hour more or less after the robing and investiture of his tribesmen, the children burst shouting into the clearing, each carrying one or another living sample for the gods, a baby frog, a speckled bird's egg, an assortment of crickets, but their shaman was lost in prayer, his arms upraised to the sun, his face covered with a glaze of reverence, about his feet seashells in which powdered paints of red, yellow, blue, black, white, which he had mixed with water, awaited the magic brushes that lay crossed before his feet, and what he spoke sounded strange indeed to their ears. "Great spirit of the Iroquois who lives behind the lightning bolt and the rain mountain, who gave us the game of the forest as our hunting grounds, save us from the sick face of the white man." The young Count continued his prayer, adding to the bounties of the great spirit, the gods and goddesses of fire, water, moonlight, corn, canoes, and the great healing power of the medicine man. When he had completed his litany, he signaled to his tribe to bow before the sun and stare into its rays, and while they did he drew emblems upon their foreheads and covered the rocks with glyphs he had seen in calotypes of Altamira—hunters shooting game, braves in twos and threes cooking around fires, gleaming suns and graves in which the dead sat upright as if awaiting a great visitation.

The ritual painting completed, the visit to the underworld past, the young Count put down his brushes and broke into a bright smile, his lineless face creasing for an instant, lips parting, and his mouth opening as though to eat the sun that shone upon him, saluting his prayers through the aperture of bowing pine trees.

At that instant they all heard a shout, accompanied by applause. The father of the young Count appeared in the clearing, his face contorted with pain, although he continued to applaud his son and laugh with apparent pleasure in his ritual. The Count, his children and nephews returned to the lodge more silently than they had come and that evening the Count, unwell, did not appear at table. His absence was not mentioned. It had become commonplace to pass over his distempers.

At Christmas of the same year, his father gave the young Count a hunting rifle whose stock was beautifully tapered to his size and embossed with the family crest, the eagle in profile, the serpent in its talons. Stefan Friedrich already knew how to hunt, having accompanied the game warden of the estate several times when the latter went in search of deer and boar to supply the Count's table and his own, but he had coveted his own rifle and when it was unwrapped he was exuberant and hugged his father mightily, although the Count drew away from his ferocious affection. A week later, early in the morning of New Year's Day, as he had been promised, he joined the party of a dozen hunters for a day's shooting in the forest. It was planned that they would divide into three groups that would converge about noon for lunch at a cabin at the base of a mountain, known in the district as Kleinfeld because one side of it was an almost naturally terraced field, which the local farmers cultivated. Although Stefan Friedrich was anxious to be with his father for their first hunt together, the Count inexplicably sent him off with his brother, Uncle Jonas, and the game warden who had trained him, insisting that it would be best if he were really on his own. The young Count protested, but the

Count was adamant; and at the last, exasperated, the Count humiliated him with an insult that was as cruel as it was effective. "You're not a Sunday medicine man any more, Stefan Friedrich. Go off and be a man!" The young Count winced but did not reply, turning back to join Uncle Jonas and the game warden as they were about to set out on a path that led into the snow-covered forest. The game warden greeted him warmly and soon the insult was forgotten as they made their way steadily into the forest darkness. It was just after dawn and little light found its way to their path. The game warden held a lantern in one hand, his shotgun loosely slung over his shoulder. The young Count, next in the file, was covered in a bear coat whose collar rose up to the Russian shapka that plunged low over his forehead to the level of his eyes. He was warm from his head to the bottoms of his fur-lined boots. Behind them, Uncle Jonas continued to twirl his black moustache, thinking of something clearly irrelevant to a hunt at dawn.

It was nearly eleven in the morning when the little group heard in the distance the sound of shots and was delighted that someone had sighted a quarry. Until that moment they had had no luck. They had seen deer tracks (even "a large elk," the game warden had thought), but after these were followed a quarter mile they disappeared into a snow drift and the hunters dropped the pursuit. A gust of ducks rose from some hidden pool and flew overhead, but they could barely focus them between the overhanging branches and none had fired although the young Count had raised his rifle for a sighting. Shortly before noon, having made slower progress through the snow than they had anticipated, a strong east wind having blown the snow in large drifts across their path, the group came to a halt in a small clearing among the rocks that began to form the outcropping of Kleinfeld. The young Count was seated on a boulder, otherwise obscured by snow, when a rifle shot sounded. The game warden turned to the right in the direction of the shot, which seemed unusually close, and noticed immediately that the young Count had slumped over, gripping his arm. The game warden shouted and rushed to the boy; Uncle Jonas began to shake with fright, ducking his head low in fear he would be the next mistaken for an animal. The two realized quickly that it was only a flesh wound, the bullet having cut the skin for two inches across the upper arm near the joint, but the young Count was in shock and the blood, even from a minor wound, soaked the right side of his bear coat. The game warden gave Uncle Jonas his gun and lantern, and picking up the boy, put him on his shoulders and carried him the last two miles to the cabin. When they arrived, the other members of the party were already assembled and anxiously awaiting them. They had heard the shot and placed it correctly in their vicinity, but had decided not to go off in search of them until the Count himself turned up. The Count had apparently missed his party a half hour before and knowing the forest well had not bothered to call out for them. His companions thought nothing of it. He was hunting on his own, which he did from time to time when he wanted to be alone. However, when they saw the wounded boy, the hunters realized the shot could have been fired only by the absent Count, as it was unlikely that poachers would have penetrated so deeply into private property. The thought was so appalling that none dared to voice it, although the idea was lost on none of them, including the young Count, who bit upon his glove, holding back his tears. The company fell silent; none had appetite for the hot game soup, rich with fowl and vegetables, the loaves of fresh-baked bread, and the flagons of red wine, which an old peasant had left for their table. It was nearly two, the young Count, bandaged and feeling more himself, was resting on the bedding of a cabin bunk, when the door flung open and the Count entered, rabbits tied to his belt, a doe hanging about his neck like a shawl, the blood dripping down his front. His face, what one could see of it through his fur, was streaked with blood where he had rubbed it with his gloves. He was absolutely silent when he entered and not until he saw his son, his bandaged arm hanging from a sling of colored fabric, did he sound his anguish—a cry broke from him and, throwing himself at the foot of the young Count's resting place, he burst into tears.

It was no longer possible to reach the Count. He had passed into another region where the interior connections, familiar to ordinary life, were no longer made. He was no longer eccentric, erratic, occasionally confused; he was, quite simply, mad. When the Count had entered and confronted his wounded son in the cabin at the base of the Kleinfeld, whatever slender filament of sanity passed like luminous copper through the swelling bulb of his dementia had snapped. There would be no more light. His weeping had given way to slow pounding of his head upon the floor until at last, fearing that he might harm himself, the hunters had tied back his arms with a belt and restrained him. The following day the family returned to Vienna, accompanied by several relatives who saw to the Countess and her children, while making arrangements for the Count's admission to a private sanatorium favored by the rich in the mountains near Salzburg.

In the months that followed the accidental shooting and the collapse of his father, Stefan Friedrich himself changed. The disposition of gravity, that meditative quality always signaled by his darting eyes and immensely open, cream-colored face, lowered precipitously. Stefan Friedrich, already called, in the absence of his father, Count Stefan, became irritable and fretful, prone to sudden rages and bouts of fury. "It came at a bad time," Mr. Richards explained to the Countess. "The boy was coming nicely into his own maturity and now this. You must be patient with him." But it was difficult. The young Count adopted even more solitary habits, riding alone in the woodlands during the early morning, returning to the house and refusing to change out of his riding costume even for lunch, leaving the table in the midst of meals to go painting, refusing to continue any longer the study of German or German literature, announcing that only French mattered and even more heretically that Italian was preferable to German, accusing his older sisters of being snobs, seeking out only Jewish students at the gymnasium for companions, even insulting Aunt Sophia for making some palpably banal remark about gypsies and freemasons. But all the while, as these gestures of rebellion settled into his ordinary behavior, he was aware that the principal issue in his life and the motive cause to his moodiness and irascibility was that he missed his father and could not believe that someone who had been throughout his childhood and youth so affectionate, forbearing, and tolerant could have tried to murder him. In his mind there was no question of accident. The older Count could not have mistaken a bear coat of reddish-brown fur topped by a shapka of black lamb for a living animal. The sightings of his father's hunting rifle were splendid, he knew perfectly well. The only misjudgment was the deflection of the bullet by some moving branch or a sudden wind of the forest. He was wounded by his father; however, two inches more to the left and a bit up and it could have been his life.

Clear though his father's intent had been, uncertainty about its motive baffled Stefan Friedrich, immobilizing him with ambiguous conjecture. Mr. Richards guessed the young Count's difficulty and, daring one day, despite his habitual reticence, to speak openly about his suspicion, urged him to visit the sanatorium where his father was confined, to speak with the resident psychiatrist and ascertain the answer. Mr. Richards was being optimistically empirical. He presumed there was an answer and that the psychiatrist would know it. In all events, Mr. Richards agreed to be the accomplice of Stefan Friedrich's visit to the sanatorium. He promised to devise an excellent excuse for his two-day absence from the household.

The following week, it was already August, Stefan Friedrich presented himself to Dr. Arnold Mauritius, to whose eminence and reputation the clinic owed its name and success. Situated on a bluff overlooking the city of Salzburg, the natural setting, the spacious grounds with walks and trees and abundant rosebushes, more than compensated for the weary interior of the establishment, smelling in equal measure of medicines and old age, since the principal clientele of the sanatorium were less the aggressively mad than the declining and feeble. Seated in the doctor's office, having telegraphed to announce the exact time of his arrival, the young Count, well dressed in a suit *à l'anglaise*, holding his cap on his knee, and looking quite convincingly sixteen years of age rather than just a bit beyond thirteen and a half, waited nervously for Dr. Mauritius to return from his round of the patients. An attractive middle-aged woman, dressed as a nurse, but obviously a secretary, for her makeup was more elaborate than usual among professional nurses, showed him into the doctor's office and offered him a chair. Actually Stefan Friedrich preferred this bit of fraud; it comforted him to be in touch with something so lighthearted and voluptuous in an atmosphere otherwise so studiously severe. The moment the door had closed behind the secretary, Stefan Friedrich got up and walked

36

about the office, admiring the solidity of the furniture, the fresh-scrubbed leather chairs, the strangely sexless silver women who supported candle holders on either side of the fireplace, the uncomfortable wooden chairs on which petitioners, relatives, patients were obliged to sit before the renowned Dr. Mauritius, whose Biedermeier desk supported nothing more at present than a silver inkstand, a stationery divider, and a large folder across which was written *Von Mauger, Count Peter Nickolaus.*

After more than a half hour of waiting, during which the young Count had settled uncomfortably into the chair assigned to him (although he would have preferred the settee against the fabric-covered wall of the office), he heard a bustle in the outer room, low voices, the distinct mention of his name, and Dr. Mauritius was upon him.

A bulk of a man was Dr. Mauritius, not small and minutely proportioned as the young Count had imagined was right for a psychiatrist. Vast, in fact, not merely bulky, his weight surely exceeding ninety kilos, the doctor wore a beige-colored smock over his black jacket and vest, from which cascaded a gold watch chain inset with small diamonds. While his right hand gripped that of the young Count, the left was removing the watch from the vest pocket, checking the time, reckoning it against the eighteenth-century water clock that burbled less accurately behind his visitor. All of this presence, the bulk, the gestures, the time check, put the young Count off stride, and by the time the doctor had settled behind the desk, drawing his hands under the folds of his beard, curled in the Assyrian manner, where they remained hidden, and fastening his black eyes like water leeches directly upon his visitor's own, Stefan Friedrich was somewhat agitated. He determined, however, not to speak first. He would oblige the doctor to begin the interview.

"So, young man, what is it that you wish?" Dr. Mauritius began, at last persuaded that his visitor would not yield.

"As I wrote you, Doctor, I wish to ask you some questions about my father, Count Peter Nickolaus von Mauger, who has been a patient here for the past eight months."

"Yes. I know the case quite well. In fact, I visited with your father just a short time ago. I told him that you were due to arrive for a visit."

The young Count's eyes lit up and he asked, with a spontaneity more touching than prudent, "Was he pleased?"

"That's hard to ascertain. I can't be certain that he even heard me."

"Well, in that case, you repeated it and he heard you the second time, didn't he?" the young Count persisted, obtusely optimistic.

"I'm afraid you don't understand, my young friend. Your father doesn't respond to human conversation at all. He hears perfectly well, but his responses are virtually nil, normally speaking. I could fire a pistol behind his back and he would give a start—but that only because his nervous system gives a shake now and again. A normal person would go through the roof with fright. Do you see? Your father, I am afraid, is gravely ill."

"I understand that. I do. The question is why and for how long?"

"Why he is ill, we cannot know because we cannot communicate with him. If we are ever able to find out why, then we might be able to describe procedures—baths, shock, conversation, exercise—which could restore him. For the present—and it has been only eight months—we can, at best, forgive the unscientific locution, pray for him. There's really little more we can do."

"All you do then is maintain him and keep us alive on hope."

"Rather metaphorical, that turn of phrase, but accurate. Yes. Maintenance and hope."

The interview was hopeless. They chatted amiably a bit longer, the clock sounded the quarter hour, and the nurse entered the office to call the doctor to the dispensary to authorize a sedation.

The doctor left the office hurriedly, promising to return, but Stefan Friedrich had no further interest in the portentous Dr. Mauritius. A minute later he left the doctor's office, bowed to the nurse as he closed his overcoat and put his cap to his head, thanking her and the doctor for their courtesies. When he was seated again in the carriage he had ordered to wait, he opened his coat, withdrew the folder he had purloined from the doctor's desk, and began to read his father's history. The medical report was annotated and initialed in many hands, among which that of Dr. Mauritius was absent. It comforted him to know that his father was examined by others less unctuous and condescending than the founder of the Mauritius Sanatorium. He read the report through twice, noting various facts that had been previously obscure, the phenomenon of mounting blood pressure, which created the sensation of immense pounding and was often accompanied by hallucination of voices and inner promptings, the terror of stationary objects becoming aggressively animate—of trees attacking, of mirrors choking, of statues crushing. Apparently his father had not taken shelter in his impenetrable fog until several weeks after his arrival. In that early period he had rambled constantly, rarely sleeping except after the administration of a sedative. During that period a nurse or floor doctor had always been near at hand to note down his words or a description of his behavior. Twice he had referred to his "bloodied son" and each time had begun to cry with evident remorse. Through the months the Count had lost weight; he refused nourishment. He was fed artificially, but the prognosis was now poor. The consensus of the attending physicians was that, without some dramatic change, which could not be planned or controlled, the Count would not survive the winter. Whatever the degenerative process that had begun and whatever atrophy of his nervous system had occurred, reversal seemed unlikely. He appeared, they thought, to be suffering from a schizophrenic dementia grounded in some pathogenic predisposition no one seemed prepared explicitly to describe. There was, of course, a recurrence of technical medical terms, invariably abbreviated (either because they were so well known as to be immediately recognizable to the trained or because they were so deplorable as to be unmentionable in other than medical code), which the young Count passed over, never committing them to memory.

The young Count finished the dossier and closed his eyes. He was not enlightened; at least, however, his confusion was shared by the most eminent doctors. There would be no answer to his question, nor any elaboration of the predisposition that even he—he shrugged wearily—might have inherited. In all events, in the passion to know the truth, he overlooked one aspect of his conduct, distinctly odd for a young Count, even a Count of the lesser nobility. He had committed a theft.

The decade that followed the death of Count Peter Nickolaus von Mauger marked not only the decline of the House of Mauger, but an alteration in the fortunes of Europe. A curiously inverted proposition, this, but one not essentially at variance with the accepted manner of receiving the dismays of history. The assassination of the Archduke Ferdinand, the mobilization of the Austro-Hungarian Empire, the outbreak of war, the death of two dozen million Europeans and the dislocation of many millions of others, uprooted and torn from their homes, is registered in every life on a less magnified scale. For each single recipient of the tremors and shocks of the historical, what is retained is not the mutilation of nameless millions or the destruction of cities and the wasting of countrysides, but the death of one or two, the loss of a home, its familiar furnishings, its mementoes and photographs, or perhaps, with more insidious implication, the loss of wealth and the trappings of power. It is only when all of these are aggregated—the millions upon millions of individual losses gathered together in the encyclopedic eye of history—that one has the judgment of world tragedy. Until that artificial unity is wrought by historians patiently accumulating evidence and proofs, what is perceived is small and private and the perception of tragedy is modest from the perspective of the larger whole, very modest.

The decline in the fortunes of the Von Maugers, although in great measure attributable to the catastrophe of war, the blasting of the forests of Silesia by the artillery of Russia and Germany who fought their battles in its clearings, the flooding of the phosphate mines which made them all but useless, and the burning of the winter lodge of the Von Maugers, all these demonstrable losses, which cost the family millions upon millions (whether accounted in marks, shillings, or our own currency), were nothing when set beside the death of Count Peter Nickolaus von Mauger during the spring of the year of war.

During April 1914 the Count died. The circumstances that surrounded his death, the last week of lucidity, the desperate pleading that he be allowed, like his great-grandfather, the befitting dignity of suicide, had been refused by medical prurience and the Count returned again to the befogged despair from which he had so briefly emerged, succumbing to a more patient and protracted suicide, refusing the benefits of nourishment even though it was injected, willing himself by denial into a death that received him at the close of his fifty-second year.

The news was brought by cablegram from Salzburg to the Von Mauger mansion in Vienna late in the afternoon of April 17th when the young Count and his sisters were gathered for tea in their mother's apartment. The Countess had aged astonishingly since her husband had taken ill. She had retired into gray silk nightgowns and blue satin robes and for weeks on end, hidden from the day, she had been sustained by light food. Everything had been done to relieve the severe migraine headaches that had begun the year before, but every tremor of the city, a passing lorry, reading the newspaper and its almost innocent recital of the omens of disaster, a particularly loud voice, would set her head to shuddering with pain. Not massages or cool compresses or even the vials of morphine to which she had, it was thought, occasional recourse were sufficient to break the deadly vise of pain that clamped her head like a steel helmet. Although that particular April day had been glorious for Vienna springs, cool and cheerful, sun having been allowed for the occasion to come into the Countess's room— a rare event; she had risen that morning without the slightest pain—and although she continued throughout the day to touch her forehead with amazement as though delicate fingers would probe the secret source of her malady, she seemed to be recovered when her little clan gathered for tea in the late afternoon. Mr. Richards (whom the Countess treated with ill-befitting irritability, excluding him as well as all grown men from her company) was not present, although he had warned the young Count of what procedures he should take if his mother became difficult to manage. After bows and kisses had been exchanged, the young

Count rang for the tea and while his sisters chattered excitedly, speaking with particular animation of a Hussar Captain of their acquaintance who had just departed for maneuvers near Budapest, Stefan Friedrich examined his mother with an especial attention. It was not that he had any foreboding, although it should be acknowledged that ever since Dr. Mauritius had advised him that his father's days were numbered, he had been awaiting the grim telegram that he had no doubt would one day arrive. Whatever glorious day had occurred during the previous eight months since his August visit to the sanatorium the year before, young Stefan had prayed that it would not be on that day. It was enough in his view that his father was mad, but he was still alive and with life he was allowed to hope that around a bend in time there might be illumination and renewal. And so he would pray each morning, invoking his several deities—a caged oriole who chirruped the moment its night shroud was lifted, his painting tools, each of which was invested with a magical potency as though his own hand did not guide its movement, and finally when he took his early morning gallop in the forest outside the city, his Arab pony, Suleiman, who if not a proper god, was a worshipful ephebe. No wonder then that on that glorious day in April he had not expected to see upon a silver salver beside the credenza piled high with cakes and cream puffs and tortes oozing jellies, a blue-enveloped telegram. The servant nodded ominously to him as he pushed the tea caddy into the room and Stefan reached and took the message.

"What have you there, Stefan?" his sisters called out.

"Read it out to us, your secret message," the Countess added, smiling an exhausted smile, touching her forehead lightly with her pinky finger as if to smooth an uncoifed hair.

Stefan Friedrich opened the telegram and withdrew the folded message and, whatever its consequence, began to read, his voice firm and clear: "It is my sad duty to inform you that your father, Count Peter Nickolaus von Mauger, died this morning. May we extend our deepest sympathies to the Countess, your sisters, and yourself upon your loss. At the end he was reconciled and he received the sacraments of the Church. It would be appreciated if a representative came to call to complete the arrangements. Dr. Mauritius."

As though carved from ice, features fixed when the cold waters rose, skin transparent before the late afternoon sun, the Countess and her children were frozen, each child awaiting the other, all awaiting their mother.

The Countess lifted her head and tried once more to renew her smile, parting her lips, showing the edge of whiteness, but at once biting her lip, clasping her hands before her, bunched, rising to her mouth where she bit them; dropping her hands, now ringed with red, into her lap, she began quietly to weep. Both daughters rushed to her and clasped her, comforting her and asking to be comforted. She did not speak for some time, the scene of weeping and comfort, the family "Pietà," as Stefan would later come to describe it. The children dropped their heads and each, not knowing the nature of death, began to cry, for they knew loss, but not death, and for each of them it was not death, but never seeing again that struck them, loss without good-bye but no different from weeping over the lost in every aspect, the lost trinket, the lost doll, the ruined, the dried out, the thrown away, those little gestures of dematerialization that occur in the normal run of days instructing children slowly in the erosion of life that ends in death. The family sat magnificently and wept, beautifully dressed, the tea warm in their cups, the cakes like pretty stuffs becoming soft in the warmth of the sun. But the Countess did not abate her tears and a half hour passed, the children drying their eyes, the Countess caught breath and strangling upon old tears renewed and deepened her weeping. At last, when she had bitten enough into the knuckles of her hands, the anger that lay sleeping beneath the headaches and the tears burst upon them. "God should not pardon that man," she shouted and stood up, throwing open her arms before them. The children shuddered with horror; before them was no longer a dear and suffering *maman*, but a woman enraged by a secret that she no longer needed to keep hidden. "Never, never, no pardon for him, even in death no pardon."

It was not until a decade later that Stefan Friedrich von Mauger, Count von Mauger, as he became known immediately after the burial of his father, learned the secret that his mother had contained until her own death. During those years, the years following the war and the financial decline of the Von Maugers, the Countess had lived in the more modest establishment that he had provided for her in the vicinity of the cathedral, where she spent her days in vigils and fasts, never missing Mass, keeping close to hand Anna Liselotte, whom she had prevailed upon by threats and promises to become her handmaiden, allowing Franziska to marry her Hussar Captain whose only triumph of the war had been to be wounded early and discharged. The fortunes of the family, their real estate gone, their equities and holdings bankrupted or dispersed by war, were reduced to the jewels and treasures of their Vienna household, not inconsiderable, one can imagine, and securities and bonds, most of which had fallen in value, but which still allowed a modest income, enough to maintain their mother's station and provide Stefan Friedrich with an allowance which enabled him to travel and study abroad. It was during the early twenties that Stefan Friedrich was recalled from London to Vienna for his mother's funeral. She had died quietly in her sleep in her sixty-first year, having outlived her husband by a bitter ten years. Among her papers, there was a letter addressed by her in a firm and unmistakable hand, dated in some confusion, either 1914 or 1924, the 1 having been altered, it appeared, by a later pen into a 2, although perhaps it was written only weeks before her death. It could not be confirmed with any certainty whether the letter was written in the months immediately after their father's death in the sanatorium when the Countess was relieving the anger and frustration to which her migraines had borne witness (for they did not trouble her in the last years except when one or another relative turned up to cheer her with reminiscences of the days in their Silesian lodge or of the splendid galas with which they had charmed all Vienna at the turn of the century) or whether it was a letter of disclosure written by her in anticipation of her death. It was the case, in all events, that in the Countess's will, which bequeathed to her son the remains of her estate with charge for the keeping of his unmarried sister, a letter was found addressed to all three children, with the instruction unmistakable, that it not be opened and read until after her death.

The letter, slightly hysterical it must be concluded, although the hand that wrote it seemed even and unexaggerated, was not read aloud, as had been the telegram announcing the death of the Count, but was passed from hand to hand and read in solitude.

"My dearest children,

I had resolved at the death of your father to carry our secret to my death without revealing its sordid nature. Unfortunately at the time of learning of his passing I was unable to control the rage which overcame me, torrentially, if I remember the moment correctly. I alluded to his sin and I invoked God to punish him, an invocation I have sorely regretted. It is not our place, sinners all, to tax the good Lord with the obligation to retribute others lest he deal us a more mighty blow. It is bad policy to come too closely to God's attention. However, having alluded to your father's transgression and planted that rage in your midst, I have equally no right to pass out of this life (into one I trust will be an improvement) without relieving your fantasies and suspicions. The news I confide to you is not minor. Nor is it such as to be concealed forever lest one or another of you be marked by its taint. I would have remained content to be alone beside himself in knowing of his great sin, had he not died hopelessly insane, a victim it appears of what Doctor Mauritius described in the papers which our son, Count Stefan Friedrich, not too skillfully concealed from my discovery in his desk, of the possible consequence of that indiscretion. Your father had become involved in the early years of our marriage with a Rumanian opera singer, a woman of no particular talent, who played I am told minor roles in operettas of the day. Apparently your father contracted from her a disease which was concealed from me until after the birth of his son. The Count, it appears, cared more for the birth of an heir than he did for his children's health. I tell you this lest you undertake to give birth or father children without proper precaution. I have no knowledge of medical science, but what need have we to give birth to broken or crooked lines? I never forgave your father his deception. I never loved him again from the time of the birth of our son and I will die unforgiving of him. I have cursed him enough. May God have mercy upon him, upon myself, and upon you, dear children."

The disclosure of the Count's affair with the young soprano, although it explained much of their mother's behavior during the concluding years of her life, did not appear to agitate the children. Franziska took the news with equanimity, for she had little choice, her own stomach already swelling in the third month of her first pregnancy when the Countess died. She preserved the optimism, wholly ignorant of the course of the disease, that the palpable virility and good looks of her husband would overwhelm the deadly spirochetes, as in fact they did, assuming, to be sure, the accuracy of her mother's revelation. There was no way of verifying the charge, nor for that matter was any effort made to seek out the relatives of the singer who had long since passed from the active roster of Viennese performers. Anna Liselotte was depressed, however, less by the letter than by the loss of her daughterly vocation and she, more out of confusion than from religious conviction, determined to enter a convent in St. Pölten. Only the Count, Stefan Friedrich, was left to settle the affairs of the family, and having reorganized its finances, investing the principal of their capital in businesses he regarded as somewhat more familiar and congenial, he made plans to leave Vienna and never to return. Such finality was accompanied by an ever more stern and absolute resolution: to one and all he announced that he was no longer a Count, that the family was dissolved by death, that his sisters were occupied elsewhere (one wedded to a military man whose connection with the nobility of Austria was at most tenuous, the other to a divinity without aristocratic pretension, although the convent of St. Pölten had been the refuge of many a disconsolate daughter of the Empire). He alone was a nobleman and he alone was in a position to abandon the title. The problem, of course, was that in an age that had grown weary of aristocrats and irritated with the pretensions of little noblemen (waxed moustaches and exaggerated manners, clicking spurs they no longer wore, and clanking swords long since melted down into automobiles and airplanes) it was difficult to renounce nobility. There was nobody to receive the renunciation, no one to frown with displeasure, no majesty anywhere who would even notice, much less care, that the recent (for the late sixteen hundreds is quite recent) family of noble Maugers was being dissolved. With the inevitable result that since it no longer mattered, the decision of Stefan Mauger to regard himself with democratic simplicity—stripped of numerous subsidiary names that narrated his line and divested of noble prefix—was noted while he remained in Vienna, but ceased to be of significance when he departed. The consequence of this was that although concierges and maîtres d'hôtel were embarrassed when they addressed the young man as Count Stefan only to be told with stern (almost noble) authority that he was Herr Stefan Friedrich Mauger, it became useful in countries where the family was completely unknown, where strangers were treated with rudeness and indifference, to employ from time to time the noble honorific.

In the months that followed his mother's death and his reluctant installation of his sister among the Englische Fräulein of St. Pölten, Stefan Mauger found himself still sulking through the streets of Vienna, walking out of perfectly splendid performances of the opera, turning his back on old acquaintances who asked to join him for a coffee on the Graben. He had lost interest in his past but he had not yet departed it. He had returned to Vienna to finish with it, but he lingered on as though awaiting a visitation that would clarify his next move. He had been unable to draw since his return, although he was endlessly tempted to try. But there seemed no point to it; drawing had come forward out of his childhood as an assertion of solitariness and self-exclusion within a household dominated by aristocratic assumptions which he had already forsworn. He was an aristocrat without portfolio, hence the ease with which he abandoned its nomenclature and honorifics. He had stripped himself, flayed off the outer layer of skin, only to find beneath layer upon layer of tissue and texture that had yet to receive the definition of character and purpose. He had returned from England to Vienna, taking the night train from Calais, changing trains at Paris without leaving the station, and arrived not long before the Requiem Mass in his mother's memory was to begin. In London, during his absent years, he had taken classes at the Slade, improved his technique, mastered shadowing and relief, but his drawing had progressed little beyond the point of gifted amateur. In short, Stefan Mauger concluded one afternoon that he was a dilettante, competent, mannered, intelligent, but finally dilettante. He could imagine remaining a dilettante for a few months longer, but not much beyond that. Without the passion to compel himself from dilettante to obsession, he could contemplate a few more years before boredom or an unheroic bullet would overtake him. He shuddered at the prospect, put down his coffee cup just as an elderly Baron who admired his youthful charm approached to strike up a conversation, bowed solemnly to the Baron, returned to his hotel on the Ringstrasse, packed his valises, and departed for the train station. He wasn't certain which train he would take. For the moment it didn't matter. It only mattered that he leave, then, immediately. He paid the taxi, rushed into the station, and consulted the schedule of departures. One train was about to leave for Warsaw, another for Paris. It was fortunate, he thought later, that he knew no Polish.

2

Collecting and Making

In the early afternoon, having watched the launch through his binoculars slow and discharge Gutiérrez's troopers to wade ashore into the jungle, Stefan Mauger commingled the expectation of ready cash with embarrassment at having once again committed a theft, a spectacular theft, which only the delivery of the single figure he had selected for his own delight would appease. The only portion of his labor that escaped the system of distribution and sales he had devised was the single piece or so that he retained for his own feast of eye. But he knew, whatever he called it, that he had become a collector, that he had passed through complex and artful rationalization, from thief and businessman to collector, holding on to the marvelous and the exemplary not because it held no temptation to his own carving, not because it did not compete with his own gifts, not even because it compelled his eye to the scrutiny of his own interior landscape, but quite simply because it was perfect and hence desirable to others and hence dear. Despite the

51

opinion of Alicia's father, the Judge of Lyons, who thought him a prodigal (although he had repeatedly assured him that without living parents or patrimony he hardly qualified) for having continually instigated his daughter to appeal for handouts in the extremity of their precarious finances, he was quick to observe that he never asked (and indeed was quite a bit more capable of doing without than was Alicia, who always converted his moan and desperation into an urgent telegram for funds), he did congratulate himself in the midst of his Gulfside depression that the Jaina treasure was extraordinary and would certainly fetch a splendid price.

That is, if he wasn't caught one day. He temporized, seated before the water, watching the soldiers wade ashore and the treasure boat turn and head out into the sea where he soon lost it to the horizon. And why not now with this theft? But so far, to his knowledge, not a breath of suspicion. Of course it had been prudent to suborn the chief of the constabulary, to draw him into the business, acquaint him sufficiently with the rudiments of the enterprise, until (indeed, not long ago) Gutiérrez caught a petty Guatemalan runner of artifacts, confiscated his stock, and permitted Stefan Mauger to select from the constabulary storeroom the only decent piece—a handsome onyx monkey bowl—and buy it from him. Gutiérrez was not essentially corrupt. Rather, he was bemused that anyone should regard the artifacts of old Mexico (which he thought ugly) as valuable—they were fit only for *gringos*, whom he imagined more stupid than the objects worthless. Gutiérrez regarded Stefan Mauger as a fool, a handsome, quiet-speaking, untroublesome fool, who paid well and promptly for clay pots and grotesque figures that could be of no value, since, if they were valuable, the Captain rationalized, they would be displayed in churches or hidden in the storerooms of the latifundia to which he sometimes gained access, but in neither place were they to be found. Nonetheless, Gutiérrez figured, here was someone who paid to be protected from inquiry, who occasionally conscripted a constabulary officer to accompany a shipment to the border, who employed indigent peons to make digs and return their findings to a shed along the dirt road to Stefan Mauger's hacienda, where they were collected. Stefan Mauger was good for the economy. Only Captain Gutiérrez knew his identity and, for his part, Stefan Mauger had only to deal with the ignorance and cupidity of the Chief of Police. There seemed little to fear.

On the outskirts of Campeche, along a dirt road that leads into the shantytown where the hovels of the poor may still be seen, there was a little cantina, cheerfully called El Cantinflas. It was there that Captain Gutiérrez had agreed to meet Stefan Mauger just before midnight. Stefan did not arrive on time. He never imagined that the Captain would be prompt. No one was prompt in Mexico; nothing ever needed to be done on time. After five years, *más o menos*, of living in Campeche he had absorbed the ritual indifference to time. People awakened when they were up; ate when they sat down to table; went to bed when they fell asleep. Time was descriptive, the report of actual facts, never promise or routine. Gutiérrez had merely said *"antes de media noche"* when they spoke on the telephone. He took this to mean any time between eleven and twelve, with arrival acceptable as late as twelve-thirty. He had intended to arrive early, content to sit on the back porch of El Cantinflas, which was raised on pilings above the mud, and scrutinize the jungle not fifty feet away, drinking his tequila and beer under the glow of a dozen painted lights, wondering whether the Indian girl with whom he had slept fitfully some months before in the tiny brothel that Tia Clara, the proprietor of the cantina, had fixed up in a secluded clearing, had had her baby. But Stefan Mauger was late. He had knocked on Alicia's door to tell her he was going off, but hearing nothing, decided to write a note and leave it on her bed. He thought that Alicia and Maria had gone for a drive, but when he entered, the two women were fast asleep, Maria's black hair spread over Alicia's face like a veil. They looked very beautiful, he thought, bunching the note and stuffing it into his pocket. Perplexed, he closed the door and sighed. His eyes passed desultorily over the occupants of the hallway—papier-mâché Judas figures with bat wings, wooden saints, a Santos Virgin stripped down to painted wood—until they settled upon his marble of an outstretched index finger on which Stefan had carefully slid an ancient gold ring. He had brought the work into the house from the studio that evening to show his women and, discovering a rough passage where the finger neared the small block from which it had been carved, he began to polish it with fine sandpaper, cradling it in his left arm and working on the rough passage with an application of thumb that was both tender and alive with affection. It was after midnight when he looked up and saw the clock reproving him. He had completely forgotten his appointment with the Captain.

Capitán Gutiérrez was seated on the back porch of El Cantinflas drinking beer and fingering *tapas* when Stefan Mauger entered the bar. His visored cap was on the table; beneath it his garrison belt, harness, holster and pistol. On the floor near his foot was a straw basket covered with newspaper. It was very late. Capitán Gutiérrez wanted to be home, in bed with Asunción. His finger was poking among bits of stewed squid floating in a brine of onions and vinegar when Stefan, wearing his habitual sneakers, approached quietly and put a hand on his shoulder.

"Ah, Señor Mauger," Capitán Gutiérrez acknowledged, not disrespectfully, his yellow teeth glinting dully under the canopy of colored lights. "You are very late this evening."

"My apologies. Work, always work."

"Will you drink something?"

"I don't think so. Not this evening."

"Have something. On me. It's been a fine day for all of us," the Captain continued, winking at Stefan.

"A beer, then."

"*Una cerveza,* Tia Clara."

"*¿Dos Equis?*" a shrill voice called from the darkness of the interior.

Stefan glanced indifferently at the captain. It didn't matter. He was thinking of Maria's hair, its rich blackness hiding her face, and Alicia, small, delicate, her reddish-blond short-cropped hair hugging her head like a bangle bracelet, her red lips moving quietly, a strand of Maria's hair falling over her closed eyes, another fanning her chin and neck. Stefan shook his head in disbelief. They looked like exhausted children.

"You shake your head. Not *Dos Equis*?"

"It doesn't matter. Of course *Dos Equis*. Why not?" Stefan temporized, suddenly weary.

"*Dos Equis*, Tia Clara," the Captain called, almost whistling. "Sit down, my friend. We have things to talk about."

Stefan Mauger had almost forgotten why he had come. He continued to think of his two women, and for an instant the marble sculpture, as though an endless woman, cylinder upon cylinder of graduated whiteness moving up from a base of hips, came before him and he began again to polish the imperfect finger.

"Those *ídolos* from the island. They are valuable?"

Stefan Mauger laughed. He had returned and was scrutinizing the Captain sitting before him, his head tilted to one side, almost lying on his arm, inquiring with that astonishing canniness which Mexicans confuse with innocence whether the treasure was valuable. "What do *you* think, Capitán?"

"I'm asking."

"But does it matter? You get paid even if they're not valuable or if they all break before they reach the *gringos.* *¿Verdad?*" Stefan Mauger had been dealing with Mexicans for years and before them with the Kwakiutl in British Columbia and dealers in Paris and New York. It was still a surprise.

"*¿Verdad!* But I'm still curious."

"Well, you tell me. What do you think?"

"I think they are very valuable, those pieces of clay we brought off the island. (And it was easy, I can tell you.) Very valuable. It took six policemen and an officer. Very valuable. Would you believe it if I say they must be worth something like one hundred thousand, no, more like a hundred and fifty thousand pesos to the *gringos*? You get very rich on my work, no?"

Stefan Mauger was no longer surprised. It was all familiar. In every dealing with the Mexican professional—businessman, official, thief—he knew it always cost twice as much as the original price. That was part of the normal transaction. It was still necessary to go through the formalities of a protest, to show anger, to induce threats, to mollify them by compromise, and finally to pay.

"What's all this, Capitán? Whose work? It's not nineteen ten any more. I'm not Díaz. I'm not Madero. You know that! And you most certainly are not Hidalgo or Juarez. You agreed to a price, and a damn good price it is. More than you make in three months. In fact, you've made from me this year more than a year's salary. And here's the money I promised." Stefan Mauger reached into his jacket pocket and slid an envelope under the Captain's holstered pistol.

"I understand all that. Very good talk. But you are too quick for me. You think much faster. You have to let El Capitán of the Campeche Constabulary think slowly." It was all familiar. Begin with arrogance and end in stupidity. Stefan sighed. Suddenly he wanted a drink very badly. Tia Clara shuffled toward the table, her swollen feet in begrimed canvas moccasins, their bottoms cushioned with strips of rubber tire. She smiled, her features stretching, her gums empty except for the blackened stumps of a half-dozen front teeth. "The gentleman has joined us, I see. Very good. It's always good to see you, old friend. How are the women?" She pulled over a rush stool after putting the bottle of chilled beer on the table and lowered her considerable weight.

"*Muy bien*. They flourish in the humidity," Stefan replied.

"Good. I saw them both last week. We had a brandy together, but they didn't say much. I think Alicia is becoming too thin. Like a chicken, I think. It happens to everyone in Campeche except me." She thought this uproarious and began to laugh, her body shaking under her long print skirt. A bottle was pounded on the table near the bar, but Tia Clara ignored it. The second time the bottle sounded, she turned and good-naturedly called back into the gloomy interior. "Wait your turn, you drunken pig. I'm talking. Don't you hear Tia Clara talking to her guests?" There was silence.

"We have business to talk, Tia Clara," Captain Gutiérrez said quietly.

"I see that. Such *señores* are rare at El Cantinflas." She exaggerated *señores* with remarkable sarcasm. She was probably a bit stiff herself, Stefan thought. She had the habit of drinking the dregs from every glass, which, even if imprudent, saved her the trouble of washing them. "I'll catch up with you again. Bring back your ladies, Señor Stefan. I love to see them." She rose and shuffled off, but as an after-

57

thought, called back, "Hey, you want one of the girls to-night?"

"Not tonight, Tia Clara," both replied. She shrugged and passed through the beaded curtain into the interior of the bar. They heard voices again and Tia Clara's rumbling laugh. A breeze rose from the jungle, but it quickly died. It was time for the rains to return, but they had not yet begun. It was cooler than usual in Campeche, but still humid.

"The money. We were talking about the money. Thank you for the envelope, but I don't think my men and I find this acceptable." Capitán Gutiérrez pushed the envelope back across the table toward Stefan.

"Your men have nothing to do with it. I'm sure your men don't even know the arrangement. You give them whatever you know you can get away with. Ah, Capitán, why must it always be this way?"

"I don't know, but it is," Captain Gutiérrez answered sadly. "Nobody can be trusted. Not you. Not my men. Not even me, I think. The only thing reliable is passing the money. When the money is taken, it's done. Until then, we, how should I put it, we bargain mistrust. I need more. If it's fifty thousand pesos we got for you, I need at least ten thousand for my men and me."

"Nobody in all Campeche has ten thousand pesos, Capitán. Nobody. You want money like a partner. You're not a partner. You did work for me. You did it well. You get paid what we agreed. I think you deserve something extra. I will give you something more. A thousand today, this minute, and another thousand with the final payment next week. But that's all."

Capitán Gutiérrez was not really as grasping as he would have liked to appear. He didn't, it is true, trust anybody, but then he was a policeman and policemen trust nobody, not the bosses in Mexico City, not General Julio of the Federales, not the officials and deputies who swarmed his office like flies, and certainly not his *chamulas*, his fellow-Indians who were scurvy and disease to his mind. He begrudgingly admired Señor Stefan because that man, at least, was not a Spaniard, lived with two women, and made incredibly large statues (*"ídolos"* he called them) with his own hands, cutting and breaking and chipping stones and trees until miraculous shapes appeared. In the eyes of Capitán Gutiérrez, Stefan Mauger was remote, remarkable, a little mysterious. When it came to money, of course, Stefan Mauger was no different from any *gachupin*, but on the whole he was a decent man. He paid well and what he did with those clay pots and jade necklaces and *ídolos* was no concern of his.

"For the moment I agree with you. Give me the packet for my men and the thousand extra. We will speak again. Next week. Perhaps before." Stefan Mauger took another packet from his pocket and laid it atop the first. He did not slide it this time. Once was enough for that mean gesture.

"And thank you for this, Capitán," Stefan said quietly, reaching down to pick up the basket in which he could trace the shape of the Jaina figurine he had marked for his own collection. The Captain's foot moved the basket out of reach. "Not until we finish our business. Only fair, no?" Stefan Mauger flushed with anger but said nothing. He found his posture, bending to the foot of his confederate, disgusting, but even more, he found himself humiliated. "Yes. Right. When we meet again." There was no hurry. It would cost more, but Stefan Mauger had vastly more to gain than a hundred and fifty thousand pesos. A slow and clumsy dance. Even then, the steps had to be followed carefully.

Mauger said good night and stood up, stretching his arms wearily. Touching two fingers to his forehead in a kind of salute to the Captain, he left El Cantinflas and started out in the direction of the jungle clearing.

Inspector Mariposa sat at his cluttered desk, momentarily becalmed, at his elbow a cup of stale coffee already mottled with drowned flies. It was not yet mid-morning and the sun was already bleaching the light of the capital. There had been rain, but insufficient. It had been an exceptionally hot season. Fortunately it had been quiet, *"muy tranquilo,"* the Police Commissioner had reported with satisfaction. Inspector Mariposa had hardly expected, therefore, the call that came from the department shortly before six on Saturday morning. Nothing like that had happened in years. He was sleeping quite soundly when the phone jangled. He couldn't imagine it was for him. The air was so clear in Tepotzlan, he thought it might be ringing in the house down the road. He sometimes heard their phone very late at night; they were Americans. But the phone persisted and he retreated from a most attractive dream—he was once again exploring jungle ruins and finding the most astonishing carvings—rubbed his eyes, grunted, and eased himself out of bed. He listened to the voice with increasing astonishment, almost excitement. Normally the drive from Tepotzlan to his office in the Central Police Station took something over an hour. It was usually a leisurely drive from the Valley of Mexico to the high ground on which the capital city had been built. Sometimes he amused himself by counting all the unexcavated sites of Aztec and before them Toltec ruins that dotted the landscape, covered with scrub grass and cactus, healthy from the humus of bones, concealing, he surmised, small temples, a necropolis, a provincial treasury, a sacrificial altar, something that when covered over with earth would age down to the shape of a fattened cone or miniature pyramid. There were more than ten thousand unexcavated archaeological sites in Mexico. He knew hundreds of them by name, their origin, their history, and more to the point, the date of their opening by the government or sack by robbers. On the road from Tepotzlan, once a major center of Aztec power, dominating the whole fertile valley from which the maize crop that fed the kingdom was obtained, Inspector Mariposa had identified and documented nearly three hundred, had explored a score or more himself, adding handsomely to his own and the nation's collection.

It was a curious arrangement, not at all common in richer nations where the national treasure belonged only to those who could afford either to acquire it or to bequeath it. Poor nations (and Mexico was among the poor) had to make more ingenious arrangements to insure that the mining of their resources would be accomplished with the least investment of the national treasury. Of course, one of the characteristic oversights of poor nations is to prize as real only wealth that is visible. Wealth that required planning and expectation, long-term investment and speculation, indeed, deep digging of any order, was thought to be fanciful, almost arbitrary and irrational. No wonder then that only the shallow wealth of the nation had been exploited over the centuries since the occupation of Indian land by the Spanish conquerors—silver, lead, mahogany, rubber—but even these had been conceded to foreign interests for development and only in the present century had such concessions lapsed or been expropriated and returned to Mexican ownership. The deep assets were still in the hands of foreigners in those middle years of the nineteen fifties—oil, iron, minerals, phosphates, and, of course, the buried treasures of the ancient past.

When Baltásar Mariposa was a young man, just past his twentieth birthday, come up from Veracruz, one of the few major cities in Mexico that barely antedated the Conquest, an early center for the true Cross come into the midst of the hard Indian world, he had never seen a ruin of his ancestors, although he might have found, had he been curious, incomparable examples. He had heard of them; he had read about them; but he had never seen a major city of the old times. He had intended to become a lawyer; indeed, the scholarship that he had won to the University of Mexico City stipulated that he would pursue courses in commerce and economics and then continue on to law. All that ended quite by accident. It happened one day during his second year in the capital that he was in a restaurant, seated within earshot of a table where the great Alfonso Caso was discussing with some associates the nearly disastrous retrenchment in the federal allocation for archaeological research, a retrenchment that eliminated most of the quasi-skilled sorters and cleaners, those semi-literate workers who took from the shovels of the peons the shards they had uncovered and by familiarity with the rudiments of style, design, materials of fabrication, could generally guess to which stratum of the classic culture they belonged. Baltásar put down his glass, turned his chair toward the table at which the gentlemen were talking, and quite simply joined up. He announced that he was qualified—indeed, fully literate as far as the general subject matter of human civilization was concerned—that he would work for the barest pittance, that he would in fact give up the study of law if the gentlemen found his talents promising to the service of archaeology.

The truth of the matter is that Baltásar Mariposa was a young man in search of an obsession, something worthwhile but obscure, underpaid but requiring great skill and devotion, intellectually challenging but beyond the possibility of exhaustion and total mastery. Nothing could have suited his requirements more completely—the civilization of ancient

Mexico could never be mastered, its language never fully deciphered, its mathematics reconstructed, astronomy recalculated, mythology adequately described, and hence its art and architecture would forever retain the aura of mystery. With every discovery not only old questions were reformulated, but a dozen more were posed that could not yet be answered. It was a Chinese puzzle, except that at its core would be found not even one single box, but a proliferation of tiny boxes, none of which could be opened. The mysteries of archaeology, unlike the law, promised ultimacy and it was the hunt for ultimacy that this child of Veracruz shopkeepers demanded, although from where that urgency derived is hard to estimate—from the dark room overlooking a dank courtyard in which he passed his youth? from the unreasonable penalties inflicted by the irritable brothers of the monastery school in which he had had his education? Who knows how it comes to pass that plants grow in desiccated soil.

The proposal of young Mariposa was first treated with amusement and disbelief. One of the gentlemen laughingly called him a *novillero*, and another suggested, extending the disdain of his colleague, that his "joining up" was no different from those young urchins who occasionally vault the *barrera* at the bull ring to make a few fledgling passes—and he pointedly reminded Baltásar that such urchins end in the police guardroom being beaten senseless. Fortunately, Professor Caso, already an eminence, indeed, at the zenith of a long and distinguished career—it was he, it should be recalled, who had opened in 1932 the miraculous tomb at Monte Alban where the richest hoard of Mayan artifacts was uncovered and it is to him that the establishment of an indigenous discipline of Mexican archaeology may be honorably credited—regarded young Mariposa's suggestion with less cynicism. When he began his labors he had been little more than a passionate amateur. He could hardly have been anything else, since those early days were marked by disrespect, confusion, prejudice, and the virtual monopoly of his vocation by German, English, and North American scholars with pith helmets, breeches and boots, camp stools, and immense theories, behaving as though they were movie directors instead of scientific investigators of a noble and unrecovered past. Alfonso Caso, not less than Baltásar Mariposa, was in search of an origin, a definite moment riddled in the stone stellae and the few parchment codices not burned by the monks of the Conquest, which would reveal to him why it was that the Mexican landscape was so brutal and extreme, why it was the Indians were so handsome and so despairing, or for that matter, why it was that his ancestors produced the wheel but reserved its employment for children's toys while favoring flat bed boats and human labor to move from the riverside to the temple site slabs of stone weighing as much as five tons. Those were questions which had, *mutatis mutandis*, crossed the mind of Baltásar Mariposa and when, responding to Caso's questioning, he revealed a mind sharp and clear, perspicacious and inquisitive, Professor Caso grunted to his companions, *"Muy bien, guapo, muy bien."*

The school holidays began normally in January and with his legal studies adjourned and his future now in question, Baltásar had joined a small group of student archaeologists who returned to Monte Alban near the city of Oaxaca to tidy up after the celebrated opening of Tomb 7 two years earlier. Nothing could have been more decisive. It might have been different if he had been assigned to an expedition in search of a discovery, the cutting of one of the myriad known but unexplored sites for example. There, with all the precision of soothsayers, a summer could be passed with nothing to show for it but a scar upon the earth; deft opening, weeks of digging and shoveling, and at last, at the very end of labor, they might find an abandoned room, a jar or two, faded cloth, a string of glass beads, emptiness and void. Deserted once more, the site would be described in the official records as having been stripped of its contents either in the ninth century or in the twelfth or after the Conquest. Such an experience could damage the enthusiasm of the novice, avid for the recovery of a segment, even a repetitive segment (and therefore a confirmation), of the continuity of the past. As we have said, Baltásar Mariposa was on the track of an obsession and a series of empty tombs would not have sufficed. Monte Alban, however, was a revelation, a capital city of a monumental culture, with temples and sanctuaries, palaces and a necropolis; founded and flourished under Zapotecs, conquered and reemployed by Mixtecs, disdained and abandoned by the warrior Toltecs, the city was intact.

The first month at Monte Alban was like a dream. The young man (he was then twenty-two with almond-color skin, soft brown eyes that glazed over with wonder, and black hair thick and combed back from forehead to the nape of his neck) worked like a demon. Nothing was too petty, nothing too insignificant to be ignored. He was everywhere, carrying sacks of dirt when the peons broke for siesta, sorting and classifying, checking notes of his fellow-workers after dinner in the cantina, and reading constantly, whenever a moment permitted, catching up on the waste of having had ordinary ambition. At the end of the probationary novitiate he returned to Mexico City, enrolled in the fledgling program of archaeological study, and spent the next three years deliciously engaged, doing what is permitted to few men—exactly what he chose to do.

It is perhaps even more remarkable that the young archaeologist, this *hombre de obsesión*, should find himself, not eighteen months after his leaving the university, attached to the police, in charge not simply of routine investigation, but most particularly of the rising traffic in contraband, whether of textiles smuggled during the European war to a woollen-starved North America or diamonds to Europe, or the treasures of the archaeological past to private and public museums, university collections, and individual fanciers all over the world.

It should not be thought that traffic in the ancient patrimony of Mexico was regarded in those early days as an authentic crime. There were few crimes in Mexico in the early decades of this century, with the exception perhaps of politics. Theft, corruption, murder were unexceptionable exaggerations of the means that the rich and landed employed to contain the zealous enthusiasm of the poor; the poor, of course, had no privilege but numbers. They, those desperate *campesinos*, rebelled, murdered, burned, looted. Embattled Mexico moved decade by decade to a more stable form of corruption, graduated, leveled, complaisant to sufficient popular needs as to insure that the rich remained rich while the poor were better fed and worse led. There were, of course, what are called idealists, that is, individuals who were curiously indifferent to the wealth that could be secured without labor or the labor of those without ambition to better themselves. The idealists (and many became the nation's teachers, doctors, researchers, poets, painters, and archaeologists) inserted themselves into the system while remaining marginal to it, paid their bribes (however modest) in order to vault the order that required bribes, and flourished in the cracks like wild flowers that will occasionally bloom on dung heaps.

Baltásar Mariposa, confirmed in his obsession, was among these idealists. Ambitious and inexperienced though he was, he had no employment when his studies were completed nor had he devised the service that he could render the system without joining it. He was offered a modest post that might have allowed him from time to time to join an expedition, but in those days he would have had to contribute his keep since he was neither a university teacher nor attached to the Instituto. He was merely one among a growing band in the late thirties who believed that the Mexican past was not so ignominious, savage, decadent as the Spanish overlords had for centuries described it. It was not only that Cortés with monumental horses, unknown to the continent, had conquered by a confusion of myth; that paranoid Moctezuma had mistaken his advent for the return of the sun god; that anything as tawdry as a misreading of the mythic apocalypse could explain the collapse in a few years of one of the great civilizations of the past. The mythic confusion had helped Cortés, but something more was involved in the decline of the past of his race which needed to be recovered. It was impossible then for him to accept a position at a provincial university, indeed, a university located in an area of the nation where he would have little opportunity to walk out into his past and to explore. His enthusiasm would have been drained by little essays, brief scholarly notices; indeed, as Baltásar expressed his refusal of the position: "I have no intention of clerking my past."

The year after his graduation from the university, Baltásar Mariposa stayed on instead in Mexico City, living penuriously in the old city behind the cathedral. He had almost returned to the humid rooms of his childhood, but he was awaiting an opportunity that had not yet shown itself.

It should be noted that during this period Mariposa had contracted the disease of Mexican antiquarians, the disease from which there is neither recovery nor death. The disease of collecting is like malaria, quiescent for long periods, activated and virulent in the right climate and vulnerability, in Mariposa's case the proximity of a quested treasure: It all began with the accumulation of bowls, for Baltásar could only afford bowls at the beginning, drinking bowls, thick bowls that had kept pulque cool, offering bowls, bowls in which rare perfumes were stored, flat bowls for burning copal, and the rarest of the bowls in his collection, a flat serving vessel decorated with the Ollin sign, an abstract butterfly symbolizing the god of fire (for do not the flickering flames of a newborn fire resemble the beating wings of a butterfly?). With that rare bowl, garnered from an excursion to the site of Tenochtitlán where he exchanged two packets of raw tobacco with an Indian to secure it, Baltásar had assembled a collection of twenty-six bowls. A modest collection to be sure, at a cost not exceeding fifty dollars (U.S.), but nonetheless the collection of an obsessive, a man who adored roundness, soft curve, grace, and magic intent. But more than these sensual affections, his instinct to possess these objects, to arrange them upon a shelf above his wooden bedstand, to acquiesce to them when their surface (glistening with moisture during the most humid months of the year) required deft sponging, to examine them repeatedly under the loupe in order to appraise the incising lines of the artisan and discern how the form had been molded, to draw large on a note pad the intricacy of their decoration, to annotate modulations of technique and minuscule variances that suggested the presence of a different hand rather than the individuation of a different vision —these time-consuming labors on behalf of twenty-six bowls drew energy from Baltásar's capitulation to the ancient aesthetic of his race. Neither name nor stylistic signature of any artist has survived and Baltásar well knew that it was not merely a question of loss, the forgotten name of the Master Builder of Uxmal or the Sculptor of La Venta, but the rather more simple fact that every artisan was like his Lord a religious man, that these objects were made not to beautify or ornament, not even to celebrate, but, quite simply, to keep the universe going, to feed the appetites of the gods, who otherwise, but for the service of men, would not carry the sun through the heavens, nor feed the earth's creatures, nor enable them to be born—and these, not simply because the gods were capricious, but rather because without service and sacrifice the nutriment of the universe would be wanting them, and panting from hunger, weak from the previous day's exertions, the sun would not be renewed, the gods who carry the universe would falter, the earth would be riven with quakes, and the crops would dry up from the prolonged slumber of an enfeebled rain god.

Baltásar stayed in his rooms most days, continuing his studies, admiring his little collection, reconstructing more and more faithfully the mentality of his ancestors until one day he was even of a mind to buy a dove in the market and offer it to his invisible pantheon, removing its tiny heart and serving it up with incense upon the flat offering bowl. But the despair of that day, raining and cold, with few pesos left him from a week of Spanish teaching to visiting Americans, ended on his way to the bird market. He stopped into a café and was seated on the terrace drinking a coffee when he observed a startlingly handsome Indian, with gray hair and a thick black moustache, whose serape identified him as coming from the south, huddled over a sack which he kept on the table while he spoke to the well-respected Professor Y whom Baltásar had known from the university. He disliked Professor Y, a sententious survivor of the old revolution, who taught agronomy with a code book of slogans, concluding each session on strains of wheat, the problems of Mexican water distribution, the climatic ferocity of bleak Tabasco with a strophic salute to a generation ago. *"Tierra y libertad,"* he would exclaim, removing his eyeglasses, saluting the little photographic diptych of Juarez and Karl Marx that he kept like an *ex voto* on his desk, and then dismiss his class. This academic revolutionary was also a secret collector but, unlike Baltásar Mariposa, not at all an obsessive. He bought cheap to sell dear, inviting foreign visitors to his home each Saturday, collecting them from lectures he gave to visiting delegations, meeting them at the Sindicato de Artes Populares, where he managed to stroll at least once a week to strike up idle conversations—one day the police had even inquired into his insistent importuning of a young American with red hair, all quite innocent but for the purposes of commerce. Professor Y's practice was to invite a half-dozen visitors to drink coffee and sample tequila in the Mexican manner at his apartment and, having turned the conversation to the ancient past, fascinating his guests with the sacrifice of princesses and tales of Moctezuma's wealth, he would show the unwary visitors his collection, indicating that some of the pieces he was reluctantly disposed to sell because his nonexistent wife needed medical attention. Naturally he had prepared everything in advance, the half-dozen Colima and Tarascan figures, the smiling girls of Remojadas, the Olmec fragments (too rare to be intact, he averred); at the end he would reluctantly close out the bargains, averaging more than one hundred dollars a gathering. His dream was to own a bit of *tierra* in retirement *libertad* near Cuernavaca and he was almost there. He intended to open a little museum of art where his collection would be on view most days (two pesos *entrada*; a little booklet three pesos; copies, fakes, and minor artifacts for sale in the back room). Baltásar Mariposa despised him.

At a certain moment the Professor opened his briefcase

and withdrew a neatly banded packet of pesos from which he counted off a number of bills and dropped them atop the straw hat that the Indian had left beside his chair. Without a word the Professor rose, gripped the neck of the sack, and disappeared into the street. Baltásar could not account for the impulse. He had, however, sniffed the wind for destiny and found it laden. Following the Professor to a small house at the beginning of Pedregal, he slipped into the garden from an alleyway and peering over a hedge saw the Professor deliver the sack to an elderly gentleman whose identity he did not at the time suspect. The sack was opened and the elderly gentleman looked inside; pesos were again exchanged and the Professor left. It was only after his departure that the sack was slit open and its contents removed. Baltásar saw exposed before its contented and smiling owner the most astonishing bowl he had ever seen, superior even to the single example then on view in the National Museum—twenty-four inches in diameter, Baltásar estimated, rising almost six inches in height, absolutely round and without lip, and incised with the most complex interlacing of hieratic figures, integrated by the undulations of the plumed serpent, burnished red ceramic, and immaculate, immaculate, the serpent moving in and about the legs and torsos of a procession of priests, warriors, dancing maidens, all ascending to sacrifice at a tended altar.

Baltásar Mariposa did not learn until a week later that the elderly gentleman was a former Senator to the National Assembly from the State of Chiapas, and the principal conduit for the sale throughout Western Europe of major objects of ancient Mexican art, selling them at considerable prices (even for those days), maintaining a network of forwarding agents, suborned customs officials, bribed airline stewards to transport the work from Mexico City to the capital museums and collectors of Europe and the

Americas. The downfall of the Senator, although precipitous, was not unusual. The Senator had failed to pay a sufficiently large bribe to the Secretary of the Minister of the Interior and, for his niggardliness, had been anonymously denounced. When the case came to trial—it was at the beginning of 1940 and Mexico was in the throes of its own precarious neutrality—Baltásar Mariposa presented himself to the government prosecuting attorney and supplied him with the only eyewitness testimony to a major transaction. The glyph bowl had not yet left the country and was recovered in a locker of the Senator's storeroom. Mariposa's detailed description of the work confounded the Senator's lawyers, in the process Professor Y was disgraced and dismissed from the university, and Baltásar Mariposa found himself a month later being interviewed by Colonel Francisco Vidal of the Special Police.

"You were brilliant at the Senator's trial." Colonel Francisco smiled with an almost lubricious succulence, as though he were complimenting Baltásar's gentle eyes and good manners. "We might not have brought it off without your help. A fine eye for observation and detail. Patriotic zeal and such like. Incomparable. We have few young men like you in the nation." Baltásar Mariposa could not have returned the compliment with equal enthusiasm, but he managed to express his thanks. Colonel Francisco did not have a reputation for justice, although his efficiency was above question.

"You see, my friend, we are coming into a difficult period in Mexico. We are cluttered with extremists of all kinds, Spanish Republicans, out-and-out Communists, Nazi sympathizers, traffickers in goods and materials for all the sides of good and evil and profiteers, marauders, old-fashioned pirates looking to bend any principle for the sake of more pesos. Obviously we can't stop it entirely. There are too many people involved and the people go very high, but we have to make certain that the distribution is fair, that Mexico's neutrality isn't compromised. That means control, occasional crackdowns, and so forth. You understand, don't you?"

Baltásar Mariposa understood only too well. Colonel Vidal was interested, like any engineer, in decent grading, making certain no road was too precipitous or too steep. He wanted evenness and maneuverability. As he always knew, the administration of Mexican law was based on equity, not justice, the proper distribution of crime, no runaway statistics, no blatant favoritism. The trial of the Senator had been a great success. The newspapers approved; the people approved. The idea of a peculating official delighted the public, which regarded courts of law as descendants of the ancient arena in which gladiatorial combat was waged to the death, in this case, the death of an old, disused Senator. And for what corruption? Dealing in the ancient past of Mexico. "To trade the nation's patrimony for money. How disgusting! How loathsome!" Colonel Vidal was eloquent on the subject. All the while Baltásar Mariposa nodded approvingly, wondering only whether the Colonel's passion would be quite as vigorous if the commodity had been oil or rubber or iron, where the monies involved ran to many millions a day. No mention of these, however, only clay statues —*ídolos*, as the Colonel also called them—pots, bowls, gold pectorals, stone figures, a contraband that involved then— how much? Several hundred thousand dollars a year, all told, everything counted.

The offer was exhilarating. Destiny had come forward to embrace obsession. Colonel Vidal invited Baltásar Mariposa to join the special investigative branch of the Department of the Interior, to be a working detective, so to speak, on the trail not of murderers or housebreakers, but of subtle thieves, whom the Colonel analogized in his summary to "termites in the beams of the national establishment."

Baltásar Mariposa accepted but in the spirit of the occasion tried his own surprise. "A splendid opportunity, I think. A really splendid and generous opportunity, Colonel."

"I thought you would find it so."

"And the pay? How is one paid to be a special investigator?"

"A fair question. Quite fair. You begin at a modest level. I believe it is thirty thousand pesos annually with extra allowances for sick leave, health benefits, and, of course, ten working days holiday with pay. The usual. From there you can ascend. The top, unless you aspire to my job" (needless to say the Colonel laughed when he said this), "is at present ninety-five thousand pesos, but by the time you reach that level, undoubtedly salaries will have gone up."

Baltásar Mariposa calculated quickly, trying to figure how cheaply he could live while continuing to provide medicament to his disease. After rent, food, modest entertainment, what remained was trivial, almost too trivial. It was then that he proposed the scheme that makes his involvement in our story so decisive.

"It strikes me that your proposal is fair and correct. I deserve nothing more than any other civil servant, but for one fact. May I be permitted to speak to you with utmost frankness and without prejudice?"

"By all means, my young friend. All of our communications should be frank and nothing you could say would be prejudicial to my view of you." At this point, as if to insure the privacy of their conversation, the Colonel rose and went to the door, opening it and closing it as quickly, returning not to his desk but to its edge, where he seated himself, almost head to head with Baltásar, who felt the toe of the Colonel's shoe brush lightly against his thigh.

"It is embarrassing to say, but I am aware that one of the principal predicaments of our enforcement agencies is that our harried public servants, underpaid as is all Mexico, are sometimes driven by need to accept little presents and gifts, which enable them to make ends meet. It is corrupt when it is done on a large scale, but quite innocently predictable when modestly proportioned. Now I think to myself. What is your temptation, Baltásar? None, except a near-worship of ancient Mexico and its art. Do you begin to understand my drift, Colonel Vidal?"

"Almost, but not completely. Continue!"

"Well, I should like to propose a not uncommon arrangement. It is used in Egypt and Iran and throughout the Middle East. It has been used in Italy although no longer openly. What I request is quite simply this. Any time that I recover for the nation an illegal hoard of ancient objects, I want the privilege of selecting—of course after the museum has had its first choice—several objects of my particular fancy to add to my own modest collection. I am a special collector and as you know, a scholar of sorts. I wish to form a fine study collection in my lifetime. After my death it is agreed that my collection would revert to the nation. What would you say to a ratio of one object to every twenty recovered?

"Ingenious. Clever. I think easily arranged and quite fair. Agreed." The Colonel extended his hand to Mariposa and it was received. While the clasp lingered, the Colonel asked, "What, my friend, is your special fancy?"

"Oh that. Bowls and female figures, Olmec and Tlaltilco at present."

"I see." The Colonel released his grip, apparently disappointed, perhaps expecting, but who knows what Colonel Vidal was expecting?

Inspector Mariposa appeared to doze. A familiar mode

of his procedure, he sought to appear disengaged, almost distracted. Witnesses and bystanders brought to his office for discreet, informal questioning found his shaded eyes, his nervously twisted gold ring, his slight build a little swollen by a small paunch, disarming. He seemed reassuringly un-threatening, but that is precisely what the Inspector intended, his eyes pitched above the head of the witness, examining a spot of dirt, circuiting with the flies the dizzying heights of his gabled colonial office in the prefecture. Inspector Mariposa, it appears, employed his mind like a poised cat. At the center of his phlegmatic impassivity was caged a tiger, only too ready to spring. The devising and refinement of these maneuvers of self-awareness, the flattening out and elaboration of its many subtleties and divagations were appropriate to a man who had remained through the many years of his maturity until his fortieth wrapped in solitude, conducting a life increasingly eremitic, one could say reclusive, living amid flowers and the artifacts of his obsession and passing the considerable hours of his freedom when other men were engaged in fruitless conversation with wives and children, regarding the motions of his mind and sensibility, as though he would—attending closely—discover some ruse of demeanor, an arched eyebrow, a pouting lip, an unfocused eye, which tactfully employed would set his interlocutor to speaking unselfconsciously secret truths.

The years had produced, it may be gathered, only modestly. Inspector Mariposa was by 1957 a fully sinecured official of the department, beyond ninety-five thousand pesos, but with only a hundred or so objects won by zeal added to his collection. It is no wonder that he received the telephone call of that early morning in March with intense emotion, completing the drive to his office in less than a leisured hour, arriving within the precincts of the city some minutes before the traffic lights renewed the imposition of artificial order upon its familiar chaos. He immediately went to the communications room, where he picked up a copy of the first report received from Campeche and there, stirring a cup of coffee that had been left upon his desk awaiting his arrival, began to consider the case.

Baltásar Mariposa marveled at crime. He regarded theft as an essentially uninteresting transgression, motivated as it is by aggravated need. Crime, however, was something quite different. The thief stole a single thing—the loaf of bread from the baker's shop, the warm winter coat, or, in the case of more exaggerated needs, the vial of morphine. Rarely did it happen that the thief took two coats, one to wear, the other to sell. When such occurred, Inspector Mariposa would usually remark with disgust to the arresting officer, "Throw the book at him." He had grown conservative in the department, acquiring rigorous definitions and a battery of distinctions that might have been more subtly refined had he enjoyed at least the second year of legal studies when the parsing of torts entered the academic agenda. Instead, Inspector Mariposa organized distinctions in order to dispose of them, relegating intellection to the attic of his mind where the trunks lay open, the disused furniture gathered cobwebs, and the old books and memorabilia were occasionally consulted for refreshment. His workaday life was consumed by petty thefts, and he despised them. Crime, however, was, at least in principle, of another order. It entailed a vision, however terrestrial, of an arrangement of life substantially different from the one enjoyed before its commission. The large crime, successfully realized, carries with it the possibility not merely of bread on the table or warmth on the back, but a complete change of circumstance, an almost galactic orbiting in which another planet, perceived once from immense distance, is now suddenly at hand. The criminal was not simply greedy or avaricious.

It wasn't like that at all, Inspector Mariposa reflected, considering the facts before him. A genuine criminal is in some way moved by the substance he steals. Most criminals steal money or materials to be converted into money, and when the money is in hand it is buried, hidden, deposited, sequestered for a greater or shorter period of time, which suggests that at least briefly those floridly printed bits of paper are desired for themselves, as though to be pasted in books or displayed in showcases. The thing in itself—the hundred-peso note, not the conversion potential of cash—is most immediately imagined by the genuine criminal. And if not money, the contents of an island, the ransacking of shelf upon shelf of a single item, in the case at hand, ancient clay sculptures.

"Whatever else he is, our master criminal of Jaina must be a collector. And what else?" Mariposa hummed, rising half out of his seat and stirring his coffee cup, about to drink, until he observed the drowned flies.

Stefan Mauger was in his workshop by six in the morning. He had no interest in the early light, only in the morning cool that suppressed the cramping dust of the studio, keeping chips and shavings, still damp from the night air, uncirculating and still. Those early hours, before his women had arisen and old Martina and her man were about on the grounds, singing to each other, were a kind of relief, as if the sun were not yet up, and everything before him—*"mes vaches,"* as he called his sculptures—were restful, ruminating before him, awaiting his pleasure and attention. Examining his creatures in the rising light, Stefan recalled a story heard in his Paris days, that once, when he was a young man, coming up by foot from Rumania to Paris, Brancusi, the Carpathian sculptor, had taken a wooden flute he had carved himself and, seated in an open field, begun to play a tune. Not yet a metaphysician, Brancusi had imagined that a cow which came closer and closer as the music flowed from his flute, approached as an appreciative listener, until he realized that, on the contrary, the cow had simply consumed the grasses as it came and the freshest swathe was near Brancusi's feet. It was reported that Brancusi laughed. Since that time Stefan had taken to calling his sculptures *mes vaches,* and although the collective noun was never applied precisely (for his subject matter was not farm animals) it was one among the strategies he employed to contain the enmity that often arose between himself and his unfinished work.

The workshop had once been the cattle stalls on the colonial ranch Alicia had bought for them four years earlier; they had converted it along with everything else in the sprawling house from the utility of farmers and ranchers to the rhythmic disorder of his own need, removing the stalls but leaving the hard earth floor, which rose above the prevailing terrain to insure drainage and dryness, expanding a small fireplace that the cattlemen had used during the rainy season into an immense hearth where a fire burned most mornings and where during the cold season into which southern Mexico was already well advanced, a large blaze pressed out waves of heat, which shimmered on the whitewashed walls. Stefan kept an area of the wall empty. Nothing hung behind him, neither working models nor drawings nor the tools of his craft. Entering the studio each morning, he felt his way through the gloom to the fireplace and struck a match, setting ablaze the timber he had prepared the night before. Turning sharply, he would seat himself on the stone lip of the hearth and watch the flames, creeping up behind him, rise upon his creatures, illuminating them in its darting light, mingling at last with the natural light of the rising sun, which rarely struck his corner of the workshop before a half hour from his entrance. When heat and light embraced, he changed his seat to the empty wall and examined the dumb show of his creation.

The workshop contained more than a score of sculptures, large and small, fixed upon their bases, themselves sculptures fashioned to extend and elaborate the line and mass of the work. The objects were continually rearranged. Rising with a grimace of irritation, Mauger lifted a zoomorphic crane carved in marble and moved it behind a smaller creature, a perfect ovum—it would have appeared, in fact, an egg, but for the slightest circumferential line, which alluded to the half-closed languors of an eyelid, resting on a sandstone cube until that moment obscured by the hieratic bird. No longer obscured, the eye opened in the day.

Creatures, creatures, he thought. All my creatures; creatures visited unobserved; shaved by the mind's blade; gentle and peaceful in their nudity. I am bound to feel for such beasts (who have now no fear of me) a kind of compassion so different from the violence of my trampling their sacred ground in the Kwakiutl country of the northwest, where I trapped them unawares and then, pinioned by eye, an image was roughly drawn, an impression of arc, curve, line, circle, beneath which seethed an invisible density of sinew all in motion, which was communicate to a feathered, hided, skinned, furred exterior, and I became joined to that other race of magicians (I remember you, old shaman Giraud) who divine with them, read fatidic omens from their aspect, and dream of honorable deaths.

This, from a stool against an empty wall, examining a theater of his own creation, thinking of his creatures not as things made that are now unalterable (except, of course, to reduce and to reduce, for nothing can be restored to sculpture and failure is always absolute) but, rather, as he often supposed, as things that somehow come alive. It was then he remembered how old Giraud had brought him among the Kwakiutl of the northwest and restored to him the passion and ferocity of sculpture. I am filled, Stefan thought (regarding his congerie of beast helmets and figures, totemic all) with the sense that I am there with them, invoking the dead men who were once animals, whooping cranes, cannibal ravens, vast bears with red faces, walruses with sad green eyes and ivory labrets, my familiars and friends, (grant, good Lord, that they are really friends and protectors of my Silesian tribe, remnants of my race who went down into the icy waters to forage for food and came up no more as men, but as fish in the mouths of birds, caught in the swiping palm of bear, my spirit painting the faces of my sisters and cousins, who were once, as was I, an old animal) and of them all, only I survive.

Stefan looked harder at his creatures than he had looked in many weeks, examining them with an eye that saw no longer simple form nor admired the deftness of his own hand, but attended rather to a motion that arose somehow from inside the matter and agitated their surface until by noon of that day he was utterly exhausted from looking, weary, almost deaf to Alicia's voice calling to him, *"Stefan, viens vite, viens vite."*

The old General sat on his bench cleaning the tarnished spurs he wore with his tattered costume each Sunday afternoon when he joined the *charros* in Chapultepec Park who rode out to celebrate colonial days, unaware that their pride amused the tourists who stood along the bridle path snapping photographs. They were in the guidebooks, the General photographed alongside a middle-aged millionaire who had bought his costume from a shop near the Teatro

Municipal and a young garbage collector whose claim to be a *charro* hung by the most slender thread of lineage.

Inspector Mariposa entered without knocking and the General (for his name had been long forgotten, although history books described him leading a charge against the loyalist regiments of President Díaz in the days when any man with enough money to pay his troops could be whatever he wished, conservative loyalist or revolutionary general) looked up in surprise. The General had been a passionate youth gone meaty and soft with age, drifting about his apartment lined with cupboards and breakfronts stuffed with broken vessels, bits of jade, gold ear plugs (one of which he wore as a ring). He had served under Pancho Villa and once blew up a stretch of railway track near Brownsville. He had, in other words, been to the United States, which already earned him credibility when he talked about the oppression of the *gringos* (which he did with fluency), spitting out his words between lips narrowly opened, holding fast a stump of frayed cigar that he plugged between his lips each morning upon arising. It was still early in the morning by the General's standards when Inspector Mariposa entered the cluttered apartment.

"*¿Qué pasa,* Inspector?" the General growled in a low voice, not moving his head, working intently the rowels of his spur, one by one, turning the silver in a rag.

"Nothing you don't already know, General," Inspector Mariposa replied, coming around the table and seating himself before the old head.

The General laughed. "You're always right, Inspector. Of course I know. The Jaina. I heard late last night. I expected your visit earlier, but I suppose they allow inspectors to sleep longer than old generals."

"And so? Who do you think?"

"It would be so easy for you if I guessed. Why should I tell you? They don't pay me for the criminal."

"But *I* do. I pay you well. The bigger the name, the bigger the price. This is a big name. On the market, how much do you think? I guess, fast money, the right distributor, quiet buyers, two hundred thousand pesos, maybe more. Each year it will go up twenty percent at least. If the newspapers get hold of the story, an article or two, some photographs, the price will go up faster. What do you think, General?"

"Right now. Even more. We have some Mexican collectors who would pay handsomely for a modest piece, and abroad—the museums, those clean *gringos*, washing their hands before holding a piece—well, I think much more. The *gringos* are beginning to go crazy for these things. I had three new runners here during the past month. Heh heh. How they love those ugly Aztec pieces. Pepe makes beauties for me. They know nothing. Shit. The runners. They're all thugs, although there's one new boy from the States who's pretty smart. An eye without a mote. No, no, my friend, I'd say with a little publicity—and the theft is good publicity—right now wholesale more than three hundred thousand pesos, maybe more. Some of those pieces were big, I'm told, big, whole, beautiful, beautiful."

"Yes, yes," Mariposa nodded thoughtfully. "May I use your telephone?" The General nodded and Inspector Mariposa opened an armoire behind the table. The General's costume, the tight leggings tricked with silver decoration, hung from a wooden peg, and beneath the foot the black telephone was hidden. The Inspector bent down and dialed. "Mariposa. My office. Sergeant? Mariposa. I want a complete news blackout. Nothing. Not a word. Yes. I know it was already out in Campeche, but if it's not on the wire, keep it from getting there; and if it is, kill it. Not a word." He replaced the receiver under the General's pant leg and shut the armoire.

"Exactly. You did right," the General muttered, lighting

a fresh black cigar. "No point sending the prices up before we've gotten our share." The General gleamed at the Inspector and sent his spur rowels whirling with his thumb.

"Yes? And so? Who then, do you think? Marejal? Arroyo? Blañes? The old-fashioned impresarios?"

"No. No, Inspector. Too fresh and ingenious. A troop of our own Federales. A captain. The phone lines. No. No. Those others—they fence, everything, nothing, treasures, junk. They have no intelligence. They deal in mass. No. I think we have somebody quite new to us, but I suspect someone we know, someone around, under our glass, but not in focus."

The General's perception was almost autobiographical. That was precisely the reasoning the Inspector had used five years before when he first became aware of the General's own activities. The General never dealt in the open. He was too clever for that. Everything went under the guise of the great bluster, the *charro* costume, the immense sombrero that covered his full head of white hair, the gray moustachios that he had only recently abandoned for the semi-retirement of his seventies. He was a nibbler at the edges of the powerful, supplying everything from fine objects to an occasional passport. He had no expenses but his apartment and his white horse, his black cigars, and an occasional Indian boy whom he mounted behind him on a pony for his Sunday rides. The Inspector had known about the General. There had been no charges against him, but the theft of fifty negotiable bonds had led the Inspector by stages to his door. Then he arrived and introduced himself, the General had embraced him, shouted "Bravo," and presented him with a large Veracruz figure in gray volcanic stone, and stunned by the manner of the General's confession and the immense thoughtfulness and tact of his bribe, the Inspector had merely wrung from him the names of the fences down the line, recovered the bonds to everyone's delight, accepted the figure as his due, and impressed the General into faithful and collaborative service.

"Suggestions?"

"I have none, none, at the moment. What do you say? One hundred and eleven stolen. We recover, let us say, eighty, ninety, and divide the rest? What do you say?"

"It depends on your work. It depends on your work." Inspector Mariposa repeated the phrase, as though magically intoning the General's investiture, but in fact distracted by a different thought—the majestic calm of the Jaina figures, their immense impassivity, as though death had come upon them like the lava of Popocatepetl, slow and inexorable, but still slow enough for them to put on their final garments, to compose themselves, to paint their faces and adjust their serenity.

"I suggest that you leave me for an hour and return at exactly nine. Take a coffee at the corner. A few telephone calls may give us some news."

Inspector Mariposa accepted the General's suggestion and went down to the corner and called his office. Colonel Vidal had been looking for him. As well there had been a telephone call from the Instituto inquiring about progress. Perhaps it would make some sense to inquire at the Instituto. It was such a new excavation, perhaps others had at one time been involved. Remarkable. The entire island empty. Only the young wife of one of the diggers, illegally hidden on the island, had observed the soldiers and had been too afraid of discovery to reveal herself. What a witness, the Inspector thought. But how did they know the island would be deserted? That was worth investigating. They must have known. But then, why cut the telephone wires? But they wore uniforms? Why uniforms if they knew the island was empty? The time passed quickly and an hour later he entered the General's apartment just after the phone had been replaced in the armoire. The General was amused.

"The first and only useful piece of information that I have is this. Our thief, whoever he is, does not intend to offer the objects at home. Strictly for the *gringos*. Indeed, there is a good chance that the Jaina figures have already left the country. I know this from several sources. One of our collectors went down the line to his contacts in the field, jumping all the intermediate runners. He flew in on his private plane to Campeche early this morning. He tells my friend here that nothing is known, that the constabulary in Campeche is not very cooperative with the Federales, who are embarrassed by the Indian woman's confused report of the thieves dressed as soldiers. Very clever, yes? But most interesting is the statement of the ranking officer of the constabulary when asked whether he thought the goods might be turned up. No, he said, one of our police motor launches was found abandoned on the coast fifty kilometers up from Campeche and under the gunwales they found several empty wooden crates and, miraculously, fallen between the cracks in the floor boards, several unmistakable clay fragments. He deduced from this that the Jaina treasure had been transferred at sea to another vessel, probably one belonging to the *gringos*. The captain's name is Gutiérrez. I think you should leave us behind immediately and go to Campeche and Gutiérrez. Don't you think? Yes. Tomorrow I ride in Chapultepec. You can call me afterward."

Stefan had no intention of hurrying, even if Clemens Rosenthal had arrived from New York. Alicia had acquired the habit, he suspected from her mother, of attaching urgency to everything. *"Viens vite"* meant nothing more than "pay attention," something is about to happen, anything would do, from the sighting of a buzzard over the chicken house to one of their pigs getting through the slatted sty into the flower garden. It was never urgent. What was really important was the coming, not its speed. Stefan stretched himself. He had been sitting before his creatures for more than six hours, lost in a reflection as concentrated and energetic as the act of making them had been. Indeed, as he had often been at pains to explain, thinking was one of the most exacting of an artist's occupations, particularly exacting because its process and conclusion could hardly be described. "You see the very end of thought," he once explained to his Parisian dealer, Monsieur Baguerre. "The first carving is done in the head and everything else, every movement with the chisel and hammer is a reply to thinking, a working out of the argument that began ages ago." Monsieur Baguerre shrugged, which was precisely the reply that pleased Stefan the most. The last person whom he expected to understand what he was about was his dealer. Moreover, Stefan had an unerring sense of fitness. The work of dealers was to keep slogans in mind, to have neatly sorted and at hand a supply of notions to enable them to explain to the wary what it was they were supposed to see. Stefan remembered Monsieur Baguerre with genuine affection; the fat man with his thin moustache and soft gray alpaca jacket had died on the way from Drancy to Auschwitz, undoubtedly wondering to the very end why Stefan always rebuked him when he told clients that his work resembled Medardo Rosso's. "I resemble no one, not even myself, and certainly not Medardo Rosso," Stefan commented acidly when he overheard Monsieur Baguerre explaining to an Englishwoman who wore a flowered hat of pink watered silk that she was looking at a sculpture "by this generation's Medardo Rosso." The Englishwoman said that "it didn't matter as I have no idea who Monsieur Rosso is and in all events I am looking for something to put in the rose garden."

Sitting and looking for hours at the sculptures was a kind

of labor, "making the fire," he said as he came out of the door where Alicia was waiting for him, looking incredibly cool and beautiful, her golden hair held with two white plastic barrettes in the shape of butterflies, wearing one of his best white shirts, pulled tight around her waist and flattened inside a pair of khaki work pants. She wore a shapeless pair of men's shoes, an item of apparel that Stefan thought outrageous, but as her feet were large and she nonetheless moved with grace, he never commented on them. "Just stoking coals," Stefan muttered, looking away from her over the high grass toward the jungle, which pressed against the clearing as though waiting for admission. "But my dearest, we have a visitor. I've never seen the limping creature before, but he says he must see you, utmost urgency, hence my cry for *vitesse*. It was the least I could do."

Stefan nodded and smiled. He was about to reply, something tart came to mind, but he decided against it. He had no right to complain. It was he who had brought Maria home, but that seemed so long ago, although only ten months had passed since he had rescued her in Mexico City. Would he have behaved differently if he had imagined that his two women would become lovers? He rationalized with considerable facility. He spent so much time in the field, buying from runners, checking the digs around Campeche, organizing the theft at Jaina, and when he wasn't chasing the past he was "making the fire" for his own. Obviously, he neglected them. The two, Alicia and Maria, were as different for him as, no doubt, they were for each other, not fire and water, passion and cool, but alternations of intensity. They weren't concubines. He knew that perfectly well. It wasn't as though he needed them all the time, that he went from one to the other, or even that he summoned them to do his pleasure. He would have thought that vulgar and demeaning. Actually, the truth of the matter is that his needs for each of them were intimately connected to the desperation of his work, the inevitable failure of any of his sculptures to testify with accuracy to the idea that had engendered it. He called upon his women instead of weeping. Most often, when a work was finished, when the carving was completed and the polishing not yet begun, he found his capacity to love immense. Before Maria arrived, he would spend several days with Alicia, making love to her often and passionately. When he finished the giant crane, the year before, the first of a series that had not advanced beyond a second smaller version—"a domestic crane," Stefan said contemptuously, sensing perhaps that the series was going stale—he had spent the day in bed with Alicia, hugging her endless times, asking her to hold him, to cup his prick like a flower, to go down on him, and only reluctantly, without much interest, had he fucked her. She had screamed with an astonishing mixture of pleasure fugued with pain and asked for it again, but Stefan had turned away, lit a cigarette (virtually the only one he smoked, keeping a single pack, nearly stale, in a shell-covered box on her night table). The next day he glared at the crane and went off into Campeche in the pickup truck to Tia Clara's and didn't return for two days and when he did, pathetically drunk and exhausted, Alicia put him to bed. But that became his way of doing things until he met Maria in Mexico City and brought her back to the jungle. Instead of his unpleasant remark—the one he had conceived and dismissed—Stefan asked, "Is Maria awake?"

"I think so. I left her early this morning. She sometimes snores, that big woman," Alicia replied, chuckling happily.

"I've heard her. I know. She wasn't snoring last night when I went in. I'm sorry about that, but I thought you'd both gone out."

"No matter. Let's hurry. The boy was impatient when I left him. He won't steal, but damned if he couldn't break something." Alicia turned away from Stefan and hurried to open the door to the living room, with a gracious gesture exposing its contents—colonial furniture of severity and mass, each individually splendid but in aggregation a bit ponderous, bright cushions of varying shapes and sizes covered in a variety of peasant fabrics, a cut-up poncho which Alicia had bought off the back of an Indian, serapes, Guatemalan mantel runners, bits of Moroccan rugs flecked with sparkling silver bangles, all neatly sewn together and backed, covering the wicker benches, the adobe wall-seat built in by the previous owners, and beyond, against the wall, on tables, massed in groups upon the floor, peering from wood and marble columns cut by Stefan Mauger, some fifty or more treasures of ancient Mexican art, a Coatlicue of monstrous horror like a guardian near the fireplace, the Xipe, groups of Olmec women forming a stone sodality, a Tarascan dog showing signs of starvation, a Teotihuacan mask carved from neither life nor death, and before them all, his white hands nearly invisible against his white trousers, as though armless, a young man. What was he? Seventeen, but no longer a boy, standing with obvious pain, leaning upon a single crutch, the other beneath the bench on which he had undoubtedly been seated until he heard the noise of their approach, his shirt opened to a religious medal, his hairless chest as brown and dry as a dead leaf, neck and head forming a unity without apparent seam or differentiation, the skin rising from the neck with a strain brought on by the pain of standing, struggling for a composure in his handsome face. Alicia's open arm, introducing the room to her husband, at last came to rest upon the boy.

"Yes?" Stefan Mauger inquired, that curious interrogation of Europeans sounding strange in the upward inflection of the two Spanish letters, signifying not question but acceptance, although the question remained. The boy did not understand. *"Sí"* was not a metaphysical affirmation like uncertain proofs for the existence of the external world, but then it was the assertion of something perhaps more threatening. Existence is granted, indeed, taken for granted, but why, the acknowledgment asks, is there this something, you, boy, before me, rather than nothing at all? The hardness of Stefan's *"Sí?"* baffled Alicia and confused the boy. He hopped and transferred the crutch from one armpit to the other, shifting his weight.

"Señor?" the boy began. It was immediately clear. Stefan looked at him closely. There could be no doubt. The Captain had once been as handsome as his son. This was the maimed youth on whose account the Captain had been so quick to accept his invitation to remove the Jaina treasure.

"I am," Stefan Mauger replied, his voice more even and curious than before. "What is it that I can do for you, young Gutiérrez?"

"Juliano, Señor. You know my father. It was he who thought I should come." The boy grimaced with pain, but Stefan did not invite him to be seated. Alicia motioned him to a chair as though continuing her hospitable graciousness, but the boy ignored her.

"And why did El Capitán think that you should come?"

"He said that I should show you this." The boy leaned his weight upon the crutch and with his back against the mantel of the fireplace, dividing his weight between crutch and back, he freed himself to move. Bending down, he lifted the loose white pant that covered the crippled leg. Holding the fabric with his left hand, straightening up to composure, he waited for reaction. Alicia gasped and turned away. Stefan, however, was hardly capable of the response that Captain

Gutiérrez had anticipated. He looked at the horror and realized instantly that part of its grotesqueness was undistinguished and the rest quite beautiful. The leg was mending. A month ago, perhaps, Stefan Mauger might have been nauseated; the first few days after surgery the wound still oozed, the skin had not adhered, the line of the sewing was vivid like marks of scarification; but now that the boy was somewhat recovered, able to move about at least on crutches (he knew perfectly well that somewhere out back, talking quietly with his Indian domestics, Captain Gutiérrez was waiting to help his son return to Campeche), the wound had a certain elegance; covered with a purple disinfectant, the clean line of the machete's bite was easy to see, running about eighteen inches down the outer line of the boy's leg, the neat stitches like the track lines of an ancient railway, closely packed.

"A terrible wound," Alicia said gently, quite recovered and able to look upon the boy who continued to hold up his pant with an almost inspiring indifference to his pain. He did not appear to understand the purpose of his visit to the Maugers.

"Thank you," Stefan said with a dismissing gesture of his hand, the irritability of his European manners returning. Alicia was dismayed by her husband's apparent indifference. The boy was, nonetheless, impassive. Once again, Stefan's Spanish, however flawless, was incapable of conveying the formal intention of his feeling. He wanted done with this display—this presentation of the wounds of Jesus, as though he were among the unbelievers who required the demonstration of the multiple wounds to shatter his dubiety. Not at all. Not at all. Stefan Mauger understood the performance. Alicia was moved only by pity, not even by embarrassment, only by pity.

"Juliano. Bastante! Gracias. Muchas gracias."

"For what, Señor?" the boy asked, not yet understanding, although he realized his own discomfort and began again to shift his weight, this time to ease a cramp in the injured leg, suddenly numb from prolonged standing.

"I have seen your wound. I am deeply sorry for your pain," Stefan replied gravely, looking for the last time at the leg. The boy released the white bottom of the garment and it dropped like drapery over the wound.

"Thank you, Señor. My father wanted you to see it. So did my wife. My child cannot speak yet, but I am sure he would want you to see it."

"Why? Why do all of you want me to see your terrible wound?"

"I am not certain, Señor," the boy said quietly, but with confusion.

"I think I understand. I do understand, which is all that matters," Stefan replied in a low voice, almost addressing himself. "This should be enough. Tell your father it has to be enough. There is no more to give." Stefan had gone to the desk, opened it, and removed from the cash box he kept for the expenses of the hacienda ten one-hundred-peso bills and gave them to the boy. The boy, remarkably, seemed humiliated and dropped his head with shame.

Stefan Mauger turned away. The boy whispered his many thanks and hobbled to the door, opened it, and stepped down to the corridor below. As it closed behind him, he heard the severe voice of Captain Gutiérrez greet his son with that endless "*entonces,*" a curious word used to pause in the midst of narrative, to effect transition, to call for air and patience, but he heard nothing beyond this as the boy lapsed into dialect, speaking the wholly unintelligible Tsoltsil language to his father.

Stefan was immensely weary, suddenly exhausted by his situation, not only the hopelessness of dealing with these people, of doing business with nameless agents and dealers who sent him cryptic messages, embedded in chatty letters from Paris and New York, and while extolling the merits of his own sculpture, would insert mention of their wish that he supply them with "something not too horrible for my apartment." Not too horrible? It was all horrible! He would never have been able to collect these things, much less to steal them, if it weren't for the horror. Somehow the mere fact that everything made in the age before Cortés was not made as art, but only to keep the universe alive and consoled, rationalized his crime. He was certain of this. He knew the connection, but couldn't quite explain it, certainly not to his friends, to Alicia, who was civilized, or his old friend Clemens Rosenthal, who had cabled that he was flying from New York to interview Stefan about his recollections of the aged and dying sculptor, Brancusi. Perhaps Maria could make sense of it. She was part of them and part of his world, his own *négresse blanche*, as he had named her that first night in Mexico City. Stefan went to find Maria in her room, calling to her, in rhythm to his step, "Maria, Maria, Maria," a low call, plaintive as a shepherd calling to sheep who need no strident invocation.

3

To Fabricate in Volumes

It cannot be said with certainty that Stefan Mauger's decision to begin to carve—to fabricate in volumes—to become, in a word, what is called, not quite accurately or adequately, a sculptor, had its origin in a specific event, a particular meeting, a discernible suite of reflections, an identifiable psychological machinery; or, lacking the certainty of one of the aforementioned, in all of them, and then, none of them at the precise moment in time at which he put away his paints and brushes and took up knives and hammers and chisels. It cannot be said with certainty; it remains unhazarded. There are, however, a number of episodes that deserve the telling, not only because they bear upon the result, quite independently of the more subtle process of arriving there, but because they are interesting; that is, they stand forth, delineated and remarkable, from the gray passage of ordinary days.

Up to the time of his coming to Paris, Stefan Mauger had been, whatever the drama of his childhood and growing to maturity, a youth of privilege. However much he might have denied this fact, contending as he did on many occasions that neither his money nor his beige suede gloves were more than accouterments, having little relevance to human substance, offering little qualification to decency or to talent, he was hard-pressed to make his views stick. No matter with whom the argument was undertaken, he was instantly on the defensive, obliged by either the scruffy shoes of his interlocutor or the threadbare cuffs of the accountant's shirt to concede that life undertaken with an income certainly left more time free to be attentive to art or philosophy than having to earn it daily in order to keep the self whole and in good repair. The argument, whatever its merits and however one devised from contentment or envy the equities of the dispute, proved irrelevant by the end of the twenties. Stefan Mauger—who had by that time passed five energetically indecisive years in Paris, moving between his studio on the Rue des Saints-Pères, where he lived and painted modestly, small canvas in a small room, making friends with remarkable women and intelligent men, mostly English and American, and the life of the boulevards where he could speak French with the animation and vivacity of a native, entertain the Parisians with descriptions of the decline of German-speaking cultures, join with the competing ideologists on the left and right who menaced each other with fists stuffed with manifestos and denunciations, and occasionally treat his circle, a half-dozen acquaintances none of whom were friends, to a decent meal and a *grand cru classé*—was informed by his Viennese banker that he was virtually without funds in the fall of 1930. It wasn't that Stefan's precautionary investments early in the decade had been imprudent. They had not been. It seemed perfectly sensible to maintain a portfolio of public service bonds of the Vienna municipality, to own the securities of several industrial corporations engaged in factory construction and the processing of cement for the building trades. Unfortunately these (and they numbered more than a half-dozen securities and obligations which until that year had paid a steady and invariant income, without attrition of intrinsic value) were apparently undermined by the inflation, the abandonment of public works projects and industrial expansion in a time of increasing costs, dizzying prices, and contracting demand. In a word, following virtually the same explanation as has been set forth, Herr Martin Andreas Maywald concluded his letter by informing Stefan that, acting upon his power of attorney, he had that day, November 11, 1930, sold him out of his entire portfolio to conserve his remaining assets and would for the time being await Herr Mauger's instructions as to the disposition of the remaining funds, the $34,383 in our currency that survived after deduction of fees and services, before determining upon alternative courses for its "gainful employment." Stefan had no further interest in considering the possibilities of Herr Maywald's conception of "gainful employment" and cabled that the funds should be transferred immediately to the Saint-Germain branch of the Crédit Lyonnais.

The decline in Stefan's fortunes, undoubtedly upsetting to those of his friends who derived especial pleasure from their association with his unfathomable wealth, his readiness to loan a ten-franc piece and to inquire about the return of sums only when they surpassed fifty, his affability (and even his good looks), which some among his acquaintanceship ascribed to the fact that he had no financial worries, hardly bothered Stefan. To the contrary! Although he had over the years argued the independence of character from wealth, contending, as though fighting for the ground beneath his. feet, that the possession of inherited means did not drain character of its capacity for sacrificial assertiveness, that however much the having of money might hasten betrayal of one's class, it need not entail the loss of integrity. Notwithstanding that the view was self-convicting with Marxists (for whom the betrayal of class *was* the betrayal of integrity), it was unusually persuasive to the circle of young painters with whom Stefan traveled, who could observe that the career of their companion, Stefan Mauger, advanced no more quickly than their own for all his possession of money. They imagined, not differently than is thought today, that money is magic, that it buys and constrains influence, determines publicity and attention, whereas the truth is that the artist of independent means has only one advantage over the impecunious—given the same amount of talent (unmeasurable though that is): he can wait longer. Money supports nothing more than patience, and as far as Stefan Mauger was concerned that advantage no longer existed.

As of November 11, 1930, Stefan Mauger had sold exactly one painting, two small collages torn from a notebook and sold for forty francs each, and a half-dozen pen-and-ink drawings, all of the last to the same collector who, it appeared, owned a restaurant above whose rose banquettes Stefan Mauger's drawings were framed and displayed. Not exactly an income, not quite a reputation, but then, until that date, neither was necessary. At least the pictures were properly sold, not interposed in the manner of bohemian vendors who dropped a drawing between the spoon and the lip and often failed to remove it until the irritated diner had acquired the mock Vlaminck or Utrillo. The few collectors of Stefan Mauger's work had encountered it socially, and given Stefan's charm and the trivial price he asked when pressed, it was not hard to sell. It would have been more difficult had the enterprise been serious, had Stefan wanted to sell his work in order to live on the money it earned. It was one thing to charge for works of art like leaving a franc piece in the lavatory attendant's dish—not much service, not much value—and quite another to advance a work of art in contention with the whole of the established culture, to set a price that of necessity obliged a client to consider whether he wanted a half-dozen Maugers or a single etching by Max Ernst. But it hardly mattered, even if Stefan had needed the money in those years. In the absence of genius as a painter, he contented himself with intelligence, with the omission of excess, with diminishment and constraint, which at least endowed his drawings with a modesty not at all typical in Paris during those years.

Stefan Mauger was learning. When he was asked what he did for a living—an inevitable question that was pursued relentlessly until the questioner was informed, usually by someone eating at Stefan's table, that he was "independently wealthy"—Stefan would answer reluctantly that he was "learning to see." Of course, "learning to see" was a turn of phrase wholly compatible with independent wealth and only rarely did the reply evoke a real exchange and from modest beginnings a durable, even if contentious, friendship.

"And what in heaven's name do you mean?" the questioner persisted.

"Does it matter? Do you seriously care what I mean?"

"But of course I do. There's nothing idle about me, my friend."

"In that case. I think of sight as history. Seeing is as much conditioned by the history of the artifacts of vision as the use of language is shaped by the history of literature. Most people who speak the language—any language—are unaware of the extent to which the very phrases they use, the urgency or elaborateness of their syntax, are influenced by the prevailing literature, by the moods of culture, by its most profound practitioners or its most flamboyant exhibitionists. Who would doubt that Oscar Wilde obliged the English to talk differently, which is only to say that he made a certain kind of social observation virtual in the diction and usage of the English language, or Stefan George, Hugo von Hofmannsthal, Nietzsche, Rilke for modern German. And for the French, obvious to say, *les poètes maudits* supplemented by the earlier Sainte-Beuve and the later (I should think by now) Marcel Proust. If clear for language, no less clear for painting. It would have been easier to be a painter in the nineteenth century. Easier, but dull and boring! I could have survived on pastorals with an occasional study of an absinthe drinker. No one would have reproved me then by mentioning Manet. Hardly anyone knew Manet at the time and those who did were not quite as certain then as they are now. But today, with numberless masters—cubists, orphists, simultanists, futurists, metaphysicals, surrealists, with Europe literally bursting with visual invention—it's impossible to lift up a pencil and make a mark on paper without being aware precisely where the mark comes from, whose style it suggests, which sensibility it enfolds. Indeed, a painter today has no choice but to recapitulate the whole modern movement. Only if he has a real gift can he exceed it. It's a fateful obligation to be responsible to the whole of modern art, don't you think?"

"And also, dear fellow, quite liberating? I mean to say there is a point—isn't there?—where the consciousness that one contains the whole history of art—a 'fateful obligation' as you put it—also implies the possibility of chucking it and cutting out on one's own."

"Where would that take you? You think there's something new, never tried, never put to the wheel. I doubt it."

"But here you show—say, what's your name?" ("Stefan Mauger." "Swiss?" "No. Austrian.") "—Stefan Mauger, that you are over-educated and that may well be as much a curse as knowing nothing of the past and being fated to repeat it. I mean, sir, that even the view that there is nothing new, or else that everything has been tried, is as historically conditioned as the art itself. If someone had proposed to Jacques-Louis David that his Napoleon should crown himself in Notre Dame with the visible passion and ferocity of the *Nude Descending the Staircase,* he would have argued that the task of painting was to narrate and celebrate, not to beat the speed of light. The vision of art is always a combination of vista and visitation—the historical possibilities that exist before the brush is loaded and the miracle which is simply doing one's work at absolutely the right time."

It had been at a small table indoors at Les Deux Magots, to the right as you enter, facing the church, the marble top covered with note paper, newspapers, piles of books, Clemens Rosenthal writing in a ruled ledger, consulting his sources, drinking his coffee. Stefan Mauger had joined him by accident; he had been late for an appointment with an older woman, a sculptor, who wanted Stefan to model for a bust. They had agreed to meet for coffee at Les Deux Magots at eleven o'clock. Stefan had arrived a few minutes past the hour and when he came inside, a piece of swirling newspaper clutching his ankle, he saw Diana Middleton at the table of this man, this Clemens Rosenthal, who simply said, not rising, but extending a fat hand bristling with hair, "Clemens Rosenthal. By the way, friend, you have *Le Monde* underfoot." He never asked Stefan's name, nor did Diana Middleton (a single-minded American who made Stefan think of cameo portraits of Frederick II, shoulder-length hair, unstyled, framing a flat face cut in low-relief)

bother to introduce him. Stefan, having long since abandoned the mild shock and reproof that accompanied bad
manners, did not offer it in response to Rosenthal's extended hand, having acquired the empirically incontestable
conviction that names are always revealed if they are necessary and, otherwise, are so much additional and useless
information; moreover, at the point at which Clemens
Rosenthal had required his name—already curious about
his intelligence—the request was prelude to conferring upon
him the only benefaction that he possessed, his friendship.

The breakfast ended at the moment that lunch began.
Diana Middleton had long since departed, content to meet
Stefan Mauger at her studio the following day, for he could
hardly refuse her request that he sit for her and, moreover,
Stefan already admitted to curiosity about sculpture. It was
not easy, however, extricating the whale-like mass of Clemens Rosenthal from behind the somewhat fragile marble-
topped tables of Les Deux Magots. The first attempt to prize
him loose failed dismally, the table almost crashing to the
floor, books sliding to the banquette. It was not that Clemens had difficulty managing the disposition and movement
of his weight, for it was neither that grotesque nor intrinsi-
cally unmanageable. It was rather a case of the kind of
indifference to body that obliged all the machinery of
movement to be ill-timed and consequently at loggerheads
with the intention of other people, other, more modestly
proportioned, smaller people. For instance, at the first movement to leave, Stefan had risen, pulled out the little marble
table to facilitate Rosenthal's easy egress; however, at that
precise instant, Clemens noticed an elderly gentleman of his
acquaintance three tables down the line and turning to
wave an arm to him, nearly destroyed the frail woman who
had been sitting meekly at the table alongside his own, feeding her Pekinese bits of croissant. Clemens had simply not

seen her; his eye-level was pitched to a region that did not include creatures smaller than five and a half feet. The second time, while he made apologies to the woman who was by then protecting the Pekinese with her own body, Clemens Rosenthal, books and papers clutched in disarray, pressed his frame between the tables, gasping from the exertion, at the last seizing Stefan Mauger's arm and propelling him through waiters and tables to the boulevard.

They lunched together and visited museums and returned to the cafes in the early evening to meet artists, and dined together and passed through La Coupole for a brandy and only after midnight parted, laughing with pleasure at having met and agreeing to meet the same day for supper. They were incommensurable and hence immensely compatible, the one finding in the other every alternative to himself that expressed an unrealizable option and therefore fantasy unaccompanied by envy. Clemens Rosenthal, born in Posen and raised in Long Island City, where his father was an upholsterer and sometime house painter and his mother a seamstress who taught piano at night, spoke English with a richness that can be described, not as natural, but forced like *foie gras*. His family determined from the day of their arrival in America to speak English, to drop every solecism of Eastern European speech, to discard Polish and even Yiddish and force themselves to master English. The house abounded, Clemens described with an immense laughter, in dictionaries and word books, every imaginable tract on usage and grammar, and it was family custom, each evening, to offer in place of an earlier tradition of blessing, two English words that each of them, father, mother, and Clemens, had employed that day for the first time. On occasion, when the day had been busy and the dinner smelled particularly delicious, Clemens would find his father hiding in the bedroom just before the call to table hunting for his words, knowing full well that his wife, stern curator of the new language, would not feed him until he had supplied her Cerberus with the two coins of passage.

"I, I haven't told you," Clemens announced when they were seated for dinner the following evening. "I edit an art magazine in New York. And what does that mean? What *is* an art magazine? Is it like," he continued familiarly, posing the hopeless question, inspiring the rhetorical transcendence, "the various trade magazines in which our industrialized nation abounds—like *Automobile Age* or *Architectural Forum*? Sometimes I think so. We are besieged no differently by artists than business magazines are pursued by inventors. But it's still pretty tame, the United States. It's just beginning, just now, for the first time, small rustles in the tame underbrush, nothing like a Rousseau tiger in the forest, nothing that large, nothing that magnificent, but beginnings. There are some remarkable painters, young ones who have been to Europe and come home, some stunning photographers, but it's still pretty tame. The speed is there, the machinery is there, the crush and crash of the city, but we're still waiting for a visionary transfiguration, somebody who can find a paint language for it all. In the meantime, I write marvelous essays on Europe; I create little hymns to what no longer interests me, and all the while I keep waiting for the sign that something is breaking through to us. It's good to be as young as one's culture. The lucky idea of making it to the United States at the turn of the century, of being thirty-one (like yourself) when the country itself is thirty-one years into a new century, of being there at the right time and with the right spirit to watch the country grow up."

It was like that with Clemens Rosenthal, every question became a thesis demanding examination, and if not an antithesis, at least the suggestion that life was not all reconciliation and clarity, but a series of tentative propositions that required formal presentation and defense. Clemens Rosenthal was no Hegelian (although he had read more than an abridgment of the *Philosophy of History*, itself an achievement considerably greater than the domestic Hegelians of Greenwich Village who, he reported, had mastered a few formulas but didn't have the time to read the grand passage of the dialectic through classic civilization to its apogee in Prussian Germany, a consummation that might have disarmed their enthusiasm), nor for that matter a Marxist, although he had read Marx and admired his rage for justice. If anything, Clemens Rosenthal was simply, uncompromisingly, a *tour de force Pascalien*, that is to say, he was a man who found reality unnerving, which, if not Pascalian doctrine, is quite Pascalian sensibility, and, as an art critic, an "aesthetician" he called himself, he found the postulations of the world unsettling, and found art—the ancient trickery, the primordial charlatanism—a source of anxiety which impelled him to take it with a seriousness and fatality that were much more than making it its own justification or regarding it as the only ransom for a corrupt civilization. "No, my new friend, I tell you," he said exuberantly, "making an authentic work of art is like making the heavens and the earth. It's the last activity for a religious man who values the creation of the new as more important than the salvation of the old and fallen."

On the face of it, it was only good manners that obliged Stefan Mauger to show Clemens Rosenthal his paintings. This seems a disingenuous, even a deceptive, explanation. Not really, however, if one considers the state of Mauger's undertaking up to that time. For one thing, Stefan Mauger never described himself as an artist or even claimed that he was seriously engaged in making pictures, although that was precisely how he passed most of every day. He would, challenged to reveal himself to his acquaintances, smile, pause, and reply in a vague and abstracted tone, "I read a great deal and I paint, some." That was the English-language version of what could be easily transcribed in German or French, a mode of concealment, an evasion that was nonetheless absolutely faithful to Mauger's diffidence, his refusal to take to himself a state of being when, at most, he was engaged in a protracted and to that moment unfulfilled process of becoming. Not a single one of his pictures pleased him; they were all the mild-mannered adaptations of the over-influenced, the artist so impressed by the achievements of modern art that he could do a canvas in virtually any mode—cubist, surrealist, futurist—and so convincingly as to be readily identified as having been inspired by another, but without sufficient definition to compel the viewer to ask, "How did you come by *this*?" or "Pretty risky, don't you think?" Of course, Clemens Rosenthal said nothing of the kind. He had come to Stefan Mauger's paintings after having first been attracted to his mind. And, besides, Clemens Rosenthal was an intellectual, a critic, an Eastern European Jew, and an American, all patents of an uncompromising directness, and moreover a large man, who had no fear of speaking his mind once he had made it up.

"None of it works as painting, my friend. None of it, I'm afraid." Clemens stood up suddenly and paced about among the paintings that Stefan had pulled out and leaned haphazardly about the small room. "No. Not this one. Not that one. No," and turning in a half circuit, his large gray eyes traveled the room, swiveling upward to where a painting leaned against the bookcase wall, and downward to a diptych of portraits, yoked together in the same frame. "No. No. Not a single one. And yet, failing though they do" (he allowed no possibility of a different view and quite correctly

Stefan Mauger concluded) "I should say that there's an immense talent here that hasn't found itself, hasn't found the correct format—'the field of battle' I call it in criticism —and quite possibly hasn't even found the right medium. Let's be straightforward and to the point. Quite true. Diana told me all about you before we'd met. It wasn't all that accidental. She wanted me to meet you. Seems she thinks very highly of your talent, but like myself, thinks the energy's misplaced. Look at the work, would you? Technically it's all over the place—heavy paint, light paint, underpainting, delicacy, gruffness. Pyrotechnics. Flaming audacity, but to what end? Does it add anything more than a bit of trick, a fillip of surprise? Not really. And the subjects come from everywhere, you know as well as I. But then, let me say something, very positive, very assured. The interesting thing about all this pastiche is that it is quite aware that it's fabrication. I know that—I can dare saying it to you, Stefan—because every single painting is unfinished. There's not a single picture here that you would let out of the studio this minute, without working on it again and again, maybe even remaking it entirely. I can tell that because there are passages that have simply not been completed, as though each painting—like the unfinished foot of every life statue of the ancient Pharaohs—was left unfinished to remind you of its mortality. In short, I believe of your work that you have real gift and, every bit as important, you understand that making art—despite the formidable opposition which such a view provokes today—is a moral undertaking."

Stefan Mauger was several days late to the studio of Diana Middleton. He had first to change his apartment, to find a different, an uncluttered studio, a space with even less view in which to recommence the enterprise of his life, recommence, that is, having abandoned everything that he had set down to that date. Funds depleted and certainly without visible warrant to the hubris of his decision, Stefan Mauger had, the morning following the devastation of Clemens Rosenthal's criticism, abandoned his apartment, taking with him only his clothes, his books, his sketching notebooks, pens, pencils, the equivocal equipment of his craft, but behind, against the walls where they had been examined the day before, Stefan Mauger left all his work. He had no further interest in it. It was a gesture he would repeat several times during the coming years. "It's not the failed work that needs to be recalled, only the failure. And that," Stefan would explain to amazed listeners, "that, I keep in my head, just behind my eyes."

It was an argument he refused to join. He knew, quite well, that the discussion had begun among the ancients, acquired intensity and elaboration during the Renaissance, and among the moderns was fiercely, often intolerantly, pursued. Stefan Mauger, however, had no interest in considering painting's superiority to or dependency upon sculpture. Diana Middleton had tried—employing a rhetoric of seduction—to persuade Stefan that a modeled head was vastly more persuasive than one painted. Her arguments were predictable, their rebuttal no less predictable. Stefan Mauger merely grunted, shifted his position in the chair that she had placed upon a rectangular dais, and lit a cigarette. "None of this matters, Diana. It doesn't matter to you and certainly not to me. If it could be proved that one was absolutely, incontestably superior to the other, can it really be imagined that either painter or sculptor would convert? The truth is more devious than Plato imagined. The problem isn't verisimilitude, but illusion. It isn't at all that we wish to make the birds peck at the fruit, but rather —more Promethean—to make certain that the same birds tear at our livers. We are all interior estates looking for a fiefdom in the real world, trying somehow to make a connection which catches and holds. No. I take it back. Not even illusion. Making art, however one makes it, is rather more like God brooding the waters in creation, brushing his wings on the waters, so to speak, bringing them to rest from their agitation. Art is, forgive me, a way of making silence, commanding silence. Man Ray, I'm told, wanted to make a picture so powerful it could kill. What a dramatically dumb conceit! The idea that a painting can do something which ideologies and armies do more efficiently is a stupidity. It's merely an expression of the temptation of the Dadaists and the surrealists to make art into an auxiliary of power, to endow it with the power to outrage, embarrass, humiliate, and destroy. It disgusts me."

Diana Middleton worked throughout Stefan's reply, laying clay in strips upon a mold and then working with finger speed, occasionally interrupting the process to pick up a charcoal and draw a series of lips or eyes, as an aid to memory when the living subject was gone. She hardly listened to Stefan Mauger; indeed, the provocation had been clearly intended to distract him from the discomfort of posing.

The following day Stefan Mauger arrived at the Louvre shortly before it opened. It was a familiar strategy. Virtually every artist of any importance in the century had used the Louvre as a treasury of the imagination, either to confirm or to rattle received opinion. Over the years since coming to France, Stefan had been there a score of times: Ingres and Delacroix, the Italian painters, the Dutch and Germans. But it was the first time that he had come specifically to see ancient sculptures. Of course, he had seen them, passed his eyes over them, wandering casually from room to room, moving down one vast escalier and up another, but he had never seen them, that is, had never seen into them.

It was overcast and the Louvre was cold. The guards tugged at their scarves, winding them more tightly around their necks, moving slowly through the enormous rooms, estimating the few visitors, peering them out to guess the reason for their presence in the rooms of the Early and Middle Kingdoms of Ancient Egypt. Stefan Mauger's purpose, an extension of his familiar explanation, the education of sight, involved as well more subtle and up to that moment inexplicit inquiry.

Where then but in the Louvre would an aged couple (his head shaped like a pomegranate, the wood burnished, arm about his ancient woman, wife of more than half a century, staring straight into the void, but still alive, blood coursing through wooden veins as though these were their channels of affection—the wood itself sustaining that affection, the knife of the carver, himself a man of affection who perceived the bond permanent in the wood and had carved in love about love, permanent, ageless) encounter Stefan Mauger in the cold morning and become for him a reminiscence of what he desired now and in that hour to understand and yet come forward modestly, out of the daytime of more than three millennia, to be a reminder in miniature that the claim of affection endured. Not alone they, hugging, but beyond them scores of deities—bull heads, monkeys and ravens, crows and eagles, surmounting bodies of exquisite modeling and strength, fatal masculinity, nippled breasts and pelvic asseveration, legs forward-striding, yet rigid, seized in the instant before dying and frozen into wood ice, the carver making sculpture by chipping away until the figure was released and mounted to pedestal. Between the aisles of cases, carved in diorite or obsidian a monumental Ptah, an Apis, Ra and Osiris, gods and divinities of another contention, ruling over civilizations that moved slowly from life into death, investing each hour of enterprise with anticipations of the long death and the even longer journey to still kingdoms where the acanthus waves, the papyrus grows, and the gold-backed ibis bears the promise of immortality.

Stefan Mauger was transfixed by Egypt. In fact, the transfixion lengthened into an inquiry, accompanied by many books and considerable research. It seemed for a time that the research intended the obliteration of his own activity, but that is mistaken. It was in fact the indispensable foundation of that activity and when the inquiry broadened to include the great Gudeas of Sumer, the Achaemenid gold helmets, the worked swords and bridle bits, each representing the divinities of nomadic Luristan, passing through the Near East to the settled idols of Anatolia and the Cyclades, simplification and abstraction, the reduction of individuation without loss of concreteness, Stefan Mauger was persuaded that he had come upon the elemental genius of classic art, which more than interpreted its religious sense, its intimacy with nature without naturalism, its hieratic abstraction without loss of passion, indeed precisely, its removal of everything which suggested that a single human being was astonishing or marvelous for having been named Socrates or Ramses or Alexander, but what was transmitted (more than a likeness) was that Socrates was ugly and wise and Ramses a ruler and Alexander, quite simply, Great. Sunk into each creature were the lineaments of essence; what the sculptor sought, irrespective of his material, was that nothing trivial should be made eternal. Even in those tender portraits so common in late Roman art and Egyptian Hellenism of the dead child, the youth or the maiden who had not survived to adolescence, the task was not the perpetuation of sweetness or a simple praise to innocence, but rather a commentary upon the unformed essence, the frail connection to the child, not yet awakened to the trials of the matured, but prescient, asleep but awake, as though early morning dew had not yet been dried up by the blanching sun of regular days.

"But you must see the sculptures of the living, as well," Diana Middleton chided Stefan, irritated by his single-minded preoccupation with the hoardings of the Louvre and his even more stunned discovery of the Musée de l'Homme to which she had introduced him, bringing him one afternoon to the office of its director, Monsieur Leiris, who had conducted him exuberantly through its collection, remarking to Stefan Mauger's delight upon the resemblances between the tribal arts and what were conveniently described as ancient civilizations. The coincidences of the imagination, the willingness to carve in the dried-up lands of the Dogon the same intimacies that he had observed in the old couple of affection in Middle Kingdom Egypt, the Queen mother of the Senufo holding the animal babe to her pendulant breast no different in spirit from Michelangelo's grieving mother holding the dying Jesus beneath the cover of her once flowing tit and beyond these, strange cultures of the Mayans and the Aztecs, whose arcana he could not fathom, monumental and grotesque, evidently ministering to a theology that had no European earth for nurture, and the even more stunning, but sparsely represented, masks of the Indians of the Pacific Northwest, of whose tribal spirit he remembered something from his youthful days as Silesian medicine man, but whose actual carvings he had never seen until that day. M. Leiris made astute comment about the capaciousness of his institution, its service to Frenchmen being at last brought under rein of a larger ministry, the human race. It was a brief visit, too brief, and Stefan Mauger returned for weeks to its collections, acquiring as he had earlier done for the ancients an appropriate library of postcards, ethnographic manuals, and books on tribal religion until Diana Middleton, wearied of his discussion of the sculpture of the ancient world and now of the tribes who had fed the cubist fracture, insisted that he consider the achievement of his own day, the Rodins, Maillols of the city, the sculptures of Picasso, Matisse, Giacometti, Gonzalez, and the many others who described the modern sensibility, and if he would trouble himself with a visit, the single public work of the Rumanian sculptor Constantin Brancusi, which served as headstone in the Montparnasse Cemetery.

"It has all come together, Clemens, and although I can claim now that I am ready to begin work, it is a work wholly different from what I had imagined at first. These past months of watching the traditions of sculpture rising from their ancient precedent have at last found a model and an end. I understand how very great and how very modern was Rodin. Certainly, he rescued sculpture from banality, removing it from decorative statuary—little pieces of sentimental cultural flatware—and restoring to it the mark of individual genius, but Rodin was too ardently genius to be a model. In wishing for myself a model, it is not the desire to become a disciple, to grow under another man's tree (quite impossible in the case of Rodin as Brancusi observed of himself when he declined to work in Rodin's studio), but rather to propose for myself an inexhaustible goal—a goal which cannot be reached except by self-differentiation. In choosing the work of Brancusi as the model for my own I am not moved to imitate, but to combat. It all became clear yesterday afternoon and I have been dizzy from the encounter.

"Do you know the Montparnasse Cemetery? A splendid walking cemetery, where the dead congregate, falling upon each other for consultation and comfort. It's an attractive place to await the resurrection, somewhat confused, in disarray, that is, with far too many gravesites, crowded and impatient, not at all the severe cemeteries I have been used to—where my own parents lie rather too rigidly at attention as though awaiting not the trumpet of Gabriel but the cornet of a well-accoutered Imperial guardsman who will raise the dead row by row, in stately array, instead of tumbling them out into the radiance of eternal life. I came early in the afternoon to the cemetery and asked where I might find the sculpture which Brancusi had called *Le Baiser*. A gatekeeper pointed vaguely in its direction and I set out to find it, tracing my way through Virgins and burnished crosses. I came around a particularly ugly mausoleum and there, set in a nondescript corner, was a concrete plinth surmounted by its Brancusi headstone. A woman had died, a woman whom Brancusi had known, a woman married, a woman pregnant (I suppose), a woman beloved, and for her, to her memory, Brancusi had carved from a block of sandstone the enlaced couple, the man of powerful chest, the woman of subtly protuberant belly, their faces conjoined, their lips tenderly touching, their heads like thirteenth-century carvings of Adam and Eve with plaits of hair and shaping of cheekbones scoring their gender, descending until the sheer linearity of legs positioned to touch and caress, bound together by forehead, by knee, by chest and stomach, by kiss, and then by arms enfolding, seizing, hugging each other, hugging each other forever. That single work told me something which the past six months of reflection and study had all along prepared. Not a single image of what endures in man has really died and cannot be brought again to life. *The Kiss* is three thousand years beyond the Egyptian couple of the Louvre bound by a single arm of affection, beyond the African sculptures of groping intimacy, beyond the Adams and Eves of all the ages embracing in their paradise. In other words, Clemens, by becoming a sculptor I am training to become a medicine man, a shaman of our western tribe. And like the great shamans of whom we know, I hold out for myself the promise of Brancusi's triumph of humility, that humble, tender work which roughly carved, unsweetened, surface rough and scaly, restores an aesthetic sanctity, a kind of holiness no

114

less impious and quizzical, which is absolutely ancient while being completely modern."

"It's perhaps my American pragmatism, perhaps the skepticism born of long attendance upon the celebrations of my ancestors, whatever, the interpretation you give the enterprise, Stefan, dismays me. Medicine man and shaman, however connected in the history of religion, have it seems to me little to do with the making of our art. Once, long ago, making art was the preserve of a special class of artisans who, in addition to the mastery of craft, required as well theological training to understand not only what was made, but the correct attitudes of the maker, the right times and fortuitous conjunctions which attended the making, in other words the sacred atmosphere of art. But in our day, how can it be said that any of the same conditions obtain? The shaman exists, I am sure, among many tribes, and efficient, well-trained, and thorough he remains, but it cannot be thought that he produces high art, which to my view is an art of the free imagination. The sand paintings of the Navaho, the poles of the Kwakiutl, the cornhusk masks of the Seneca, and I am sure countless artifacts and ritual dress-ups of all the extant tribes of the Americas, Africa, and the Australian archipelago are undeniably powerful with a terrifying beauty, but they are an art of magic. Are you interested in becoming an artist or a magician?"

"I refuse the distinction, Clemens. I refuse it. All the years that I made pictures, I felt that my fingers were trying to claw the edge of the canvas, to pry it loose, to lift the surface I decorated and look behind. It is the looking behind that I think sculpture entails. Obviously both painting and sculpture are desperate measures in the absence of an acceptable metaphysics of the unseen. The artist tries to make us see differently. Regrettably most modern artists lack a metaphysics. Many to be sure are engaged in some species of theosophical arrangement—Kandinsky, Mondrian, Malevich, Klee—but they, I suspect from reading their aesthetic notations, are merely trying to

115

supply their work with a canon of criticism. They make the work and interpret it, as though jittery that the work will be misunderstood and lost without their annotation. None of them needs to worry.

"When I write to you about my wish to be a medicine man, I am supplying a different connection entirely. I am not arrogating to myself the potency of magic or the healing ministrations of the shaman. I am only suggesting that I wish to pursue the connection between my own contemporaneity— as a man of this century—and the ancientness of my being. I contain (as do you) connections with the beginnings of the race. The same birth and the prospect of the same death bind us to the earliest moments of the species. What I do now has as much connection with the modeler of the Venus of Willendorf as it has with Maillol and Matisse. The ancient carvers not only believed in the gods when they made their votive idols, they were in some small measure possessed of the gods, themselves little gods and divinities, who knew pretty well what the gods required and how much the gods enjoyed of their portion. The connections are thin, the bonds frayed, and what we retain is not much more than an unperverse fetishism. But that's it!

"I want to make sculptures that I can rub and touch like theirs. I'll never make sculptures like Michelangelo. Don't want to even if I could. He's too grand, too tragic. But sculptures that I can hold in my hand and carry in my pocket or sculptures I can mount on marvelous bases and walk around and lower my head to, upon whom I can smile and whom I can salute in the morning, and even vaster sculptures that I can situate in the woods where people can come upon them like benign monsters in whose presence one is both afraid and comforted—that's the extent of my shamanistic ambition.

"Have I made myself clearer? And, let me add, it connects with events of my childhood, all this. My childhood, my own phylogeny, recapitulating my own ancientness, had its moments (I dimly recollect) in which I am certain are lodged events which explain these discoveries of mine. One day, perhaps (more than 'perhaps' I hope), those deeps of mine will be touched by something in my making and then, as if the right word had been spoken—if this magic applies as it does in fairy tales—something that had been held fast will be loosened and will float free to the surface. And the images I catch and hold are those which I find absolutely familiar, like houses visited in the forgotten past and then suddenly recalled. Plato called it *anamnesis*, but it's more than recollection. It's not that I knew everything before my birth, that I forgot, and that the passage of life is recall. That Greek version of the fall of man into the world—fall as birth rather than error—is the invention of philosophers. Artists work differently with the myths than do the philosophers. Artists, I think, fabulate; the philosophers interpret."

"Right, Stefan. Of course, the artist succeeds in his ambiguities while the philosopher is repaid for his with chastisement. It's permitted the artist to be ambiguous. Not the philosopher. The only relevant question is whether we're talking about ambiguity or confusion. Is it a muddle in the nature of things (read ambiguity) or simply an example of poor thinking? Of course, even this distinction—elegant though it may be—will not persuade thinkers with a system (for Kant and Hegel, there is nothing so elemental as an ambiguity or so vulgar as confusion—they, to be accurate, speak of antinomies and contradictions). Philosophers think themselves compromised if they are obliged to admit that they don't know. It takes a rigorous mind with an unhappy sensibility, like your countryman (Wittgenstein his name is) to say 'I'm absolutely clear and lucid about the mountain, but it's this small pile of stones I can't fathom.'"

"Which is, you must admit, rather a good case for my pursuing the myth. And it's not even the myth. I don't know what a myth is except an explanation which the myth-maker no longer believes in or perhaps, I should add, believes a little or a lot, but doesn't dare to admit in public. No. This won't do at all.

"Bear with me a little, Clemens. Myth is explanation as story. The story varies from culture to culture, but given the perception of certain common problems and the available language, imagery, material culture on which language builds its structures, myths will tend to overlay each other and explanations for fire or drunkenness or fertility or grain will have some interior resemblance. The words will translate from one mythology to another and only in cases of psychopathic cultures will we get a mutation of the myth which reflects its abnormality. No. It isn't the myth as such that I can deal with as a sculptor. The pot painters of antiquity could unroll the myth. Any Corinthian olpe is grand enough in scale (although its shape is pretty pedestrian) to permit one of the master painters to tell a whole saga, unraveling it like an early piece of silent film, one frame after another, disjunct, but unified; beginning, middle, end; origin, development, dénouement. But the sculptors? The sculptors aren't engaged in the mythic telling, but rather with the mythic form. They arrest the essence of the myth and offer to the traveling eye, the eye that leads the body round (and here I have some simple discoveries to note), a hypostasis—the whole at one instant. Sculptors who worked from the myths, making the idols to be worshiped, cutting the great narrative glyphs and friezes, these were artists of the deep forms of man, the ulterior structures that lie hidden under the paint and color of our sunlit days. And that is what sculpture is about, first and foremost, primary form, essential form, the interior life of form which the sculptor is obliged to bring to the surface of the wood or the marble."

"Interesting that you speak of wood and marble (stone) and not at all of metal or the fusion of materials. Primary natural substances, primary forms, and primary methods of getting hold of them—carving directly. Have you begun to work? I know that you've left Paris, although you've told me nothing about 'Le Vrai Presbytère,' the pugnacious name which your return address mentions."

Le Vrai Presbytère was located off the main road that leads into the village of Les Herbiers, itself the point of conjunction for several tributary highways that link the city of Nantes and the towns of Cholet to the north and La Roche-sur-Yon to the south. There is no particular mystery to Stefan Mauger's discovery of this small village in the Vendée to which he moved in January of 1932, carrying only his few belongings, the tools that Diana Middleton selected with him, and the first cast that she had made of his head (his look aloof, but as he came to feel later, studying himself for his own self-portrait, insufficiently abstract). It was more a question of having attended closely to the names of the principal real-estate agents in the ninety-five departments of France, eliminating those in whose region he had little interest in living and addressing letters to the fifteen or so that remained. It wasn't long before the letters began to arrive, brochures with photographs appended and brief descriptions of less elaborately endowed offerings, of which one was Le Vrai Presbytère.

Le Vrai Presbytère was certainly to be preferred to the abundance of encumbered chateaus and deserted manor houses in which the agents of the untrafficked regions of France specialized. It was only when he confronted Monsieur Louis Dampierre, the director of the real-estate agency of the same name, in his office in the old quarter of Nantes, that he learned why he had chosen to include in his reply to Stefan's inquiry the description of a property as modestly proportioned and as modestly priced as Le Vrai Presbytère.

"Mais, c'est évident, Monsieur. J'ai pensé que vous étiez Protestant." And indeed, that would have clarified it, had the explanation been sufficient and accurate. As it was, Stefan Mauger's family was quite Catholic and if theology rather than space had been the issue, poor M. Dampierre,

himself a Protestant, might have failed once more to relieve the burdened treasury of the local Protestant mission of one more piece of useless and draining expenditure. "I couldn't understand anyway why the old pastor thought it was good evangelism to establish an outpost at Les Herbiers. Wanted a summer place outside the city, if you ask me. Place to recreate and disport himself, if you understand my meaning?"

Stefan Mauger understood something, if not quite M. Dampierre's meaning, but after a short drive from Nantes to Les Herbiers, the distance of forty-four kilometers, going very slowly indeed, allowing M. Dampierre to indite the virtues of several other, more expensive and available houses along the way, his wish being to sell dear, even if he failed in his service to the encumbered mission, they arrived in the village, where several townspeople shouted greetings, and turning to the right off the highway, down a steep cobbled road to a narrower dirt path on which they continued by foot, M. Dampierre finally announced—as if dropping a cover cloth from a monument—*"Voici Le Vrai Presbytère."* And it was, in truth, splendid, a perfection of containment, a Presbytery, a summer house, with a garland of crosses, turned so that their cross-bars formed a rectangular opening emplaced beneath its gables, advertising its function, circulating the breeze, permitting the birds to enter and flee the large and empty single room, which had served the summering pastor.

"Modest and unpretentious," M. Dampierre interpreted, observing the obvious. What could have been more modest and unpretentious than the large and empty room in which the departed pastor had summered, conducting his religious services in an atmosphere uncongested with religious bric-a-brac, neither altar nor tabernacle, neither pews nor benches. The few itinerant Huguenots of the district who came to church Sundays on their way to picnic grounds in the wood found the pastor awaiting them, seated on a floor covered with scatter rugs, and abandoning winter formality for a summer holy spirit, he would discourse for an hour, sing a bit longer, and then dismiss them with a blessing into the bee-filled atmosphere of hollyhocks, climbing vines, and bougainvillea, that whorish purple beauty that will grow anywhere and grew abundantly at Le Vrai Presbytère. It was a foregone conclusion that Stefan Mauger would rent the abandoned church; the price was small and M. Dampierre was delighted to let it by the month, since Stefan was uncertain how long it would be required.

The following morning, after Stefan Mauger had installed himself, stacking his books on the window sills of the Presbytery and arranging the contents of the small foot locker against the wall near his bed, he went for a walk about Les Herbiers. The walk, more important than it appears, indispensable for a sculptor in fact, since it traced the dominion of nature from which fallen trees are cut and carried to the chisel's place and beyond these, the accidental troves of farmyard debris—a broken adze, a disused shaft, a wooden pail, a series of mallets, graduated in size, which the village carter threw into the bargain when Stefan Mauger hired him to carry the carcass of an oak tree, felled the year before, to his front door—confirmed the correctness of Stefan's decision to settle in Les Herbiers. The only things that Stefan bought, aside from food and supplies, were an astonishing variety of tools, sturdy knives, a two-handed peasant's saw, a claw hammer, another large chisel which virtually matched those he had brought with him from Paris, although there was the slightest curve in the metal, which he imagined could be used for routing the wood.

"What are you planning to do with all these tools, Monsieur? Rebuild Le Presbytère?" the merchant asked as Stefan counted out the money.

"Not at all. I'm a wood carver, you see."

"You mean a sculptor, don't you?"

"That remains to be seen. I begin as a carver," Stefan replied, laughing.

"Show me when you need an opinion," the merchant offered.

"If it's worth showing. If it's worth an opinion. By all means, Monsieur . . . ?" Stefan inflected, hoping to be rewarded with the merchant's name. The merchant, however, had already turned away from Stefan Mauger, having arranged his purchases in a wicker basket. A young boy—he could not have been over nine—took the basket and followed after Stefan, obviously deputed by the merchant to accompany this new and undoubtedly steady client to the Presbytery.

It was late afternoon when Stefan was alone again. The Presbytery was large and almost empty, clean and almost unused, the tools were hung, the mallets arranged, the chisels disposed, the accidental finds of the day—adze, shaft, pail—lay to one side in a corner, castaways from the center of the room. Before the open doors of the Presbytery Stefan examined carefully the five feet of oak trunk that, rudely dumped by the carter, rested upon a bed of leaves as though a hobbled beast awaiting the hierophant's knife. Stefan knew already that the essentiality of wood was different among all the species of tree, the woodness of oak ribbed and veined differently than beech or ash, the sap and stain of sycamore variant from that of cedar or mahogany, and with alterations of color, grain, hardness, decisions of form would vary.

Stefan sawed the stump in the dying sunlight and watched with pleasure as a small mound of cream-colored dust rose like an ant hill beneath its bite. He had worked furiously against the descent of the sun, drawing on the rectangular saw, back and forth, occasionally stopping to rub his damp forehead against a shirt sleeve and estimate the distance he had come and had still to go; when it was sundown and only a glow broke the horizon, he heard the stump groan and snap. The pieces parted, three feet and some to the left, two feet to the right. And cleanly parted. With chisel and mallet, by the vagrant light of a kerosene lamp, he skinned the stump of its bark and revealed, shivering in the evening cool, the naked oak, distinguished only by a brown birthmark, a whirlpool of subtle color whose rivulets streamed out from the center. Stefan Mauger admired the immaculate stump and appraised its life, its color, its surface toughness, and, beneath, the forms it might yield. Not everything can be made from everything. Certain materials reject certain forms: too delicate, they deny ferocity; too obdurate, they refuse sensuality. Only by experience could Stefan come to know which material is right for which form, which wood among a hundred woods, which stone among stones. Note-takings of experience; the sufferings vary as do the sculptors. As the materials differ, so too the hands. Not alone the impassivity of the matter, its supine reception, beckoning while concealing, allowing the hand to work its pleasure or its rage, cracking, seaming, splitting, the pressure too great, the force too unrelieved. Not only the matter, but the hand and beyond hand and matter, the mystery of form, the living form, for carving has no dealing with still-life.

It was this strange absence from the historic repertoire of sculpture—the absence of still-life—that moved Stefan Mauger to the first of what were to become the remarkable series that are still identified with his reputation. The first series, only latterly named by him *Imagines Mortes* recalling a medieval tradition, allegorically warning the human species about the attentions and ministrations of the sepulchral skeleton with scythe and hourglass, was used by Stefan Mauger to suggest, almost as though by means of a pun, that the *nature morte* of the sculptor was the modes of death by which the human face (and by implication the body) might be stripped of its various skins, molted and transformed by the imagination. And this idea, sculptural as it is, did not entail, as might be thought, a series of portraits in which the head is gradually peeled of its flesh— the imaginings of death expressed in earlier days by the removal of skin, the wasting of eye, disclosure of the rippled brain, crease of skull, until stripped of surface what remained is what always remains, carapace and bone. Not at all. Stefan Mauger's imagining was not fixed as it might have been, had he arisen from a fantasist's tradition, an Archimboldo of sculpture (making the human head an architecture of vegetables or a construction and decomposition of bricks and mortar) but from the earliest originations of man, and hence for him the imaginings of death consisted not in the stripping of the face of its natural covering and color, but rather in the overlaying of the face, nature built with masks which disclosed the extremity and variety of human affections, the kingdom of feelings and the exaggerations of temperament, which, were they frozen to an instant, could as well be painted. The innovation of the series and indeed its ultimate terror and success lay in the fact that the mask was in place upon a sculpted head with only suggestion of neck (as though a bust portrait) and upon that naked hairless skull the mask hung, only a hairline of discrimination marking the discrepancy between face and its dissimulation.

The series, begun the night of that first day during the winter of 1932, was completed by the end of summer,

twelve masks, the first being the self-portrait of Stefan
Mauger, as nature described him, deftly and by suggestion,
not at all with the comprehensiveness that ordinary viewers
call face, but as the face is viewed in reduction and con-
densation, simple line, overhanging forehead, lips that part
but rarely laugh, eyes that suggest but do not guarantee the
possibility of sight; with hair, the arranged ordinariness of
classical hair; and ears that do not stand forth to hear but
are adumbrated, flat and against the skull; and upon this
mask of nature, Mauger then laid upon his portrait the
masks of feeling, conjuring extremities and versions, parodies and exaltations, which mask, becoming the face from
which the same invariant wooden neck descended (not his
own neck as a photographer would observe, but neck as
bearer and base of head weight), and hanging upon head as
though no other face but that of the mask existed, transforming the true face into the mask's or the true face which
is a mask upon the false face which is nature's (when death
drains it of animation), he elaborated a suite of self-
portraits until by the last the mask was no longer visible as
mask, but the face of Stefan Mauger had become the
permutation of the mask and no longer sculpture of face
wearing mask but face become mask remained, and these,
at the very end, he called Imaginings of Death, the *Imagines Mortes*, by which title the series of sculptures was
known and exhibited at the Galerie du Cherche-Midi, on
the street of the same name, to whose director, Monsieur
Théophile Baguerre, Clemens Rosenthal had introduced
him.

Clemens Rosenthal had been moved by Stefan Mauger's
first sculptures. He sat before them on a ludicrously insub-
stantial chair, his large frame drooping over its sides,
his face slack from concentration, the tufts of hair that
fringed his premature baldness pulled by habit as Clemens

thought, pulled and twined in the absence of a beard, and after an hour of searching examination, occasionally falling upon one or another sculpture to shift its presentation, or walking around the table on which Stefan had disposed them, arranged first by order of making and subsequently, after their conversation, by order of their interior logic, Clemens pronounced his "superbs" and "splendids."

"They work. They do really work. You've brought it off and it's not without its own originality, genuine originality. Not cleverness and absolutely nothing chic about them. But one question comes to mind. Wherever did you get the idea of painting the masks and highlighting the carved volumes? Of course, it was done. We know that, but it's unusual, this combination of the painted and the carved."

"I'm not certain any more."

The reception of the exhibition was encouraging. Monsieur Baguerre, a tasteful sparrow who knew precisely where to feed, presented the exhibition in the fall and Clemens Rosenthal, although completely unknown among Paris collectors, had a sufficient camaraderie with Parisian painters and critics, that his little essay produced their attendance and small cries of approval. The work was alluded to quite explicitly, but unfortunately without name, in an essay that Christian Zervos wrote for *Cahiers d'Art* on modern masks and totems; the surrealists approved the exhibition, relating its subject matter to the world of dreams and the unconscious from which in large measure it probably derived; four of the works, including the prototypical self-portrait, were sold for modest prices; moreover sculptors visited the exhibition and signed the guest book.

"You may consider the exhibition a success, a qualified success to be sure, but nonetheless a success," Monsieur Baguerre confided.

They were seated in the office that the small director of

the Galerie du Cherche-Midi had contrived to excavate from the remains of the kitchen that had once occupied the space. "Four pieces well placed. Not bad at all for a beginner," he continued. Stefan Mauger had come to collect his funds. He needed the money. Monsieur Baguerre presented him with an elaborate rendition of his expenses, explained his deductions, and passed along an advance against the final reckoning. The pieces were sold well, but in those days, selling well meant little more than having persuaded casual collectors to risk a modest sum on the whim of enthusiasm. If they could afford to visit a gallery to offer praise, they were pressed to confirm their daring. In this consisted the success of Monsieur Baguerre and, however honest, he was essentially a mountebank like all the dealers, even the most honored, who considered the task of presentation, display, publicity, and business as somehow more a sign of quality and discrimination than the artist's making of the work.

"Yes?" Stefan replied to Monsieur Baguerre's disingenuous report, once again affirming, while querying the truth.

"Mais certainement, mon ami," Monsieur Baguerre continued, his voice rising to higher pitches of excitement. "What more could you wish? Four pieces out of a dozen and surely more to come. We are delighted," he continued, retiring for reassurance to a majestic impersonality of address, for there was no Madame Baguerre, "but then, I know, you wished the pieces sold as a group. Quite impossible as I explained. That would have taken more than twenty thousand francs, and who has that for art these days?"

The Galerie du Cherche-Midi was not without reputation. It was to be sure a gallery without innovative intelligence—a defect that Monsieur Baguerre was incapable of recognizing, but nonetheless being second-rate or second-rank meant at worst that its director pursued the epigones of whatever movement dominated the season and in the course of such pursuit, having learned well the persuasive marks of a well-concealed imitation, he often chose well. He never showed the masters, for they were all taken, nor did he ever manage to organize about a specious concept an exhibition of masters in the manner of galleries who built their reputation on borrowed glitter. Monsieur Baguerre did, however, take chances on younger people who in due course took hold, sold for several seasons at the Galerie du Cherche-Midi, and then left for more established dealers and more generous guarantees.

"And they all came to call. *Tout le monde*. Think of it," Monsieur Baguerre leaned forward and tapped the desk as each grand name fell from his lips: poets, painters, sculptures, and at the last—"even Brancusi who never . . ."

"Brancusi? Did Brancusi come to my exhibition?" Stefan asked hoarsely, his throat suddenly tightened.

"But of course, look here." Monsieur Baguerre lifted the imposing leather-bound journal and there beneath the day, "15 novembre 1932" on the first line of faded blue, there, heading the column of eight visitors who had bothered to sign their names, was "C. Brancusi." Stefan took the book into his hands, but his head began to spin and a giddy feeling that he rarely experienced apparently drained his face of color, for Monsieur Baguerre brought out a bottle of brandy and delicately ignoring his consternation, proffered the drink, instead, as celebration. Calm returned, the excitement congealed, and Stefan began again to examine the name and the signature.

The initial, which is all that remained of Brancusi's connection with the illustriousness of its origin, was even there truncated, the upper curve, like a swooping swan's neck, reaching forward to the smaller majuscule as if to nip it in its beak, reaching forward and rising off the base of its lower curve so that the latter, the bottom of the *C*, was no longer comfortably balanced upon the imperceptible horizon of blue, but stretched as if poised to fly, straight line of flight, the swan about to depart into the air; and separate from it, beneath, huddled and compressed (it could be said), if not in fear of the swan's motherhood then at least awaiting her ministration, the fullness of the brood, the eight children in their order, the crushed *B* upon whose head pressed the weight of sixteen centuries of memorials to Constantine. The signature of a man suggested the lineaments of character, pressing into this speedy, undeliberated assertion of presence an unguarded description of C(on-stantin) Brancusi. Stefan shook his head in disbelief, examining it before him, the letters all run together, each distinct, but nonetheless butting against each other. The *C* dominated everything, holding the man Brancusi at bay beneath the cover of the swan or perhaps the ibis or the firebird or his own Maiastra. Beside C. Brancusi, Stefan Mauger's name seemed to him merely an identification, a signature for checks and documents, but not yet a name that spoke an authentic tracing of the self, a ghost printing of the soul. It was all this, the name a scintilla of the person, the bearded man shambling beneath the cover of his Constantin; the modesty and elation of his patronymic circling from its letters into his work.

"Did he say anything, Monsieur?" Stefan asked some minutes later. Monsieur Baguerre was busy with the mail, opening announcements and examining papers, no longer aware of the overwhelming impression that the presence of Bracusi had made upon Stefan Mauger.

"Who? Of whom were we speaking?"

"Brancusi."

"Ah, Brancusi. A decent man, but he works too slow to really matter."

"Monsieur Baguerre, forgive me, but I'm not curious about your opinion of Brancusi, only your report of his visit to my exhibition."

"I am sorry," he replied archly, unaware of Stefan's agitation. "I wasn't aware that my opinion counted for so little."

"No, no, Monsieur. It's simply that you have no idea what Brancusi's interest in my work means to me. Did Brancusi say anything, anything at all?"

"Nothing, I'm afraid. Brancusi speaks very little in public and with all the artists who come by here, I hardly have time to collect their droppings even if they did. But I *can* say he stayed quite a time, standing with his hands to his face in an almost mournful contemplation—yes, a most dolorous contemplation of your pieces. Once only, I recall, he touched one of the painted masks, hoping—if I interpret the gesture correctly—that the paint would come off. He looked at his fingers afterward. But no expression, I'm afraid. He doesn't like to paint sculpture, you know. 'Direct, direct. Only the stone, the wood,' he might have said, 'reveals the creature.' "

"But he didn't say that. Nothing at all. He only studied and touched and looked to see if the paint came off on his finger."

"*Vraiment, c'était tout.*"

The visit of C(onstantin) Brancusi to the first exhibition of Stefan Mauger, wholly unexpected—what is called correctly a fortuity—transformed his dream and expectation. However tenuous the connection (for what is fifteen minutes, at the most, that Brancusi spent before the suite of the *Imagines Mortes* wondering who knows about what? whether the paint would peel? or whether the paint was oil or solvent? whether the sculptures possessed tactility, the pleasure of touch and rubbiness? or whether they were as severe as their masked faces proposed?). Indeed, it was certainly possible—and Stefan Mauger considered it ruefully —that the sculptor, then a man of fifty-eight, had only come out into the maelstrom of the city from the quiet cul-de-sac where his atelier was located to purchase some necessity or simply to visit, so to speak, abroad, in the world of which he was an intimate and to which he was a stranger, and passing the Galerie du Cherche-Midi had entered and examined. Whatever the occasion of Brancusi's visit, it was now an ineffaceable fact that his small eyes had passed over the surface of Stefan Mauger's sculpture and those dozen pieces had been seen, into their very heart had been seen, and his own heart discerned and estimated.

It was a slow and painstaking resolve, the process of several years, but Stefan Mauger determined somehow to apprentice himself, if that were at all possible, to Brancusi. It was not the case that Brancusi's visit had dammed his energy, filling the pool with still waters awaiting the propulsive force of an open sluice gate, indeed, the unavoidable surmise about apprenticeship. Not at all. Stefan Mauger's need for Brancusi was less that of the young artist who requires an accomplished example in order to motivate his art, compelled by the concentration and assiduity of the *pater magister* to be a dutiful and domesticated son; Stefan knew perfectly well that art is as much the offspring of vagrancy as of settled habits and housebound discipline. The body stays put, constrained by requirements of work, but the imagination wanders, picking up the colors of the world without needing, necessarily, to step outside the studio. Inspiration was not at all the issue of his wish for apprenticeship; it was more in the mode of a submission, a joining of himself to another who conducted the life of art sternly, even eremitically.

Stefan Mauger learned all this over the succeeding years, as he gathered every essay about the man Brancusi and his works, every magazine photograph of his cluttered studio, committing to memory the exortia and epigrams that had come from his mouth (and they were very few, the canon profound but brief), and traveling long distances by car and train to visit any museum in the accessible provinces of Europe where one or another of his sculptures was to be seen. He contrived to secure the address of the young Rumanian, Margit Pogany, and called upon her to inquire about Brancusi, but she had gone out and he never returned, suddenly embarrassed by his forwardness; he wrote to Edouard Steichen to ask permission to visit his garden where the first *Endless Column* was installed but he never replied; and he wrote to James Joyce and Ezra Pound who had contributed to the legend of the artist, hoping to secure evidence whether one or another quotation of Brancusi's words was accurate or their own paraphrased embellishment, but in both cases his letters were returned, one in the original envelope stamped "Addressee Unknown" and the other, neatly inserted in the recipient's envelope, presumably read, and, as he understood, answered by dismissal, for the name and return address of the sender were not supplied.

The enterprise was a circumlocution, for Stefan Mauger was then a modest man. He did not feel he deserved Brancusi or, more hubristic still, that Brancusi deserved him. Quite the contrary, and in its very contrariness lies the explanation of the length of years that elapsed between seeing the signature of the master in the guest register and his first meeting with him. Stefan Mauger was tired of having struggled out of doors; his search for Brancusi was therefore an enterprise of coming inside, finding, so to speak, his own hearth and his own fire. It was not necessary over those years (and there were five of them) to meet Brancusi, to wait outside the passage that led from the Impasse Ronsin to the Rue Vaugirard as many did and fall upon the man as he came out to walk his dog or to buy his provisions.

It could be done that way, waylaying, so to speak, Brancusi. It was done often to Brancusi and to others—to the other masters—but Stefan Mauger regarded such devices as treacherous and considered anyone who contrived by stealth or pretexts to insinuate himself into the presence of another artist to be a robber who deserved all the punishment the world could devise (and, of course, the world did not even regard it as a crime). He once overheard a young Berlin journalist who had come to Paris to write a contemptuous article for a popular magazine describe how he had, in his words, "spun a web about Max Ernst. I dazzled him (I knew more about him than he knew about himself) and he fell into my lair where I devoured him." The young journalist was so amused by his conning that he fell to chuckling with his cafe companions about his great success. Stefan Mauger had been taking a coffee at the next table and although he loathed the sound of his own language he could not avoid hearing the little recital of fatuities. "You are contemptible, sir. The only spiders that do as you describe are human and they, not poor Max Ernst, should be devoured." He was protecting Max Ernst, whom he did not know and for whose work he had no particular feeling, but he was also protecting the privacy of his own Brancusi, whom he wished guarded from everyone else, from any other interloper, feeling himself in some sense already both his guardian and his most particularly appointed robber.

During those five years, Stefan Mauger worked constantly. The more his work diverged from that of Brancusi the more relieved he became, knowing that his discipleship was not in the manner of a copyist who, slow-witted, considers fidelity of repetition to be the mark of intimacy with the master without ever realizing that repetition, whatever its compliment, renders not only the copy but the original turgid and slightly boring. Originality, then, originality of subject matter, originality of technique, discriminated Stefan Mauger's achievement from that of most other young sculptors. He learned to carve directly into wood and stone; he rarely prepared a maquette to enable him to transcribe in miniature what would eventually be seen in grandeur, although very often he would make a whole series of drawings in which he would try, by shading and modulation of perspective, to see around the curve, to suggest, as it were, the volumes and the fall of light that would be the condition of their realized expression as sculpture. The drawings were ways of seeing feeling, setting down instantly a mode of care and solicitude for the line of the creature-subject, and in sculpture, it was all creature.

Sculpture, Mauger came to realize, mediated between painting and architecture. Whereas painting describes both the living and the dead, the human and the inanimate, setting to both the limit fixed by line and color, animating and suppressing life by turn, making the fruit live as warmly as the young boy at the piano, it could not make architecture. No painting could hold up an arch, and if that illusion can be suggested by painting the arch or converting the wall into mural, such enterprise is of a species of illusion verging upon deception. The painter may try to think architecturally, but the transcription of space—open as a canyon and deep as the valley—is accomplished only by an abstraction, where not the whole of that immense space is offered but only its sign and symbol, a mere suggestion that space is deep and vast, and that the eye must travel through the limits of the color and the bounds of the edge to the blue sky and sea beyond. Can it not be said, Mauger generalized, that the painter who makes the familiar *nature morte* alive and vibrant no less than the tableau of persons or the lady in her green hat, is a specialist of time, caring that time be stopped, that every instant in its sequence swell with the pride of eternal life, whereas the painter who sheers off to architecture describing visionary details of imaginary cities and impossible connections, building constructions that no eye but his own has ever seen, considers the prospect of eternity less bracing than the monuments that time fits into space, making space the proper receptacle of time, the endless home of the race, the major mother of all the rest that comes into being and passes away. Despite all this facility, painting cannot do more than suggest the world of space in which architecture lives and into whose midst sculpture is placed. Sculpture, for its part, can make no bowl of fruit nor carve in marble the hanging goose or slab of beef; it has no gift for the luscious, no talent for skin and flesh tones. It is an art that obliges the eye to fabricate from the inside, to tease to the surface the life that is virtual in the matter.

These are the notions that Stefan Mauger expressed when he found the energy to speak, for during those five years, except when Clemens Rosenthal came to Paris, he had few friends and spoke little. He worked; he struggled with the making; he worked, and the uses of the world (as Monsieur Baguerre described them after each of his increasingly successful exhibitions) interested him less and less. The inquiry of art, no differently than the occupation of the alchemist who as well had no interest in exhibiting an even more refined example of fool's gold, was all that mattered. The research had no end; it was still fool's gold.

By the spring of 1938 Stefan Mauger had written Brancusi no less than forty letters. The fact that none of these were mailed should not be surprising, since he had no justification, given his view of molestation, to send them. Brancusi had no need of Stefan Mauger's patronage nor even of his praise and consequently the letters accumulated, written it appears in a special notebook, where Stefan noted down remarkable findings, events, comments, apocrypha, ascriptions or pasted clippings, photographs, postcards of Brancusi's work. It was only by chance that Stefan learned during late April of the year that an astonishing project of Brancusi's, little publicized or remarked to that date, was going to be sited and made during the summer and that Brancusi was leaving Paris in June to supervise its preparation. The notice had appeared on the art page of *L'Aurore*, a small notice, neither lengthy nor detailed. It observed quite simply that the noted sculptor (Rumanian-born, but naturalized Frenchman) had accepted a commission from his natal country to design and execute in a public park at Tirgu-Jiu an ensemble of sculptures to commemorate the fallen of the World War and was returning at the beginning of summer to oversee the cutting and casting of its principal works. Simple, spare, quite flat, but sufficient to afford Stefan Mauger the occasion that he required in order to make himself known to Brancusi. Since he had no wish to offer himself as an equal, that is, as a fellow-sculptor or worse, as a hierophant (which, indeed, to some degree he was), he realized that the only representation that could possibly be meaningful would be that of worker and therefore (it was on a Friday) he carried a letter to the Impasse Ronsin and slipped it under Brancusi's door. The letter stated that its author was an artisan who worked in wood and stone (preferring wood, but carving with equal competence in stone), that he had a particular interest in the recipient's methods of carving and an unequal, but genuine, attraction to the peasant styles of wood-carving still employed in the region in which the war memorial (of which he had read in *L'Aurore*) was to be erected. He asked, therefore, to be accepted as a worker. He did not expect any payment; it would be sufficient reward, etc., etc.

The letter was not fulsome; it was, however, round, and although he had no reason to expect an answer, he hoped that Brancusi would reply. Ten days passed. Stefan Mauger had determined by then to forget his aggressive overture, rationalizing that Brancusi had no need to bring an entourage to Tirgu-Jiu and certainly not a young sculptor whose credentials were at best dubious and untested. For nearly a day, therefore, he ignored the blue-enveloped *pneumatique* that the cleaning woman had placed upon his desk, supposing it was only an urgent invitation to some unnecessary dinner party. Not until late in the day, when he broke off work and brewed a pot of tea, did he bother with the letter. It invited Stefan Mauger to visit Brancusi at four o'clock the following afternoon. It concluded, "You know the address," and was signed.

Stefan Mauger arrived at the Impasse Ronsin at precisely four o'clock. He approached the wooden doors thinking to knock softly, but was forestalled by a note addressed simply to "Mauger" and run through a rusted nail. It advised him that Brancusi was away, but would be back shortly and requested that he enter the studio and await his return. Stefan Mauger put the note into his trouser pocket and entered the atelier. It was not as he had imagined it from the many photographs he had seen, for none of those carried with them the force that fell upon him, unexpectedly alone in the studio of an artist whose presence he had only conjured. The photographs revised the reality, selecting from the dominated disorder this or that sculpture which Brancusi had learned to photograph in order to effect a simulacrum of objectivity; however, each time, having chosen one or another work to distance with the stern glass eye, the shutter closed and seized more than its intended *Torso* or *Bird in Flight*, leaving over in the shadows undulant woods and carved stones whose identity one could only guess in outline and relief. Stefan Mauger had correctly guessed that the studio was a workshop in which nothing was called art, but all was described as having life, whether grown up and matured by sun and rain, or else animated by the cut of a metal implement. Encountering all this with the ordinariness of eyesight, with the ordinary level of the eye (which however high it pitches its focus retracts every majesty to its own level), Stefan was stunned, able neither to move into the studio and take a seat to await Brancusi's return as he had been asked to do nor to flee as he felt prompted. Instead, for those minutes he waited, his back to the entrance doors, a hand to his mouth, transfixed and immobilized, peering through the muddied light of a gray day into the expanse of the atelier.

It was not only the presence of all the sculptures he admired, a profusion of sculptures and a profusion of versions of sculptures, that overwhelmed him, but even more the wall of tools, the wine press, the baker's oven, the carved chair, the ascetic bed upon wooden planks up the narrow flight of stairs, the chaste kitchen from which the famous feasts had been produced, and everywhere work commenced, progressed, interrupted, unfinished, taken up again, and marble and limestone bases and natural and hewn wood bases, and before him in the area where they might sit a vast stone wheel, like an immense tambourine, on which stood *Yellow Bird* and a glass jug filled with white flowers. He rubbed his stunned eyes and suddenly the sun broke from behind the clouds over Paris and flooded the studio: metal dazzled, marble hummed with warmth, ancient woods and polished cedar shone like bodies running with oil, and all the creatures of the atelier began to move, as if all that was needed for their awakening was a sunburst. Released by the sun, Stefan began to move slowly through the studio, touching and feeling surfaces, rubbing and smoothing, picking up tools and feeling their weight, gripping the handle of the peasant's saw no different from the one he had used at Les Herbiers; and by the time he noticed Brancusi who stood behind him near the door, watching him intensely, not having removed his soft sun hat of calico, he had completed the passage from the work to the hand of the worker. When he came forward to take Brancusi's outstretched hand they both smiled, for each of their palms was browned with the same dirt and a delicious odor of wood oil rose to their nostrils.

It was in the month of June that Stefan Mauger, traveling by train, came to the city of Tirgu, situated on the river Jiu, in the southern reaches of Rumania, bounded by the Carpathian Mountains through which the Roman army had been forced to travel in its pacification of the frontier tribesmen of the eastern Empire, leaving behind them the fragments of speech that in the mysterious ways of language would compel Rumania into the similitudes of the Mediterranean. There, once arrived, Stefan traveled the region, visiting the farmhouses, granges, and wooden churches of the region, examining closely and remembering beams intricately carved with rosettes and doors paneled with abstract reliefs, their sides thrusting carved diamonds of weathered cedar forward into the light and graveyard crosses irregularly carved, protected from the fierce weather by little houses of their own.

All this peasant architecture embraced small hamlets, within villages, within districts among which were the hamlet of Hobitza, in the village of Pestisani, in the district of Groj, not far from Tirgu upon the Jiu, where Constantin Brancusi had been born in the first year of the concluding quarter of the previous century, one child among seven children of poor peasants, from whose care he fled when still a boy, becoming by stages a sculptor whose first work was considered by the academy so perfect an anatomical replication that it was used in lessons at the local medical school, where frustrated by his failure to secure a scholarship to continue study in Italy, he abandoned the land of his birth and walked to Paris; arriving there a year later, he began again to work from models, achieving modest success, but soon lost his way once more, regaining it after a long illness, persuaded (like the artists of Africa whose work he had learned to admire) to carve directly and carving directly, with ever more careful attention to the reality out of which one carves, the matter under knife and the urgencies of self-consciousness, he arrived at this point in his sixty-third year, come home to Tirgu-Jiu, to elaborate a complex of sculptures that would commemorate the living and the dead of all those, compatriot and enemy, who had fallen in the Great War.

It had been arranged that Brancusi would meet with his workers about the middle of the month to traverse the existing park, which extended from the banks of the Jiu, and to discuss with them the scheme of the project, to describe his sense of its ensemble, and to establish with each of them their responsibility for overseeing the carving and fabrication of its principal elements. It was the first, and as it proved, the last such project to be undertaken by Brancusi.

Other of his works had found their way under the sky, but they had been conceived and executed indoors, carved in the atelier on the Rue Montparnasse or in the first studio at the Impasse Ronsin. Not until that moment, however, had Brancusi's work been acknowledged by a nation, his own country, indeed by an organization of women whose care for the dead of their commune of Groj undoubtedly outweighed their admiration for Brancusi, but who nonetheless, urged by higher auspices, had seen fit to commission one of their own sons to consummate the memorial.

It was densely humid the day of their walk through the park, the cedar, oak, even the cypress bowed under the heat, moving listlessly, and the park, empty of strollers who would find no comfort beneath their boughs, left the landscape without human movement other than the foreman of a shop of stone carvers who had cut headstones in the district for more than a half century and an engineer whose task became quite specific as the tour progressed, and a handful of craftsmen in stone and metal who worked for the stone carver and the foundry; these, and Stefan Mauger whose function was obscure, walked beside Brancusi as he strode up from the river.

It is a whole. It is a whole. No part may be seen outside the whole. Truly whole. It is seamless, each part moving to another, communicating and transmitting life from each to each, speaking of parts and wholes, as he spoke softly in his own tongue, addressing himself at the beginning to the chief of stonecutters whom he preferred to any professional sculptor for the cutting of those cylinders, which became what is now called *The Table of Silence* and its twelve stools, each fashioned of a stone ball of modest circumference cut in half and superimposed one upon the other and placed equidistantly around it, distant enough from each other as to be solitary, distinct from the table so that it could serve no purpose to the seated but to think upon its circularity and its voided function, and yet an imagery which in its simplicity of form and abstractness of relation, its numerical suggestiveness and its mythic adumbration supplied every visitor, the summer traveler or the winter mourner of recollection, a construction that removed both —traveler and mourner—from any other sensation but one of having stopped in the preparatory antechamber to the precincts where any and every rite of attention and fidelity was appropriate.

It was exceptionally hot. The heat bore down upon them as though the sun at the center of its cavernous vault had no other purpose that day than to illuminate their conference. It meant nothing to Brancusi. His head covered by his sun hat, his short body confined by his buttoned work suit, he continued to walk, stopping only to examine each tree and remark upon its health or its need for attention, turning back at last to observe the distance they had come from the siting of the *Table of Silence*, and, returning to the group of workers, he spoke with soft precision of what was to become the *Gate of the Kiss*, grown from the simple *Kiss* of the Montparnasse Cemetery until it, too, received the expansion to monumentality that brings with it repetition and simplification, the reduction of gender to indifference, the concreteness of form become symbolic only if one fails to realize the absolute singularity and immediacy of any abstraction become circle in stone, become line in stone, rectangle in stone, all placed above and beside each other to suggest what is not given and what needs no words to be explained, and at the last permits those who celebrate and those who mourn to pass beneath, to move around, to stand and gaze at the binding of earth and sky, transitory kiss in slowly weathering travertine, life and its unfrightened passage into death. He made no mention of these, but only of

142

the conception that entailed placement of plaques of stone in the travertine of Banpotoc around a cement foundation supported by an iron armature which would serve as the superior relief resting upon four blocks of identical stone carved with the glyph of the kiss, emplaced upon a pylon of faced concrete, the whole situated upon a slightly raised platform that described not an elevation to which one would be obliged to ascend (for this was no sacred grove), but a station of the way through which one passes.

Passes, as they continued down the pathway lined now with trees, passing down the center where the sun burned through still trees, until they came to the Church of the Apostles Peter and Paul which Brancusi circled until he regained the path once more, trusting, as he had been promised, that it would be moved so that the eye might wander unimpeded through the *Gate of the Kiss* into the expanse above, enlarging, growing until it ascended to the *Endless Column*, to be placed—there—upon a slight rise, sixteen rhomboids of brass-sheathed steel, reaching to a height that would impress the sky and needing no base until, as Brancusi repeated himself, "it is put forever in a special place, supporting a special thing," as it will be now, he added slowly, showing with a gesture the grassy knoll into which the column would be set. The *Endless Column* planted there, supporting sky and earth, would hold up a universe.

Stefan Mauger worked alongside the carvers of the stone for many weeks chipping carefully, polishing with an intensity as though each curve and cut now mattered to the earth and to the sky. When his task was done, he was paid by the stonecutter not more than any other worker and when he said good-bye, Brancusi smiled and wished him in Rumanian something that he later learned was "God protect your way."

4

Exhausted Days

The Mauger hacienda, abandoned for more than a generation, had almost returned to the jungle when it was acquired by Alicia Mauger. Once the plantation of a wealthy merchant family in Merida, who maintained their residence in that steaming city to insure the education of their children among the families of the *gobernadores* but made their wealth from sisal and chicle holdings in the jungle, the hacienda had been crudely formed of adobe walls nearly two feet in thickness and floors of unevenly cut mahogany planks, room upon room, each with a raised fireplace, all looking out to a central courtyard where the horses had been tethered and watered from an ornate well that echoed voices from a depth of more than ninety feet. Cut from the jungle over a period of seventy years, the hacienda had grown from an agglomeration of huts dominated by a single dwelling built upon a rise where the overseers of the Campos family of Merida were installed. Alejandro Campos had received a vast land grant in the vicinity of

Campeche from President Benito Juarez in 1867 in return for the support that he had (quite unexpectedly for a family of Merida) given to the revolutionary cause. Not only had Señor Campos denied Emperor Maximilian his welcome, refusing to join the other merchants of Merida in the subscription to welcome the Emperor and his entourage when they visited the capital of the Yucatan, but later when he had undertaken to supply the besieged General Díaz, then making his stand against the Expeditionary Army of Napoleon III at Oaxaca, with shipments of maize and hemp shoes for his soldiers, he earned the debt of the revolution, which was richly repaid. It took the family of Campos more than a decade to make their holdings secure and profitable, to subdue the Indians and indenture them to service, but by the eighties of the last century it was accomplished, and Alejandro Campos, then a man in his early fifties with short-cropped gray hair and uncommonly blue eyes, disposed of his import-export business in Merida and removed himself and his family to the plantation in the jungle, clearing the huts, relocating the miserable hovels of his Indian workers to a campsite deeper in the scrub jungle, and by enlarging the simple adobe dwelling where formerly his overseers had lived, had fashioned the remarkable hacienda in which the Maugers were now installed. The hacienda was remarkable, not because of size or the salubrious proportion of its rooms, for the Campos had neither the inclination nor the necessity to entertain. It was not then the number of its rooms or their commodiousness that one would find impressive but rather the sense, quickly acquired, of a house inspired by an obscure principle not usually associated with the arts of building since neither comfort nor clarity of design was its motive, but fear. The central room, the original overseer's dwelling, became the large living room whose high ceiling was turreted with openings now covered with glass, which had once allowed watchmen positioned on a catwalk to police with guns at the ready the open land that surrounded the headquarters of the Campos plantation. Since this dwelling place was built upon a rise, the hacienda that grew up about it was lower by nearly two feet and it was necessary to step down from the living room into the kitchen, dining room, sitting rooms, library, and bedrooms that formed what became, after the arrival of the family of Campos, the hacienda of the Señores. But not only this was indicative of the atmosphere of fear which suffused the hacienda's construction, for within each bedroom there was a smaller room, pierced to be sure by openings and doorways in which the beds were situated, forming so to speak a maze, walls within walls, light coming from the piercings of the roof, windows situated not within bedrooms but in the alcoves and corridors that linked each box of space to the next, as though the original owners sought to protect themselves doubly from scrutiny and malevolent intrusion. The hacienda was formed like a unit of children's blocks, thickness protecting thickness, warm bodies and weary souls dwelling within, far removed by cool adobe from sun, from scorpion and tarantula, from the avenging families of Indian workers who died of disease and starvation during the rains.

The Campos were evicted from their lands during the later revolutions of the twenties, the old man dying in Cuba, his children dispersed, his wealth and booty dissipated. The hacienda was empty, as we have said, for a generation, cactus growing up beneath floors, breaching the adobe, windows battered, courtyard tiling cracked; the Maugers happened upon it when they came down to Mexico from the north, and Alicia, cabling her father, paid the money and acquired the property.

Understandable, given the principle of fear that governed

the construction of the hacienda, that salubrity would give way before security. Each of the bedrooms, hewn within a room, was unbearable during the heat; at night the breeze would need its own intelligence and sight to keep from buffeting helplessly against the adobe walls that surrounded the bed itself. What cool the winters brought made these nooks dank in summer and only by the deliberate refusal to close doors and windows—in a word, to ignore security— could the bedrooms open and invite the night air.

The door to Maria's room was open. She never closed it except at night. Night, she claimed, was everywhere and her doors were closed only at night. "To make night smaller," she would say in her curious speech, a Spanish obedient not to the rules of grammar but to the requirements of feelings that worked her lips long before sound began to hollow out the regimen of words.

"To make night smaller," she had said to him the first night at the hacienda, when she shut the door after he had come to her room in the early morning. At that hour—it was past three—the invading darkness of the jungle still occupied every corner of the house. Her combat with the darkness lay not in modesty, for she also abhorred drawing the curtains. (In Mexico City Stefan had brought her to his room at the Maria Cristina, which looked out over a patio, an old room with brilliant fabric and heavy colonial furniture, and she went to the window, looking down upon the few late drinkers talking quietly below, and removed her long cotton dress, her breasts bristling in the night cool. "Close the blinds and come to bed." At first she ignored him, but she closed them after he extinguished the bedside lamp. She felt the night like a blanket covering her face, a stifling that frightened her. He had observed to her smiling: "Not the darkness, dearest. You never push your hair back. With all that black hair falling over your eyes you always think it's night." She laughed and admitted it was the truth.) It was not strange, then, to find her door open in the morning and Maria standing at the window watching the animals in the pen being fed. She was naked, but then, to be precise, Maria was rarely clothed. It wasn't a matter of provocation. It was simply her abhorrence of the night wrapping her in impenetrable fabric that had no density or weight and the day requiring, in the orders of modesty, a swath of cloth to serve the body as did the night. It was against the daytime eye that Maria struggled.

Within her room, tucked as it was at the back of the house, a half-step up from the level of the hallway, as though long ago it had been determined to pitch under the wooden eaves of the hacienda a room where someone would be lodged, someone particular, to whom access would be by rising and ascent. But it was day and Maria stood at the window, examining her breasts in the late morning sunlight. Stefan had come down the passageway calling "Maria, Maria, Maria" in a voice so low she could not have heard it. He was speaking her name to himself, in rhythm to his walk. He stepped into her room, lowering his head, which grazed the door jamb.

Maria turned away from the window and looked up, indifferently passing her attention from her body to his face.

"Maria, Maria," he continued, coming to embrace her.

"I never see you. You keep to yourself these days." She wasn't angry. It was a statement of fact.

Stefan said nothing in reply. He had learned over the months that when Maria spoke this way she meant nothing severe, however much her language was heavy with assumptions of delight or irritation. He had to remind himself that when Maria spoke she was simply vibrating to promptings that moved in a region of her mind to which no one had gained access, not even, he supposed, Maria.

He continued to repeat her name—a single word of familiar comfort entailing by its use an order of possession he employed (as earlier he had learned to use his tribal masks and totems) to specify and master an uncertainty about the space he occupied in the world. The masks and totems, gathered in his journeys, enjoyed position and honor in his life less because of beauty than because they contended with his own phantoms and demons. And, indeed, this was the task for which their carvers had intended them. The Kwakiutl crane—vast jaws incised with undulant stripes, immense eyes flat against the cranium retained the memory of the carver's hand, cantilevered above the studio fireplace—watched him and the Senufo rhythm pounder, slammed against the dry earth to mark the fall of dancers' feet, all legs, spindly wooden legs, mere posts with only knobbled indication of knees, entering the attenuated rib cage where on one side shriveled breasts reminded of woman, and on the other, flat concavity of man, surmounted by a head of majestic simplicity, drawn down to pointed chin of beard; skull to one was also high-boned woman's face, the chin of beard yielding to delicacy of coiffure. The vision and the regard joined in these things: crane disappeared into an unseen world and rhythm pounder, hermaphrodite, sustained the ideality of the race, reaching back beyond division to a unity where differentiation was hardly symbolized. Standing erect, hands covering her breasts against some wind from the fields, Maria was not simply beautiful; no hand, however agile and informed, could succeed in setting down with a single stroke the lineaments that delighted. What confounded Stefan was that the sharp and clear Maria, a name marking out a space in the universe occupied by her, her alone (the Maria who was lodged deep within him), had become the name of a conjuration before him, right there, her bare feet, like the rhythm pounder, rubbing against the wooden floor, a toe, a single toe blushing with vermilion caught his eye.

"You've painted only one toe?"

"You like it?"

"I don't know. I'm not used to a single toe painted red."

"But *you* artists do that all the time. Yes? You showed me in the books. An eye painted like a diamond. A hip like raw steak. You artists do that kind of thing. So I do one toe."

She carved herself like I carve wood. Why not? But I may have missed the point. Maria moved her feet apart and turned slowly, once and again, swiveling on a base. He had no need to move about her, stationary, observing the immobility of sculpture, the eye animating, implying movement in the dead thing by moving. She moved, turning about, circling herself, while he watched. She knew he was delighted by this. It was among their games, her left leg sweeping a small circle while the vermilion toe of the right held her weight and served as fulcrum upon which the mass of her moved. As she turned, an arm rose to hide her eyes and then ever so slowly the arm descended and, hand asplay, she guarded her pudendum. She mocked him, making herself a moving sculpture, modeling for the sculptor, turning on her base, shifting her postures, a small smile widening as her game progressed until she collapsed laughing upon the wooden floor and he joined her there and they embraced, laughter subsiding into small grunts of pleasure.

All instinct before speech, Maria attended to Stefan like a mythic playmate, a child before adolescence, playing, playing games of fantasied desire and service, unable to say what it was that drove her to such exercise. Stefan supposed that in her family shaping words had been useless to describe a need or an affection. Among the dozen of her brothers and sisters eating from the same bowl, pushing corn mash into each other's mouths, they learned that speech could not address hunger. If there was no food, there was little need beyond the scream of eyes to announce it, for speaking the name of hunger or the exalted sophistication of appetite brought not another drop of milk from their mother's breast nor another kernel of corn from the grinder's stone. Long ago she had learned that speech was nothing. If the hands could not seize it, it was not there and all speaking—summoning out of darkness what could not be seen or touched—was unavailing. Her father, a man not more than thirty-eight at the time, had been paralyzed when a falling tree had broken his back while he was clearing a field behind their mountain shack, and he had also given up speech, nourishing his daily portion of pain as he and the other children had contained theirs. But not all pain. There had been a brother, Tino, whom Maria had especially loved. *"¡Qué diablo!"* Maria would describe him, smiling, whenever she reminisced about Tino. Tino had been her baby brother. All of the children had their own, their own baby brother or sister, the next beneath them, or skipping one, the next, and some competed for the same, and one or another neglected by the misfortunes of placement were stunted out of life, dying and being replaced by yet another. Their mother bore them, sometimes assisted by a wet nurse, sometimes replaced entirely by a concubine, by whom three children were born. She, Fidelita (they all called her), continued bearing and working until their father's accident. Then, as if relieved by a mighty sigh, she gave up giving birth and simply worked, up long before dawn to make tortillas and a hot brew to warm her children against the day. The boys went down the mountainside to work on the latifundia or in the towns, some of them not returning for several days on end; the girls cut wood, mashed corn, tended their own half-acre of garden, fed meager livestock, or rode about on the lone donkey—he was called Chulo—trying to look busy, one eye watching to see their mother's frown. Maria was the next to last and Tino was the real and rightful last, the baby of the family, the final gift—*el último regalo*, Fidelita called him affectionately, her expression mixed with an irony and a contempt that presumably only the special saint of the village, San Isidro, would understand.

"*¡Tino. Tino. Qué diablo!*" Maria burst out laughing when she described him to Stefan. "What eyes," she said with admiration. "Enormous, I never see such eyes. Everyone who look at Tino had to laugh. Those eyes of Tino's are more than beautiful. Brown, with enormous black dots and lashes long like feet of centipedes. They were so alive. By the time Tino was ten, the last of the babies, the rest of them—not me, not me, *¿comprende?* (I am still different than they), were all but dead. My sisters! You couldn't imagine they were my sisters. My God, their breasts were wasted like udders, shriveled up and worn out. They were all exhausted. It isn't poverty that's bad. It's how it uses us up. But Tino? He refused to be used up. I saw it in his eyes. He saw more of the road than all the rest of us, saw what was going on to the right and to the left, up in the skies birds and along the road scuttling lizards. All the rest of us, carrying water, wood, corn, always carrying like animals, what chance did we have to look up or watch the life underfoot? But Tino was carried everywhere—the youngest, hidden in Fidelita's poncho, peering out all eyes—he had the chance to see. As soon as Tino could walk he would go off. I mean young, young, Stefan. When he was four years old he stayed out a whole night. He was holding on to Mama's skirt when they came down from the fields, cutting sugar for one of the bosses, and the next minute he was gone.

'Christo, baby Jesús,' Mama wailed through the night, but the next morning there he was sound asleep in his hammock near the fire. 'I wandered off,' he said simply, proudly I guess. And what could she do? She slapped him about but Tino stood his ground and even though he cried, it was a kind of silent crying. His eyes filled with tears, rising like a flood that never cleared its banks, his lashes fishermen's nets holding the catch of tears from spilling out. It was marvelous to watch Tino. By the time Tino was ten he would go off for a day or two but always come home for eat or sleep and he never looked hungry. He stole birds' eggs, he tell me, and pick off the right leaves when he want to chew on something and even find water in the desert, knowing—strange, no?—which plants hold water and which dry as bone. We call him *brujo*, magic witch, you know, but I still say, *diablo*, when I think of Tino. In the past? You say, I speak most in the past. Yes. Tino's dead, like my mother and father, and eight of the twelve of us, dead and gone, swallowed up. Winter fever. That's all. Winter fever. He came down with it the day after he loved me the first time. (That was the best love of my life. He knew what it mean to love me. My lip's bleeding? It always bleeds when I think about Tino loving me.) When he died—he was seventeen ten years ago now—that was the end of us. Within two years, my parents die and seven others. Various things. Accidents, fevers, exhaustion, mostly exhaustion. I think Tino held the key to it. If I could understand what Tino knew about this world I could understand why he had the key. Isn't it strange? They all die within three years and at the end most of them mentioned Tino. Those that had a chance to collect themselves before moving over, they all said something about Tino: 'Will I be with Tino?' 'Tino will meet me, won't he?' 'Tino's waiting to show me the great paradise.' "

When Maria finished she was not in tears. The contrary.

She smiled with a deep and contented pleasure. And it was not the last time she spoke of Tino. It had become her habit to mention Tino oddly in the conversation that passed between her and Stefan in the hour or so after their passion had expired. Once she went to wash out her mouth and came from the bathroom and remarked that Tino always drank water after eating chiles. He used to say, "It's not the hotness, but the bitterness that upsets me." Stefan didn't question the association. The curiosity was the mention of Tino as though what Tino did excused her imitating him. "We had artichokes last night," Stefan said, explaining, but it was lost, a bit of knowledge he had garnered elsewhere. "It's still bitter. I feel better now," she replied, returning to him and burying her head in the crook of his arm.

"Do I remind you of Tino?" Stefan asked indifferently. He didn't care if he did, but it would have secured him if the answer had been unambiguous.

"No. Only your eyes. But yours not big like Tino. You have wise, sad eyes, but careful and small." Before he could question further, she was asleep.

The following morning Stefan had telephoned Alicia, who had remained behind. She was expecting a truck from Campeche to move a sculpture which had already been crated. Stefan had sold the work from a photograph to a collector in Chicago. He had exhibited there two years earlier—a group of smaller versions for larger pieces that he had been anxious to cast. It was his practice to make two versions of every substantial work, one in bronze, the other, more difficult, in wood or marble. He was very happy when the collector commissioned a casting in bronze; unfortunately the price was not immense, a few thousand dollars was all, but it pleased him that the work was ordered. The difficulty with all his commissions was that he often ended up losing money. Alicia knew this. She calculated the loss.

She knew it was a losing venture, but there was no way to avoid it. Ridiculous, a poet married to a sculptor, living like retired rich in a Mexican hacienda they could hardly afford. Ridiculous. "If you can't get at least twenty dollars an hour, we'll have to steal." She had laughed when she said this long ago, winking at Stefan, her short blond hair shaking about her head, as if it joined in the subversionary wink.

Inspector Mariposa preferred the provinces to the capital city. The provinces sheltered the past, whereas the capital, impatient with the obstructions it presented to the vast land movers, plows, and cranes of progress, regarded it as something to be pulverized. Or if not pulverized, then tagged and hedged with the elevating analogies of higher civilizations and in consequence suppressed (he recalled in this connection as the plane hesitated over the Pyramid of the Sun before it turned south for the short run to Campeche that the first time he had visited the tombs at Mitla after they had been opened to the public, an Indian guide—an Indian, mind you—had first warned the assembled knot of tourists, most of them in flowered shirts and print skirts from north of the border, that what they were about to see was the execution chamber of the royalty of the south, but that even then, despite the fact that in those ancient days the dark interior walls were bedaubed with human blood, let it be noted that on various capstones—which he would indicate as they passed through—there could be seen the Cross of Christ, suggesting that even then, dim in the unconscious of his ancestors the prophecy of the great savior was already anticipated; Mariposa had snorted with contempt to the embarrassment of the guide and the annoyance of the visitors and now as the plane paused, he imagined, to absorb the vistas of the great capital framed in the little window of the aircraft behind the splendid monument of Tenochtitlán, he snorted again, recollecting his disgust). "The Cross of Christ indeed." He knew perfectly well that it could not be otherwise. Revolutions were made only by breaking eggs, he recalled, forgetting as he often did the structure of the symmetrical analogy, but drawing the conclusion correctly. "Break up the past. Break up the past," he muttered as he turned over on his lap photographs of Jaina figurines that had previously been delivered to the capital before the theft of the island. *"¡Qué maravilloso!* One miracle after another," he said fanning the photographs so that they fluttered in his hand like the stills of an early movie, one after another, views and angles of the same work succeeding to another, until the whole fistful of images had been reviewed. "I marvel at them, marvel at them," Mariposa began, addressing the earth below, rushing by beneath the low-lying clouds, desiccated earth, the mountain passes through which the insurgent troop of Cortés had marched from Veracruz, occasionally interrupted by a patch of planted soil on which he could see the smallest dots of color—a bent back protected by a poncho dyed with the symbolic frets and serpents that memory preserved as the earth guarded shrines whose significance had long ago been lost. "Mariposa guards the Mexico nobody remembers. All alone. I do it all alone. One day they will want to recall what nobody cares about any longer and they will thank Mariposa for vigilance."

The plane banked toward the small airfield outside Campeche and settled down, taxiing to the tin-covered arrivals hut to discharge the mail, produce, several wooden crates, an old woman, and Inspector Mariposa.

An automobile, dispatched by Captain Santiago Gutiérrez, was awaiting him near the runway. A young policeman, only six months on the force, held the door open for him, saluted smartly, and motioned Inspector Mariposa to the back seat. It was not, however, Mariposa's way. He acknowledged the salute with a nod, came around the other side and joined the driver in front. After a few minutes Inspector Mariposa began, hoping to secure not information but a sense of the situation. "A remarkable theft, don't you think?"

The policeman shrugged, knitting his black eyebrows with evident perplexity. "I don't think so. Why get excited over a mess of clay statues? They can't be worth all that much."

"It's not the money, you know. Not the money at all." Inspector Mariposa had been through this countless times. No one really understood such a crime. "Let me ask you something. If a thief stole the altar cross from the cathedral in Campeche, what would you think?"

The policeman thought a moment and replied, "Terrible. It would be a terrible thing to steal a cross. There could be no Mass until it came back. Everything would be undone, you know? We need the cross to pray."

"Precisely. You need the cross to pray because you are a Christian. Once upon a time, my friend, you and I were not Christian. We were worshipers of the sun and the moon, and the god of good harvest, and rain, and all of those gods had their own statues, which not only stood for them—like the cross stands for the Savior—but were really the gods—more like the wine is the blood and the wafer the flesh of Christ. You understand? It's just as terrible to steal those statues as it is to steal the cross, perhaps even more terrible because it means stealing something that you and I were long before we were actually born, stealing our past and smuggling it out to sell to *gringos* to put in their living rooms or in their gardens."

"It's terrible to steal a cross, much more terrible." The policeman insisted. It didn't matter finally. Inspector Mariposa drew in his line determined to fish nearer land. "Any leads in the case?"

"I don't know, Señor Inspector. Captain Gutiérrez doesn't tell me such things. Usually I work traffic in the downtown."

"And the Federales, have they been in touch?"

"I don't know, Señor Inspector. We don't really like the Federales in the police, you know. They're a pain in the ass. Most of us started out in the army, you know, and then when we got out joined up in the police. That's the way I came. But there have been so many calls from Mexico City. They seem to think up there that this theft is important."

"I know you don't, my friend. Well, enough for the moment. Thank you." Inspector Mariposa had grown tired of this ordinary boy. The car was already nearing the city and Inspector Mariposa fell silent. He had an immense amount to accomplish in a few days.

Clearly they had arrived at the police station. The automobile glided into a vacant space before the building that fronted the coast road, and the large double doors, held open by two helmeted guardsmen, admitted Inspector Mariposa whose hand was quickly seized by Captain Gutiérrez who drew him up a short flight of whitewashed stairs into his office. Mariposa seated himself, lifting his briefcase to his lap and pretending to busy himself with its contents. The Captain was arranging for coffee to be sent in, speaking on the telephone, issuing trivial commands, obviously unsettled by his visitor. Inspector Mariposa was struck less by the Captain's nervousness, which as an officer of the Special Branch from the capital he took for granted, than by the fact that no one else was present, no introductions had been made, no subordinates engaged on the case summoned, no representative of the Federales waiting. He found that curious procedure.

The coffee arrived and after a minute of sipping and cigarette lighting, Captain Gutiérrez settled into his desk chair and awaited Inspector Mariposa's first inquiry.

"Have we a written report of the inquiry so far?"

"I'm afraid not, Inspector. We're very short on writing in Campeche. Most of the girls out there do clean-up work. We get reports done only when the men come off duty and volunteer an hour or two to write up their duty sheets. We are, you understand, Inspector, in the provinces." Captain Gutiérrez smiled.

"Well, if no written report, may I have an oral one. Then I would like a quick tour of the Isla Jaina and afterward a meeting with the young girl who was found on the island, and later Professor Hermoso, who ran the excavation."

"You're all the same, you officials from the capital," the Captain commented sourly.

"And you, my friend, are no different from all the provincials. So let's be done with that kind of observation. It gets us no place. I am not here to check up on your efficiency. I'm here to catch a remarkably intelligent thief. So let's begin to catch him."

"It would appear to be more than one, Inspector. We assume that a landing vessel came to the island some time during the early morning—leaving the mainland under cover of darkness. How many thieves were involved we do not know, but it would have had to be at least three and possibly as many as ten. We found many footprints, but nothing remarkable about them. They found the store shack of the expedition locked, but unprotected. They broke the lock and as a precaution cut the telephone lines from the island to the mainland, carried the *ídolos* to their boat, and left. The boat—a police vessel, remarkably—was found fifty kilometers up the way late yesterday afternoon.

It was then that we guessed the connection between the theft of the police ship during the previous night and the clearing of the island. You see, under the gunwales of the boat there were some packing cases and at least one broken piece of ceramic, a piece of something—I don't know what. Would you like to see it?"

Inspector Mariposa nodded and the Captain removed a fragment of ceramic from an empty cigarette packet that he kept in the pocket of his blouse. He handed it across to the Inspector, who emptied the contents carefully onto the desk. The fragment, about two inches in length and not more than an inch in width, appeared to be a piece from a ceremonial headdress, a lozenge of beige ceramic, one of whose sides appeared to be pigmented mustard yellow. "A ceremonial headdress perhaps, but then perhaps a ritual baton or a weapon of some kind. Very beautiful, no? It either rose from behind the head of a woman, a young woman, a princess perhaps, or else was carried in the hand of a warrior, a standard of office. We will know when we recover the treasure."

"You seem confident of that, Inspector. I am not, I'm afraid. I think the *ídolos* are already in the States."

"How can you be certain, Captain? Yes, I know, the boat fifty kilometers up the coast. You imagine the loaded vessel left the island and made contact with a ship at sea, which removed the material and made for a Gulf port in the United States. Very likely, but I think some of the treasure, perhaps even much of it, will reappear here in Mexico, perhaps even in Campeche. It is certainly easier to sell Mexican treasure to Mexican collectors than to North Americans and much easier to bring Mexican objects across the border into Mexico than to smuggle them out. Well, we shall soon see. Catch the criminals and we catch the treasure, so to speak. It will be easier to recover the treasure

160

from the United States if we can prove to Washington that it is stolen. *That* we can do! You see, the treasure is the largest group of Jaina figures ever to reach the market at one time. If we find the thief and locate the whereabouts of the treasure in the U.S., we can certainly prove it was stolen and transported illegally. . . ."

Inspector Mariposa temporized aloud, projecting one speculation after another, counting the uncounted treasure, examining in his imagination one after another of the pieces, selecting those he would retain as his percentage, dismissing out of hand the possibility that he was working hopelessly, that the treasure had fled, the thief unknown, his accomplices unidentifiable. Those considerations were not even entertained.

Hombre de obsesión. He was most certainly an obsessed man, but curiously uncertain at this juncture of his life in what the obsession consisted—in his avarice to augment his collection, to add yet another suite of objects to those that already constituted his motley. Tagged, numbered, dated, and identified by the name of the thief with whose capture each acquisition was associated—Mariposa's collection was a kind of museum of rogues, each object connected by a strand of recollection to the thief, the dealer, the runner from whose hoard it had been plucked. The unity of the Mariposa collection was no longer simply an inventory of the past—although it was to the honor of the past that he dedicated his rhetoric—but crime and the capture of the criminal.

"I suspect you may be right, Gutiérrez. The treasure is gone north. All that we have is the prospect of the criminal and he, I should imagine, will prove interesting if we can come close to him."

Captain Gutiérrez had listened to Mariposa with half-hearted circumspection, sipping his coffee through cupped

161

hands, while the Inspector wandered and returned, projecting alternatives and fantasies that seemed to Gutiérrez happily remote.

"What shall we need to begin our work? I should think an interview with the Indian woman on the island. Bring her in for a conversation. She will tell us nothing, but she might remember what one or another of the soldiers looked like. There must have been someone in charge, an officer for the detachment. Professor Hermoso, he's another. He's not really important since it was obviously a surprise to our thieves that he and his workmen were off the island, but then who knows? And I have a personal interest in meeting him. It may lead somewhere. And the boat. It came from your own docks, Captain. It was one of your boats. How many police vessels do you have?" (The Captain held up three fingers, but Mariposa ignored the answer and moved on. He was not interested in replies, only the inventory of questions.) "Where are they berthed when not in use? Where are the keys kept and who had access to them? Someone from the police department would have to be involved, even if the keys were stolen, but not really. Negligence, stupidity, the common defects of bureaucracy. No matter. And then the ultimate question. The lover of Jaina. Who is he? Who collects the arts of Mexico in Campeche, although that, too, is a dubious assumption. He may not be from Campeche at all. He could be from anywhere, but we begin in Campeche. Are there any shops that sell antiquities in Campeche, any tourist shops where they have bits and pieces for sale along with ponchos and serapes? Get me the list, all right? And so we begin, my friend, we begin. Such investigations are painstaking, boring, little bits and pieces, end to end, until, within the maze, a trail is plotted."

"We'll have to steal." She repeated the phrase again, smiling into the telephone, but after countless repetitions over the years it had become the code of her own anxiety.

Five years earlier Stefan Mauger had begun his distinctive enterprise of theft, although at the time he had hardly regarded his activities as illegal or his diligent research into the antiquities of ancient Mexico, his hours of gazing in the Museo Arqueológico and reading in the National Library, his exchanges of letters with Caso, Bernal, Westheim about the complex aesthetics of Mayan art as preparation for his thoughtful and judicious accumulation of an inventory of bought and stolen artifacts. In those days—it was at the end of 1951 that Stefan and Alicia arrived in Mexico City, having passed more than a year driving slowly from Vancouver (where they had recovered for a month after their encounter with the Kwakiutl) down through Portland to San Francisco, with an extended stay in Los Angeles where Stefan exhibited and met exiles from Europe with whom he spoke German and French—Mexican law respecting traffic in its ancient art was still flexible. It was quite permissible then to collect the historical patrimony; indeed, it was hardly noticed and certainly unexceptionable in the homes of the great Mexican artists, all revolutionaries and none of them thieves. It was not yet asked—in any considerable detail—how one came by such imposing sculptures, competing as they often did for refinement and mass with the objects coveted by the nation's museums. The museums were poor, archaeology was poor, and there could be no complaint if private collections were founded whose contents would one day spill over into the ample skirts of public institutions. The private collector, it was temporized officially, was doing the work the government was too poor to pursue. It was in those days—not too long before the events of this telling—that the sites of unexcavated tombs and monuments were documented, that the Indians, like ants in a file to a droplet of honey, began their trek to the collectors of the city, bringing each week at appointed hours their backyard findings, selling them for small pesos and smashing with disgust the contemptible little objects no one wanted to buy (including undoubtedly objects from subcultures not yet known and identified and hence regarded as deformed hybrids or worse, as ugly fakes, which had as well begun to make their appearance).

The trade in the arts of old Mexico was growing but undisciplined; it was the recreation of the cultured, the avidity of new artists and cognoscenti discovering delightedly that the miseries of their Mexican modernity possessed an imperial past. It was not yet an international traffic in those early years: there were, to be sure, pre-Columbian *ídolos* in the anthropological collections of most great museums, treated under the same rubric as skulls and flintstones, reminiscences of the early unfolding of the race, improperly documented, fancifully dated and described—but there were signs that it was beginning. Notwithstanding the fact that Europeans and Americans had dominated the exploration of Mexican and Central American remains, their own countries (excepting universities and what were ineptly called institutions of history and folk culture) rarely coveted the bizarre works. The explorers—they, too, displayed private perplexities—had photographed, cleaned, identified, and left *in situ* what they found: Stephens returned with little more than his drawings of the monuments, and Catherwood spent as much time battling fever and the jungle as he did annotating his discovery of mysterious ancient cities. It was all very slow—this movement of international culture—and only the disappearance of patrician collecting and the expansion of personal wealth opened the need for new dominions of aggrandizement. But it was beginning. Indeed, the very year that Stefan Mauger arrived in Mexico City, he met a remarkably farsighted American at a cocktail party in Cuernavaca to which he and Alicia had gone, thinking perhaps to rent a house there for the winter.

"A newcomer to Mexico?" the voice inquired brusquely. A short man with florid complexion in marked contrast to a nondescript alpaca jacket that hardly closed around his girth handed Stefan a drink he hadn't ordered. Stefan took it politely and placed it on the low wall surrounding the patio overlooking the city square below.

"And you?" Stefan replied without much enthusiasm.

"I'm here every winter. It's good for my lungs and good for business."

"What do you do?" It seemed a more promising question than the short man's lungs.

"I deal."

"What's 'deal'?"

"Deal. You know. Deal in art, of course. Buy and sell. But it's becoming difficult now. My collectors are off painting. I've had to improvise. When Chagall passed through in the forties I showed his drawings and they took and also the French surrealists, who didn't, so I went back to the masters. The impressionists. Do nicely with them, but it's hard to work up enthusiasm nowadays—with the world what it is—for shimmering trees and windy beaches with girls in pretty hats and all the men looking like idlers out for a Sunday walk. Modern art is hard work, you know. So I'm trying my hand down here."

"And what's in Mexico that anybody wants in New York? I presume it is New York?"

"No, L.A. Los Angeles is where I deal."

"Oh yes? I was in your city for about ten months."

"You? What's your name?"

"Stefan Mauger. I'm a sculptor."

"Yes? Do I know you? Or should I know you?"

"I don't care one way or the other."

"Well, that's straight and clean. I like that. Mine's Burl Hendel. I deal mostly from a nice gallery on La Cienega, but when I get bored with it, I close the place and sell from my house in the Canyon."

"I see," Stefan replied, using an expression he delighted in employing, since Americans are often claiming to see when in fact they are stunned with incomprehension. "And it's not going well enough, so you've come down to Mexico to find something else to sell. And have you found it?"

"Yes sir. I think I have. I really think I have. They call it pre-Columbian art. You know, the statuary and artifacts made by the ancient Mexicans before Columbus opened the continent and Cortés demolished it. It's wild stuff, *really* exciting."

Burl Hendel began to tell Stefan Mauger everything he knew about pre-Columbian art. It wasn't much, but it was passionate. The pronunciation was execrable, the accents misplaced, but the enthusiasm for the numbers was infectious. Stories of movie stars and interior decorators discovering Tarascan figures and Tlaltilco maidens, each tag-lined with a price. "This one was delighted to pay five bills for it" or that one "dropped a grand that day" consummated with a superb name-drop—the first that Stefan Mauger recognized—"Little Caesar stopped by. You guessed it. Edward G. Robinson himself, and paid four big ones for the seated figure. I couldn't believe it. And all the stuff had just come up with a runner I knew from Mexico City who asked me to try and flog the stuff on the off-chance it might catch on. It certainly did and here I am, looking for more, for great pieces, not little bits of worked clay with a mouth or a hairdo. I want sculpture, big sculpture. You know what I mean. *You're a sculptor.*"

"Yes, I am a sculptor, but for the moment out of work."

"Sorry to hear that," Hendel replied with a register of

consolation. He had, of course, missed the point, but it hardly mattered to Stefan Mauger, who was already considerably beyond the commiseration into his own speculation.

"You may not be aware, Mr. Hendel, but I think this pre-Columbian art is beginning to take hold in Europe as well, or at least it was when I was last there in the early forties. The Vatican—yes, Mr. Hendel, the Vatican itself—has just had an exhibition of pre-Columbian art from its own collection—the gifts of the grateful Spanish kings at the time of the Conquistadores. Very well received, I'm told, and fulsomely reported. And earlier the French surrealists who didn't sell became very enthusiastic about Mayan art—the violent dreamworld of the new continent they called it. André Breton, the surrealist impresario himself, returned to France in the thirties with some splendid examples and did a little exhibition alongside Mexican photographs. His infectious stewardship of old Mexico—even though it failed with collectors—nonetheless persuaded French art historians to take a look, and articles followed in all the magazines. So, you see, Mr. Hendel, you're not completely alone."

Burl Hendel watched Stefan Mauger as he spoke, examining his face intently as though trying to decide whether to move on and try someone else, or, indeed, whether Stefan might not be just the right person for a perilous inquiry. He apparently decided that it was worth a try. "Do you mind talking a bit longer with me?"

Stefan Mauger noted with quizzical delight (for he had anticipated his interlocutor) the change in tone from Hendel's earlier address. No less clotted with solecisms and ponderous toughness, Hendel no longer touched Stefan Mauger as he spoke, grappling with his lapels or tapping the pocket of his white shirt to insure that Stefan was listening. From across the patio where Alicia was speaking with the handsome wife of the American dental surgeon to whom the house belonged, she winked at him with amusement, aware of his entrapment but unwilling to rescue him. He had been particularly remote that week, wandering the streets late at night, even rising one morning just after dawn claiming he wanted to be at the Museo when it opened although she knew perfectly well that he wanted to walk and breakfast alone. She found him later, his head bent over a vitrine that housed dozens of small Olmec figures of exquisite complexity and abstraction, although at first sight they appeared as though modeled after a ward of hydrocephalic cretins, all of them with elongated pointy heads, slant eyes, and stippled and slashed pudenda. Stefan had merely whistled with amazement as he studied them, commenting no further. Of course, the Maugers were without money. Alicia had cabled her father to send the annual income from her trust fund as speedily as possible, but he had neglected to make the transfer by cable, regarding air mail as quite speedy enough. His diligent indifference to speed was of a piece with his sedate black suit and severe four-in-hand, which befitted an important legal eminence but hardly enabled Alicia to cover their hotel bills. Stefan, for his part, was nearly broke, although the Banco de Mexico would shortly receive from his Vancouver account what remained of a check Clemens Rosenthal had forwarded from his New York gallery. At the conclusion of an unjustifiably expensive luncheon on the Paseo Reforma, Stefan had bolted when the check arrived and returned smiling, a half hour later, his shirt cuffs, withdrawn from his jacket, flopping over his wrists, his father's diamond cuff links absent and pawned. Alicia laughed and kissed his hand while he drank off another brandy. They were, unmistakably (not he alone, but both of them), spoiled and, as the ermined Judge of Lyons had contended, prodigal. So Alicia let

Stefan endure Burl Hendel. "He deals in art," Señora Small had explained. It was enough to put Alicia's mind to rest. "Oh, an art dealer. It will be pleasant for Stefan to argue about art for a change."

When they had reached a corner of the patio protected by a grove of flowering avocado plants, Burl Hendel motioned Stefan Mauger with proprietary assurance to be seated on the stone wall and pulled toward them a gray sandstone receptacle, carved dimly in the shape of a turtle, which Hendel identified as being a *metate*, a sandstone platter on which the ancient Mexicans ground their maize— "common as dishwater," Hendel confided—lit a cigarette, and threw the match into its antiquity. When he had determined that Stefan Mauger was comfortable and attentive, Burl Hendel began his remarkable suggestion. "Now, I guess, Mr. Mauger, that you are probably in a bit of financial difficulty. No money is what I mean, to say it straight out. And I guess you could use some. No doubt about it, is there? So let's come to the point. What say I make you my agent down here for buying and delivering pre-Columbian art. For starters I'll tell you where you find the shipment, tell you whom to pay and how much, and through whom to ship it. You simply follow directions, keep your nose clean and the right palms crossed with gold, and you can make a quite decent living. I have no doubt you'll begin to get interested in the stuff yourself. Should be interesting for a sculptor, don't you think?" Burl Hendel sat back, tamped his cigarette in the maize grinder, and waited with a smile of satisfaction, biting his lip with conspiratorial smugness, while Stefan composed the answer he had prepared well before the proposition had unfolded.

"My friend, it's an appealing offer. No doubt in my mind, quite appealing. I love antiquities and I assure you, Mr. Hendel, I am a good bit more knowledgeable than you suppose. I know a lot more than exhibitions and art magazines. I have done virtually nothing since I arrived but haunt the Museo Arqueológico and study its collection. And, sir, I am, after all, a sculptor. You may not know my work—and, as I said, I couldn't care less if you do—but I have some reputation in Europe and North America. My eye is for volume, cunning volume, illusions of volume. What is remarkable about Mayan sculpture is that its similitudes are not with Greece or Egypt but with the sculpture of ancient Japan and Easter Island, the Haniwa and the giant stone plinths of that virtually deserted Pacific island (so close to South America, you know?), but not with European antiquity, with which its origins are roughly contemporary. It's a mystery to me and hence I am delighted to confront it and study it while I, as you say, deal."

Later that night, restored to the Maria Cristina in Mexico City, Stefan described Mr. Hendel's proposal in detail to Alicia, examining its expanse and its implication. Stefan knew that in six months he not only would know more about pre-Columbian art than Burl Hendel could ever hope to master, but also would be dealing on his own, using Hendel's resources when they were needed and supplying more than Hendel could absorb. It was a convenient presumption on Stefan's part that Burl Hendel had anticipated precisely such an outcome, hoping and indeed by the end of their conversation (which continued over dinner in the town while Alicia stayed behind with Señora and Doctor Small discussing Cuernavacan real estate) quite assured that he had found in Stefan Mauger a cunning, sophisticated, and clever European who could manage the Mexican sources and officialdom much more intelligently than he could, who knew finally only how to reach into his billfold and keep paying. Alicia put her hand to her mouth, aghast, when Stefan elaborated his suspicion of the enterprise's illegality and the likelihood that he would be paying off shippers and customs inspectors, but he assured her that Mexico was a nation of shoeshine boys awaiting a tip and that the tip was all that mattered. "Everything can be legal, if you are prepared to pay to have the law changed," he concluded, not a little sententiously. But then his desperation to be engaged and change direction was immense. He had, moreover, a growing contempt for Mayan art and its imagination, which facilitated his commitment to its plunder.

It worked precisely as Stefan Mauger had imagined and Burl Hendel had schemed. Stefan started out with modest enterprise, collecting four crates of Tarascan figures and Colima pots—all of modest value and putative elegance—and drove them across the border in three days, collecting from Burl Hendel's agent in El Paso about five hundred dollars for his trouble. This was followed by a small package of carved Olmec jade plaques, which Stefan handed to an airline attendant at the last minute before the departure of a Pan American flight to Miami, and the following week his bank account received a deposit of nearly a thousand dollars.

During the first year Stefan Mauger had made a reasonable sum of money, perhaps six thousand dollars, more than enough for him to keep Alicia comfortable while she scoured the countryside of the south looking for a place to live (Cuernavaca was too close to guests, cocktails, dinner, wasting time) and work. But more than the money earned, Stefan had noted the names of virtually all the collectors in Mexico City who bought and sold works of art, all the receivers and shippers, the several Indians who regularly brought up the treasure from the country, and more important the sites of several significant tombs that the government had begun to excavate and abandoned for want of funds.

It was during the fall of the year after his arrival in Mexico that Stefan mapped out his first extensive operation—the clearing of a modest burial ground, whose principal mausoleum had been marked and sealed by the government four years earlier and completely forgotten. It was thought to be the grave of an important Mayan provincial governor and tax collector a hundred kilometers from the hacienda the Maugers had acquired near Campeche. Stefan hired seven diggers from a small village a short distance away, paid them in cash and drink, treated them decently, rigged up lights, which he attached to the generator of his pickup truck, and set them to work, watching them carefully throughout the nights of their labor, attending to their bruises, feeding them hot coffee and tortillas at the work break, and at last entering the tomb alone to gather up the ceremonial *hacha* that he found, numerous jade pieces and semi-precious beads—the latter distributed among the workers to allay their greed while he helped them pack the remarkable statues, utensils, bowls, which lay in orderly display around the wound bones of the ancient notable. Honorable, however, to the discipline of archaeology and respectful of those he plundered, Stefan took photographs in the early morning, wrote up his findings on the tomb, and six months later, long after the peons had forgotten or could be identified, sent a descriptive article and accompanying photographs to a German scientific periodical under the pseudonym of Dr. Levis Glyphstein (the former after the denims that he had begun habitually to wear and prudently Biblical sounding and the latter a portentous conjunction of the two principal features of his thieving—that everything he robbed was essentially carved stone, stone in relief, glyphic stone, stones telling the story of ancient American man). Since his note-taking was precise, his language colorlessly scientific, and his reports dryly informative, they were all published and in due course, the name of Levis Glyphstein acquired some reputation in archaeological circles. Unfortunately the post office box in Merida to which Inspector Mariposa had assigned a watch when the articles were traced to plundered sites proved fictive and though letters arrived from Germany with several academic inquiries and bundles of periodical offprints they were never collected (for his vanity Stefan had arranged that Clemens Rosenthal would take a subscription to the *Zeitschrift für Wissenschaft und Archäologische Forschung in Alt-Amerika* and pass them on to him from time to time with other clippings regarding the American cultural banquet). Stefan Mauger continued to service his obligations to Burl Hendel, although his own initiative was vastly more productive and the objects he supplied to his North American agent afforded him by the middle of the fifties a not inconsiderable income as well as a remarkable personal collection that he augmented by the purchase and delivery of a number of northwest-coast carvings he had put aside at Father Benno's Kwakiutl mission when he and Alicia had departed two years earlier. He was not a rich man; indeed, riches had no particular part in the scheme of things other than for the critical fact that making his art continued to consume more than he could possibly hope to earn either by his thefts or by his talent. The only hope that he possessed of overcoming the discrepancy between the immense expense of conserving, remodeling, and furnishing the hacienda and its lands, and his income, was by stealing more and hence having less time for the exiguous requirements of carving and casting without exhibiting and selling.

Those early years in Mexico were a frenzy, virtually unrelieved by the sanity of retreat and consolidation. No sooner had he settled down to his own work than he would receive word from one among numerous contacts in the field that a remarkable "*obra*" (the agreed code) had turned up; these contacts knew only that he lived in Campeche and would from time to time apply under various identities to the telegraph office for messages as to where and how they might be reached. Only the girl in the telegraph office was startled by the variety of his names, but Stefan assured her that he was a famous writer, living incognito, and tipped her grandly while he flourished before her an authentic passport and she would pass along the messages. A telegraph girl knew who he was but had no idea what it meant for him to be summoned as Hernández Secundo, Juan Roncón, or Blas Alemán to call Pepe in Merida, Julio in Jalisco or the others who scoured among the Indians for rumor of a promising jungle find. The thefts were always well managed and executed without the rapacity that became characteristic in later years—he never destroyed a dig trying to cut loose a carved wall or broke down large pillars to secure an imposing lintel. Quite the contrary, those architectural carvings he dutifully photographed and sent along with his articles and, in the course of time, a number of these were properly removed and subsequently exhibited, one even noting (accidentally, he was certain) that it had first been excavated and photographed by the German archaeologist, Dr. Levis Glyphstein. And, moreover, the actual thefts—thefts as distinguished from legitimate purchases of single sculptures or groups of objects —infrequently came to the attention of the Federales and its special officer, Inspector Baltásar Mariposa, except as they were connected with the illicit excavations and academic essays of Levis Glyphstein. Hardly anything could connect the fifteen or more archaeological excavations that had been conducted in the interest of theft and scholarship with the sculptor of Campeche, Stefan Mauger.

This, of course, did nothing to relieve the anxiety of

Alicia Mauger, who continued to observe that the cost of casting his sculptures would bankrupt them, that every sale to a collector worked out to be a loss, and that it would be necessary to begin to steal to cover their substantial expenses. Her bourgeois confusion of tenses—insisting upon the volitive future for their illegal traffic when in fact they had been stealing now for more than five years—exasperated Stefan as profoundly as it amused him. It was not that her desperate turn of speech communicated a frustration with the habit of their living or even that she expressed concern that one day her husband might be caught, their property confiscated, and after fining or imprisonment or both, they would be expelled from the country without a penny; it was, rather, a stylistic turn of speech intended as ironic comment upon what might be supposed to be a complaint that such a risky and precarious existence had only produced a decent income and a private collection of domestic grotesques, when she might have wished for great wealth and an end of Mexican provincial life. His reading of Alicia's invitation to theft—her repeated "we'll have to steal"—was as far from the mark as was her own anxiety that Stefan enjoyed stealing sculpture more than making it. Such misconstruction is hardly shocking if one remembers that the anguish of criticism, personal no less than historical, invariably connives to read the metaphor as though it were literally true, ignoring all the gestures of ambiguity, incertitude, despair that would—were they metaphors of our own making—guarantee to the interlocutor that living speech is hiding and substitution, concealing what is the depth of the truth, unspeakable truth, riddling the gut where it can hardly be cut loose from the moorings of privacy and secret pain.

During the five months passed in the northwest among the Indians of British Columbia, before their Mexican days,

Alicia had neglected to make the connection between Stefan's astonishment and jealousy and their devolution into crime. She had missed the link between his rage and the immensity of the native long huts and men's houses, each one a monstrous achievement of sculptured architecture, massive bears holding up the roof, walls paneled with plaques of birds molting into men and men becoming eagles and fish, and within, dressed in garments of painted pelts, each incanting another vision of the first tale, the elders and initiates danced out their intricate hymns, singing in a voice that seemed to consist of grunts and groans, drinking a native brew that at first taste made a stranger wish to vomit, smoking a tobacco laced with some obscure drug, watching for hours while the theatrical expertise of the Kwakiutl prepared for the coming of that monster man who could in himself and person bring up from below unrecognizable voices, descend with the dead to pass time in high conversation about origins and beginnings, and retrieve for the old initiates and the young about to join, versions and prospects of a universe that, despite jagged rupture and seismic disorder, despite white man and gold and drink and disease, was still a unity, potentially unifiable once more. And then, when the Indians were not about their tribe's work, they were raveled within themselves, observing Stefan Mauger and his young wife move and talk, eat and smoke, laugh and touch, impassive, without comment, as though they, as well, were exemplifications of an unseen order about which information would be forthcoming if the shaman chose to beseech it. This world of mists and cold, white rock, spruce forests, waters blue as a knife blade, made Stefan jealous, and from jealousy—in that alembic of the humors, where fires habitually consume and transform—jealousy became rage.

Stefan Mauger had continued his rage against the Kwakiutls, carrying it with him to Mexico, diffusing the rage, sophisticating its dimension and inclusiveness, distancing himself more efficiently from the violence it had produced there, north in the forest beyond the clearing where the tribesmen had danced, wearing their incredible masks. It wasn't enough that Alicia had stood by, trying to understand the reason for Stefan's pursuit of the shaman's grand-daughter and watching as the rage against the Kwakiutls —quintessential carvers, for whom every nick of blade, every cut and chop, yielded an image that purported the universe—mounted to greater heights of intensity. Those primitive sculptors of the north, whose tales and sagas hid from view their mastery of all nature, yielded place to the unseductive brutalism of Mexican art. The Aztecs had made an art of which Stefan was not jealous; he experienced no fierce combativeness and anger when he looked for the first time on the museum collection of Mexico City. Those objects of clay and stone, even those small hand carvings of serpentine and jade, provoked in him no comparable emotion to that which he experienced when he watched a server lift an intricately carved ladle (fish molted to bird with eyes of mother of pearl) and hand it to the shaman to spoon him a cup of the sacred beer. The Indians of the north allowed no room for the intermediate fabrications of history, no accounting for real events, the rise and fall of dynasties, the coming and passage of armies, the building and rebuilding of temples and holy cities. They, residents of the north for no less a time than the Indians of the south (indeed, perhaps their racial kin), dealt with their world in a slow dance of affection, gathering little information beyond the necessary, content to observe the heron, the salmon, the bear and out of their migrations to construct a sufficient vision of the universe which enabled them to hunt, trap, fish, preserve, gather, and reproduce the essential provender of the wilds. The Indians of the south, after the earliest periods of severity, pure line, simple carving, hyperbolic modeling of the species, went baroque, and as their sense of doom increased in the centuries before the appearance of the white Spaniard, their gods and their human creatures became interfused, ornamentation exceeded substance to the point where the subject of the vision was lost in its style of execution.

Stefan had remarked that the late Mayan Empire seemed in panic. "It shows in the art. Look at it. It's all so desperate. The victims show agony and the gods seem so wild and ferocious as though they have put on more and more horrific masks to conceal their own fear. It's a civilization that had to die. Even without Cortés it would have died." Stefan said this exuberantly, exulting that at last he had found a great civilization, one that had endured and produced a splendid and complex art, for which he had contempt.

It hadn't always been so, this working of contempt. For years he had had no occasion for its expression, no anguish before genius, and no dissatisfaction before the prodigies of the ancient world. That too began in the aftermath of Tirgu-Jiu. When he had returned to Paris just before the war he'd tried to return to work but it wasn't possible. He exhibited for the last time at the Galerie du Cherche-Midi but when Monsieur Baguerre complained that most of the pieces were old and had previously been seen, Stefan Mauger arrived with a truck, removed the sculptures, and closed the exhibition. He had lost the energy to carve. Everything he had made until then seemed so constrained by human scale, his eye at a level with the eye of the creature (his arm resting upon the shoulder of a bronze woman) and even where the series had been partitive, an element of the complexity that was whole creature—the *disjecta membra* of arm, foot, cheek and ear, phallus, breast, suggesting the angle of the living but nonetheless cast and resting upon an unpretentious base, all of these died after the summer of 1938. They seemed to him clever investigations, caring examinations of the living creature, but somehow demonstrably fashionable, although no one had ever accused his work of that artificial self-consciousness that made so much sculpture either mannered or artificially tough.

Stefan held the phone from his ear. The connection to Campeche had begun to hum. He laughed to himself, thinking for a second that it protested against Alicia's renewal of her formulaic invitation to steal. He had heard her say that phrase—"we'll have to steal"—so many times, throwing up her hands and laughing when she dropped a bowl in the kitchen, crying over the bills that arrived unpunctually whenever a tradesman or worker thought to run after them in town or call on the telephone or—like their woodsman (who could neither read nor write)—pile up twigs in a basket and present the amount of pesos he required in the form of sweet-smelling pine kindling. "We'll have to steal" was her ritual, their secret, a special cipher of discontent.

"Yes, dearest, I'm sure we'll have to steal. Next month, perhaps."

"I'm not serious," she replied, although she knew quite well that Stefan had gone to Mexico City to make certain that Hendel had transferred funds to his account and to arrange for shipping an especially large Teotichuacan mask to his North American receiver.

"It doesn't matter for the moment. Good news. It's all taken care of up here and I'm coming home."

"Oh, that's so good. I've missed you."

"I'm bringing a guest. She won't be much bother. You'll like her, I think. She's not too strong, but she's lovely and needs a rest."

The pause wasn't noticeable. "Is she good in bed?"

"You'll have to judge for yourself." Alicia wasn't annoyed. Whenever she questioned Stefan he would answer in this way. Flippantly, rudely? Not really. Accurately? It didn't threaten her. She had some idea of the way men behaved. It wasn't errancy or obtuseness or the mysterious meanderings of the lusting organ that she once fantasied as having a life and intelligence of its own, swelling and despairing, curling and bending, probing and stiff in the underbrush of the world. Not these things which in childhood she had compared to her own wretched little thing, touching it, losing it, finding it, hunting it like huntsmen seeking out small quail, almost invisible in swampy waters. No. Stefan wasn't one of those whose reality was dominated by his sexuality. He was sexual, "Oh yes, God, his body seems to me in the morning when he's asleep—blue veins ribboning his white skin like a chart of Vesalius—beautifully sexual. If only I could love him then. If in those hours I could come upon him and seize him so he would never know, so he would go on sleeping while I took him and left him, but for that, I know I would have to be someone else, someone else, in fact, a man." It was this way that she thought of beautiful Stefan, beautiful to her, but not to everyone; others often found his glares and rages and subtle withdrawals frightening. It was Stefan who denied that men were equal, telling a friend one day that he had no right to make a certain request for reciprocity—whatever it was— because they weren't equal. The friend left in a rage, thinking him an arrogant bastard, but the truth was that Stefan, left behind, muttered to himself, confused by his friend's outrage, "But nobody's equal, damn it. The fool thinks equality really means no one's anybody. I just meant that it's not necessary to figure out who's superior."

Alicia usually left Stefan to his waifs. There weren't many, but they were persistent over the years. They didn't

last, but they recurred. And it wasn't even the case that
Stefan cast himself as guardian or, worse still, as docent,
guiding his young loves through the thickets or shoals to a
firmer and more responsible maturity. That would have
been so boring. She suspected, finally, that Stefan was the
waif or rather that there was in him that spot of essential
forlornness and disconsolation to which the visible confusion or mystery or incomprehension of his Marias was a
temporary solution. One vermilion toe, turning in the
morning sunlight. A throbbing of a single note, invariant,
soft or loud, but one note in a chord of complexity was all
his Marias played. Alicia, for her part, was whole composi-
tion, the range and texture of his days, and she could abide,
often biting her lip, often biting her uncolored, unpainted
lip, waiting to see what would come, wondering about who
it would be this time, whom he had uncovered and brought
today, leading her by a towline, something like a bowed
captive, noosed and straggling behind, the rope tied to his
leather belt. The first time she had had to cope with his
Marias—it was shortly after they married, when they first
came to the Kwakiutl village in the north—she had complained bitterly, taking the presence of that flat-nosed
Indian girl as a reproof to her own womanhood. Unfortunately, that week her flow had begun and hadn't stopped for
nearly three days, accompanied by horrendous pain that
left her miserable and exhausted. She had thought that
Stefan was simply voracious and cruel, unable to bear the
waiting until she could receive him. She had offered to help
him, deft fingers and agitant nails, but he had simply replied
that she didn't understand, that it had nothing to do with his
impatience or, worse yet (for she accused him and implic-
itly herself of being bored), indifference. "No. No. You're
making it all into something it isn't. She moves me, that's
all. She makes me weep." It sounded to Alicia's ear like

sentimental romanticism, the kind of nonsense one could hear on the boulevards any day, intense men leaning forward over small zinc tables toward vacant beauty and announcing any and all nonsense, all varieties of *"tu m'excites"* delivered elegantly, raw fingers touching gloved fingers, holding stem glasses, holding frail and perishable sentiments. Even in that wild north country, just barely in thaw from an eight-month winter, she burst out laughing, thinking not of tall Stefan and his Indian girl, but of the French making love like sonatinas on a harpsichord. It was only later, weeks later, when she had come to know that the Indian girl did not leave, that she padded beside them as they went off to visit the totem field, that Stefan loved her no less intensely, but that indeed something of him had, if not been given to the young girl, at least been received from her—that single note throbbing when the girl turned back from a long gaze into the ocean and seeing his eyes upon her turned away ashamed at being caught. Alicia composed a notion that seemed to fit. It was, she devised, her fortune to be loved by a man who, like ancient mountains, wore upon his face the marks of all his trials, wearing like skin the rough and craggy extrusion of old quakes and tremors alongside gentle and pleasant knolls, all a single mountain, a single face, but no less the production of millennia of growth and maturation, leaving nothing behind, and however suppressed or masked it might be, the ancient stuff, the earliest level, the oldest stratum was closest to the surface. This European refinement, these splendid manners, those incredible features of aristocracy and grace, that youth and beauty were, Alicia devised, merely what was shown; in fact, she fantasied, if Maria or that Indian girl could have said the one right word, magically Stefan would vanish instantly and in his place an immensely gifted wizard would appear who would carve sculptures that would make the world blaze with understanding and settle into peace and speechlessness. Alicia believed in Stefan's gift rather more than she believed in her own.

"That's not quite right, love," she chided, when Stefan criticized her inattention to poetry during the previous months.

"But the truth is you haven't written a single poem. I haven't seen a word in months."

"The world will survive," she replied, laughing.

"I'm sure of that, but will you?"

"I'll have to, don't you think?"

They had been standing in the patio before the sunset. The theft was done and Stefan was relieved. He had returned from the late-night rendezvous with Gutiérrez and taken a pitcher of hot coffee with him into the studio, where he remained for hours, until Alicia had called him to come quickly. Alicia had driven into town for supplies after the meeting with the wounded boy and Maria had gone to the kitchen to make bread during the afternoon, relieving old Martina to fetch kindling and work in the garden. When Alicia returned near sunset, Stefan was sitting in the patio. Alicia waved to him from the truck and he ran to greet her, his face briefly lighting into a smile.

"I've missed you," he said.

"Yes? Did you, Stefan? I had no time, I'm afraid, to miss you. Too much to do in town. Not a word yet. I went everywhere hoping to hear something. Not a word. More cars than usual at the police station, but who knows what that means. It's undiscovered, I imagine." Stefan took her about the waist and hugged her. It was such an unfamiliar gesture, Alicia resisted. "Did it go well?"

"Not really. I just stared at them all. I don't seem to be able to finish an old piece or begin a new one."

"You've been worrying again. About money still. I can always cable Papa for another check."

"It's not the money. We have enough. When we get paid

for the Jaina we'll have plenty. I'll pay something to every-one and they can start waiting again. It'll be all right, I should think."

"Yes, but the money will take time to come home. They keep asking in town when we'll pay. The *mercería*, the garage, the electrician, and they're the large ones. I should think between them—and the contractor (we still owe him for tiling the studio)—more than eight thousand pesos, and that's without food and clothing and Martina. We don't live cheaply, my darling."

Stefan hardly listened. He endured talk of money badly, impatiently. Not that he didn't understand its abstract scarcity or abundance. It was abstract, he claimed, and hence as intelligible and unreal as any abstraction. Alicia was fortunate, he once told her, to be raised by a bourgeois. Her father was *Chef de la Cour d'Appel* in Lyons, a re-spectable eminence, with honors, titles, rosettes of ac-knowledgment, investments in land and ownership of a herd in the Camargue. Alicia had never had to scrape or aspire. Solidity was given with her morning coffee. The sus-picion of poetry was her only transgression against her paternity. Poetry, formed not casually as one takes a hobby or a relaxation, leading threaded needles through a pattern to distract one from the necessity of perceiving or reflecting. Alicia composed poetry in her early twenties like a dancer working at the barre, continually exercising the power of imagining, like a muscle that demanded flexing and stretch-ing. Poetry was for her not simply a craft of ingenuity or a gift, but a stratagem of survival. And who threatened Alicia? Her father? The head of the Court of Appeals in Lyons in his ermine-trimmed robes and his oddly shaped cap? Perhaps, but not he in his own self, in his method of loving or caring, which he did splendidly well; but if not he in his own self and his method of loving and caring, then what? What would commend poetry to a young girl of

Lyons, and not only poetry but the poetry of the surrealists, and before them of Apollinaire, Cendrars, Max Jacob, Tristan Tzara, vaudeville and circus poets, men who balanced words on the end of their noses and juggled them in the air like flaming swords. Psychology isn't everything. It leads us by the nose when we move on the trail of disease, but it hardly helps at all when we are obliged to deal with a well-loved young woman, beautiful, educated, who made poems out of necessity. It should be made clear, however (and perhaps this is the relevant codicil to this aspect of description), that Alicia's talent, though genuine, was not large. But what then is largeness or smallness of talent? It resides not in the energy of application, for many minor artists work with dedicated attention, breaking themselves long years to produce the inconsequential—perhaps it is there, in the notion of consequence, which suggests range and extent, the visionary dimension. Alicia produced poems whose imagery was drawn largely from the barely visible, the kingdom of insects, colonies of wasps, small birds, the fortifications and domiciles of ants, and the instinctual amity of honey bees—these were her poems, and there were many, several books in fact, one published by Editions Surréalistes with a paragraph of affectionate congratulation written by André Breton, with whom she claimed to have had a romance as intense as it was brief, and another illustrated with etchings by a surrealist painter who interpreted her imagery as glittering lights and fluttering winged substances rising from a dark ovoid miasma. Alicia was, it will be apparent, held together by her life of dreams, dreams whose filaments of illumination irradiated from the disconsolation of childhood contentment. It had been so easy—Alicia's childhood in Lyons—that only the rivings of art seemed to raise the appropriate finger of protest, as if to contend that this daughter of the bourgeoisie required something more to affirm her distinctiveness. The vision then was small—those small creatures of her imagery, obliged to sustain not more of the universe than could be borne on microscopic feet and translucent wings—but they were enough to set her apart. Her poems were small and modest, finished, well turned, admirable, but still small and modest.

Alicia's joining up with Stefan Mauger six, nearly seven, years earlier dissolved at least one of the uncertainties that had compelled her to attend to poetry, to listen to her dreams, to observe and note the couplings of her fantasy that allowed her insect world to copulate so ferociously, for Stefan had at least removed from her the vague burden of boredom, the malicious revenge that reality takes upon the excessive contentment of childhood.

"Not cheaply, at all, but the way we want to live." Stefan said this last severely, his face turning upward to the light, if not to catch the sun, which he habitually avoided, then at least to celebrate the last hour of the day.

"I would be a lot happier, *mon cher*, if I could be certain you believed it."

"Believe it, Alicia! Do believe it! Isn't it so? Isn't this precisely what we want?"

Alicia smiled, graciously, her large eyes opening to even greater amazement. "Yes, it is, Stefan, but each year it becomes more difficult, incredibly more difficult to maintain it."

"The money again."

"No, not money."

"Then what?"

"You're being obtuse. You always make me say out loud things that are already understood."

Stefan paused. Of course, she was right, but the choice of language made the hurt more precise.

"The stealing. I detest it."

"That's all?"

"For the moment enough."

"And not Maria?" Stefan asked softly.

"No, not Maria."

"Not Maria, I see." Stefan wanted to continue. It dissatisfied him that Maria had not come between them; it alarmed him that Maria and Alicia had obviously formed a compatibility, an alliance that excluded him. It disobeyed the mechanism of his intent; it was unexpected. He had known nothing of this side of Alicia, indeed, he could barely identify it. It meant nothing to him to speak of its sexuality, for he conducted his own sexuality with a kind of unknowing—unreflective, more accurately—as though making love were really at the surface of things, a species of webbing that he flung over his women to settle them down, to pacify their scrutiny. But that was lovemaking, making love to a particular woman who had already settled into loving him. The vagrancy of his sexuality—its ardent vagabondage—arose from other sources, obscurely anxious and unsettling, shimmering reminders of discontent, uncertainty of vocation, the terror which he knew to be increasing that the talent might not be equal to the vision, which is only a way to express the fear that the vision was confused and the talent paralyzed. That was one difference he knew between his own and Alicia's art: she could replace poetry with taking care of him; the ardor was the same, the diligence, the fantasy, while the more he doubted, the greater became the silence and the deeper the abyss. It was at those times—lengthening shadows of his Mexican days—that he would gaze upon his creatures and shift uncomfortably before their lifeless rebuke, stir the cold coffee, pace the studio, and straighten the tools and at last discover himself meditating an unexcavated site where buried, buried deeply in the earth, he would find a whole culture of lost objects awaiting the digger's spade.

"No, not Maria, Stefan. I've discovered that I can·love that woman." Alicia was clear, her voice strong and un-apologetic. "I begin to understand what it must mean to you to care for someone forlorn."

"Yes? Well." The phone sounded in the house, the long trunk-line jingle, unbroken for a full twenty seconds, as though a hand bell were being rung uncertainly. "It's prob-ably Brownsville. I have to take it."

"Mauger here," he said quietly. The voice replied. It in-troduced itself, announced its intention, paused briefly to await a reply. Stefan had little more to acknowledge than his recognition. He had heard the name. It was hardly pos-sible for someone as knowledgeable as himself to pretend ignorance of Baltásar Mariposa. No one engaged in his particular line of work (as he sometimes described it) could be unaware of the Inspector. He replied slowly: "Indeed. Inspector Mariposa will be welcome." Nothing more needed to be said. It was all there; already, it was all there.

Stefan Mauger worked late into the night. The thickness of the jungle night, the invisibility of angles and contours filled with shadow, returned nature to an unparsed simplic-ity, eliminating the grammar of declension and elaboration by which each thing acquires a specific character that leaves behind line, circle, cone and affords it definition and partic-ularity. If the morning visit to his creatures was marked by the lighting of the fire and the building of warmth, the nighttime hours began with the contemplation of darkness and shadow, the presence of his creatures in the lurk and gloom of the studio, the fire banked and dying.

Stefan had passed Alicia in the patio where she had awaited his return from the phone; she had wanted to talk further but Stefan had moved already to the other side, beyond love and domesticity to a region where the free actions of destiny so often threaten to become fate. Inspector Mariposa was coming to call. Convergence and dissolution. The time of his "creatures" had returned.

He sat with his back to the fireplace and watched the beasts move among each other, birds and women, crooked arms, phalluses at ease, hands asplay, face masks in stone carved not in death, with the pain of death, but into life. Abstract smiles. Too many shadows in Rodin. Nature has no shadows. Obscurity does not mean confusion, but our sculpture and painting represent the potholes in nature as though my doubt belonged to it. It is not permitted. Deep down, beneath the surface of things that fill with shadow, nature has a unanimity, each speaking to each, like my young bear, which stands with a calm and grace no less imposing than a young lord presented to royalty. Creatures interlock and what is wildness to human sight is only, I think, the incomprehension of speech. All the wise teachers knew the language of animals. Tigers rolled over to be tickled by the Buddha. These sculptures, this life work of mine, a form of speech that allows me to walk around instead of seeing into things like theater. Sculpture I have always thought Copernican, painting Ptolemaic. Yes, yes, the Renaissance began all the new work, allowing rose and mustard yellows, and vermilions and greens to stand in for the shadows of our finitude, pushing back Egyptian flatware until the more glorious perspective of near and far, at hand and distant, visible and hidden could be tolerated again in our universe. Those who think the age of faith stood at the beginning of our history are wrong. There is hardly a bristle on my bear's back. (Anyone who sees him would know simply by touching the grain of the wood that his back is covered with a ferocious fur. Sculpture's a walk-around.

Never against a wall even when carved for the wall. Walk around and around and touch, stroke, my hand with agitant pulse vivifying wood and stone, receiving their impulse—is there a significant difference between flesh and bone and wood and stone?) Easy for the great believers since they thought there was nothing besides themselves and God. What an arrogant universe was the old world of faith. I began with the Renaissance to celebrate color and depth, which is, after all, different from man and God; I allow nature to shimmer off of man, to diffract his light over everything, to make up a new skin for the world and to color it brightly and to see beneath everything not a message, but a form. Down with instruction! I have always been amused by the paintings of Jerome writing at his desk, translating scriptures, with his benign lion at the hearth or in a corner or resting beneath his feet like a cushion. It always means the same thing in those paintings: look how grace sedates the violence of the beast? look how the wise man thinking wise thoughts is calming to the terrible beast? But I marvel at the intelligence of the beast and the vanity of the man. I read it differently. Look, I say, isn't it splendid that the beast forbears to gobble up that wasted man, how kindly he regards him, how intelligent that he lets the man alone to make up his words? The lion, stretching out noble head upon his crossed paws, lying quietly, enjoys the aura of power constrained, mystery of gentleness and ferocity, and the man, center of his universe, works on announcing his revelations.

Sculpture is my parlous art—the more abstract (cutting back the world to its elements), the more divine; and the more it copes with luscious skin, the more it celebrates its maker. I've no vision worth talking about—anyway, talking makes it as stale as yesterday's bread. It would have been terrible if Brancusi had known to speak in more than little epigrams, if Rodin had been able to say straight out what Rilke devised into a book about him, if Michelangelo had left more behind than his poems and the work. Màtisse was right: artists should have their tongues cut out. The public needs help from the artist, thinking all the while that he has something secret or special that he knows. I can testify that I have no message, no information, no secret that isn't right in front of everyone. What I've got—the privilege of my carving—is that I am never bored by the rite of passage. The worst artists are those who imagine they can hold off death by saving someone besides themselves. They end up making their words into puffballs, sculptures into heraldry, paintings into lessons.

Me? All I'm looking for is a connection, the link between myself and everything that has been. I don't care what happens after me. It's what I ravel into myself that interests me. I painted my sister's hands with little circles within circles, red circle within black circle within yellow circle, and on her forehead above her beautiful eyebrows I drew the outline of a pyramid, a simple triangle, and then discovered in the north that the Indians carved their masks with the same device, but they intended no theosophical pyramid (perfect form of ancient architecture) but the unnatural emphasis of what nature had devised as hairy undulance, green triangulated, bar-thick, and the eyebrows painted to instruct us that the shaman's face had wise eyebrows and the wooden mask powers that concentrated hoary wisdoms to its brow. (Dear sister, I didn't know that. I was a copyist when I was a boy playing Indians in the wood.) And the circles, spindly whorls, which every Mayan knew as the symbol of the universe. Everything basic implies.

It's getting cold in here and the fire's almost out. The wind's brisk, but no longer warm. Smell of dead fish brought in from the sea. I can smell the salt this far inland.

Almost surrounded by jungle, I can smell the sea. Jungle of beasts and men, stiff joints and seamless, nighttime shades, arms reaching across the ceiling, the flames begin licking themselves, lashing themselves, flicking tongues at the arms, circling stone torsos like vines, tentacles of vines circling, trying to seize hold. Dumb show of light. Somnambulism. The enmity of fire and moon contest the field of marble men and wood beasts. They resist, standing fast before the assault, fire gaining against the pale white stream that flashes like a tongue of silver across the beak of crane, the chest of bear, the thigh of man, the woman's breast lying upon its marble rest, weary adornment, illuminated nipple. Cut by fire, the stream breaks up, overwhelmed and weakened; the circle of defense against fire dissolves and the fire rising in strength and temerity moves and warms, compelling the creatures to doze, animating the face, wiping from it the preoccupation of distant danger, men with weapons, authorities who search, accomplices who threaten, and shining, ashine with firelight, warm with fire warmth, an arm, unenlarged by illusion, pulls the drop cloth that covers a vast counter on saw horses behind the ring of beasts, sheltered by beasts and men who are weak from fire, and a microcosm in stick and matchbox, flour and water, modeling clay, and the smallest of worlds pushed with fingers from little molds of metal assembled with a tinker's delight, madness of the minuscule, dreaming as model-makers dream not of miteness and fragment, but of construction large as the mind's scale, flying from finitude toward an infinity from which the gods have withdrawn, leaving space upon the flat board of the world for men to fabulate. Minuscule vision in wood and clay, there against the background of the house called "hacienda" and "the atelier," named the same, the borderline of jungle marked by trees of wire, aflame even with parrots and colored specks for fruit, and winding aboveground a sculptor's conceiving of the cavern formed by King Argos to keep his Minotaur craven, awaiting idle visitors and knowing thread-bearers, but what's all this aboveground? What's this? A maze. Not quite, but then astonished by the complexity of the underground, where cities and civilizations are buried, he cuts them out of earth and turns them right-side up—walls of city hewn of stone, seamed with candle wax and lying in the way, as the foot would pass, treading upon the path, lost in the maze of streets, unmarked, without sign, leading inexorably toward an exit into the jungle (where fancy dictates the building of the car park beyond the precincts of the sacred rendition), out and away from a whole universe fashioned by a sculptor making architecture: an architect carving space with a sculptor's knife, cutting out of walls figures who pierce the wall and yet sustain it, part of wall and part of man, the architecture of the body united with the sculpture of walls, doors opening upon hinges nailed like fingers to the jamb, handles turned like testes, and the maze unfolds toward vistas where a woman's body bearing the head of an eagle throned, appears to deliver eulogies to the visitors and obsequies to the open sky; and continuing on his way to the sculptor's maze garden, the visitor tightens his grip on the cord, threading it around his finger, winding it around his wrist; at first frightened by the eagle woman of perspicacity he moves beneath an arch designed of broken stone, fallen into place, piled up as though by the archaeologist's earth mover, with seams and junctures so interior that the eye beholds only crack and fissure, imagining the whole will bash his head when he passes under, but will not, since it is formed by pairs of nature's beasts, simplified to bone and claw embracing, hugging gently; united in the lips where the mixed spittles of affection are shared and supped, through, beyond the arch coming to a strange confection, city of an earthly passion which ascends by turret, circling turret, circling turret upward, passing the tops of the jungle trees, illusion of height upon height until the stars would be touched and singing soothsayers (some thought) would force the benefice of one audible word (his name perhaps?) into the ear of creatures who acquired ancient wisdom through the circuitry of the fleshy ear, but the visitor passes beneath this turretry, through courtyards and passageways, through circles and beneath arches of linked hands, through mouths with cupped hands calling, a minuscule of the dreams of the species, he believed, watching the phantasmagoria, examining, appraising, figuring the time and immense cost that the building of his visible maze would consume, checking it with a sigh, at ten o'clock in the evening against his fifty-seven years and his situation.

The fire slumbered and the moon rose, burning through the window in a steady stream of silver. Stefan Mauger lifted the drop cloth high above the maze garden; it fell upon it, billowing slightly in the night breeze, settling in a second, covering his imagination like a veil. Times of resolution approached. Brancusi was dying in Paris; Clemens Rosenthal was coming to speak with him of his recollections of Tirgu-Jiu; an inspector was calling in the morning, and the maze garden of his sculpture appeared improbably magnificent in the moonlight. Consinnity approached; the old time of rage was coming to an end.

He heard a knock at the door and as usual did not answer.

5

The Mean Kwakiutl

The silence of the frozen nights of the north was broken only by tremors of thaw. The earth, which for months had held its breath, stopping its mouth against ice and snow, had gasped, responding to temperate currents from the far Pacific, which arrived at last to bathe its extremities. The Indians knew that it was no earthquake (only the coming of spring) and smiled, saying nothing, when Stefan Mauger and his bride, Alicia Lurçat, straightened up with fright as the small trading post that served as meeting place and general store for the Kwakiutl village shook to its foundations.

The Indians continued to smile long after the episode had concluded, their narrow eyes creased by a webbing of crow's feet. Long after. The wooden house had shaken some time before, in fact had shaken several times since, and the Maugers now forewarned remained sternly calm, pretending to indifference. The Indians, however, once amused, continued to smile, if indeed it was smile and not, as Stefan came to think later, the endurance of expression long after its sense and affection had changed.

The Indians watched them; the Maugers thought of them as Indians. They were *the Indians*, as abstract and generalized as gypsies, even though Alicia watched two young boys moving bone counters on a board grooved with deep ridges and Stefan's curiosity alternated between a young woman with long black hair that fell down her chaste gingham dress and two young hunters wrapped in fur. That assembly (with the exception of a white trapper who never acknowledged them) simply stared at Stefan and Alicia and smiled. And they were the Indians, the scenery of the world to which the Maugers had come with indefinite expectation. They were not indifferent to the Indians. It is rather, one presumes, that for those who have only dreamed of Indians, to be one was sufficient to appear unique. Not quite the same, of course, for the smiling Indians, members of a small sub-tribe of the great nation of the Kwakiutl which once numbered tens of thousands of fishermen and hunters who had, through perilous descent into civilization, become listless in the pursuit of traditional ways. The nameless village had once been prosperous, located as it was some miles north of the large settlement at Alert Bay on Vancouver Island: in the past trappers congregated at that season and the Indians brought dried game, smoked fish, and frozen bear steaks to trade for knives, deer leggings, and beaded singlets, but now in the middle of the white man's century as it was called along the northwest coast, population had thinned, women died in childbirth, more often from loss of interest than from disease, and disease cut through the Kwakiutl nation like the fires of the potlatch.

It had all come to pass (some Indian savants had theorized) because the potlatch had been outlawed.

The launch arrived at dusk not long beyond mid-afternoon. The Maugers had been traveling since dawn, having left Nanaimo, the principal town of southern Vancouver Island, the previous day. There was no destination in mind, only as Stefan had put it vaguely, pointing to the little pile of illustrated pamphlets they had gathered in Vancouver during three days of touring that provincial capital, that they wanted to be among them—the Indians, most specifically the Kwakiutl, the people of the giant crane. They could have gone farther north among the Bela Coola, the Tlingit, the Tsimshian, the Haida, but it was the Kwakiutl Stefan had settled upon, fixed in expectation of some discovery that was certainly unavailable in New York, among the friends of Clemens Rosenthal.

Of course he had taken away Alicia Lurçat with him, taken her away like pelf, plundered in the living room of Clemens Rosenthal. While Clemens spoke, and smoked, and drank from every glass at hand, lecturing his assortment of Sunday guests on everything they claimed to know better than he, Stefan had observed in the corner of the room near the kitchen a woman in her thirties (her blond hair shifting and glinting, moving and shining about her face, hiding and suggesting small nose, blue eyes, shyness and smartness) passing in from a disembodied hand that appeared and disappeared again, plates of anchovies bathed in oil, mussels pickled in red sauce, tuna with rings of green pepper, cheeses and biscuits, platters of salami and wurst until all of them disposed upon a table not far from Clemens Rosenthal caught his attention and he speared a fillet of tuna and dropped it into his mouth, pausing only briefly in a run between Monet and Matisse, to swallow, to interject (interrupting his own circuitous passage of thought). "Who needs to go out to supper?" Clemens smiled, supposing that the plates, enough for his own appetite, would appease the growing pangs of his guests, who had gathered to celebrate some cultural triumph or other to which Clemens had bidden them—the appearance of a new writer or poet or painter or, as on a previous occasion, a new girl friend, Alicia Lurçat, the French surrealist poet, who had come from Paris to Clemens to make verse. Enough for Clemens, the thin fare was insufficient for his weary guests and so, while one hand would seize toothpick and slice and mouth worked over the syllables of the culture, guests would catch his roving eyes, nod farewell, and proffer a hand of good-bye which his other received with anchovy paste. At last, marked by lipstick on forehead and cheek, exhausted by drink, nine o'clock passed and his new mistress and old friend, Stefan Mauger, just arrived in New York that day, were left alone. Clemens Rosenthal, no longer leviathan come to beach in Les Deux Magots, lay snoring, curled into his fiftieth year of speaking in tongues, most of them not his own.

"He's gentle and he makes no demands," Alicia exclaimed while they drank coffee, passing the cream over Clemens's sleeping hulk.

"Not a recommendation of bliss," Stefan replied, already moved by the young woman, who struck him (vulnerable to love) as being that curious French type, rare but not unique, who in the absence of experience had nonetheless imagined all its possibilities and dismissed many she had thoroughly conjured.

"Nor its denial. Depends what you want. For the moment bliss doesn't happen to interest me. Never has, I'm afraid. Bliss? As you use it, Monsieur Mauger, it's pure rhetoric, but in fact bliss is hopelessly Elysian. Good for a diet of nymphs and satyrs, but hardly for an exhausted child of this century."

"Dear woman, you can't mean that," Stefan responded with paternal warmth.

"But I do, I do. You're not French," she said, ignoring

the sequitur, but acknowledging his excellent French, which Stefan spoke without accent (indeed, Clemens had once called his an "anti-accent," since it possessed rhythm but no melody).

"Austrian. Austrian and Polish. Austrian and Polish with an English tutor who spoke German, English, and Italian with me. French I added to my repertoire after I repudiated being an Austrian nobleman and denied the existence of German. However, before you force me to hunt the thickets of my own past, I have to lead you out of your own. What's this 'exhausted child' nonsense? You don't look at all weary, beautiful woman, and you're most certainly no child. Old enough to have found your way to the New World and into the indiscriminately affectionate arms of this vast creature."

Alicia Lurçat watched Stefan as he spoke, observing how he chose his words, plucking them breathlessly, slowing down precipitously to refuel his vocabulary, and then rushing once more as the French idiom returned. "I apologize, Stefan Mauger. I loathe self-pity, even my own. I'm tired, that's all. Tired sometimes of trying to settle in, make my life fit. But what's all this? Why am I confessing? Change the subject. Abruptly. Clemens says you're a great sculptor."

"Did he say that really? Did you really say that?" Stefan slapped Clemens's heaving belly and the whale moved, shifting to its side, its gull fins sucking the air stale with cigarettes, a large arm rising and falling to Alicia's knee where she stroked it, smoothing the disgruntled hair. Calm again, Clemens resumed his contented snoring.

"Are you?"

"What? Am I what?"

"Great sculptor? Worthy successor to the 'aging and dying greats of Europe'?" Alicia laughed, as she repeated

Clemens's enthusiastic formulation when the cable announcing Stefan's imminent arrival had reached them from the ship three days earlier.

"Clemens wouldn't tolerate me if I were no good. That I'm sure of. He suffers only the great or the helpless to approach him or if not great or helpless then at least powerful or rich or admiring or young and dutifully attentive. And which are you, Madame Lurçat? You are married, aren't you?" Stefan had become severe. Clemens's praise embarrassed him; he thought it gratuitous and unsupported, as he had made little sculpture recently and only now the anger against his inability to work, anger against praise for work that had no currency, anger against all those sculptors of whatever age and time who had left behind them a body of work was finding its way to the surface.

"Which question first? In order? None of the above and no."

"Not great, rich, powerful, or disciple, and unmarried. So be it. But something that calls you to his side. What is that?"

"I don't want anything. *Rien du tout. Rien du tout.* And I don't propose to stay for long."

"Passing through?"

"Yes. He couldn't stand it if I proposed to stay on. It would frighten him, you know."

"Come to bed with me. Right now. Under his very nose, if you will. He wouldn't mind. In fact, he'll never know. He sleeps through until morning coffee."

"You know him terribly well."

"I should, I've known him for years. We met long ago when we were still trying to grow up."

"Are you grown up now?"

"Not yet, but I wear fewer skins than I did. Sculpture. That fits, at least, even if it requires alterations."

"And the others? You're beautiful, you know."

"It's no beauty contest," he replied irritably. "I found that out during the past years."

"Were they hard? The war years. You didn't have to fight, did you?"

"You think not? It isn't always in battle."

"I'm asking."

"Beauty. My beauty, as you call this pleasing undergarment, is a handicap when one is otherwise stark naked. Had I already been a hero of culture like the rest of the Paris *métèques*, I could have gone on doing my work and the Germans wouldn't have bothered. But I wasn't. They let Picasso and Brancusi alone because they were great and foreign and never qualified for being Aryans. The Jews they destroyed because they were Jews, and all the French artists and intellectuals had two, three names with which they used to live above and underground. But I was an Austrian and hence part of greater Germany and Aryan and the son of nobility. No choice really.

"In late nineteen forty-one I fled, walked out of Paris, south to the border carrying a small suitcase with some notebooks, my father's loaded revolver, some papers and photographs, and whatever bits of family jewelry I hadn't already sold. In Port Bou I learned my lesson. I stayed in a cheap hotel for one night before I crossed over the border into Spain. The hotelier gave me a room in the back over the courtyard. '*Voici. La chambre d'un jeune suicide.*' He announced this with dramatic pleasure and told me the story of a German writer, probably forty years old, he imagined, who had shot himself the year before, believing he would be turned back and delivered to the Gestapo. He had noticed my revolver when I opened my case to show him my documents. 'Don't do it, please, Monsieur. It causes people to think poorly of my little hotel. It's very clean you know,' he added as a mitigating afterthought. I searched that room the whole night for a trace of the suicide, something that would tell me the extra lesson. (You see, I had wanted my father to die the same way—with a revolver—but he wasn't permitted such a justice.) And now, nearly thirty years later, I was being warned not to kill myself like my predecessor in the room. I realized then that it was for this reason, perhaps, that I had carried my father's silver and enamel revolver with me over the years, never leaving it when I traveled, always carrying it with me as a precautionary gesture. All along I had held out the privilege of killing myself when it became impossible. But it wasn't impossibility that confronted me (as it confronted the German writer). Hopelessness. Despair. But not impossibility. My papers were in order. I had visas and stamps and documents that the French police would accept and I had a perfectly satisfactory name. In the morning, I breached the pistol for the hotelier and gave him the bullets. He complimented the beauty of the revolver. I paid the bill and crossed the border. Much later, after several years in Portugal nearly at the war's end, when I was making ready to return to Paris, I met a German diplomat at a bar in Lisbon where he was waiting for an appointment. We began to talk. A message came that his appointment would be very late. We continued to talk. The plot against Hitler had failed and reprisals were going forward. The diplomat with whom I was talking told me quite frankly that he had been a supporter of the plot and that he expected at any moment to be recalled to Germany to stand trial. When that moment arrived he had his cyanide tablet in the change pocket of his jacket. I asked him why he didn't flee. He said, quite frankly, that flight was an option he had no training to entertain. A month later I read that he had taken his life. Another impossibility.

"The suicide of impossibility is quite other than the romantic suicides we celebrate. The one kills himself to make death certain and painless. The other makes his own death into a commentary, a gloss on life, a startlingly indulgent interpretation and hence a gesture, a question, a further conversation with life. No. I have contempt for any other suicide than that of the young intellectual or the diplomat. All the other suicides—the one I contemplate daily—are precisely that, contemplations in order to strengthen life, to clear up irresolution, to remind myself that beauty is an undergarment, that the real work is undone and will never be done with a bullet in the head.

"We, dear woman, you and I, are among the most fortunate of creatures—there is no necessity that will ever compel us to confront impossibility. We are not demons or monsters; we belong to no loathsome tradition; we hold no contemptible doctrine. There is nothing about us that can ever make our life a hell beyond choice. That happens only to natural martyrs and implacable enemies of whatever order is running things. We are neither—which makes life both possible and predictable and hence often not worth living. I wish sometimes that I were like Clemens here, always nervous and unnerving, always gobbling with two hands, always speaking, eating, belching, dropping his turds wherever he feels they might be at home. He's vulgar and real and I fear I never am." Stefan Mauger drank off his coffee and stood up. He smiled at Alicia, embarrassed at having talked so long. He blushed, his fair and orderly face filling with the blood of too much confession.

"Come, sit down and let me kiss you." Alicia Lurçat took his hands and gently pulled him beside her. They made love quietly. Clemens Rosenthal never awakened; once he tugged at his cheek furiously, perhaps when the remarkable odor of sex rose in the room, but otherwise he snored, while

Alicia lightly cried her pleasure and Stefan bit his lip so as not to cry aloud.

Stefan Mauger wearied of New York quickly. He admired its energy, its absence of artifice and secrecy, its lethal pace, but quite as readily admitted that precisely those virtues which he admired he had no wish to emulate. He spent his time close to base, hidden in the library of Clemens's apartment, turning the pages of picture books, waiting for Alicia to return from the long walks she took daily to the Cloisters, after which they would find a small restaurant for lunch, and at the hour when Clemens would be entering into phonic communication with the world, stretched out on his library divan, eating almonds and dialing one friend after another, making and abrading reputations, advancing and repudiating ideas, reviewing and disseminating art, literature, culture, Alicia and Stefan made love. Clemens didn't mind. When Alicia announced to him that she was in love with Stefan he replied querulously, "But we're *both* invited to dinner this evening." Of course they were, and three of them went; indeed, for the months that followed, whenever a social engagement expected two, three would appear until in the weeks that remained before their marriage and departure for Canada, it became customary at breakfast for Clemens to inquire of his house guests who would be available for the social engagements of the day. He didn't mind; at least, he didn't appear to mind. Clemens needed women about to bring to parties and leave in corners, to separate boring couples at dinner, to light their cigarettes and open doors for them when he remembered, to have them listen and serve, and from time to time, rarely, to make love to them. He expected them to base with him and relocate periodically. He had married twice disastrously and had no intention of marrying again. It rather pleased him therefore to witness the marriage of Alicia Lurçat (his former mistress, who had never married before and had passed thirty-six avoiding marriage) and Stefan Mauger, approaching the half century of his life without a gray hair, quite marriageable but resolutely unmarried, who presumably, come to a new world, had agreed to new possibilities as well, of which marriage was the first in his desultory list to be realized. The second, obviously, was to travel among the Indians of the Pacific Northwest, a dream from childhood, reawakened by a picture album of turn-of-the-century photographs of the Kwakiutl Indians, sepia drenched, all tonalities of brown and black, mist laden and masked, huddled in the wet and cold, but making immense wooden sculptures that had no parallel in Stefan's imagination other than to the canny sophistication of Brancusi's Tirgu-Jiu.

"Tomorrow we marry and in three days we take the train to Chicago and then to Seattle, plane to Vancouver, and by boat, pony express, dog sled, whatever it takes, we settle in among my Indians and take photographs of their sculpture, and arrange to buy some for ourselves, and make notes and watch them and learn everything we can about them. It shouldn't be all that difficult. It shouldn't take too long. After all, they're dying out and they're said to be uncomplicated people."

Smile or grimace, whatever expression they put on, the natives of the village were taciturn. The language of their faces bore no relation to the words they spoke, the few words they addressed to each other in the public places of the village, along the shallows where they had gathered to await the docking of old Giraud's launch and pass from its hold cartons of dry goods for the general store as well as mail and newspapers for the youthful priest whose servant (an Indian girl with long black hair running down her gingham dress) received them wordlessly from Giraud, afterward kissing his hand affectionately; even along the rise the growing children silently threw balls and skipped through metal hoops of disused barrels; silently the old people stood out before their huts on the bluff overlooking the ocean sorting vegetables and tying them in bunches or beating on skins with slatted wooden implements, curing them for the traders who would come up in six weeks' time to barter.

Spring was coming in the north. The blue ice, not appearing to melt, only retreated, yielding place to mud; inland behind the settlement, the eye met the tops of spruce trees, whose separation from each other implicated spaces where wild apples grow and berry trees budded in late April. They disembarked there because old Giraud had said it was good. They had listened to him for ten days. Garrulity awakened from winter somnolence, Giraud was anxious to start the cutter launch through the thawing waters, to move up the coast from Nanaimo visiting the dozen or so settlements to whom he was the other world, the familiar who brought them bits of news, their kind of news—word of weather, births and burials, migration of seal and salmon, the movement of fishing fleets in their waters. Giraud —he allowed only that name (his other name he said would be useless to them)—had been traveling the coastal waters for forty years, ever since the power launch came into general use in these regions. He was born north of Quatsino, not far from the village where he put them down, but ever since the government had asked him to join the Indian Bureau during the First World War (the white man before him, who had covered the district overland and by long boat, had enlisted in the Canadian Air Force and been killed over the Somme) they had turned to him.

Giraud was inexplicable. Like the Indians, his broken French and English bore no relation to his mood or the set of his face. Angered by the falling of a late winter snow, the last to fall on Nanaimo, Giraud had rattled through a litany of Anglo-French curses, calling the sky and its Lord to account for disgusting vices, while his face remained impassive, his high, almost oriental cheekbones calm beneath the thin webbing of olive skin, the strangely thick lips, wholly out of keeping with his narrow eyes and delicate bone structure, asserting the curses monosyllabically, rhythmically, but without emphasis, each curse against the wet snow sounding precisely as its predecessor, indeed a litany of curses rather than an explosion of wrath against the sky's indifference to his need to get out of Nanaimo into the open, onto the waters, bearing deliveries and news to the Kwakiutl settlements that stretched for several hundred miles on both sides of the Queen Charlotte Straits. Stefan, remembering the winters of his childhood, knew the difference and reminded Giraud that so did he. "It won't last, Giraud. By tomorrow morning it will have stopped. It's lumpy mush. Go out and see. And it's not even cold."

"All the same. All the same," Giraud replied, the words vindictive, the tone even. "It *vraiment trop. La neige. Maintenant. Trop. Trop.*" It was understandable. Usually it started snowing there in late September and snowed off and on until March. Then the temperature would rise slowly, moving beyond freezing during March and up to thirty-five, sometimes forty or even fifty, by the time the cutter launch began its six-month season up the coast, twelve circuits annually, each two weeks up and back, with two, three days at the Catholic Mission near Margaret Bay at the border between the Kwakiutl and the Owikeno tribes, which shared the flange of land that descended into the sea. When Giraud reached that point, signaling to the weather tower above the last settlement, he'd put in for the night with the Mission, get back his land legs, and then walk off into the forest where, he insisted, his work awaited him. After his mysterious furlough ended, he would return to the Mission, covered with little bags of berries and herbs, and several lengths of unstripped red cedar he wished to carve.

Old Giraud liked to carve, he told Stefan Mauger when the question of Stefan's work came up. Giraud didn't know what sculpture was. It was a word that had no echo in his language, but when Stefan said he made up animals or better still when he struggled to explain how sculptors try to make what's inside the wood and stone come out, to express what it feels like to be given a certain kind of grain or vein, Giraud understood perfectly, his crow's feet creasing to tiptoes as he nodded vigorously. "Me get it," he announced definitively and went to the other room where he tugged out from under the bed a battered suitcase strapped with leathern thongs. He was very excited as he undid them and opened the case. What it contained was not immediately visible, for it, too, was wrapped in a striped poncho also tied with thongs. He carefully undid each of these, circling them one after another around his finger, all the while cradling the hidden contents, until at last, lifting the poncho from its painted face, he remarked matter-of-factly: "Great-great-grandfather. Mine. Very long ago. Two, three hundred years, yes."

What Giraud meant was immediately clear. The curious statue of his great-great-grandfather, come back to this world in the guise of a seal, had no need of the carver's art to reveal his glorious tongue, for a swath of darker-grained wood, interior to the tree section from which it had been cut, was perfectly employed by Giraud, ridged at the edges where it lightened, shaped and gouged to the interior sightless region from which it had emerged and dropped into

208

grotesqueness, becoming the creator fish which descended to the navel of the little effigy. "A marvelous invention," Stefan saluted, taking Giraud's hand and shaking it with passion. But these compliments meant little to old Giraud, who only replied, "All great-great-grandfathers same like this. All from great seal. Not same with you?"

As the launch approached the settlement, shrouded in the mists of the coast, old Giraud became suddenly agitated. He began a curious dance before the steering wheel, his eyes barely visible in the reflector mirror, his lips pressed together in concentration. After some minutes he cut the motor far out in the bay, maybe nine hundred yards from the landing dock that swayed ominously in the wind, and motioned to his two passengers, who had been standing on deck peering into the mist struggling to make out the village, to step down into the cabin. Giraud waved them peremptorily to a bench and seated himself before them on the wooden floor of the launch, his legs drawn up under his chin.

"My name not really Giraud. You guess that. Me Kwakiutl, great-great-grandson of the seal. My father was French trapper who came and went. He gave me to my Kwakiutl mother. When he died he gave me his name, a good rifle (which I sold long ago), and a letter to the old priest up north at the Mission who taught me French and English. I old Kwakiutl (more than seventy now I think) and I know many, many things. Good Kwakiutl. Sometimes bad Kwakiutl. Do bad things. This my village. Young girl here who work for priest—she my granddaughter. Her father—my son—and mother, good woman, killed in rock slide when she little baby. I gave her to Mission. She work for priest. Now that Giraud's story." Carried on the tide, the vessel moved toward the coast but Giraud ignored the steering wheel, beginning to speak again after a few minutes of silence during which his eyes remained closed. "Now listen to Giraud. We come to land now. Last word. You watch your step. You make carve. Good! Watch how my people make carve, but no steal from them. No steal from them. All right? Many white man come here steal things. When I was little boy they come steal skins and fish. Now they come steal ancestor poles. We weak now. No potlatch. We weak. But I tell you, Mister. There be potlatch deep inside where white man not walk. You see potlatch, but you no steal from us. Giraud friend to you, but he be mean Kwakiutl when mad." Giraud finished, expelling his warning words with much emphasis, the face impassive, although his hands sometimes took the words from his mouth, cupping them and throwing them at Stefan and Alicia where they were received with fascination and worry. Giraud's admonitory confession confirmed what Stefan had already sensed: there was much hidden in Giraud's otherwise frank and open generosity toward them. He had kept them well for the ten days they had spent with him, giving them room and breakfast, allowing them several times to cook a makeshift stew, which he ate with enthusiasm, permitting Alicia to clean up and make the beds while Stefan walked around Nanaimo in the morning, laying out the general path the two would explore together in the afternoons. But on the very last day of their stay, before the unwanted snow had passed and the cutter launch was being readied for its spring departure, Stefan had asked Giraud to see the seal effigy again. Stefan had made the mistake of asking Giraud to see his "carving of the seal figure." Giraud looked at him, his lids curving downward, his eyes filled with a sudden sadness. "Wrong name, Mister. You no see. You no understand. Bad mistake. That thing not seal. That great-great-grandfather. You name him bad. When you see him, he seal. When he hides, he my ancestor. You get it. Things change. Not everything the way you think. Things change. You get that straight."

It still wasn't clear, but Giraud had said all he intended to say and that was that. It left Stefan and Alicia with something of foreboding, as though they were missing a critical turn in the path, which, like missed road directions, might lead to desert waste rather than the springwater clarity they had purposed. But Giraud offered no further explanation and they never saw the seal effigy again. And now, drifting on a light current toward an unknown land, they were being warned about elaborate crimes against the Kwakiutl nation and promised mysterious punishments should they transgress. And the potlatch? And the old man with the inexpressive face who alluded to the knowledge of deep matters no white man with millennia of civilization in his memory could claim? The usually inquisitive Stefan Mauger was silent when they parted, and Alicia Mauger solemnly shook hands with Giraud after he had handed down their stuffed duffle, the camera case, and the old suitcase filled with warm trousers and thick wool shirts and sweaters. They planned to stay three, four weeks, until Giraud descended a second time from his rounds. As it turned out they stayed much longer, a whole season in fact from April, that is, until Giraud's last trip that fall. They might have stayed even longer, having all along fantasied how they would stand up against the sleeting rains, lowering mists, and snows of the region, had it not been for what Stefan insisted, despite the evidence, had been really an encounter with a ferocious bear.

It all began—if that is what this seems to be, an ordinary story with beginnings and conclusions—the very day of their arrival in the village to which none referred by name (nor in the mapmaker's art had it been identified and marked with signifying dot upon the inland crook in the arm of land that bent around a forest rise behind which rose several ranges of spruce- and cedar-covered hillocks). The village, if that is what it is, perhaps for that reason defying the obligation of name and solidity of naming, had less than a dozen houses in which the principal families of the settlement made their residence: on one rise, the family of the great bear hunter Nauka and his wife and children, and their wives and husbands, in all a large family cared for by a formidable sodality of old women and servants, occupying a vast lodge subdivided with skins and hangings; on the other, the rise that turned southward toward Nanaimo, stood another lodge, distinguished from Nauka's by the artfulness of its decoration, its assertion of endless variety and invention, each plank of its structure yielding to the carver and painter's hand a field for imagining and devising, not a single image or a sufficient totem, but a complexity of interconnection, whole fields of animals, whose histories— if they could be read—rose from heads, emerged from ears, dropped from mouths, grew from all the bellies and anuses of the world, until one was amazed that the lodge and its small tributary lean-tos and outhuts were ever finished to be occupied, so complex was the carving, the workmanship, and the colors in which they were disguised. These latter, situated on a planted hillock, which in contrast to the muddy mount of Nauka seemed ready to show the rich green of spring, were the sprawling domicile of the family of fishermen and planters called Shunesh. In all, the two families and their lodges numbered more or less seventy people. These and the few others (strays adopted into the clans of Nauka and Shunesh) and the forest Indians unseen by the coastal eye, made up the congregation of the priest, a Salesian missionary father, whose own rooms and church occupied a lodge stripped to yellow sap wood, undecorated but for a sequence of crosses, thorn crowns, dove birds, fish, and other emblems that Father Benno had undertaken to burn into the wood with a heated poker the second month after his arrival in the north. But that had been more than ten years ago. The emblems had weathered, the lodges of the principal families were worn but well repaired and beneath them at the lowest level of the ascent, a dozen feet above the ocean, were several smaller huts whose inhabitants tended to the dock, kept the fishing boats in repair, worked in the general store where on cold nights Indians from the interior slept in a sprawl or, as now, in the time of thaw, met to stare and smile at Stefan and Alicia Mauger who had just arrived among them.

"I am Father Benno," the voice announced, and a rough hand lightly tapped Stefan's shoulder.

"We're grateful for a voice we understand. Won't you sit with us and have another coffee?"

"I have coffee enough for all of us," the priest replied firmly but not impolitely. "You and your wife will stay with me. I have quarters for visitors. No bath, but ample bed. Out back there's a latrine of sorts and once a week the Indians let us use their sauna in the forest. Very healthy. Very simple." Father Benno gathered up their belongings and opened the door, nodding first to the Indians, none of whom came forward to help him. Stefan reached into his pocket for change to put on the table, but Father Benno called back. "Not now. At the end. Before you leave, I'll tell you what you owe. Take whatever you want. Even if no one's here in the store, take what you want. They always know who takes what. Sensible procedure. No one takes what they don't need and there's nothing here that isn't needed by someone. Since they know everyone's needs, what's left over is charged to me and I'll charge you." He smiled warmly and led them down the steps into the mud.

They climbed straight up a path toward Father Benno's lodge, clean and orderly as a worker's house, nothing free-spirited, nothing carved or native. It was, as the Indian girl later explained to Stefan, just what the Indians thought of the white man—"clean and bare." They adopted the assumption from the huts they had seen nearly a century earlier when the railroad was built through the Canadian wilderness and the Chinese and Central European workmen had been put up in easily forsaken wooden shacks, brought out on flatbeds almost prefabricated for cheap construction and inexpensive abandonment. The Indians copied the way they thought the white man lived, but only for the white man. Everything that made the priest's lodge intimate and warm was Father Benno's doing, from the graven emblemata to the furniture—sturdy and unadorned, but clarifying the Calabrian ancestry of the red-haired priest who had grown up in the cramped toe of the Italian boot and had learned to do woodwork and carpentry to earn something for his large family. His being sent among the Kwakiutl, he explained ruefully, was modeled upon the wisdom of the U.S. Army during the war. If thousands of pairs of tennis sneakers and shuttlecocks could be sent to the recreation centers of the Aleutians, the Salesian Fathers can send a Mediterranean child to the fasts of the north. "It may be the case that the Americans couldn't play badminton on the ice drifts, but I think I have done well among the Kwakiutl. I like them at least, and what's more, admire them, and more than this, I've learned a great deal from them. It's made me, if not a better Christian, at least a more curious one."

Father Benno and Stefan Mauger were sitting at the dinner table finishing a large fish soup, soaking up the remains with lumps of corn bread and talking into the early morning. The priest was obviously overjoyed to have visitors.

The Indian girl (her black hair festively plaited and wound with a colored ribbon she had not worn earlier on the docks or in the general store) had gone off early to sleep in a room off the kitchen, and Alicia, weary and unnerved by Giraud's parting admonitions, followed her shortly thereafter.

"Ten years you've been here? Astonishing. Don't you get cabin fever?"

"Not often. Not often. I had a leave about two years ago, which was to have lasted three months. Originally I thought of going home to Calabria and visiting with what remains of my family, but a week before I was to leave Vancouver for the flight to Montreal, word came of some trouble in this area and I came back. Never wanted to leave again."

"Trouble? What kind of trouble?"

Father Benno ignored the question, stood up from the table, and went to a cupboard where he kept his pipe and tobacco and occupied himself some minutes filling the bowl and lighting it. But Stefan was aware that the decision to smoke was an evasion of his question, and he repeated: "What trouble?"

"Nothing very serious, but I'd rather not discuss it."

"You know, Father, you're the second person today who seems to be warning me to stay off what isn't my business."

"Yes? Well then, shouldn't you listen to us?"

"You know the other one."

"Of course. Isn't it obvious? Giraud. Couldn't be anyone else. And we both have our reasons for putting you off, even though our reasons converge."

"Converge, do they? It becomes more and more mysterious."

"Doesn't it?" Father Benno laughed, amused by the intricacy of the situation but still serious and unyielding. "The truth is we are both putting you on guard for religious reasons, for reasons of his religion and mine, and as you may

215

suspect they're not the same religions. Giraud, my friend (and this I tell you and it is all I tell you), is a kind of priest in their religion. It's one of the reasons he loves his work. He's a real missionary, unlike me. He wanders in search of his flock up and down the coast. I wait for them to come to me. He agitates that his faith be witnessed and all I do is offer witness, very passively, very quietly to mine. Naturally we're in combat, mortal combat if you will, but still respectful of each other. Put another way, I respect him because I choose to respect him and he is obliged to respect me, because he's an Indian and I'm a missionary protected by the government. I think it's a dirty piece of business, but that's the way it is. Not at all like Elijah and the priests of Baal. But then the difference is that his faith is so direct and primary and my own, by comparison, so immensely sophisticated—even though I myself am a fairly stupid man—I think I would lose if we had to put out fires by faith."

"But why me and my wife? Why the suspicion of us?"

"Not you or your wife particularly. Any visitor would be treated the same way. We don't have many, you know. An occasional government official, a university medical team, or an itinerant anthropologist who knows no Kwakiutl. Not many more. All very boring by and large. Old Giraud doesn't bother them, but people like yourselves, husband and wife, artists, with cameras and sketching notebooks, and particularly you, a sculptor, that suggests a different sort of thing."

"And which sort would that be?"

"Well, how should I put it. They believe, for instance (and it's only one example) that when you take a photograph you steal their face. The fact that when the shutter has clicked their face has not in fact vanished, that when the picture is made and they examine it, their own face persists, does not prevent them from believing that you have stolen it and that only by the efficient working of their own magic are they able to get it back. They're already in the forest making ready for your visit."

Stefan laughed, flattered, but nonetheless concerned, since he was visible to all the Indians, but they—with the exception of Giraud and perhaps the Indian girl whom he knew to be his granddaughter—were obscured by the generic nomenclature of Indian, which prevented him from identifying persons, naming those who were benign and those of whom he should be wary. "And need I be afraid?"

"Not really. They won't harm you physically. That's not their way, but they will—if they become unnerved—attempt to frighten you, to blunt your anger by the monstrosity of their own."

"Anger? What anger, Father Benno? Why do you single out what you call my anger?"

"I have no right to discuss these things. They're certainly not my business, but dealing as I do with these odd natives of mine who speak little, who show their emotion not by face but by body, by odd little finger gestures and the movement of their arms in relation to chest and stomach, I am acutely aware of everything that the body does, how it speaks. And yours could not be more rigid, more unyielding, in a word, more angry. You are angry, aren't you, Mr. Mauger?"

"You astonish me, Father Benno. No. I won't deny it. Were I a man of ordinary pride, I would deny all you say, accuse you of stupid chattering, even pull the rank of age or accomplishment, but I can't because you're right. I am angry and for the most foolish of reasons, I suppose. I can't get it right! Not my life, not my work. I can imagine the perfection, sometimes dreaming it so accurately, so precisely I can almost touch it, but at the very moment when I come to say it—to work it out with my chisel or my knife or the rubbing edge of my thumb—it resists, everything gives way, and matter triumphs over spirit, remaining formless, the void, chaos before God first began to speak over the waters. Do you understand what that means? To have worked at sculpture now for two decades, to have made a hundred works and destroyed a hundred more, and to know that not a single work is right, that the vision is right here— just behind the eyes—and that as hard as I've tried to force it beyond the eyes into the horizon where the artist works it out, I have failed. Of course I'm angry, sometimes so angry I could die, or as I'm doing now—forgive me—raising my voice at three in the morning."

"But instead of dying, you've come here, more than four thousand miles from New York, twice that from where you were born. And why? Because they do effortlessly what you've been trying all along to do—to make the essential forms animate in carving. But, let me tell you something, my friend, that isn't at all what they think they're carving and so far you've seen nothing. I'll take you one day to the totem field and you'll see carving that touches the hem of the universe. It works for them because they think that what they do is the only way to do it. The role of talent, ingenuity, novelty (everything that makes your world of art hum) is for them simply the need to adapt the stories as they remember them. Talent, genius? Meaningless! Accuracy and truthfulness in telling the great forms: everything. Actually they're not as good carvers as their ancestors were, because thirty, forty years ago it was even more difficult. Then they still carved with bone implements and the colors took months to make from saps and grasses and berries. In those days, the thinking process was longer, the great myths were without alternative from people like myself, the forms were everywhere, and the carving was utterly profound because the thing that emerged under the knife was as real as the imagination decreed it. Now? It's faster, less reflective; the categories a bit more uncertain, the alternatives vivid, the tribal strength less secure. And hence, the carving will not make you quite as angry. It will leave you with some hope. And, with those comforting words, I have to go to bed. I say Mass tomorrow for the fishing fleet of the village. Tonight their own benedictions are being said out there in the forest where I am not permitted to go after sundown."

It was not far from dawn when they broke off their conversation. The blue black of the night was shattered by a soundless crack of white that appeared suddenly in the distance, far beyond the arm that Stefan stretched out into the darkness from the open window of his room, saluting the deep of the forest, the singing that he could not hear, the wordless totems telling stories in the claustral field within the wood, acknowledging unseen eyes that surely watched him.

The days that followed the Maugers' arrival among the Kwakiutl were indistinguishable. Not that they were boring or uneventful. It was rather that the habitual conventions which define the usages of civilization no longer applied. There were, for one thing, no clocks or watches in the village and so it happened that, forgetting to wind his watch before going to sleep, Stefan awakened to find it had stopped. Sighting the sun in its relation to the horizon he reset the watch and promptly ignored it, for no one asked the time, no one consulted its legislation, no appointments were made or broken on its basis, and so after several days Stefan Mauger put his watch away and forgot the matter of time. He and Alicia, moreover, found themselves compassed by terrain more than by time; it delighted them, in fact, this charmed indifference to proper times and right moments. Those early weeks after their arrival, they spent walking long distances through forests and along the coast, following the spruce ridge behind the village, until out of sight of the smoke of its fires they would settle into making their own, some days not returning to Father Benno until dawn or even late the following day, carrying only their sleeping rolls and simple provisions for soup made thick with potatoes or a chunk of lard. They would watch for hours in a blind the sporting of seals at the edge of the ocean, or climbing an ancient pine find in their sights all the animals of the forest clambering by, smelling their odor, but unmindful, moving off to find their own provender. And the Indians, those other inhabitants of the forest, were everywhere, as ubiquitous as its wildlife, sometimes gathered into small interior settlements of three or four lodges, or scattered distances a mile or so apart, keeping their lives separate and private, stringing lines into the forest from which salmon hung to cure in the air, and tending to vegetable gardens cleared near lodges crafted of cedar logs and stretched skins. For the Maugers it was their own suspended time, season beyond seasons, just married and come to the wilderness of their world in celebration, an intervening whorl inserted into the vortex of time, protected like a cocoon, while the ordinary forces of erosion continued to abrade their exterior; within, of course, caterpillar becomes butterfly, Stefan Mauger and Alicia Lurçat become husband and wife, become integer without unity, and beyond even that transformation (since the butterfly cannot become caterpillar again without dying), having joined together, separate once more.

Giraud had come and gone twice. A month had passed. It was May and beginning to warm up; trees had put out leaves, the forest was flowering, mushrooms were everywhere. Giraud had come and gone twice, but the second time had stayed to eat at Father Benno's table; Alicia had made him a rabbit stew, which he savored, licking his fingers when the bread was exhausted. With all they had come to know of him, Stefan and Alicia treated him somewhat differently than they had previously, regarding him no longer as a simple Indian who could be talked about and around, indifferent to his actual presence, but with circumspection and solicitude, having accepted from Father Benno that he was an eminence with secret powers. It was at the end of the meal, shortly before he was to leave, that Father Benno asked Giraud if he thought the time had come to show Stefan and Alicia the totem field. Giraud looked at them both, peering intently at their faces, already weathered and tanned from their time outdoors, and after some reflection, nodded affirmatively. His granddaughter, the young Indian girl with the long black hair, stood at Giraud's side throughout the meal, eating where she stood, removing the plates, washing them and restoring them heaped with different vegetables. Her eyes moved about the table, watching Father Benno whom she clearly respected, her relative Giraud whom she well knew to be a habitant—beyond gentleness and affection—of a region where simple generosities were able to move trees and shift boulders, to Alicia whom she thought strange and unfamiliar, although in some dim canon of estimation, carved with pleasing orderliness, to Stefan Mauger whom her eyes circled and evaded, casting down when he looked up, aware as they both were, as they both had been, of each other's presence from the very first. It was agreed that the following day Father Benno and the Indian girl would accompany the Maugers upon their walk to the totem field. Stefan had expressed particular curiosity about its location, since during the month they had been in the village they had walked continually in its environs, covering an area probably ten miles in circumference. "You've passed it countless times,"

Father Benno asserted laughing, "but it's concealed with great subtlety."

"At one time, not," the girl contributed, "but some time during past fifteen years—when I was baby girl—they think to hide it away from what Indians call 'poor sight.' "

It was Alicia who asked her to say her name. It was Sahué. They had heard the priest call her by the name; they had never learned it. It was a lovely name, but to master it they asked that she write it for them. The writing was labored and difficult, but when it was finished Father Benno congratulated Sahué on her script. "She was sick for much of her childhood and only recently she's started school again with me. We do English—even though Giraud thinks she should learn French, but there are so few French around here and most of them are trappers—and numbers and religion. In a few years when she's old enough, she'll go back to the Mission School if she wants and learn a trade— the brothers teach them some useful things, but it's still a European notion of what women need to survive among men and not a very accurate register of what an Indian woman needs to survive as an Indian. What do you think, Sahué?"

"Not leave you, Father Benno, unless you send Sahué." The girl said this with obvious feeling, although it was clearly a cruel game in which Father Benno continued to prepare the girl for the inevitable departure and Sahué responded with a charming, but obligatory, resistance. Her eyes had filled with tears, but Father Benno kissed her forehead and reassured her. "Not for a time yet. Don't worry, Sahué."

The next day was unseasonably chilly; a fog had come in during the night and dropped over the village. Advancing in the mud, one thought to pull at one's face to remove it, but the fog hung close as breath, and only by holding a battery torch low, near the ground, where the fog made room for the heat of the earth, were they able to find the path upward and out of the village, beyond the rim of the forest, down into the next valley, four miles off, where the fog had not penetrated. There, not fog, but early morning mists prevailed. Father Benno had taken Sahué's arm; behind them, Stefan and Alicia, with camera and equipment, moved forward toward a coniferous wall—young scrub trees near the path and rising beyond them, taller and taller trees, graduated in height suggesting a mountain rise, but all densely packed and impenetrable. At a certain point the path that they had been following appeared to break off, leading as it did into the seemingly impassable density of forest, only to resume more sensibly a few feet away, directing the commonplace traveler upward and in a different direction from the pine forest. It was here, in fact, that a complex lattice of boughs parted with ease, the bottom yielding to Sahué's grip, the others following, untangling and pulling apart, as though the old trees had grown together by happenstance, rather than design, and behind them other trees, more than a dozen, placed and rooted in such a way as to conceal a well-trod footpath that led further into the forest. Emerging from the wood they entered the valley of the totems, beyond which was the graveyard of this Kwakiutl tribe.

Stefan Mauger gasped.

It was an unequaled presentation. Different by magnitudes from the monuments of Stonehenge or the Greek and Roman architecture of Southern Europe, or (he numerated in his head, counting up the experiences which resembled the totem field without overwhelming it) the Brancusi emplacement at Tirgu-Jiu. The carved wood trunks, reaching upward like an endless column, although each had an origin, middle, end (and hence were finite), were nonetheless circular, beginning at any point, read in spirals up and down, down and up, or read from bottom to top and then down again on the other side, or wherever the eye fell—upon tail of lizard or mouth of bear or heron's beak, the eye continued the narration, disclosing to the memorial function of unmasking that before the eye is no bird, insect, animal, but leader, parent, child, wizard, trickster, each of whom has told his totem beads, each recalling to the knowing eye an aspect of the immemorial past of yesterdays and millennia ago, indifferent to measurable time, telling the ancient inheritance of nows and forevers, and even if, not knowing their significance (as did Sahué who stood before one small and modest carving, her head bowed away from the white men around her, wondering whether they recognized beneath the red forehead furrow and triangulated eyebrows the lineaments of her dead father, son of Giraud, the shaman of the tribe), they walked slowly through the totem field, threading themselves through the small passageways that marked at some points the extreme density and packedness of images, three four totems, jammed together so that they breathed upon each other and made passage through and about them impossible.

Stefan lost himself in the totem field. The forty-three poles reached various heights, some striplings of nine feet, while the most ancient were the most immense, weathered of color, making do in grandeur by massiveness, thirty feet or more as the eye estimated, surmounted by a hooded bird (the Rumanian cupola that cradled a broken divinity passed quickly before his eyes) whose claws held fast the frog face of sagging jaws and bulbous eyes, drained down to the serene and gentle bear paws that almost touched the earth, flattened as though waiting patiently its feeding, holding as by air, a wizened Indian, all eyes and lips, beneficently enchanted before being lifted and engorged. All these, a thousand sights of telling, telling ancient truths again and again, motifs repeated but with renewed vigor, for all men have mouths and eyes, and all beasts succor and destroy, but each effigy changes, each animal has spirit, and the narratives were made over centuries, "over many years, many years," Sahué said in a low voice, saturated with wonder, leading Stefan by the wrist from the small pole that Giraud had made for her dead father and mother throughout the sinuous paths that threaded oddly from the central pole in figures of eight, ballooning to include whole clusters and then, following a path whose logic was obscure, to the outer rim where Father Benno watched Sahué and Alicia observed Stefan, padding for hours through the Kwakiutl totem field.

"It's come together for me," Stefan said as they walked slowly back to the village in the late afternoon. "Every day I must go there. Every day, without fail."

Strangely excited, as though some obscure and livid fire had touched him, Stefan became ill upon his return to the priest's house. Ill with excitement, ill with his anger, ill with pleasure, feeling the fingers of Sahué lightly encircling his wrist, as though not touching him, but touching him no less profoundly, explaining to him with small words and incomplete phrases something that she knew which he had never known, but for which he had been searching—in the Louvre, with Monsieur Leiris at the Musée de l'Homme, in the bleak corner of the Montparnasse Cemetery, among his masked death's heads, in Tirgu-Jiu—but until then had never learned. Sublime, carve sublime. The reaching to sublimity could either be done if one had been (like the wood) weathered and stripped to nakedness beneath beauty, where all is the grain of seasons without time, knowing no history or civilization except the place where the ancient gods planted paradise; or else the carving is made such that the ripple of artifice never shows upon the surface where everything is borne—life and death—indifferently.

Stefan Mauger did not visit the totem field again for three days; the fever passed, the anger returned like a pit jammed in his windpipe. Alicia had left his bedside to have late tea with Father Benno, to whom she had drawn closer, and Sahué brought a damp cloth to wipe Stefan's face and a bowl of soup she had made with forest herbs, which "grandfather Giraud showed me after my father and mother had died and," she added, smiling and embarrassed by her knowledge of civilization, "became poles in the field."

It was more the case, despite Alicia's misunderstanding and Father Benno's insistence upon betrayed hospitality, that Sahué had construed a love for Stefan Mauger well before his own curiosity, intensified by carnal imagination, had brought them together. Sahué, sent away at the end by Father Benno (although he promised she could return to his service when she had thought out her penance), and Stefan Mauger, revised by terror, were the consummations of judgments prepared and executed in the absence of either witnesses or confessions, for Stefan Mauger denied that they were lovers in the ordinary sense and Sahué, having no notion of such ordinariness, contended that she loved the fair stranger without ever being asked (all being enraged, none being prurient) in what the action of her love consisted. It was enough that a girl, not yet seventeen years, slender and graceful, erect and grave, black hair plaited with flowers that descended below her boy's buttocks, breasts indited but invisible beneath a chaste gingham dress, should have encircled the heart of an older man, more than willing to imagine that anyone with secret information to impart—whether poet wife or Indian child—deserved succor and caress. What, finally, did it matter, that Sahué believed she loved the sculptor and to him, day after day, walking in the mountains and to the totem fields, she confided all that she knew of her childhood and helped him work the cameras, while Alicia wrote and threw away poems, becoming daily more sad. It would come to an end, she reassured herself. Sahué would remain behind; Stefan and Alicia would leave, probably never to return. And so, why did it matter to the Indians that a joy beyond propriety had come to Sahué and longing beyond carnality had returned to Stefan Mauger.

"It's only that I've come too late, that's all," Stefan tried to explain to Alicia when they sat one evening on the bluff over the ocean talking of the confusion of their days. The bluff had hardened; the mud was gone, baked and settled in the sun; the ice was no longer visible, drifting like becalmed monsters beneath waters greening now with driftwood and scales of gleaming fish that swam in the shoals like currents that carried reports of other water worlds into their own. August, dead-weight time, but no somnolence here, busy with preparation for the autumn the Indians predicted would come early; incomplete thaw, already making ready to congeal. "Too late. Lateness in beginning, lateness in finding, and now, hurrying everything, hurrying to do the work before my own congealment." A bar of ice, running with warm waters, bobbed in the distance, rose and sank, like a dead fish that had come to surface for a final gasp of air only then to disappear into the deeps. "That's all it means, Alicia. You? You are the double for my life, but doubles aren't all. We're permanent, but permanence even in life has the smell of eternity about it, eternity and death, but no immortality. And it's that, damn foolishness, I itch to have, an immortal ingredient that survives beyond fame and credulous acceptance. Sahué tells me things that I can't determine for myself. She is part of the inheritance of their imaginings; she is the flesh carving that they turn in wood.

227

We have nothing like that in our world. Benno wanted to know the first evening why I'd traveled, four thousand, ten thousand miles to find this and it's precisely because at the rim of our civilization (up here and alone) is a small nameless village where everything ancient is current. Not like the poor Navahos who make their figure dolls and sand paintings more and more to please us—turning them out with store paints. They're dying—those Indians—without a chance. Here they're dying differently. More slowly. The weather isn't right for tourists and summer houses; no impetus to put on culture festivals and folk dances for the white man's pittance. Even though Sahué goes to Mass and says everything that Benno needs to hear, she still knows how to listen to trees and wind; she hears odd things that Giraud taught her to understand. It's no practical wisdom she has. They know all that sort of thing without any special training. We're always so amazed that Indians can read weather and tell if an animal is wounded from its paw prints, but that's no secret information. Anyone who has so much repetition to observe and lives the observation will learn as much. Nature is only a secret to romantics who take it as a rush and then turn back to books and fireplaces. For these Indians, it's nothing special. Whenever I ask Sahué how she knows where the bird keeps its nest or why this season the beaver seems to have such thick fur, she smiles at me. It's no surprise to her. None at all. It's no mystery. The reasons are simple. It's only that we don't look at nature in detail. We treat it like a museum landscape—all grandeur and expanse—rush by clucking with astonishment that God can work such wonders. But our wonder, unlike theirs, is for the overall effect. They worry the details; it's in the details that their gods live." Stefan looked out over the bluff into the distance of the ocean where vast objects moved as specks upon the horizon, rising and plummeting; his head rested on raised knees; his hand, weary of brushing back the hair that blew down over his eyes, came to rest on Alicia's shoulder. She had said nothing. She had not interrupted, but was comforted by his hand which gripped her shoulder, strengthening her by its attentiveness and drawing her closer to him.

"Stefan, my love, all this I understand. I understand. But the girl? The girl is still beautiful. She's no natural dumb show, there, like any other detail to be observed. You hold her. You pass your hands over her breasts. You have kissed her good night as no daughter is kissed to sleep."

He lowered his arm to her waist and turned her body toward him; he kissed her as he had kissed Sahué, kissing her eyes and passing his hands over her face like falling leaves. Not gentleness with the determination to be gentle, but the caring of hands that shape as they caress. Immensity of attention in his hands, Stefan wanted to assure his wife that she was deeply loved, even if at that moment and for some weeks to come he would withhold himself.

"I can't explain more. It will come to an end."

Behind them, coming down the path, Sahué approached almost soundlessly. At the very last, a pebble leapt from her path and dropped over the side of the bluff into the water. Stefan saw the pebble, turned his head, and his hand left Alicia's shoulder and grasped the ankle of Sahué who stood above them, laughing. "A forest walk before supper?" she asked quietly and they both rose and walked with her. Sahué moved between them. Alicia, suddenly aware that the beauty of the child—indifferent radiance—was meant for her as well, crossed her arm over Stefan's and joined in circling Sahué's waist. They became three and it was easier.

Only Father Benno, removed by holy paternity from the festivity of their affection, smoldered uncomfortably. He was a good and conscientious priest, but he was young, not that far removed from tempestuous childhood, however much he was restrained and disciplined to be unsusceptible to carnal impulses recorded now only in dream and reverie. Sadly, he punished these, disappearing into the small whitewashed chapel to upbraid himself and apologize. But, although he made apologies to God and excuses to himself, he despised the easy habit of his visitors' days and the seduction into waywardness that he imagined they had enforced upon his charge. Sahué he punished by harassment, complaining about her cooking, noticing areas of floor that had gone unwashed, remarking crumbs beneath their eating table, demanding that the vegetables be better cleaned. But worse than all these, he threatened her daily with being sent away, no longer postponing to some vague and distant time her return to the Mission, but threatening gruffly that the time was coming soon, if she didn't do her duty. He knew that he was jealous of all their freedom and their indifference, their careless days, uncharged by obligation and vow. They had no cause like his and his words to them became more harsh, his impatience with their presence more obvious. He longed to reclaim his empty house, empty of laughter, empty of conversation, empty of long looks and touching hands that made every surface bristle like aroused skin.

It was during the first week in September, several days before Giraud was to return on his last journey up the coast, that Father Benno announced at supper, aware that the event would shatter the casual rhythm of their wandering days, "There's to be a potlatch at week's end." Stefan, surprised, looked at Sahué, who averted her eyes, for she had mentioned nothing of it.

"They will not be welcome," Sahué said slowly, but without antagonism.

"But why, Sahué?" Stefan asked.

"It for us only. Not for white man. Not for outsider. Not for you two." The rudeness showed, but it was uncertain. Sahué often spoke with an apparent ferocity, English being a language constructed by her as single words somehow strung upon the thread of an idea without attention to stress and movement. It sounded resentful, but it may not have been.

Father Benno knew the difficulty, but he was determined that they should not be spared. Of course if he attended, he would be as deeply compromised as the Maugers, more so, since as priest of the village he was obligated to maintain distance between the ceremonies of the tribe's people and established order, which he represented. But more serious still, since such distinctions hardly mattered two hundred miles from the nearest eccelesiastical community of the Mission, was the fact that the potlatch was outlawed. The government, under pressure from the trading companies which had acquired rights to the handicraft of the territory in the nineteenth century, had secured the prohibition of the potlatch, since by its very nature this ceremony of con-sumption literally destroyed the goods on which their com-merce depended. And Father Benno, not only priest but servitor of the government, *de facto* arm of civility and hence of law, was required by his informal privilege to re-port the imminent outbreak of potlatch to the authorities that it might be suppressed. But he had laughed to himself when he reflected on this duty. To whom would he report? There was no telephone. The wireless was at the Mission station, and who would bring the message? The employee of the government, old Giraud? Old Giraud would un-doubtedly be present himself at the ceremony. Old Giraud would dance and celebrate, say the words, cut the cord (if that's what they did) to start the festivities, light the fire more probably. Old Giraud? Would he say to old Giraud: "Take this message to the north, open throttle, no intermediate stops, go straight to the Mission and report the potlatch. Send the Mounties." How ludicrous! Old Giraud would smile his incomprehensible smile and say nothing. Father Benno had discussed the potlatch with old Giraud many times and he would calmly assert that its passing was the death of the Kwakiutl. The government had suppressed the potlatch thirty years ago, sending in the Mounties, putting out the fires where they had started, imprisoning the chiefs and headmen. No more potlatch. "You can't burn property," they asserted. "The Doukhobors can't run naked and burn down their houses and you people can't burn up your wealth. Why do you do it, Indians?" Father Benno didn't know, but he expected that it was as strange to the Indians that he held aloft a chalice of wine and tasteless wafer and made strange contentions about the power of transforming words. They accepted his contention; he was willing to accept theirs. Young priest, just past thirty-four now, but already weary of arguing points, Father Benno had grown to love his community. He had claimed all of them as Catholics when the census had been made several years earlier, but he didn't care. The important matter to him was that his presence had meant from time to time that the sick had come and he had saved some from dying, and others, alongside the medicine man and the old woman with her stinking pot of herbal brew, he had eased into dying. None of the terms were the same; none had the same value —life, death, kindness, loyalty, sickness, and transgression. He said one thing, they another; he spoke, they nodded; they prayed and he stood to one side. Being a priest, he believed, was at its finest a task of smoothing the way, picking up a stone in the path and putting down pine boughs to make the going less arduous, less unnecessarily arduous.

"No, no, Sahué. It will be fine. They will want me there and I will bring our guests. They know them by now. They've all watched you in the forest and seen you in the totem field."

Stefan raised an eyebrow. He had hardly ever seen an Indian when they'd walked in the forest. "Yes?" he inquired incredulously.

"Of course, of course. They watch to make certain you behave. Isn't that so, Sahué? Don't they watch? And of course to protect Sahué."

"From us?" Alicia joined, enchanted by the notion.

"Certainly. You think that you are thought of beneficently, walking along, arms entwined like the ribbons of a Maypole. No. No. You may not know it, my friends, but this child here, this Sahué, is Giraud's granddaughter and he is the shaman of the tribe. They are under charge from him to guard her."

"Well, that explains it, doesn't it, Alicia," Stefan announced. "Although I have no idea what a shaman is or does, I'll take it at your word, Father Benno, that it's an awesome personage who guards this child." He smiled at Sahué, who turned away, embarrassed.

"But Father, you know it not good, they come to potlatch. Nauka not like them. He think they take pictures too much."

"Was that Nauka, the big fellow with the painted hat we saw yesterday standing on the ridge when we passed?"

"Yes, that was Nauka. And he doesn't like you. He thinks it isn't right that you hold hands with Sahué. And for that matter, neither do I."

"I'm surprised at you, Father Benno. The last thing I thought was that you'd take offense. She's a child, for God's sake. What do you take me for?" Stefan laughed and turned to Alicia for agreement, but she pretended to watch an ant hobbled with an enormous speck of bread walking across the table. "In all seriousness, I am respectful of Sahué. I love her beauty and respect her unpreparedness. More than that is irrelevant. I have nothing to defend or to explain." Stefan stood up from the table, folded his napkin ceremoniously, angered by Father Benno's reproof.

"Whatever it is, I am sure your presence at the potlatch would be welcomed. The guilty never appear and if they think you guilty, they will take your presence as proof of innocence. And so come, my friends, come if you are innocent. Of course, you're innocent and so you will come to the potlatch. I needn't add—no photographs."

It was to be the first potlatch in more than ten years. The last one in the region had occurred only a few years after Father Benno's arrival. A deputation had visited him headed by the donor of the ceremony and invited him to be present. It had taken place to celebrate the wedding of the eldest son of a moderately wealthy planter in the interior, an Indian who kept cornfields and grew potatoes. The police learned about it afterward, but were never certain whether Father Benno had attended. They questioned him, but he managed to be evasive without lying and no one among the Indians had betrayed him. The potlatch had lasted only six hours and although the flames reached thirty feet into the sky and had cost the farmer many thousands of dollars, the offense was forgotten. The farmer was fined and warned; but the authorities, missing the point, assumed that once a devotee of potlatch, forever vulnerable to its temptation. They didn't know that most Indians can never afford a potlatch; the fortunate often saved a lifetime to afford its luxury. That old potlatch had been a modest affair and although the ritual was the same, its consumption was small and the scale of its disaster contained by the evident fact that the planter could replant and the house he burned would soon be rebuilt. It was to be very different with this "serious outbreak" as it was reported later in the Canadian newspapers.

It was Nauka's potlatch and it was a true potlatch, a ceremony of towering rage in which everything that belonged to Nauka was to be offered in ritual combat with Shunesh, to whose eldest son he had offered his daughter in marriage as a gesture of conciliation and been refused. It was as an assertion of honor and a rebuke to the elder Shunesh that Nauka had ordered the accumulation that was to be the potlatch, had ordered it in fact three years earlier, gathering, storing, building the reserves of skins, meats, whale oil, dried fish, clothing, hard cakes, beer, furniture, masks, copper plaques, figures, and when enough was gathered inviting the contemptible Shunesh, themselves the principal guests of the ceremony, to watch and to behold the power of Nauka and his kinsmen, the immensity of their wealth and the massiveness of the conflagration which their offering would require. Father Benno had spent hours trying to dissuade Nauka and his clan from their decision, but his word was unavailing and even though he threatened to absent himself he knew that such refusal was irrelevant, that his absence would be considered a mark of some obscure guilt and intransigence, ultimately more damaging to his work than would be his presence. He had no choice but to attend the great potlatch of the Nauka, which would take place in the depths of the forest in a clearing cleaned of growth for an acre around, in the center of which a lodge had been constructed and stocked with all the provisions of the clan; there, beginning the following day when the sun was at its daily mid-passage, the giving of gifts would commence, the consumption of beer would start, the feast would be made ready, and at nightfall the dancing would begin, and in the late evening the shaman would appear and

235

descend, and at dawn the fires would be lit that would consume rage, burn anger, reassert the generous sovereignty of Nauka, and restore peace to the seething village.

It was as though a theater had been scalloped from the center of the forest, a massive open-air theater at whose lowest point the action would transpire while the audience disposed in a semi-circle about the stage stood on gently rising ground, the most removed (and consequently commanding) locations reserved for the outsiders who stood together on the highest ground, their backs to the forest that rose like a guardian curtain to the secret action, a thick tangle of foliaged trees through which neither the daylight of the valley nor later the night firelight could penetrate.

Father Benno had conducted Stefan and Alicia in the late morning, already past the midday hour, to the site; Sahué had disappeared hours before, after first warning Stefan not to come, pleading with him briefly, but giving up, her vocabulary of remonstrance exhausted, and, shaking her head in disbelief at his foolishness and his tenacity, leaving him to his fate. Coming to the clearing, their passage through the forest noted by Indians stationed along the way to intercept strangers, the three stood at the rim of the field, higher by several feet than the participants in the theater, the principals, the special guests, and the tribesmen (more than two hundred from old people to babies) who formed orderly lines, men to one side, women and children to the other, standing in lines that ended at the wooden floor that aproned the enormous lodge in which the goods and materials of the potlatch were stored and piled.

It was an endless day; at the outset, wearying, tedious, immensely boring, the action slow and pedantic, gestures used once, used a thousand times, approaches and retreats consummated with shuffling foot and bobbing head. It was not like the theater of diversion, plotted and styled to unfold, transform, and purge, moving the audience to participate with the passions, to reflect with the head, and reconstitute themselves in the aftermath, relieved at the drastic abyss that yawned between their lives and those of the players. Not here. Not in such theatrical rituals as the potlatch. The principals were merely the donors of the occasion in which the myth was to be vivified; the symbolization of ordinary pride (burning pride) is brought into the open, enlarged, magnified, and discharged, all bursting hearts shriveled by the flames to the black edible muscle which is, after all, what ancient cultures knew the heart to be. So present the play, the visitors thought, making life into theater and keeping distance.

Not ours, not of our world, the visitors thought; even Father Benno, knowing better, thought the same, recognizing his congregation, all of it, disguised now (as he had never seen them before) by dress which was more truly of their world than the faded denims and red wool shirts, work shoes and lumberjack boots, forgone now for the most astonishing complexity of clothing and head masks—ponchos cut like episcopal robes, heavy with appliqué of colored fabric, emblems of tribal familiars and clan totems, every beast of sky, field, forest, and ocean, reduced to the right summation of eye, claw, beak, tail, tooth, and tusk, in colors as rich as an unabashed rainbow, spectrum of primacy, covering shoulders and descending like copes to stop above the feet, beneath tight leggings or ballooning skirts, and above, surmounting forehead tied by latchets behind the occipital bone, two, three, sometimes four feet of carved headdress, articulated with glittering mica and shist, colored stone slabs elaborating the border that linked each man's clan loyalty to an aspect of the greater myth—wind, sun, salmon, transmogrified fish warrior, frog sage, bear demon, rampant and wild in red, green, black, and what remained of body, naked and undisguised, was daubed with colors contrasting costume and headdress.

There, for each other, robed to the ritual of the potlatch, all members of the cast and all audience to the drama waited in their lines for the chief of the ceremony, the great Nauka, warrior hunter of the realm, to move from the interior of the lodge to the empty stage, at the corners of which several natives sat before gaint drums and young boys held to their lips, awaiting signal, long gourds and hollowed reeds from which the beat of the ceremony would be sounded. The sun had passed the meridian, dipping behind a white cloud, airy adumbration of the mountain jaggedness above which it hung. After some minutes overcast in the September warmth, the sun emerged slowly, a noiseless signal passed, and the drummers began, low drumming, slow palm upon stretched hide, sounds without melody, extended wailing notes, discrete without succession or logic of intimacy, notes of wind and thud of drum. By mid-afternoon, as the music elaborated, sound more densely packed but still not more than a beat to each three-second interval, the winds more rapidly pleading; the feet of the dancers began to rise upon the platform and fall, as slowly as the music had been; headdress lowered to hide their faces, only feet explaining, rising and falling, orderly at the beginning, but disorderly as it became, some dropping out from time to time to draw upon a gourd or spoon to their lips the sacred beer, gradually becoming more drunk, more sodden, or more frenzied as their energy died away and returned, beginning with a dance of touch, an intricate line of dancers that joined and separated, hands to another's hips, hands passing before the eyes, rising into the air, holding the headdress as it began to bob, bowing to others, saluting, reclining and rising in triumph, each portion of the mythic presence having its moment of ascendancy and submission in the ordering of the clamor, music rising, volume intensifying (more drums than could be seen, for the forest clattered with drums), first the drums and flutes of the stage followed by the stately movements of the dancers. By nightfall the dancers became wilder, the drums pounded louder, torches were lit to illuminate, not yet to burn, and from the forest came forth Nauka leading in his train the members of his clan, and behind them, as postulants to the order of his authority the family of Shunesh, each dressed in the clan garment, each submissive to the commanding gesture of Nauka, the gesture of dominion and self-destruction that was the potlatch.

The music sobered briefly as Nauka (immensely robed and regaled, his face etched in brown muscle as though teeth had ground each other to bone dust and what remained was only a jaw able to crush stone) ascended the platform and as he slowly lowered his upraised arm, the rhythm of the drums changed, and a procession of the massed members of the tribe began. One at a time they rose and passed to Nauka, who greeted each, and with the greeting a retainer of the family emerged from the lodge and presented him with a woven basket containing foodstuffs, garments, carved posts, drinking equipment, inlaid drinking spoons, and a multitude of stuffs with which the guest was draped until he was able to carry no more; the receiver bowed low, spoke some words, and retreated from the platform. The giving of gifts took until late evening when the feasting began, roasted meats and drink appearing from the lodge; there was no corn or vegetables, for Nauka was a hunter and his feast was of meats, game, and their stewing sauces. It was nearly midnight, perhaps before that hour, perhaps after.

The giving of gifts was past, the feasting had subsided,

the music slackened. Nauka, the donor, stood alone and aloof upon the platform. It was then that Stefan Mauger became aware that all the tribe had turned away from the platform, averting their eyes even as the musicians had lowered bandages over their eyes. Only Nauka stood bravely and alone. The drums from the forest began their ascendant beat, the flutes and horns blew steadily, screaming to the forest. There suddenly emerged from the forest and descended toward the slatted stage a small creature, wholly covered in fur, his hair—what could be seen of it—filthy as though the creature had dipped it in mud and dried it in the sun; shells hung from his furs, and a human skull could be seen beside a bear's paw, cut, it would appear, from the unburied animal, the flesh appearing gray and putrescent in the firelight. The creature danced about the platform, his movements unplanned, almost spastic, sometimes trailing his unkempt hair along the dusty wooden platform, sometimes rolling his body upon its rough surface, indifferent to the splinters that gouged him, the blood droplets falling from his chest to the fur about his loins, occasionally rising up and gasping out disconnected words which seemed the groanings of a body tormented elsewhere than in the September night of the north. After hours of his gyrations, during which Nauka remained standing, motionless, aware that for him and his gift of the potlatch the shaman danced, the drums stopped and the wailing winds fell silent. It was then, bent double upon the stage, the magical emblems rattling, that the dancer rose up slowly, his body for the instant slithering upward, as though mimicking the motions of a giant serpent rising up out of its fur sheathing, the plaited hair seemed smooth, the face with eyes rolled back in trance, filth and sap making its features indescribable, a voice consulting the bone of another universe spoke, few words gasped from the ventral cage; unloosed like trapped animals, the words came up, few words, frequently shattered and re-shaped by mad screams, specks of froth flying in the fire-light. At the last exhausted, the creature collapsed upon the stage, the trance continuing while the creature of deeps rested. Nauka's body relaxed and he became human again, the vast regalia once more resumed the marks of costume rather than the millennial grandiosity in which it had been borne for those hours of consultation and exorcism. The potlatch had been accepted and, although crushed into the poverty of the earth from which his wealth of pelts and game had been wrested, Nauka was assured that he was received, that the ancestors were satisfied, the pride restored, the rage becalmed. Nauka would recover and the balance of all was renewed.

The ceremony seemed at an end. Father Benno, tense with horror and fascination, had taken Alicia's hand and held it, while Stefan, comparing his own rage to the ritual anger of the potlatch, appeared calm. At last, as the conclud-ing gesture, Nauka took a torch from the leading servitor who bore it toward him, and calmly, dispassionately, went to the four corners of the lodge and lit the straw piling mounted against its walls. The sky was suddenly alight with flame, the house and its belongings, all the wealth of Nauka that remained after the distribution, ascended to the skies, the coals which would remain going down into the earth to the bones of his complaisant ancestors. It was all accepted.

The outsiders had stood above the ceremony, on a craggy lip of a moraine that descended gently into the cleaned valley where the lodge, the platform, and the In-dian assembly had gathered. A hundred yards from the crumpled figure of the shaman; perhaps more. It is uncer-tain. They didn't bother with the distance, relieved only to be at its outermost edge, away from the fright and the flames. The sky burst with orange-red light as though an explosion of dawn to greet the dawn light which seemed to rim the eyes of the horizon in the distance. They were making ready to turn away and return to the village when they were distracted by a knot of Indians turning upward toward them, as though noticing their presence for the first time. There was a shout from somewhere down in the assembly and suddenly the entranced fur creature roused itself and on feet that seemed swift as a beast ran upward toward them, howling unnaturally. The priest and the Maugers, bristling with terror, turned toward the forest and ran, the priest south, toward the village, Stefan and Alicia to the north, into the forest depths. Soon they were away from the fires of the potlatch, running hard through the thickets, tripping on roots, cutting their faces with slapping branches, their clothes torn by the brambles and barbs. Some minutes later, panting and exhausted, they stopped. For a while there was an unearthly silence. It was then they heard in the distance a large animal coming in their direction. The wood sounded only to the movement of the beast, coming toward them, moving swiftly, branches snapping. Stefan withdrew his father's pistol, which at the last minute he had taken from the duffle to carry against the ominousness of the potlatch, but it was unloaded; it had not been loaded since Port Bou. It was useless; he jammed it back into his belt. It was a meaningless appendage, no more useful than a fist would be against a mountain. They began once more to run, clambering up a spruce-covered hillock which emerged from the gloom before them; to the left, in the dawning light, they saw the outlines of a cave into which they squeezed behind a rock that covered its entrance. The animal had no interest in them; they were merely in its path and were best out of it. Stefan reassured Alicia. They dropped down with exhaustion. The forest remained still, silent before the immense beast. Nothing moved. Stefan was about to light a cigarette when as before he heard a noise, the beast's noise, but so close it could be touched, the noise of imminence, scratching sounds, the irregular panting of the beast, and finally an enormous groan and flailing against the boulder. Stefan looked up in terror and saw standing astride the crack through which their slenderness had slipped a giant bear, fully eight feet in height and immensity, remarkable in its rage, except, as he later insisted, that from its neck had hung a circlet of shells.

Stefan Mauger faced the bear, its mouth open and frothing, and unaccountably, remembering from somewhere the gesture of nobility in the face of terror, bowed his head, accepting his defeat from wherever it had come. He remained bent from the waist, succumbing to the bear's dominion, and when he straightened up the bear was gone and the dawn had come. It was some time later that they fell into a deep and troubled sleep, Stefan clutching Alicia and holding her, their arms falling about each other, their heads entwined as though grown from the same neck, the same trunk, two bodies commingled in terror and in weariness.

It was late in the day before they left the cave. Nothing seemed disturbed, no branches broken, no leaves matted. It seemed hardly possible that a monstrous bear, the largest they could imagine, had stood before their cave and threatened them. Ominous and inexplicable, the rush of the shaman toward them succeeded by a monstrous bear, pursuing like a possessed man, inflexible in its intention, larger and more persuasive than the warning words of old Giraud on the floor of his motor launch.

The Maugers came down shaken from the last hill that divides the village from the forest; more precisely, shattered and revised. The usual self-assurance that had defined their presence among the Indians, their movement through the wood to totem field and beyond to small encampments of the tribe, had been marked by an unabashed straight-forwardness, a coming forth from wood to clearing to ask for water or a place to sleep, confident of being made welcome, leaving behind in thanks (as though required) some items from the store—a knife, a tin of tea or coffee, a packet of candies for the children. When the two had moved alone (unaccompanied by Sahué, who habitually walked slightly behind and to Stefan's side of the path), they seemed independent of each other, no enmeshment of arms, no carrying of the other's pack, no hand extended to assist the mounting of a rock; they, "those two" as they were simply called by the natives, were wholly separate and confident, able to move through strange woods and among even stranger people with an assurance that most white men lack, concerned as they often are by the sensitivities of trespass and violation, fearing to step upon some concealed trap, to release the nemesis of sacred taboo. Not Stefan and Alicia Mauger, who came to the Kwakiutl persuaded that they were right to come, that it was there for them, as though the rhythm of Kwakiutl life had been invented and set in motion to afford the Maugers an instruction about their own abandoned world. Of course, had they been modest and cautious, they would have seen nothing; nothing more than the tantalizing surface, which, despite carving in high-relief, is still limited to two dimensions, deprived of that circumambience and complexity that results from having gone to the interior and worked from the depths. The Maugers had unwittingly chanced it, gone to the limits of excess and passed over its rebuke, remitted into life, the sentence lifted. Undoubtedly beneath Stefan's blond hair, the follicles of gray had appeared and lines later to show on Alicia's neck had begun to crease, but these were not yet visible as they came down slowly into the settlement, her arm about Stefan's neck, his hand supporting her waist, each holding to the other, not simply prodigals returned unscathed. They returned shattered and revised.

When they awakened from a sleep that lasted more than half a day, it was late afternoon. Sahué was gone. Father Benno admitted sternly that she was in the village, but asked that they not seek her to say good-bye. Stefan, near tears, had begged the priest not to return her to the Mission and Father Benno, at the end of his importunings, had relented, assuring him that after their departure he would allow her to return. There was no discussion of what had occurred. Had Father Benno not mentioned them, Stefan and Alicia would have forgone the few objects—a giant crane mask, two ladles cut from tortoise shells, carved with incomprehensible glyphs, and three dance masks, whose animal doors opened upon minuscule hinges revealing within other masks of the constellar heavens, sun dotted with beads of perspiration, and a half-moon, face partitioned by color and carving to suggest the moody shifts of the night—they had bartered to acquire and stored in the corner of their room. Stefan looked at them sickly, both wanting to take them and aware nonetheless that they were a portion of the terror that had been mounted against them. But Father Benno assured him that after a time their danger would decrease and one day, when Stefan wrote, he would dispatch them; even old Giraud would not mind. Father Benno was tender to them both, his own discomfort and irritation having given way before the immensity of the potlatch and its aftermath. Although he did not inquire about the night events, he was able to guess that something frightful had occurred. Its magic was too close to his own to be reviewed.

Three days passed before old Giraud returned with the launch, driving it down from the northernmost village of his territory to stop once again, to deliver messages to the priest, drop cargo at the general store, and collect goods to be sent by the Indians for sale at the trading posts in Nanaimo. It was agreed that the Maugers would leave at that time, and having settled accounts with Father Benno, they were waiting late in the afternoon beside the mooring when old Giraud reappeared from the store where he had spent his visiting hours and moved slowly toward the launch, his movement constrained and hesitant. Although he did not appear to have seen them, he nodded in their direction as he passed, acknowledging them wordlessly and with an indication of his head, pointing to the launch and telling them to board. The voyage down to Nanaimo was uninterrupted, for Giraud failed to stop at two other villages along the way. It took nearly eight hours. During that time little was said. It was only in the last hour before arrival in the port that old Giraud, settled upon his stool before the steering wheel, his eyes fastened to the night lights that flickered along the shore and guided his descent, made a few comments which stayed with the Maugers for a long time, indeed, one should think, for the rest of their lives.

"Old Giraud warned. Yes? You not hear. Not listen." He wetted his lips, his tongue rolling about his gums silently, only little protrusions of his lip marking its passage about his mouth. It was Giraud's pause, a kind of gathering of words, as though stuck to his mouth like flies immured in sugar; they needed the passage of his tongue to moisten and release them. "Not your fault only. Fault all you people. Come to my nation and spy us out. Try find something my people hide. You two think it belong to you. Long time ago hunt gold. Now hunt my people. No. No. No good." Giraud stopped and slapped the wheel, a small slap, like hitting the hand of a child who had reached for something without permission. "Giraud warn you. Father warn you. Sahué

246

warn you. You come with picture machine. Take pictures like my people nice trees or big stone. No good. Not know that tree and stone have power? Everything piece of whole spirit. Everything power. No make picture of power. No learn secret unless have secret long ago. You two found out. We old world. Old as your world. Different old. Not old things. Old spirit. We hold it. We not give it to picture machine."

Old Giraud looked at them suddenly, darting a glance at them, his oriental eyes nearly closed, the lids unlined, as serene as they had remembered his eyes. Old Giraud turned back and once more faced out into the sea, maneuvering the boat to tack against the waves, forcing the boat into the rhythm of the waves, turning the wind to its advantage and pushing forward toward the lights of Nanaimo. "Give old Giraud pictures."

The words were a command. It wasn't a matter to be argued. There was too much, Stefan admitted later, that was unclear, that would always remain unclear about Giraud. Alicia agreed, urging Stefan with her eyes to hurry before the mood of Giraud turned from explanation and command to something more. Stefan handed Giraud the little boxes, the thirty little yellow boxes, and Giraud opened the window of the launch. The spume cut through the crack, water hitting their faces, but the Maugers hardly moved: they watched as slowly, one by one, his lips moving as though counting the rolls (but he may well have been saying other words), Giraud tossed the boxes into the waves.

By the time the launch reached the dock at Nanaimo the waves had subsided and the waters were calm; a crescent moon, half mocking, was tossed free of a billowing ocean of night clouds and seemed to jest its way through the sky.

6

Mortal Combat

Inspector Mariposa was fidgeting. He had arrived early in the afternoon from Mexico City; it was already evening and nothing had been accomplished. It had taken him more than three hours to spend twenty minutes surveying the island with Captain Gutiérrez. Nothing was found. A heel print of an army boot; several cigarette butts in the storage hut. Useless information. He idled while the Indian woman found at the site was being questioned by a subordinate. Pitiless business. The Indian woman, nursing an infant, had nothing to confide other than her amazement that the empty island was suddenly overrun with a squad of Federales. She had seen nothing, observed nothing, recognized nothing with the exception, perhaps, that one of the group carried no carbine, hugging instead beneath his arm a businessman's briefcase. It was he, she said, who gave the orders and watched attentively while the *ídolos* were packed. She had counted six soldiers and the officer in charge. But for description and identification, she was useless. No one was marked with distinction, neither face nor body; no habit of speech or oddity of dress had been noticed. She was too frightened to pay attention, admitting that for the most part she had spent her time making certain that her sleeping baby was dry and quiet. Inspector Mariposa dismissed her with a wave of his arm.

Captain Gutiérrez, absent during the interview, returned to his office, where the interrogations were being conducted, and commiserated with the Inspector. "Nobody sees in Campeche," he commented drily. "They're present but they never see. Who pays them to see? They're hardly paid to work."

"And the list of dealers in the district? May I see it?"

"It doesn't exist, Inspector. There are no dealers in Campeche, no dealers worth the name. In the market there are always Indians with a broken *idolo* alongside old glasses and chamber pots. You want their names? They're nothing. What's the point?"

"And Professor Hermoso? Has he arrived?"

"This minute. The car brought him from the landing. He came directly from the island. Agitated. I should say the Professor is very agitated." Captain Gutiérrez went to the door and called as he opened it: "Professor Hermoso. The Inspector will speak with you."

"Ah, the great Hermoso," Inspector Mariposa exclaimed as the thin and undistinguished figure entered the room, peering about nervously, his eyes immensely magnified through the thick lenses of his eyeglasses. It was apparent that the Professor could hardly see without his glasses. Years of scrutiny in dark vaults and ill-lit tombs had accustomed the Professor to solitary existence where his weak eyes, focusing once, remained riveted and inerrant. It frightened him to be in a well-lit room, distracted by conversation, voices from various directions, where his eyes were obliged to move and swivel with sound. He disliked people. There was never any need to talk with artifacts.

Professor Hermoso did not acknowledge the Inspector's greeting or his extended hand. He was intent upon finding a seat and installing himself. Mariposa was indifferent, watching him with amusement as he moved with mole-like uncertainty toward the chair. Mariposa knew perfectly well that Professor Hermoso was not great, merely diligent, having acquired no reputation except for his scrupulous attention to the excavation of Jaina. Jaina required no genius, merely care, precision, meticulous annotation. But then Inspector Mariposa was disingenuous. Whatever his pedestrian talents and capacity, Professor Hermoso had nonetheless been assigned to one of the most productive archaeological sites in Mexico. If for no other reason than this, he was slightly envious of the Professor. Professor Hermoso was living the life of which Inspector Mariposa had dreamed.

"It is a great tragedy," Inspector Mariposa began, issuing the proclamation as prologue to the inquiry.

"More than tragedy. Much more. Three years work. Don't forget that! One hundred and eleven pieces of astonishing perfection; each one annotated and described; each one measured and tagged. Gone. Not a trace. Not even a photograph." The Professor blinked, his eyes opening and shutting rapidly.

"Again no photographs. When will the government learn?"

"They're more afraid of the cameras being stolen than of losing the pieces. They never issue us photographic equipment. Everything is photographed in the capital when the pieces arrive. At the site, nothing. I take a few flash pictures during the excavation, but that's all. Photographs don't matter except when a tragedy like this occurs."

"That seems remarkable."

"My work is intellectual, Inspector. Intellectual work.

Not visual. I find the words to identify what the camera could never photograph. You see the figurine. The camera records the surface. What I put down is the language of essence."

"The language of essence," Inspector Mariposa repeated with delight. "Splendid! And such language. What is it?"

"The myths. The myths. I show you a statue holding a pomegranate. But I document with time and eternity. The pomegranate. Myriad hidden seeds densely packed and flowing with juice. Ah. The stream of eternal life beneath the ruby skin."

"You make poems out of the statues. Is that the case? Poetry rather than photography. Yes. Well. Most interesting," the Inspector mused tartly. The Professor had missed the point, but not completely because he continued, "Of course, besides all this—my special speculations—I have precise descriptions of materials, color, dimensions, techniques of modeling, and estimations of the procedures of firing. You see, Inspector, I do science as well as poetry."

"It would be helpful, don't you think, if we had some photographs?"

The Professor shifted uncomfortably in his chair. His knee grazed the Inspector's leg. He smoothed his trousers irritably. He disliked being interrogated. It made him somehow party to the crime.

"And tell me now, Professor Hermoso, you work alone at the site?"

"I have peons, but no colleagues, if that's what you mean. Yes. You might say I work alone."

"And how many peons do you have?"

"Not enough. Not nearly enough. At the speed we're working, it will take us more than a decade to complete the work. A dozen workers at most and the rains will begin again."

"You have a dozen workers now?"

"No. No. We sometimes have a dozen. Now we are doing the work with eight. And look how much time we lost this week. We left the island Thursday night and here it is Saturday and the island is sealed off and policemen are examining my office and asking hopelessly irrelevant questions of my workers. The late winter rains will begin again soon and there's so much to do."

"But my dear Professor, you don't seem to appreciate that there's been a major theft at Jaina. Not a trivial theft. This was no vandalism, a minor escapade of an amateur, but a careful, thoughtful, immensely well-planned act of theft."

"Yes, yes, but I'm still losing time. So much to do to make certain we survive another season on Jaina; keeping the pumps moving out the water, preventing the Zacpool from flooding. Archaeologists end up as plumbers most of the time."

"To be sure, to be sure. But explain please how you came to leave the island Thursday night?"

"A mistake, I'm afraid. A call came from my colleagues who are digging near La Venta. It came about midnight. They wanted to borrow my workers for a few days to shore up the walls of a badly opened tomb they were excavating. It was very urgent, very alarming. They were afraid that the scaffolding they had constructed would collapse. I hesitated a moment when the call came. It was so late and I had to wake up the camp, which is always difficult. But I said 'Yes, of course.' They wanted a favor from Hermoso. One day I might need one myself. We left early before dawn Friday morning. After six hours in the launch we arrived. But it was very strange, you know. My friend Geraldo Balaguer (who conducts the dig) said that he had never called. He showed me the tomb. (Several marvelous figures and a wonderful wall frieze.) It was very efficiently scaffolded.

No problem at all. I was so relieved at being able to return the following day that I slept soundly, took an early dinner with Balaguer, and arrived back at the island late Friday evening. I reported it immediately. The phone was cut, so I had to take our launch back to Campeche. It wasn't until this morning that I began to reflect on the obvious question. We had been drawn off the island to make it easy for the thieves. But they overlooked something. They left behind all my notes. We can, I should think, have extremely detailed descriptions of each of the stolen objects in a few months' time."

"In a few months?" the Inspector exploded. "A few months, indeed. I want those notes in detail by tomorrow."

"Impossible. Out of the question. I can't make poetry and science overnight."

"But you will, Professor. You will," the Inspector replied firmly.

"No. No. No." Professor Hermoso lifted his hands and turned his palms toward the Inspector as if to push away his inundating authority.

"I will have you ordered to by the Capital if that's what you want. I need those descriptions. I need them now. Immediately. But tomorrow will have to do."

The Professor subsided, dropping his hands to his lap; the torrent had engulfed him, flooding him with a confusion and resignation he had never experienced before. "But how can I?" he mumbled to himself, suddenly miserable. It was then that the proper focus of his anger found language; his eyes narrowed and the vastly inflated pupils condensed behind their magnification to the size of peas. "Damned thieves. Contemptible thieves."

"Correct," the Inspector agreed. "It's the thieves who should have your outrage, not me, Professor Hermoso. I want the Jaina figures back home with you, in place on your storage shelves, and for that I need descriptions to circulate. But enough of this for the moment. A side issue really. The real matter is the thief. Who do you suppose, Professor Hermoso, called you and diverted you from the island?"

"The thief, of course. Most definitely the thief."

"Of course. And who, Professor, do you think he might be?"

"I have no idea. I should think someone who knows the Jaina figurines. Someone who realizes they are master-pieces, each one a masterpiece." The Professor wagged his head sadly, reviewing one by one the figures that had once occupied his now empty shelves.

"Undoubtedly. And there cannot be many such con-noisseurs, since very few of the figures were known outside the region until very recently. And who would have guessed from the several examples in the capital that your island is literally stuffed with them? The thief must be someone both knowledgeable in general and from the district; someone who knows not only your work but also, it appears, your friendship with Balaguer at La Venta; someone who could rely on your camaraderie to draw you from the island with the vague explanation of an endangered excavation." Inspector Mariposa paused briefly, admiring the clarity with which he had constructed his necklace of suppositions and waiting, hopefully, for the Professor to drop into place the single link that would transform his fabrication into an ir-refutable logic.

"I have no idea," the Professor thought aloud. "Who cares about the Jaina in Campeche? Fishermen try to barter with my workers for a piece now and then, offering a large lobster in exchange for a fragment. But I don't permit that. It's against the law, you know? Who besides them?" The Professor paused and reviewed mental notes, turning pages rapidly until, startled, he gasped, "Not possible. It couldn't be him. Not at all possible." The Professor contended with himself, his head turning from side to side, acknowledging a fact, repudiating it, reclaiming it once more.

"Share it with me, Professor Hermoso. You have a name. Who is it?"

"I met the gentleman by accident a little over a year ago. I was sitting in the park in Campeche. Reading, you know. Sometimes I leave the island for a bit of relief and come into Campeche to read. Particularly in the fall when it's cool and the flies are tired. I was reading a German magazine—a technical periodical, you know; it had a fascinating article on a despoiled excavation near Palenque. This gentleman was passing by and for some reason sat down beside me. We began to talk. He was very interested in archaeology and wanted my reaction to the procedures employed by the article's author. I was surprised. It isn't often that one meets an amateur who knows something. I don't know how much he really knew, but he was curious about the article and so I shared my views with him. He seemed delighted. Handsome man. Foreign, but he spoke excellent Spanish, hardly an accent. I didn't know who he was. He did claim, however, to have spoken with the author of the article, Levis Glyphstein. I was startled by this because I knew that Glyphstein had been somehow involved as the resident scholar to a band of tomb robbers. But it didn't matter for the moment. We talked at length and eventually I had a drink with him before I returned to the island."

"Very promising. Very promising. Now tell me, Professor, did you describe your work on the island? Did you tell him about the Jaina excavation?"

"Oh yes. Yes, yes, and in considerable detail, I'm afraid. More than I should have, I suppose."

"And did he visit you at the site?"

"Yes. How did you guess that, Inspector? He seemed

255

particularly interested in seeing our work in progress; he claimed he had never seen an actual excavation before. He came over, in fact, this past fall, wandered about, asked a number of harmless questions, the kind a condescending tourist might ask—about origins and dating of the mortuary, my view of the artistic merit of the pieces, my interpretation of their religious function and such like. I answered as best I could, taking into account that he was an amateur, but . . ."

"Did he inquire at any time about the value of the objects?"

"No. Remarkably, no. Once I mentioned that the pieces were extremely valuable, but he appeared to lack the familiar avarice of foreigners."

"Curious, don't you think? They are very valuable, aren't they, Professor Hermoso?"

"Substantial. The whole group should bring a very great deal of money, much more by far than we'll ever make," the Professor added wearily.

"And his name? He told you his name, surely?"

"He did. At the beginning when we met the first time and at the end when we parted. He used the Spanish for his first name although clearly he wasn't a native. I found the coupling amusing. Esteban, he said. Esteban Mauger. Yes. That's his name."

Inspector Mariposa could hardly contain his pleasure. He had won the prize of a name. It always seemed to the Inspector that every interrogation led to simple things—an address, an identifying scar or limp, a name. Hours of circumspection and deviousness, allowing interlocution to acquire its own pace and sinuosity, moving in and around the subject, passing from subject to subject until the whorls begin to narrow, a focus emerge and the center be dictated: in this case, he sought a name. It didn't matter particularly

256

whether it was the right name. All that counted at the outset was appropriateness. It was a name that connected. It could be the wrong name, but then one name would lead to another.

"You have helped me immensely. Immensely. By the way, my friend, you could identify him if necessary, couldn't you?"

"Possibly. Possibly. But I'm not at all certain. My eyesight, Inspector, is very unreliable. These thick lenses. I'm medically close to being blind. Except for my work. Except for my work, you understand. I see everything that relates to my work, but I hardly waste my eyesight on the world. I doubt I'd make a reliable witness."

"Well, perhaps we won't need you to identify Señor Mauger. Thank you. Thank you very much." Inspector Mariposa took the Professor's hand from his lap and shook it warmly as he conducted him to the door.

Captain Gutiérrez returned to the office a moment later, shaking his head with commiseration. "Nothing, I suppose."

"Something, I'm delighted to report. Get me the central operator in Campeche. I have a name to locate."

It was done. Not at all difficult to find. Stefan Mauger lived in the countryside, nine miles from Campeche, near the turnoff on the highway which passes through miles of forest before it descends into the dense scrub jungle through which one traveled with great difficulty to the city of Merida on the other side of the isthmus.

"Captain Gutiérrez. Please ring the hacienda of Señor Mauger and tell him that Inspector Baltásar Mariposa will call upon him in the morning. The morning will be soon enough."

"It was Inspector Mariposa. What an improbable name." Stefan Mauger had passed Alicia in the patio. She had

257

listened, straining to hear his voice on the telephone, but the windows were closed against the humidity. She had heard nothing, only a door slam, and then he had returned, bending his head to avoid hitting it on the low jamb, passing out into the declining day. She was about to ask if it was Brownsville and had everything arrived unbroken, or perhaps it had been Clemens from Mexico City, but Stefan had spoken to her, literally in passing, without looking at her, and had turned around the corner of the hacienda toward the studio. She watched him disappear without trying to speak again. He seemed to her, for the first time, drained. Imperceptibly his youth had receded. What remained was weariness, exhaustion from battle, the pool of vitality eddying about his feet. Alicia was too pained by the sight of his drawn face, his mockingly nerveless bravado, and palpable disconsolation to ask her question. She already knew that her question was irrelevant. It was an inspector who called and inspectors were all from the police. (She thought briefly that she had finally succeeded in hurting him, repaying him for Sahué of the north and Maria of the south. But she knew better. It was part of it, but not the major part. She had nothing to repay, after all; he had never construed his waywardness as an assault upon her. It was all the accident of angles. Innocence sharpens the blade; it doesn't rationalize the wound. In any case, innocence and confusion are not adult excuses. She was aware of this, often temporizing with her depressed feeling of being beside the point of Stefan's life. But she imagined no less fancifully that she was the point, although she had accepted reluctantly that the point, whatever the point, is blunted and sheathed, that no one knows the point until too late.)

Alicia continued to sit in the failing light. The shadows had begun to advance from the jungle, crawling her legs. The telephone rang again. She determined to ignore it. It rang insistently. It didn't matter to her if it was answered.

"Alicia. It was Gutiérrez, Alicia. Very excited. He said, 'Tell Stefan the Inspector knows the truth.' He begged Stefan be careful. He was almost in tears. *¿Quién es el inspector?*"

For a long time Alicia sat in the patio. It was nearly ten when she got up and began to walk slowly toward the studio, her head bent low, shaking it from side to side, as though arguing with the conclusion of finality. It surprised her that it had been so easy for the police this time. For five years Stefan had been organizing complicated thefts, involving numerous peons, sites, objects; gathering and distributing the finds; responding to inquiries from Hendel and his associates; supplying museums and collectors; but until today no inspector had announced that he would come to call.

She knocked at the door. She had no doubt that Stefan was inside, seated with his back to the fireplace surveying the creatures. There was rarely a reply. Sometimes a grunt or a low whistle, but never a word. The knock was rhetoric; a reply would be no less rhetorical. She rapped lightly, but realized the sound was no more than a small rock lifted by the wind and striking the door would make. She knocked again, twice in a row, clearly and unmistakably. There was no answer. She opened the door and entered. It was very chilly. The fire Stefan had lit in the early morning was nearly gone. Only a single log smarted with embers. She called to Stefan through the dark.

"I'm here. Over here in the corner beneath the crane." He was wedged between the brick protrusion of the fireplace and the adobe wall that ran beneath a high window. Stefan had drawn up his legs almost to his chin; he had been reading, but he knew the text by heart. There was so little light the papers could not have been actually read. He began to recite their text as though reading them, forgetting nothing, the little printed rubrics in the medical report and the filled portion in various hands, each initialed by the physician who had attended his father. He concluded the record with the painful summation of Dr. Mauritius, the jargon of the psychiatric profession, the late deteriorations of a disease that affected mind and spirit, diminishing their appetite for life, the confirming self-accusations and tears, and he passed, without pause, to unfold his mother's last letter, reciting it aloud as though reading it from an indelible script, long ago memorized and enacted before mirrors and during sleepless hours of his youth. "My line ended long ago. With these. I take them out and repeat my memory of them whenever I feel hemmed. The final night in Nanaimo before we left the northwest. That was the last time I read them. Most often a passage will do. One of my mother's choicer lines of rage is more than sufficient. But now. It's different. The shaman is about to become a monster again. The Inspector is a shaman, don't you think? Like old Giraud, but probably without mercy. The police aren't hired for acts of mercy. But it's a fitting time. Brancusi is dying in Paris, you know?" Alicia touched Stefan's leg lightly, acknowledging that she heard and understood; he could still see her eyes, the glowing log occasionally burst into a tiny blue flame and for an instant her eyes were illuminated and he could see her watching him, listening to him deeply, her eyes wide with amazement and kindness. "You can't see them, but I put up two photographs of Brancusi over the fireplace and added his dates. He'll be dead before summer, I should think. Yes. Constantin is dying. Maybe he's already dead. Clemens will tell us when he comes. You know, Alicia, I always spoke to Brancusi when I worked. He was very generous. Helped me, nodding vigorously if he liked what I was doing; sometimes even took my hand and restrained it. 'Less,' the pressure of his hand cautioned. It's not unusual. I know painters who speak to Matisse. But now Brancusi is dying. No one's left to battle. Except myself. It would have been easier if I had simply failed. Failure is acceptable, you know? It's what the world expects, demands even. When we don't fail, the world is annoyed. 'No one asked you to be an artist.' Quite so. No public whimpering allowed. But me? It wasn't enough being an artist who did his work quietly, anonymously. Do you know, Alicia dear, that we have the names of hardly a hundred artists who lived before the Renaissance? A few we know simply as the Master of this or that city or altarpiece. No names, no identities. Praxiteles and Phidias, a few pot painters, but no one from ancient Sumeria, no one from Egypt, no one from Anatolia, no one from old Africa or New Guinea. Names were accidents then. Today the name precedes the work. I've hated that all my life. It's because I was born long after I received a name. I was the Count, son of derangement. The whole of my growing up was the pursuit of the work that would become my name. Brancusi explained it to me without words. If you put the two hundred or so pieces that he made in one room, there would be no doubt that a single genius made them. If his name is obliterated, if a potion of forgetfulness is drunk by the whole race, the work will still be his name. That's what I've pursued all my life. And I haven't been able to do it. I'm still imprisoned by the knowledge that everything that I become was named long ago in the room of the lintel fireplace in the family winter lodge. The more I pondered that fact, the more I knew that I was trapped by my past, the more I came to hate what I couldn't be—I couldn't make birds and masks and human fossils that would renew ancient anonymity before names were distributed and required. The image, not the maker, needs our praise. And the stealing? I began with the illusion of work, an alternative to work, a devious method of coping with the prospect of having to live with my name, and as time went on it became a deeper and deeper way of tormenting myself, continually dishonoring myself. I never stole before now, because in every other world in which we lived I felt at home. There was no point fighting my name in Europe. It couldn't be obliterated. I was always the Count (even if I suppressed it) and there was always Brancusi to warn me, living Brancusi to warn me. But here, cut off in the jungles behind Campeche, surrounded by the artifacts of a vision I despise—no peace, no joy, no celebration—I lost compunction. Whenever I stole it was like their ancient priests tearing out hearts and burning them. All my thefts. Tearing out hearts to stoke my own courage."

"And the Inspector? Inspector Mariposa. What's to be done with him?"

"Tell him everything. But in my own way. He'll have to want the truth badly to get it. I won't give it easily. It's no truth either of us would accept if he got it easily."

Alicia felt the strain spread through Stefan's body. Every muscle of his jaw showed, the teeth grinding against each other, the words released like gusts of air. "I'm trying to work it out. It would have come anyway. With Brancusi's death. When Clemens came. I had all along decided that Jaina would be the last. It is the last. But there has to be something more. I want more than a pause, a change in the order of the rage. I want to be done with it. I owe Brancusi at least that, for all he's done for me."

"It may not be yours to manage. If the Inspector really knows, he'll just come and take you away."

"No. No, Alicia. You don't understand. He can prove nothing. Absolutely nothing. No photographs. No connections. No loose ends. I've watched my disguises like a master. They've probably come close before, but they can do nothing more than suspect. They can spend the rest of their lives watching me, but since Jaina was the last, they'll never catch me in an act of theft. Never. There's nothing but suspicion."

"Can't you let that be? Isn't that enough? Go free and stop it."

"No. I don't think I can. I'm full. The sculpture garden is ready. The creatures are carved in my head. I need to do them now. Brancusi is dead. His hand no longer has to guide my own. I think I can work without him. I've tried all these years to kill him, but, marvelous man, he's dying at his own pleasure. Isn't that wonderful? He's letting me go so gracefully."

Alicia could feel Stefan smile. The rage of years was passing at last. The banked embers of the fire glowed within themselves, but cast no more light. Stefan could only recollect the daring of what his rage had been—making sculptures and thefts, interlocking acts of seizure, trading off against ancient imaginings the fabrications of a present time when one no longer wrestled with angels, much less won from them remissions and benedictions.

"You're not afraid?"

"I am afraid. Not of the Inspector. I'm afraid of leaving Brancusi. Letting him rest in peace."

The first shock of dawn streaked through the high window of the studio. The light begins, Stefan thought as he awakened. I must see it all clearly today.

It was terribly cold in the studio. He had not prepared the fire. He reached above his head and pulled from a hook a warm jacket he kept for winter days and went toward the door. It must be just past five. The light begins at that hour, coming from the distant waters of the Gulf, spreading like a slowly unfurling pennant over the jungle until it reached his domain, where it settled down, covering the land with a purplish cast soaked up from the glistening green and brown and yellow of the dense jungle that surrounded it. The wind flourished as he opened the door and he paused a moment, thinking that he had forgotten something he intended to take with him on his walk, but he could not remember (still clotted with sleep) what it was and shrugged his forgetfulness, closing the door behind him.

There was a path through the high grass of his untended field. It had been cut a half century ago by the workers of Campos who trotted beside their donkeys hauling sisal from the forest to the cutting shed. This was to be the arena of his carved garden, still high with grass, each year growing higher until at some points of rise it more than covered his head. Each year he resolved to hire workers to clear the land so that he could begin to draw accurately its topography, determine its elevation and declivities, and oblige himself to adapt the visionary model of the studio to the space around him. It's all near at hand, Stefan thought, and reached out, touching only the fibrous, blade-like notches of massive yucca plants and the cutting edge of the wild grasses. It must be cleared, he repeated to himself. But he contradicted his resolution with the specter of a little man in uniform with handcuffs looped through his belt. It was then, plunging through the grass toward the jungle, that Stefan began to remember his night of despair, the heroics of his conversation with Alicia, the remonstrance of his dreams, which proposed to him not courage but various undertakings of aborted suicide—knives that shattered like icicles; beckoning rivers that became resilient beds of lily pads; hanging ropes which strung about his neck became garlands of gardenias that grew wild in his land; and even pistols, gilded and ornamented with his name, which, put to his temple and discharged, clacked like metal tongues, sounding, but harmless for their chambers were empty.

It relieved him to recall these dreams. They seemed then, in that early hour of the dawn, more reassuring than the specter of the uniformed policeman was frightening.

Suicide, he thought again, was idle contemplation. Suicide is done. Its something is finally nothing. It has no value as contemplation. The only incomplete suicides worthy of recollection are those realized afterward, after the crash, to have been real. (It was then—in the curious conjunction of his dreaming and his headlong plunging through the high grass—that he recalled a forgotten episode: shortly after his father's death, he had driven his horse frantically through the Wald into the traffic that streamed back to Vienna in the July before the war—artillery caissons, mounted platoons dragging munition carts, officers' automobiles, heavy canvas-covered trucks filled with soldiers. Stefan had spurred his horse across the highway to reenter the forest on the other side. He had ignored the traffic, urging his horse through the military confusion. The roads were muddy, slicked with a sleeting rain. Suddenly a motorcyclist, concealed behind a caisson, zoomed forward and Stefan's mount reared up. He was thrown into the arms of recruits who were already reaching out from the rear of their truck to catch him. He banged his head, passed out, and when he revived, lying on the knees of the soldiers, the first thing he heard was their amused laughter. One admonished him: "Trying to kill yourself, young Lord? We need you for other battles." "Did I see the cyclist and rein back?" he had asked. "Wouldn't be here if you hadn't, young Lord." He asked for a drink and brandy was poured down his throat and he fell back asleep upon their knees. Later that afternoon, put to bed by Mr. Richards, he awakened and called out. Mr. Richards came quickly. "Mr. Richards, do you know something? Do you know something I've just remembered. I had a terrible dream last night. And this morning when I went for my ride I couldn't remember it. I was miserable. But I remember it now. It was my father come to call on me, telling me how much he missed me and how he would like me to visit him soon. But Mr. Richards, Father is dead and I don't want to visit him very soon.")

Stefan began to cry quietly as he struggled through the grass to the jungle's edge. Recalling the dreams of the night —the faulty suicides—joined now with the memory of his single adventure of suicide, he realized that what he had forgotten to take upon his walk was his father's pistol, which hung from the wall of the studio, cleaned now and loaded.

Inspector Baltásar Mariposa was extremely careful dressing Sunday morning. Although he had brought very few alternatives to augment or diversity his clothing—he had left, after all, from the central police station without returning to his home in Tepotzlan—he always kept in the bottom drawer of his desk several handkerchiefs, scarves, a change of shirt and underwear, for precisely such unforeseen departures (this latter precaution having been forced upon him some years back when he was obliged to fly on short notice to Ciudad Juarez to intercept a gun runner who didn't show up on schedule, obliging him after three days without change of underwear to buy from the local haberdasher a coarse cotton pair that left his legs raw from constant itching), he did manage a kind of Mexican panache, his white shirt open, a green silk scarf covered with small yellow diamonds, a suit of substantial dark blue cheviot, and his inevitable straw panama with the high black band. His dress was never flashy, but unlike the habit of the police, it was composed, thoughtful, somewhat aloof, suggesting an ease and comfort in its authority that were often found by criminals to be upsetting. An edge, precisely the edge that a man not much over five feet, slight of build, with hair, thinning to the point of disappearing, arranged like a tracery of veins on his head, required in order to make the point of power. He never carried a weapon; he had made it clear to Colonel Vidal a long time ago that he intended to work with his head rather than with firearms.

He had it right. He flicked a speck from his lapel, smoothed down the face of his jacket, lifted the drooping ends of his shirt collar so that they lay in repose upon the mixed field of green and yellow silk, and smiled pleasantly to himself in the hotel mirror. The driver was below, the same young guardsman who had picked him up from the airport, but Captain Gutiérrez claimed religious duties that Sunday and apologized, contending, despite the Inspector's disapproval, that he had to take his wife to eleven o'clock Mass to give thanks for their son's recovery from an accident. It didn't matter. Captain Gutiérrez would be worse than useless; his insistent stupidity could be a positive hindrance to the investigation. In all events, Mariposa knew perfectly well his visit to Stefan Mauger would be a first visit. He wanted, after all, to see a splendid collection as well as to catch a thief.

The door opened and Martina entered, her thin arm perfunctorily extended to the Señores, introducing the visitor whose name she did not understand.

Inspector Mariposa was already about his work, surveying the entire room, noting and observing, his eyes darting like hummingbirds, his lips pursed contemplatively. But it was all an instant, the first pause, and then forward again to Stefan Mauger, who stood up to accept his handshake as he introduced himself: "Inspector Baltásar Mariposa of the Special Investigations Branch of the Department of Interior. Such a great deal we are obliged to say. And even, should you wish it, sir . . ."

"I am—yes—Count Stefan Friedrich Martin von Mauger. A great deal for me as well."

"Oh? Yes? Count Stefan. I didn't know. But, sir, would you like to see my identification?"

"Not at all necessary, Inspector. I spoke with friends in Mexico City last evening. You're quite authentic, I've discovered. Do be seated. There, that should be comfortable." He indicated with a slight bow of the head a large couch on which more than four could be comfortably accommodated.

"And coffee and refreshment? I'm sure you haven't lunched as yet. Only one o'clock. Will you have sandwiches and cakes with us? We always eat lightly at lunch."

"If it isn't an inconvenience? Yes. I should be pleased."

"Forgive me, Inspector, I've neglected to introduce my wife. Alicia, this is Inspector Mariposa from Mexico City." The Inspector rose and took Alicia's hand graciously. Their hands touched and separated. "Would you tell Martina that we'll have luncheon here in the living room? Tell her not to fuss. Yes?" Alicia was surprised that Stefan had rebidden the Count from the shades. She was surprised, but immediately understood. He did intend to make the Inspector work. But she was relieved that he had not referred to her as the Countess. That would have been difficult. She doubted she could have kept from laughing, although it was true that she was indubitably a Countess, even if the Count had only just renewed his credentials.

"It will be a few minutes. Will you take wine, Inspector? Red or white? Or would you prefer a sherry? Very light. From Jerez de la Frontera."

"Thank you, Madame, but coffee will be generous enough." Alicia nodded absently, determining to make herself somewhat vague and unsolid, a presence to deflect attention rather than to focus it. She ran a finger over the surface of the objects that lined the small passageway that led down from the living room to the back of the hacienda, her fingernail scratching lightly the tops of statues as she passed. The Inspector straightened as he heard the unmistakable sound. The door opened, closed, and the Inspector was alone with Stefan Mauger.

"It is an imposition, I'm quite certain, to bother you on Sunday. I presume you are Catholic and religious."

"It's a presumption, Inspector. I'm afraid not. Born Catholic, yes, but not at all observant."

"I understand. I'm no different myself, I suppose, although I never had any faith to lose, unless being descended from Indians gives one a special religion in this country."

"In what sense?"

"It's only," the Inspector renewed cannily, quite aware of the direction in which he wanted to move the conversation, "that the Indians of Mexico were once deeply religious. It was all religion. That object there, for instance, the handsome figure with the agonized mouth, covered in the skin of captives . . ."

"The Xipe, you mean? A magnificent sculpture, technically exiguous, but emotionally persuasive. All the horror of the ancient religion. Yes, what about the Xipe, Inspector?"

"I was only going to point out that my own connection to that god is probably more settled in my blood than my connection to the Church. The one came out of this earth, this misery and this grandness which is our land; whereas Christianity is a traveling religion, going from place to place in movable arks of the sacrament, opening the door, dispensing the wafer, closing it, and moving on. The Church only pretends to stay put and help. Its real concern is to move on and save. The Indians, however, have to stand fast, to cope year in, year out with a miserable climate, earthquakes, floods, starvation, drought, and to this condition they, we, I myself, I suppose, invented a grim tale of a waxing and waning creation which required, in times of particular stress, the proofs and confirmations of personal sacrifice, bloods and skins in which to nourish and clothe the gods. The Church, on the contrary, despite the gentle Jesus, burns us out and tells us to pray. What the Church can't reform it covers with prayer. But my friend, Indians like myself (and even though I have a properly Spanish name I am descended from the Toltecs, indeed, our genealogy can be traced back quite definitely to the late fifteenth century just after the Spanish Conquest) . . ."

"Quite a bit further than my own. You should be the Count, Inspector."

"And what would you become in that case? An inspector? I don't think you'd enjoy that."

"Enough of this fascinating discussion. I suspect I would agree in part, although I'd take a different religion or at least a different rite for my own. Your visit has, however, more than an ecumenical intention, doesn't it?"

"Agreed. To the point then or at least near to the point. The truth is that I need your help. Don't protest that you have none to give an inspector of the police. You do. You do. We are in pursuit of an extremely intelligent, sophisticated, and gifted thief, someone who has for many years now, with various subterfuges and disguises—sometimes as amateur, sometimes as learned professor, sometimes as private dealer, again as public vendor *en masse,* and finally as private collector—managed to skim the treasure of at least six major archaeological excavations, and probably countless others of which we have no record. Do you understand clearly? This man, whoever he is, has succeeded in going into business against the Mexican government, digging her treasures, accumulating and disbursing her patrimony as though it were his own to distribute, and I suspect doing so to very handsome profit."

"I should think the thief a clever scoundrel. I agree with all you say about him. But it's still not clear how I can help you."

The Inspector stood up and clapped his hands dramatically, pointing with excitement to a small Olmec figure that stood amidst a field of figurines, all women from various tribes and cultures of Mexico, women with slant eyes and hairdos of pinched clay, women with serene death-like countenance, women with overwhelming pudenda, women of jade, serpentine, red, brown, grayish clay. Rushing toward the heavy colonial table on which the women's assembly was arranged, the Inspector pinched her between careful fingers and laying her upon his outstretched palm returned and extended her to Stefan Mauger. "Now, do consider this, Count von Mauger. This Olmec figure, for example, was stolen. Yes. Yes. Indubitably stolen. It is identical with one that was stolen three years ago from a dig in the north. We have all the documentation in this case. The lucky documentation that in most other cases we lack. This particular tomb had been officially opened, photographed, and then sealed for clearing several weeks later. During that brief interval, the grave was robbed and the site photographed, minus its contents, and published by one Levis Glyphstein in a German scientific journal. Fortunately we were able to circulate quite decent blowups of the actual objects. This most certainly is one of them. Most certainly." The Inspector lowered the Olmec figurine into Stefan's hand. Stefan looked at it carefully and then, grimacing, raised it above his head and threw it against the wall of the fireplace.

The Inspector had watched Stefan Mauger with horror, the hand rising, the fingers releasing the delicate ceramic, the flight of the woman across the room, breaking against the stone and shattering. "I don't believe this," the Inspector gasped, passing a hand over his eyes as if to deny what his eyes had seen. "That was monstrous, Count von Mauger. Monstrous." The Inspector's voice was shrill with anger. "Such a beautiful creature. Such a beautiful creature." The Inspector might have wept; his lips quivered and a dot of saliva appeared at the edge of his mouth. "Why did you do this terrible thing?"

Stefan Mauger watched the Inspector's outrage impassively, at once both aware and unaware of the vast risk he had taken. "First, Inspector," Stefan began, his voice so low the Inspector was obliged to come to rest to hear him, "it was not monstrous. Second, sir, the piece belongs to me. I paid for it from a reputable runner of such things. And thirdly, after considerable expense and research, I've discovered beyond a shadow of doubt that the piece is not right. I believe it a fake, a perfect fake, introduced I suspect into the dig you are referring to, by precisely the thief who removed the original. The Olmec figurine is a lie. I've left it amidst all those genuine objects more as a game for the educated eye—to determine who knows and who does not. I'm afraid, Inspector, that your enthusiasm is more genuine than your knowledge. In this case, at least. At least in this case, although I am told by my friends in the Capital that you are deeply learned about many other aspects of the classic culture. Bowls, for instance, are your specialty, not Olmec figurines. Most certainly not Olmec figurines." Stefan Mauger had observed the Inspector count off with his eyes the bowls that circled the turret, his eyes lighting with pleasure and covetousness. A lucky stab, a successful recovery. For the moment, for the moment.

"A fake? And your word against whose? A photograph? Not a very good one, that's true. But smashing it? Incredible." Fortunately Alicia returned, holding open the door for Martina who carried a large tray, struggling to elevate it to the level of her eyes like the regalia of royalty. Alicia whispered and Martina put it down on the sideboard that stood behind the Inspector's couch. Soon the refreshment was distributed, little plates piled high with small open sandwiches and cakes flavored with anise. The Inspector nibbled, eating little although he was immensely hungry, anger having set his appetite in motion. "Forgive us if we continue our conversation."

The Inspector acknowledged Alicia, who settled herself beside her husband on a rush stool, her long red skirt, fringed with alternating border silk of black and gold, hiding her feet, which pushed nervously against the sides of red leather pumps. "By all means, Inspector. You won't be bothered if I listen."

"Not at all. Thank you. And now. Count von Mauger, we do have a problem. You did after all break an object, fake or not, which the police regard as having been stolen. . . ."

"Inspector. Enough of this, please. I am not being difficult, but I say again, the piece was mine to preserve or smash as I chose. If you are here on official business, I should be the first to know. If you have a warrant to search my home, let's be about it. If you wish to accuse me of something, I am at your service. I'm here. I'm not moving. I have no intention of leaving. I have nothing to confess. Much to admit, perhaps, but nothing to confess. So?"

The Inspector was again calm. He acknowledged to himself the profundity of the defeat that Stefan Mauger had administered. It was the ability to recognize defeat as quickly as success that had over the years augmented the considerable reputation of Inspector Mariposa. He knew when he was outwitted and quickly accommodated the information to a change of strategy. He determined to proceed more slowly, to allow the soft currents of the sea to gather force slowly, to pick the bottom clean of information, before assembling the overwhelming wave. "I apologize, Count. I do apologize. I overstepped myself. I have come innocently enough. For information only, for ideas, for consultation, not for accusation. I would have wished the Olmec lady intact. More because she was immensely beautiful than because I believed her real. Beauty is (what do the Americans say?) deep as skin. Of no consequence. The photograph was probably deceiving. I accept your freedom to do with your possessions as you will. But then your possessions are somehow to the point. You are a brilliant and discerning collector," the Inspector acknowledged, moving his head in a swift turn about the living room. "In this room alone—and leave aside what all the others must contain—is a treasure worthy of Moctezuma's piety and Cortés's avarice. A gold pectoral. The jade necklace in that case. The astonishing Teotihuacán onyx. The bowls, yes, the magnificent bowls. Xipe. Tlac in ecstasy. The most perfect pair of Remojadas smiling girls I've ever seen. And that Veracruz crucible. The *hacha*. Quite astonishing! And the Jaina—the most remarkable figure from Jaina I've ever seen . . . And when did you begin all this—I was about to say—accumulation? Wrong. A vulgar word. There isn't a piece here that suggests the mass of agglomeration. The criterion is perfection. The eye of an artist. An artist! But of course, you *are* an artist."

"A sculptor. Yes. An artist."

"And a very good one I'm led to understand. Is there

anything of yours here, in this room? I don't see anything here that I would call modern." The Inspector moved tentatively. He had little knowledge of any art beyond the end of Mayan civilization, regarding everything later as either a denial of his past or a modulation of its violence to a more seductive line. Modern art he considered a humanist indulgence, compelling an uncongenial reality to the round and curve of pleasantness. It was a prejudiced reading, he readily admitted when he attended exhibitions in Mexico City, but he held to it. Not even the forceful Siqueiros or the orotund Rivera could persuade him that after the debacle of Conquest must come the reversion of revolution. He wanted, unlike them, to move the clock back differently, to recover the time of the ancients not by resetting the timepiece with rapid revolutions, but by retracing slowly, obliging the Mexican to recover his primordial flesh in seasonal moltings, putting off skin pleasures and adornments until the bare bone of the skeletal vision would be revealed once more and the great god, no longer come humbly calling in a ship from the sea but striding over the waves, would march up the land to the capital. It was a fevered exaltation that animated the Inspector and he did not dare yet to share its brutal rhythms with this Count whom he took to be a gentleman of the West, exceedingly canny and elliptical.

"Modern. No. There's nothing here that's mine, but there is a great deal here that I would call modern. Much too much in fact."

"Now that's a remarkable statement. Too much modern in this assembly of work from a thousand years ago."

"Precisely, Inspector." Stefan was beginning his admission. "These works are of the modern age. My own—out there in the studio—that's the ancient work."

"Astonishing. What a point of view!"

"Not really. Convergence of intention, that's all. Your

ancients read into the foundations of the universe a myth of sustenance and loss which ours has made absolutely explicit. Tell me now, Inspector. Is there a substantial difference between a myth that would startle Cortés with a mountain of whitened bones in Texcoco (estimated by Bernal Díaz at one hundred thousand) and the mountain of unburied bodies the Americans found at Buchenwald? The difference isn't in the number. The difference is attitude. Your ancients murdered for the sake of a muddled metaphysic. Ours had no such lofty doctrine. Notwithstanding, they rationalized their paranoia in the same way. They murdered races, classes, cultures that impeded their greatness. The true difference is that in your ancient days—even cowed and terrified—the victims begged for the knife and celebrated their evisceration. I read in Westheim, I believe, that a defeated Mayan warrior nobleman begged that he be sacrificed. He was denied because he was a celebrated hero of battle. He died of grief instead. That couldn't happen in our day. It's hardly likely that a poor Jew would have begged to be gassed as an honor. No, my friend, Inspector, I find your ancient doctrine thoroughly distasteful, loathsome if you will, exceedingly modern."

The Inspector listened with an aching ear, pained by Stefan's reading of his world, the similitudes it defined, the analogies of violence upon which it rested. Several times he wanted to interrupt, to stab the air with his index finger while he refuted, but he restrained himself, allowing the Count to come to a finish. It seemed more and more to him that if not actually the thief, the Count was close to the thief, one face, at least, among others, that the thief had assumed. He realized, however, that without clear identification, a formal confession, the naming of objects in his collection that indubitably derived from burgled excavations, he had little or no hope of trapping him. It seemed, however, that another way lay open, a way more tortuous and uncertain, which could result in the same thing, the thief's unmasking. His sense of the Count, his handsome wife, whose hand rested now on the knee of her husband, the old furnishings, the bright colors, the glorious collection, which contained not a single work made by Stefan Mauger, the sculptor, pointed to something odd, something that evaded the Inspector but that he wished to grasp.

"Since I am a stranger in your home, I am obliged by politeness and circumspection to see only what you allow me to see, Count von Mauger. I have, as you pointed out, no right to inspect your hacienda without a warrant. I have none. I could return with one, but how foolish. I have no reason to suspect you of theft—of being my clever thief, that is—and even less reason, having met you, to think you so stupid—if you were my thief—as to have a closet filled with stolen objects, neatly tagged, awaiting my authorized return. It has to be more difficult than that." The Inspector temporized aloud, watching the Count carefully through half-closed eyes, daring to work upon him what he had worked upon so many others, the petty rites of indirection. As he spoke he walked about the living room, his coffee cup in hand, sipping from time to time, putting it to rest upon a table or a ledge, picking up an object and raising it to the sunlight, replacing it and continuing his walk. "And yet, however much I argue with myself, I am forced to think that somehow there is a link between you and this unknown thief. You have so many rare and exemplary objects. Not the casual pickings of the Indian runners who uncover an object in their fields, chip it with their implements, glue it clumsily, and bring it in a sack to the collectors. Such pieces —occasionally glorious—are already soiled. Surface pieces, I think of them. Buried by casual catastrophe—fire, war, the movement of the Mayan peoples—they are not like

Monte Alban, for example, laid to rest in state. They are not the pieces of royalty, portions of the treasury, the barter goods of the dead selected to keep company and enchant the gods of the netherworld. All of yours, however, are so magnificent, so perfect that they seem to have been chosen from the underground caves and burial sites of princes and governors, picked by an eye of immense discernment from among literally hundreds that even there, beneath the earth, had suffered damage through the centuries from earth falls and quakes. From whom, Count, did you acquire these? May I have the name of your principal source?" Inspector Mariposa had settled himself at the last before Stefan Mauger, his cup to his lips, his eyes fully opened at the final question, but behind, in the recesses of the brain where it would be hard to perceive the twinkle of amusement, the Inspector knew the answer he would hear, and was already beyond the answer to the larger scheme whose lineaments he had delightedly begun to sketch and examine.

"But you already know the name, my dear Mariposa," the Count replied intimately, moving rapidly to catch up with the Inspector's adroit maneuvering, determining to cover the first revelation of his inner life with its diversion. "Levis Glyphstein, of course."

"Precisely as I supposed. Levis Glyphstein. And who is Levis Glyphstein? What does he look like? Where does he reside? How may we find him?" the Inspector asked predictably, so predictably that Stefan Mauger took note of a kind of unanticipated dull-wittedness, the return of the professional to the domicile of the ingenious amateur. It was alarming to watch the Inspector's languorous lids open upon turquoise blue eyes, even more green and ominous in the bright afternoon sunlight. It seemed as though the Inspector was too eager, too satisfied with the new name, too complaisant in the information to be believed completely

and Stefan composed his answer, therefore, with less elaboration than he had originally planned. He had thought to
invent Levis Glyphstein, to give him a body, a training, a
culture and inheritance, a character and wit that would
send the Inspector tracking a very definite and precise person who never existed, but instead it seemed wise at this
juncture to evade and dissimulate.

"The truth, Inspector Mariposa, is that I've never met
Professor Glyphstein. It is the case that from time to time I
have received a call from someone who purports to be Professor Glyphstein, but even this I doubt. I have certainly
spoken to him once, perhaps more than once, but each time
the voice of Levis Glyphstein is different: sometimes it is a
voice gruff and hard; sometimes heavily accented; sometimes reedy, thin, and exceedingly cultivated; and once,
even, very amusing, it was a woman. But the procedure was
always the same. 'Would you be interested in an astonishing
hacha recently found at such and such? Yes, you would be.
An agent will deliver it to you next month. Please pay him
whatever—three thousand, four thousand pesos.' "

"And you pay him?"

"Promptly. I pay him immediately."

"I see. It's strange, however, don't you think, that a man
who can afford to pay three and four thousand pesos to
purchase a *hacha* should still . . ." The Inspector paused
briefly to withdraw from his side pocket a piece of paper
from which he read rapidly, "owe eight hundred pesos to
the automobile mechanic, fifteen hundred to the local car-
penter, more than four hundred to the *carniceria*, and even,
I note among a whole list of others, forty pesos to the
herbolaria for a potion she told our officer was intended to
combat sexual lassitude. Amusing the precision with which
bills are recorded."

Stefan Mauger blushed at the last. He recalled that extravagance with embarrassment. He had assumed that a potion of some order would be useful in the first months after the arrival of Maria. Of course, it wasn't needed as it turned out and, as Alicia, silent and attentive as she had vowed, interjected, "How unnecessary, Stefan. You've been perfectly satisfactory without a potion. Or perhaps you've been using it all the time and have never told. How sly of you!" Alicia laughed nervously.

"Tell me about all your debts, Count. They do mount up to a sizable sum. I figure them at more than fifteen thousand pesos and I'm told in town that there's talk of bringing all this credit to a halt, demanding payment, or bringing suit against you."

"How very ungrateful the shopkeepers can be, don't you think, Stefan?" Alicia purred, behaving for that instant as though she not only were, but felt herself to be, a Countess. She performed well; Inspector Mariposa was impressed by the alacrity of her response.

"We can deal with it, of course. Sell one object and all the bills will be paid."

"Precisely. Sell one object stolen by Levis Glyphstein and sold to you. Of course, we'll have to prove it—which object is stolen—and find Levis Glyphstein in the bargain if he really exists (about which I have my doubts), all very tedious, time-consuming, and unpleasant. Moreover, I doubt that we can develop the evidence in sufficient time to secure an injunction against the sale of anything. So. Go right ahead. Sell an object. I advise it in fact. But it is strange nonetheless that people of your class, breeding, education, keep poor shopkeepers waiting while they buy objects."

"Not at all, Inspector. It's commonplace behavior. Shoddy, but commonplace. The rich always think the poor can wait. And even when the rich are no longer rich—as you'll find out tomorrow when the banks open and you examine our records—they continue to behave as though they are. It reassures the once rich to believe they can still keep tradespeople waiting. It's a nasty habit. Let's pay them off, Alicia. This coming week. We'll manage without debts, don't you think?" Alicia shifted uncomfortably before this resolution. They had barely ten thousand pesos in all, between funds in the bank and what remained in Stefan's desk after bribing the Captain through his son for the majestic figure he had left behind in the kitchen; nothing had been received in advance on the stolen treasure; her father was on holiday in Scandinavia and not quite accessible to a telegraphed appeal. But then she knew that Stefan was working through some other decision than the payment of debts. "Yes, we shall manage without debts," Stefan continued, "without debts—perhaps even . . ." Stefan found another phrase clinging to the monster of his debts, but at that juncture was unwilling to speak it.

"Perhaps even—what?" The Inspector had noted the upward tilt of reverie as Stefan's voice rose to self-consultation and stopped.

"I was going to say, but resisted, that we can do without debts, but also without all this, all these weighty possessions."

"You mean sell all these, your collection?"

"Sell? Destroy? Give away? It doesn't matter, but finally lift the weight of these possessions from our backs."

The Inspector heard the words and noted their sequence, but he hardly believed him, assuming that like his treatment of tradespeople, it was only the further self-deceiving of the rich. (Mariposa, not unnaturally, discredited the rich. He regarded those who had come to settle in Mexico as frivolous people with ailments and tidy incomes, who regarded his native soil as an attractive place in which to settle down,

281

construct little fiefdoms of manipulation, and put Mexico to work making their idle time and late days pleasant before death overtook them in the sunlight. The rich—and anyone who could afford to live in Mexico without working was perforce rich—were disrespectful, and in the face of such disrespect the Inspector could be immense in his irritation and contempt.) He thought it hardly likely therefore that Count von Mauger could part with this collection, even though it symbolized for him, as he had made exceedingly clear, a world for which he had thorough distaste. "I think that hardly likely—disposing of all this, smashing it against the wall (one object is gesture enough, no?), feeding it to the ceremonial bonfire, selling it back to traders and dealers. Not likely, I think."

"You're not an artist, Inspector. If you were, you might begin to understand what moves me, my disgust with all this. As it is you are a policeman with a special passion on the hunt for a discerning and clever thief whom you think I resemble. Well, there we have it for the moment."

Stefan Mauger stood up and extended his hand to Inspector Mariposa, thinking by this gesture to conclude the interview. The Inspector, however, was not finished; although he had risen from the couch, laying his cup upon the plate soiled with crumbs and dots of mayonnaise and placing it indecorously beside him on the couch cushion, he was not ready to leave. The extended hand was acknowledged, but the Inspector received, not the hand, but the words that had accompanied it. "To the point. How should I know that you are an artist, the gifted sculptor to whom they charmingly refer in town as the maker of 'ídolos modernos'? I've seen nothing. Since we have passed for the moment beyond the business of crime to more personal and universal perplexities, I should be more than honored if you would show me something of your work. It would interest me immensely."

"I doubt it would interest you. It moves from a different

view of it all than the one that fascinates you. As I've said. I'm the man of ancient preferences. You're the modern. But you must judge that for yourself. I'm quite willing. I've begun to like my work again. Even if it will make no sense to you."

"But you must, Count von Mauger, allow me to judge that for myself. As I judge everything you say. You will understand, won't you, that thus far you have persuaded me of nothing. Everything that you've said must go away with me, stored and noted. Later, when I am calm, when I let the sands run through my fingers, I will discover from which rocks they have been ground—bright with truth or dull and lying. But it's always the same with police inspectors. We speculate our thieves—we reconstruct them and then we are ready at least in theory to apprehend them."

"So that's the way it works? Excellent. But you needn't be so avuncular. I realize that I'm under suspicion, although of precisely what I'm unclear. It will become clearer, won't it?"

"It will be made clearer in time. I promise you that."

The Inspector once more surveyed the room, noting a pile of periodicals among which he was certain he would find the German publication in which Levis Glyphstein appeared from time to time. He noted as well more than a score of pieces that tallied in style with the general contents of the digs that had been robbed, but he recognized that all this observation was circumstantial at best, hardly the basis of an accusation. He was fabricating tests and inculpations as cautiously as Stefan Mauger was devising feints and evasions. The mortal combat was joined; not yet hand to hand, without weapons and wounds, but still combat, still mortal.

"And these are my creatures."

Stefan Mauger opened his arm in a wave about the studio. The sculptures, clearly visible, were nonetheless made pallid by the afternoon light, white marble appearing gray and hard dark woods yellow like old parchment. Everything, beasts and birds, parts of body, masked heads—the congress of his creatures, dimmed and dulled in the sun—were as they should be for Inspector Mariposa, neither grand nor threatening, recumbent in the daylight, supine and reposeful. "At night they come alive in the firelight, but now they're timorous. They tend to hide in the day."

The Inspector listened closely, startled by the alteration in Stefan Mauger's voice, soft and affectionate in the company of his familiars, plangent, almost supplicatory, as though asking their permission to come upon them unawares. "They are quite alive, don't you think?" Stefan asked disingenuously, picking up from the worktable the marble of an ear from which the intricacy of audition had been reduced to layering of canals within a circular cavern lipped like the edge of a moribund volcano. "Such an immense world is the ear. Only the terracing of sound makes its construction so elaborate, but when you see the ear in removal from the sheerness of the skull, you look at it quite differently. I no longer think about the ordinary ear of man —the involuntary organ for receiving everything tender and violent in the concussion of air—but rather the modeling of levels and angles, like the sides of old mountains cultivated for centuries by terraces and walls. I think of the ear as a topography seen from an airplane, very far away, a circular system for shunting sound from confusion to lucidity and meaning. This one works. The marble is so handsome, with the slightest suggestion of a gray vein."

Inspector Mariposa was disinclined to chatter. He had heard that Stefan Mauger was a sculptor. Captain Gutiérrez, having visited the hacienda several times, had described him carefully. It was from the Captain that he had heard the phrase *"idolos modernos,"* which amused him since it led him to believe that this Mauger specialized in making the kind of adaptations of Mayan sculpture one found in the market stalls of Cuernavaca and San Miguel Allende, passing not as authentic works of ancient art, but as what were called by the artisans who lounged about the square, "free and creative renderings of ancient artifacts." Nothing of the kind, the Inspector could see immediately. Stefan Mauger was a considerable artist.

"And this work, Count? The eye. It is an eye, isn't it?" The Inspector held in his hand a small slab of sandstone into whose surface a shallow eye (much like fragmentary Sumerian glyphs, so persuasive they are preserved in the absence of the whole frieze) had been carved. "Is it an ancient or a modern treasure?"

"A half-opened eye. Much like your own during our interview. Ancient, I hope, but I made it."

"Yes. Do I . . . well, never mind that. It is magnificent. This eye. It is your eye, after all. Not my own certainly. Glorious. Glorious." The Inspector held it close to his face, tilting it in the gathering shadows to catch a shifting ray of sunlight. It glistened and enlarged, the simple line, unadorned and without natural allusion, a further reduction to simplicity of the marble eye that Stefan had previously completed in the round.

"A new series. Human fossils. Each part of the body is cut into an irregular slab of sandstone and mounted like an archaeological artifact upon rods sunk into a stone base or soldered to a metallic plate. They allude to ancient times, but unlike an eye of Horus or the genitals of Isis, their only theophany is that they are creation reduced to essential line."

The Inspector held the sculpture to his chest and turned away without comment, to wander again through the studio, increasingly excited by the profusion of works—animal and human shapes, each one straining toward a more exacting and severe articulation; ecstasy and pain (so common in the sculpture of his own tradition) wholly absent from their expression. The work was all clarity, concision, and lonely essence.

"You are a considerable artist. I am very moved, grateful even, Count von Mauger. But all the more it baffles me. I wonder? Would you allow me to ask something that troubles me now even more profoundly? How can it be, how can it be that the man who can make all this is the one I believe a thief?"

Stefan Mauger smiled faintly. His eyes, however, succumbed, becoming distant and dark. He replied with weariness.

"Inspector Mariposa. Inspector Mariposa. How can I explain to you the truth? The connection is subtle. So subtle."

"I suppose it is," the Inspector commented sympathetically. "You will explain it to me?" his voice inquired quietly.

"Tonight?"

"You would like me to return this evening?"

"I should like that very much, Inspector Mariposa. Please have dinner with us. Perhaps we can conclude our business. I promise you, if not the criminal, at least the crime."

Inspector Mariposa had been watching Stefan Mauger carefully, his drawn face shadowed in the closing day, immensely tired, looking out into a room filled with his creatures. Something stirred in the Inspector which he had not anticipated. He still held the glyphic eye to his chest; he had not replaced it upon the worktable. Stefan Mauger was trying somehow to reach him, to move over the chasm that separated the pride of his contempt from a private gift—great or small was of no importance—which enabled him to create a treasury of creatures that needed no opening of graves and no plunder.

"Señor Mauger," the Inspector began modestly, "if only I could afford to purchase your glorious eye!"

"Where have you been? I expected at least a tutti of trumpets. My God. Nothing. Alicia is nowhere. Not even a woman's squeal of delight. The house was empty. I let myself in. The door's open, you know? Don't you have ferocious bandits? Is it the right house, I asked myself? But then I knew it had to be—all these grotesque effigies. I made myself comfortable as you can see. A hug, Stefan? At least a hug for an old friend. Stefan. Look at me. I must be dying. I feel like a soggy poached egg. This suit! It hangs on me like drapery. There's nothing left of me. Nothing."

Clemens Rosenthal was lying on the couch, shoes off, his toes about to burst through grimy sweat socks, the light odors of travel, musty, clinging to him as in a hotel room with sealed windows. He talked, however, in his usual nervous manner, words of unease fingering the air to catch hold. Out of place anywhere, Clemens was also changed— the ballast of air and water of which his largeness was once composed had receded to a profile of enormity; still tall, he was without bulk, not merely thinned, but sliced, as though an enormous chunk of girth and buttocks had been pared away by a Procrustes of the circumference. Stefan Mauger stood over him and examined his attenuation, the large head, hair slate gray, precipitous cheeks descending to jowls like those of a starved bulldog, and blotches of reddening skin beneath his chin where Clemens had hacked with his razor, refusing to look while he shaved (lest he be accused, he claimed, of premeditating self-destruction), a shred of toilet paper still visible on a large nick he had taken just beneath his ear. Stefan was almost nauseated by the appearance of his old friend; he seemed so fragmentary, like a half-exhaled rubber toy, patched with bits of tubing, glue seeping from beneath the edges.

"You're a shadow, not a sight, old Clemens. I can guess what you once were but I can't see it any more," Stefan said affectionately, sitting down on the side of the couch and laying his arm across Clemens's chest. "What's wrong with you? Are you ill?"

Clemens turned his head upward to the turret, where dusk was settling like gathered cloth, a rich gray fabric suppressing the bright colors of the room to chiaroscuro. "It's nothing, really. It had to come, don't you think?" he answered sadly. "A bleeding ulcer. That's what the doctor said. Operated three months ago. The wound's staunched, but all I can have now is milk. With a little whiskey. Still permitted. A little whiskey. Too much milk. Too little whiskey. Shall we have some now? This minute. The little whiskey."

Stefan stood up, looking suspiciously at his friend, unpersuaded. "Are you sure it's all right?" Stefan's look asked, but Clemens nodded vigorously and then dropped his head back on the pillow while he rubbed a patch of stomach skin with irritation. Stefan had already bent over the cabinet beneath the sideboard near the couch; he couldn't see the grimace of pain which for an instant strained his friend's face and then relaxed as an arm extended over the sideboard to receive the filled shot glass. "Ah. It's good. It burns, but it's a pleasant pain for a change. I can have the milk later. As long as I keep the ratio three to one. Doctor says four to one, but threes are more mysterious and perfect. Trismegistus to Paracelsus. Everything in threes. Damn it all, Stefan, where's a hug? I've traveled three thousand miles to see you. Not even a hug." Stefan Mauger slid down beside him on the couch and squeezed his sagging face in both hands. Clemens lifted himself on an elbow; Stefan kissed his cheeks.

"Thank God you've come, old Clemens. No better time. The ancient Constantin is dying and so are we all."

"Won't hear of it. Not all at once. Anyway ancient Constantin has already joined the monuments of his ancestors."

"Dead? Is he dead? It's not possible. When exactly?"

"I'm not certain. Yesterday or the day before. But you knew he was sick, didn't you?"

"You wrote me that weeks ago when you announced your visit."

"The commemorative interview. That's what I've come for, isn't it?" Clemens asked vaguely, trying to recall the excuse he had given Stefan for the urgency of his excursion.

"He changed my life."

"I thought all along that I had."

"You, too, you first, but Brancusi for years after, to this minute." For so many years Stefan had pushed the expectation of Brancusi's death to the side of his mind, keeping it distant, refusing to consider it as a possibility even after Clemens wrote to tell him that Brancusi was failing. Eighty-one. He had the world's permission to die, but not Stefan's. He had had no contact with Brancusi since they had said good-bye in Tirgu-Jiu, but that did not mean that Stefan had forgotten him. When the letter from Clemens arrived, Stefan had taken two photographs from an album he kept with his boxes of clippings and articles and tacked them to the wall of the studio. He was preparing himself for Brancusi's death. He only put out photographs of the dead.

"I'm not sure what this will do to me."

"Brancusi's death? But why should it do anything?"

"Why should it? You're right, of course. But Brancusi wasn't only a genius. He was much more than that."

"We're beginning the interview. I'm not ready. I have no energy to take notes."

"Stop it, Clemens. I don't give a damn about your interview."

"Neither do I. It was only a pretext to see you," Clemens answered, his voice strained by a supplicatory inflection.

"You didn't need one," Stefan replied briskly.

"Yes, I did. We've hardly written these past years."

"I know. But nothing's changed. We followed you. We read everything you sent us. Mailed in those gray envelopes. We've loved you from a distance. That's all."

"It's different now," Clemens wanted to explain, but he wasn't ready.

"It *is* different. Constantin is dead and an inspector of police is coming to dinner."

"Who is he?"

"He suspects me of being a thief."

"Of *what*?"

"Of being a thief."

"Stealing *what*? Plantain fronds, gold teeth, what does he think you've been stealing?"

"All this. Every object in this room."

"And have you been?"

"Yes."

"But why? For money? I thought Alicia's father sent you money."

"Of course he did, and I made sculpture and sold it from time to time. But none of that has anything to do with why I stole."

"Not the money?"

"It wasn't the money. Alicia thought it was for a long time. She knows better now. No. Money wasn't the reason."

"So why?"

"You remember what Le Douanier said about Brancusi.

It doesn't matter if you do. I remember everything about Brancusi. 'You have made the ancient modern.' That's the whole of it. Brancusi did what I can't. He made everything ancient part of our world—he lived in the center of the city of cities and made it simple; he made silence out of noise; everything in his studio was white and dusty, but the flowers were fresh every day, the bread was baked at home, and the steak was cooked on charcoal; he played golf in plus fours, danced in the streets in paper hats on July fourteenth, and every day worked like a slave who ran the universe. 'Make like a God, rule like a King, work like a slave.' His motto. He lived it. Mine. Destroy what I can't make. Be angry like a Lord. Try to keep from strangling on my rage. Lived mine, too. I've been very foolish. And they've found me out."

Clemens lifted himself from the couch and embraced Stefan, holding him gently, his large head pressing against Stefan's ear, until the pain returned. He groaned and fell back on the couch.

"My pills, Stefan. In my overnight bag in the hall. There's a whole dispensary in the shaving kit—any vial will do. They're all pain-killers." Stefan went quickly to the hallway, where he found the black vinyl traveling bag. Opening it and feeling about amid crushed shirts and socks, loose papers and books, he found the shaving kit, which contained three small plastic bottles. He handed one to Clemens, who poured out several tablets and threw them into his mouth, swallowing them in a gathered hoard of spit. After a minute he lay back, smiled bravely, and began to talk again. "Disgusting, aren't I, Stefan? Pain and pills. Disgusting." Clemens lamented his condition, dismissing the pain with irritation. "It doesn't matter, all this, does it, Stefan?" Clemens rushed on, his words gushing stertorously from his fount of pain. He had been taking the pain-killers for hours, ever since he left New York; anticipating a renewal of pain, he dropped a pill into his whiskey and drank it off before the flight steward had even withdrawn the tray. Fortunately he had slept most of the way from New York to Mexico City. The connection to Campeche was lucky, only a three-hour wait. He had moved through the airport like a sleepwalker, hulking through the brightly colored waiting room, decorated with mosaics, drinking generous margaritas from the bar. By the time the flight departed, he was weary from drink and his pills. He revived while the pain slumbered, but coming home to Stefan and Alicia anguished his violated and cut innards and the pain renewed, stabbing like a cornered marmot, the rodent teeth digging into the curtain of morphia. The pain was returning. "And I come back to you in triumph. Yes, triumph, Stefan. I'm so powerful all of a sudden," Clemens plunged on. "All of a sudden. I help everyone. Museums, universities. They're rich all of a sudden and don't know what to do. And of course the artists. The artists. Oh Stefan," Clemens spat through clenched teeth and lifted himself up suddenly and fell back. Stefan watched him helplessly, horrified.

"It's not an ulcer, is it, Clemens?"

Clemens hadn't heard the question; he kept on, trying to thread himself through the pain. "I love the artists. Hopelessly. Whatever aesthetic I have—and they accuse me of having none—I keep to my notebooks. Every time—you know this, Stefan—that a critic has to write, he becomes more than powerful. A cheap god. Killing and making alive. I'm like Sainte-Beuve. I let the truth slip out only when I talk about the dead. Cowardly. But at least I kill no one. And Stefan, my dear friend, Stefan (I'm so happy to be here), I've kept my decency. I don't own a thing but my books. A little drawing Gorky gave me before his death. That's all. I praised his nostalgia in a symposium. Gorky sent me a little sketch he had made for a painting of his boyhood; for once his own warm sadness overwhelmed his paranoia. But besides the Gorky, nothing, nothing, except two works of yours from your Paris days."

"It's not an ulcer, is it, Clemens?" Stefan persisted, cutting in during a pause, when Clemens lay back upon the arm rest, his forehead damp with perspiration, but Clemens still refused the question and continued, "But I rewrote my will. I had left them to Barr's place but changed it to Boston. It wasn't necessary any more. Yes, my old friend, I *am* powerful. I got the Modern to buy two large sculptures from Kootz and placed another up in Buffalo. The check's in the suitcase somewhere. Great deal of money. You really don't have to steal any more."

"It's not an ulcer, is it, Clemens?"

Clemens looked up to Stefan, his eyes clouded from the dosages of morphine, and turned away. There were tears in his eyes.

"I don't think so, but they never tell you. They're all nameless doctors with nameless medicines and nameless diseases. It's all a code. They speak immense complexities, like formalist critics talking about diagonals and foregrounds and perspective. Who can understand them? The fact is, I know. I know everything about the limit of talent, my own and theirs. They think medicine has to do with avoiding death. They're wrong, you know. Medicine is simply the art of making death precise, slowing down its ineluctability, obliging us to wait it out. Yes. I'm dying. If you don't mind, I should prefer to die here."

Stefan was in no mood to pretend; once he might have ridiculed the drama of Clemens's dying, but now it was beside the point. Brancusi had died; so had his father. Both had died alone, he imagined, or at least out of reach. Brancusi had no lover that he had ever heard about, and he knew what his father's cubicle looked like. Clemens could die in bed, with a large and bright Mexican blanket pulled to his chin and Maria laughing at the butterflies that flew into the rooms.

Of course, he nodded grimly to Clemens, of course, of course, and Clemens received the permission with his eyes, settling his chin to chest, relieved, received, at rest. "It won't be for a while. I can promise you that, Stefan. Not immediately. Not tomorrow. We'll get done with your business first. Next week. Next month. Not much beyond that. Remissions are unlikely. So then. I won't become a burden. If it gets out of hand (*I'll scream less, you know, with someone around to hear me*), I have enough prescription to take me out. The doctor said that about eight full-strength pills a day should hold me for some time; after that I have syringes and morphine vials; deep sleep, coma, and that will be all. No burden to you and Alicia. Alicia, Alicia," Clemens roused himself smiling. "Where is she? Where is my old girl friend? Let me see her now, Stefan."

Stefan had been listening to Clemens, his weary voice trailing like a winding vine, circling the air in unemphatic whirls, gaining unpredictable strength and dying away, the voice strong on the wrong words, weakening before "morphine," encouragingly loud at "coma," disengaged and indifferent before the end; only at the very last, calling for Alicia, Clemens became familiarly affectionate and sly. He was for the moment without pain. Stefan went to the kitchen door beyond the dining room a foot below the level of the spacious living room and called in Alicia's fond phrase, *"Viens vite, viens vite. Le grand Clemens est arrivé."*

Alicia kissed Clemens ferociously, kissing his head and his cheeks, her face melting with smiles. Immense Clemens produced joy. In the time—not more than a minute—that it took for Alicia to kerchief her hair and dry her hands, Clemens sat up on the couch, even jamming his feet into cracked black oxfords. His arms were open to receive her and she laughed with pleasure to have his arms around her, his hands rubbing her back with a delight that hid all sensuality. "Oh dear Clemens. Thank God you've come," she added at the last, looking diffidently toward Stefan, who watched them both.

"I'm grateful to be here." He stopped; he was about to add something, but his voice quavered slightly and he bit the words. "Who's that beyond you, loping like a desert camel?"

"Maria. That's Maria. Our Maria," Stefan announced, introducing Maria with an exemplary smile. It seemed all right. The common love seemed at that moment acceptable to everyone, even to Clemens, perhaps because of Clemens. "Clemens—Maria Cesares. Our great Clemens. Maria." Maria came from behind Alicia and smiled at the large man who began to rise to greet her, but Maria observed his fragile largeness, and with a gentle hand of restraint upon his chest pressed him back upon the couch, kissing his chin warmly.

"I adore kisses."

While the feasting dinner of welcome to Clemens Rosenthal and Inspector Mariposa's supper of recognition cooked slowly, the old, the new friends embraced each other with many words and many smiles, only once invaded by a stitch of pain that moved in a strange diagonal from the lower stomach to a grotesque seizure of the cheek muscle. Stefan mentioned Clemens's ulcer to Alicia when she fetched a glass of water for the pill. Maria had taken Clemens's hand when the spasm occurred and held it fiercely while it lasted, releasing it only when the pill had eased the pain.

Darkness had fallen outside, and in the fields beyond the

house, wild winds, come up from the ocean, streamed through the jungle. The returning rains would start again that night perhaps, the following day with certainty.

Inversions of order. Wrong deaths. Wrong dying.

Clemens is resting in his room; Maria is telling him about Mexico. She loves describing poppies the size of melons and as tall as buildings. Maria is making up a Mexico that Clemens will be able to see. Martina is shining copper service platters that will not shine, spitting upon their surfaces and rubbing them with her elbow. Her old husband feeds the animals even when they're full; he doesn't come indoors. Instead, he brings firewood to the door of the shed and drops it for Martina to collect and stack. Alicia is making *huachinango* in fennel; she places the candles throughout the dining room. She demands an immensity of light, moving light, light that never stands still but angles and darts like speech.

Stefan Mauger waited for the Inspector in the living room. He had not mentioned the hour. Any hour would be right. The food lay in the kitchen, arranged like a window display, cooked and uncooked, parboiled and arrayed, waiting only the time of arrival to be grilled, ovened, and served.

It was a suspended time—a parboiled hour, half done, half undone. The night curled around the house like smoke, entering empty rooms and rooms closed off from the day, rooms that Stefan Mauger had filled over the years with chests and armoires, filled; filled with many stuffs and fabrics, rugs and broideries, old worked lace from Colonial Mexico found in the shops of Merida and Campeche; serapes of all the tribes, ribboned colors which caught the variety of human hues that made up the races of the Mexican Indian, walnut browns and puce, shimmering skins golden with oil, jaundiced yellow skins, mahogany skins glistening with sheep's milk, tribal colors for each skin—in purple, lizard greens, the orange-yellow of mottled mangoes, the reds of coral reefs and the reds of dried blood edged in purple and flies' wings; he had bargained with the backs of the Toltecs who stopped and spread out before the hotel porch in Oaxaca and screamed prices in wild Spanish, the pesos rising in little mountains of excess trampled like sand castles of indifference, serapes and belts, woven with silver and thonged in cured leather, silver earrings and silver necklaces, heavy with crude ambition; toys and Judas figures, skeletons of papier-mâché and cut from paper, thin like bark; dancing figures from the grave that sweetened death to benign inevitability, pressing back upon hearts conversant with dying the remarkable evenness of dying; one cupboard stacked with *ex votos* painted in celebration of a cognizant Virgin who restored all manner of limbs, limbs not even lost, limbs not even imagined possessed by men. Stuff and things, hoardings of closets, packed tight against air and the draining acid of sunlight.

Stefan bought over the years and forgot the buying, laying up these things against a distant day, he recollected, when he thought he might need them. They cost nothing in those early days and he bargained ferociously, walking away in a fury if he was refused his way—or triumphantly demanding the extra rug thrown in with two others. Only to be carried to the hacienda, folded and laid away in one of the rooms. Alicia wondered aloud and Stefan muttered. "Things for the future." He sat in his fan chair and waited for the Inspector. His eyes reviewed each closet, counting out what he remembered of its contents, and then passed down the hallway shelves, recollecting each little figure, each mask, each necklace of gold shells and bone phallus, and his eyes traveled in the turret room, counting bowls and measuring the height of standing figures and seated women

—the displays of little women and bound warriors and ceremonial axes and courtly feather helmets surmounted by ceramic plumes. He lived amidst the artifacts of his anger. Only beyond the house, in the area cleared of grass where the sisal had been dragged for cutting and the animals had been stalled, was he safe among his own making, safe and separated from all these emblems of disconsolation. He had promised the Inspector the crime, but not the criminal. He had no wish to escape. There was no reason to escape now. Constantinople had fallen again; its Emperor had died. Clemens, transposed Jew of Alexandria, born in Galicia, raised up on the streets of New York, had come to Mexico to die. Stefan Mauger, born to a line that had ended, surviving beyond the ending of the line, divested of a cheaply purchased nobility, had tried impatiently to humble the Mexicans again, putting on the regalia of his noble title and its manners. Rage become fright, that was all. Stefan smiled when he remembered the Inspector gulping to address the Count, but even he at the very last, when he admired the fossil eye, returned to the equal speech of gentleman and señor.

"Am I interrupting you, Count von Mauger?" the Inspector asked.

"Let's be done with that at least. I was a Count once. I have not been a Count for many, many years. Forgive me. It was a cheap and useless evasion. He rests in peace, I trust. The old, dead Count of mine. Stefan Mauger, that's all I am, Stefan Mauger, born in Austria, awakened in France, married in New York, struck dumb among the Indians of the north, disconsolate among the Indians of the south, here, in your Mexico, fifty-seven years old. That clears up something, doesn't it, Inspector?"

"It does. It restores the balance. We can at least match each other's derangement without fearing that we transgress unwritten rules of manners. Do you despise manners as much as I do?"

"I am unmannerly by nature. Rude, I think, is the right word. Impatient is even more accurate. I can't bear people who are polite. It's a kind of carefulness and trepidation which breaks down the fiber of the world. Manners marinate everything vital."

"You give me permission to be impolite?"

"If you mean direct. Without holding back, without restraint. Of course. I expect you to force me to my knees, Inspector. If you don't, you'll win nothing. No crime. Certainly no criminal."

It was early evening when Inspector Mariposa reached the old General on the telephone.

"You rode well today in Chapultepec?"

"Every Sunday is the same. My back is still straight and my legs hold the horse like metal hoops. I will ride until I'm a hundred," the General answered, roaring with self-approval. "But you called to tell me you've found your man."

"I have, but he's no ordinary thief."

"I never thought he would be. Who is he? A newcomer, I should think."

"We've never had his name before."

"Does he confess?"

"He will, but it doesn't matter. The confession is irrelevant. Catching the thief without the theft doesn't interest me. Besides, there's more to it than that. He isn't the kind of criminal that needs prison. Society isn't menaced, old friend. He alone is at the heart of the enmity. Anyway, I don't think we can prove it. You know how vague traffic in these things can be. It's anyone's word and without finding the cache, there's no hope. We searched the grounds during the night and I've seen his studio—he's an artist, a remarkable artist—and it's filled with his own masterpieces, not ours."

"He sounds marvelous, but hardly believable."

"Believe me, old *charro*, believe me. I'm returning tomorrow or the day after. Cook me a *zarzuela de mariscos* and I'll tell you all about Stefan Mauger."

It was Alicia's wisdom to construe the dinner as a ravishment of light and flowers. She had determined that if it was to be her last entertainment in Mexico it would be splendid even if the guests were few and the occasion of their gathering portentous. A simple candelabrum ordinarily lit her dining table; Martina was nearly invisible in the gloom beyond the narrow field of light, the food delivered and passed by brown arms that entered and withdrew between the diners.

In the past all would be muted calm. This evening, however, Alicia determined upon a brilliance of light. It might have been a thousand candles, a ballroom of candles, ringing sideboards and dropping low from thin brass tapers, for the light from twenty candles made ballroom brilliance immediately sensible in that modestly proportioned dining room with its generous oak table and straight-back chairs. Everywhere light, candlelight and the smell of flowers, white and pink gardenias before each placemat and a centerpiece of red peonies and yellow coreopsis, interwoven by a circlet of ivy. Ravishment of flickered light and drifting sweetness, and the food—the snapper of Mexico, its red and gray flesh scored with bars burned black and brown, grilled in fennel and covered with sizzling brandy, duck with figs and white turnips mashed with butter, green salad and fresh bread with cheese and the dinner was done, more than two hours of light which subsumed seriousness, putting to one side the issues that had brought the company to table, compelling the Inspector to speak of food and the customs of his own household, reminiscences of his father carving turkey on Christmas day, his mother's gift for baking, Clemens adding to the amusement with tales of artists' banquets in New York and cafeteria camaraderie where free salt, sugar, mustard, ketchup supplied many a poor artist's table with pilfered condiments, even Maria contributing a tale of her own Tino slaughtering a pig for Easter and roasting it with wild sweet potatoes. The company, embraced by light and flowers, aromas and smells, was elevated beyond assaults and inquiries. It was only afterward while the women cleaned and put away and the men had gathered in the living room to have liqueurs and coffee that the solemnity of firelight returned them to each other, Stefan looking hard at the Inspector, the Inspector scrutinizing Clemens Rosenthal.

Clemens, stupefied with drink, was emboldened to inquire, "What brings you here, Inspector?" Inspector Mariposa had not expected his intervention, and did not reply. "Some spectacular crime compels you to descend, as I have descended from the civilized high ground of the capital to the swamps of Campeche?" The Inspector looked at Stefan Mauger, puzzlement straining his face, for he could not imagine that Stefan Mauger had told Clemens Rosenthal, but then he had no certainty how close their friendship might be or indeed, whether Clemens Rosenthal might not be a functionary of the consortium of thieves.

"My friend Clemens is oblique. He's always oblique when he's had too much to drink. His speech expands like beaten egg whites—fluff and full of air. He's asking, Inspector, if you are here looking for a thief?"

"Ah, so that's it." The Inspector acknowledged Stefan's direct translation. "Actually, yes, Señor Rosenthal. I am looking for a thief, but more than the thief I am anxious about the theft."

"And what is stolen that makes it more valuable than the thief?"

"A brilliant assembly of ancient Mayan and Aztec artifacts."

"You care about such things? Or is it, how shall I say, merely your job?"

The Inspector smiled and withdrew from his pocket a cigar that he rolled between his fingers before he bit its end and lit it. "Your friend, Señor Mauger, is more direct and rude than even we contemplated."

"Rude? You find me rude?" Clemens exclaimed, annoyed; he disliked his rough manners but found over the years that he had no time or disposition to refine them, contenting himself with defending them when they were criticized.

"It's not a criticism, Clemens. Believe me. The Inspector and I had a brief conversation about manners before we came to table. We agreed that we would be unmannerly if it seemed justified. I think it wholly justified. You're not being rude, old friend. Only directness, indifference to the style of time and its slow dance, is what we're after."

"A remarkable man, this Inspector."

"Very much so. I am remarkable, despite my small height and slight build. Remarkable. That means, doesn't it, someone to be noticed and observed. Yes. Yes. Well, to the point of your question. It was my vocation—the hunt for these ancient artifacts—before it became my work. Inspectors of police, Señor Rosenthal, are not only interested in crime. Far from it. The more refined our education, the more cultivated our tastes, the better inspectors we become. But as it happens, more than all this, I began my adult life as an archaeologist. I was trained, so to speak, in sculpture. My own, of course. That is, from my Indian culture. I come from the Toltecs, as I told Señor Mauger earlier, but I did not tell him that I came to the police because of archaeology." Having won their attention with his prologue, the Inspector seized upon their interest and his personal story emerged—the peculating Senator, the denunciation, the trial, the press notoriety, the interview with Colonel Vidal. "And so, my friends, it is no surprise that I should love sculpture. It is my single passion. No wife. No mistress. No sport. No hobbies. Only the remains of my ancestors."

"And these ancestral *memento mori*, do you gather them the way others preserve their recollections of the dead: trunks of clothing, books with pressed flowers, photographs, locks of hair, and fingernail parings? Do you collect your past as well as ferret out its thieves?" The Inspector was uncomfortable; he began to fidget, first pulling at his collar and then relighting his cigar, drawing deeply and exhaling a series of circles into the air, smiling at them sheepishly as if to draw the attention of his interlocutors from the implication of the question to the single wonderful trick he had often practiced to master. Clemens Rosenthal observed the circles rising to the turret but ignored them. For the time his pain was quiet; he was relieved, the dinner was digested, even though he had only nibbled it, the wine was competing with his pain-killers and he felt almost giddy, his head roamed free, a kind of wildness invading his temples, which thumped like drums; he felt dangerously in control.

"Modestly, very modestly. My little gathering of objects are, as you say, reminiscences of the dead, but you see, Señor Rosenthal, nothing of that past is really dead to me. It is as alive as I preserve it, as it obliges me through its own insinuations to make appeal to its universe, to be compelled by its own claims to search out those who trample it, who despise it, and at the last to defend its territory against them."

"Like me," Stefan Mauger said quietly, but neither heard

him, for Clemens Rosenthal had lifted himself to a grand rhetoric.

"You don't await the great Quetzalcoatl? You aren't his devotee surely, like misguided Moctezuma?"

"And Quetzalcoatl? Is he such a worthless god, really? Look, my friend, you two gentlemen, Christians by birth" (Clemens snorted but did not correct him), "are worshipers of a divinity no less strange to my ancestors than Quetzalcoatl is to yours. We clothed our divinities with permutating nature, their bodies moulting with layers of the natural world, working miracles of transformation from serpent to bird to fish to man and through the cycles of time, repeating the investiture and disrobing endless times. Is there a difference between our vision of the redeeming god and yours which comes out of sand dunes, stubby mountains, buoyant salt lakes, bringing wine from water, striding over waves (like Quetzalcoatl, after all), reviving the dead. My friends, it's what you need that answers credo to the mysteries. Mine, my mystery is the old imperial mastery—vast architecture, golden cities, floating gardens, royalties and armies, priestly intellectuals, sculptors of the vision. I gather their emblems the way your believers keep medallions, religious pictures, bibles and prayer books."

"And you keep fakes?" Clemens renewed.

"I don't understand."

"It doesn't matter to the Christian believer, I should think, if he prays from a cheap prayer book or tells his rosary with coarse olive beads. Quality doesn't matter. Presumably only intention. Is it the same with you and your gods, Inspector?"

"It can't be the same with me, you know perfectly well. Nothing of the past is unreal. If it's past, it's real."

"And for precisely that reason," Clemens perorated, "a dead belief. If your world had endured you'd find your religion mass-produced like everything else. Fortunately for you, it's a dead belief and your ancient artisans were master craftsmen. Today, they'd be coarse carvers hard-pressed to keep up with orders for the spring sacrifices. It's all beside the point, Inspector. Don't you see that you've blunted my question? I asked if you collected. I asked if you gathered your emblems like a collector. Selectively? Carefully? Choosing the finest and the best?" The Inspector nodded, listening closely. "If so, you aren't insensible to the fact that in our world—unlike that ancient time of yours—the best is also the rare and the expensive. You must have (certainly you must have!) looked about your shelves from time to time and totaled up the value of your emblems, consoling yourself by reckoning money; delighting yourself smugly that prices were rising; that this or that god was bought for a few pesos and is now worth thousands. Yes! Surely! You're acquisitive like everyone else."

"You think, sir, that I buy cheap to sell dear. I'm not permitted to do that," the Inspector answered firmly.

"But you would if you could get away with it. No?"

"No! Absolutely no. I wouldn't," the Inspector contended vigorously, his voice trembling with anger. "Everything I own—my study collection—is willed to the National Museum. Even if I had heirs, they would get nothing of my collection."

"Only for truth and scholarship, eh, Inspector? And then, for truth and scholarship, you manage, don't you?—you must, no?—to get a little piece here and there, a bribe now and then, which encourages you to be lenient?"

Inspector Mariposa did not reply. It had caught like a fishhook. His mouth suddenly dry, he gurgled hoarsely: "It's true. It's true. I will admit something to you I've hardly admitted to myself. My collection is gathered from bits and pieces that I bought as a poor archaeologist, but it has grown immensely over the years from other sources—an object here and there, as you said, retained as my percentage from recovered thefts." Inspector Mariposa looked about the room, his eyes peering through the shadows at the congerie of objects that he had numbered in the daylight, coveting each surface, working that unconscious selection of form which countless times before had yielded one or another treasure to his hoardings; but in the nighttime gloom in the company of his accuser he could not see—the Xipe had withdrawn and Tlac was invisible—through the wall of blackness which his ancient divinities had thrown up to guard themselves from his depredations. The Inspector cried desperately, "It's legal. It's legal what I do," but then his voice collapsed and the small breath of guilt eased him to confession, "but, but, it's true, it's all corrupt. Disgusting, isn't it?" he appealed.

"Caught you, Inspector. How delicious! Caught you. The Inspector of Police no less. Caught you." Clemens roared, his powerful voice booming the confession.

The Inspector gulped and raised his hands against the tumultuous Clemens. "I never really believed them, my old gods, my little gods. I've dishonored them, picked them like spoils. How disgusting." The Inspector rubbed his eyes with disbelief, his head spinning with confusion. "It's all reversed, my friends. All reversed. I don't understand why I've admitted this."

"You don't need to understand. It's done. You've made your confession and taken a new vow. 'Never covet the old gods.' That's the way the commandment reads now." Clemens renewed his laughter, clapping his sides delightedly and then, suddenly, jumping up from the chair. The laughter assaulted the room, its bellicosity striking the Inspector with a force that caused him to redden once more and drop his head with embarrassment. Stefan, at first horrified by his friend's pleasure in the Inspector's humiliation, was about to interrupt when he realized that the laughter had changed from straining contempt to a cry. The laughter covered a shattering pain that finally propelled Clemens upward, like a fish breaking the surface of the water; Clemens gasped against the laughter for air, his hands tugging ineffectually at his belt. Exhausted, he crumbled at the last, to the floor, clutching his stomach and crying to the others, "Help me. Help me, please!"

By the time Alicia and Maria appeared from the kitchen, Stefan and the Inspector had lifted up the agonized Clemens and with the women's help carried him to his room, where they laid him on the bed and Alicia administered the first injection of morphine. After a time, Clemens's body relaxed and he fell into a long sleep. Maria and Alicia stayed by his bedside and Stefan and the Inspector returned to the living room.

"Your remarkable friend is dying," the Inspector resumed, his hand reaching out to touch Stefan's arm with uncommon tenderness.

"I know it. Within the week," Stefan acknowledged sadly. "The dead and dying are really in pursuit of us, aren't they, Inspector?"

"Me? Who are mine?" the Inspector asked with resignation. He knew that something had changed. Perhaps Stefan Mauger was right. The Inspector wished at least to know.

"The gods were alive to you, my friend, as long as you kept them alive. That was the old religion. You fed them and they nourished you—*your* rage, *your* anger. You're a Mexican with a betrayed past. But you blame me for the betrayal. (What you call my thefts.) You blame foreigners, *gringos*, Spaniards. You're not very original in that. Isn't it about time you blamed yourself? How do you keep alive a shriveled vision? Of course you have your beautiful tales and glorious ruins and magisterial sculpture—but it isn't enough for a life. Your landscape sweats the past. But the present sinks roots into a swamp. How do you expect your native imagination to thrive in a soil turned on shards and human offal? It's too ridiculous."

"Rage against rage, Stefan Mauger. Yours against mine. My myths against yours. Pointless. Look where it has brought us. I swindle my past and you, yes, *you*, Stefan Mauger, steal your own."

"It's a draw then?" Stefan importuned, observing the Inspector cautiously, for he still felt himself, even if tenuously, in control.

"Not a draw. Never a draw. We both fall. Unequally, but we both fall."

His curiosity aroused, Stefan grunted acknowledgment but waited for more. There was something that began to move inside him, a flutter of anxiety, as though a covey of birds had been set free to fly about his chest. He began to feel weak and put his hand against the cool adobe wall to steady his knees. "Yes, Stefan Mauger, from different heights, from different positions, but we both fall." Stefan wanted to interrupt, to turn his speech aside, but the Inspector anticipated him, pressing back the interjection with an upturned palm. "Let me go on, my friend. And, yes (forgive me, Stefan Mauger), but I insist we are friends. Not ordinary friends. We are joined by no affinity of history or nature and certainly not by past. Differently joined, but no less inexorably. The obsession is our common cord. We can never be separated. All we can do—all that is left for us to do—is to live within its constraint and its promise. I can no more renounce mine (and take a wife and raise children and tend a vegetable garden behind my house in Tepotzlan) than you can deny your passion to create form. My friend, we are linked inexorably. We have found each other at the time of our renewal. Shedding skins and acquiring new ones. Your friend, your remarkable friend, Señor Rosenthal, has done us the greatest generosity. He is dying, but he makes way for our life. Preparing its new foundation, I should think. I? I have betrayed my past. You are right. I see it clearly now. When I was young, before I came to the Special Branch, did you know that I wrote eight archaeological essays—technical reports, careful, detailed, cross-referenced, illustrated with drawings and field photographs? Some of my essays were published. They were thought excellent. Others were delivered at conferences and put on file in the Institute's library. I was a young scholar, full with my obsession. But when I became an unemployed young scholar, my apprenticeship over and my future bleak, despair settled down upon me. It was at that time that I began to covet. Later, when I could afford to acquire, to accumulate, to barter my services for a percentage of the recovery, I had forsaken scholarship. During these past years my library has grown immensely. I have more than a thousand volumes on the arts and culture of ancient Mexico. But all I look at are the photographs. All I do is compare mine and theirs; what's mine and what belongs to others. Envy and avarice. I disgust myself, Stefan Mauger. You will understand then why I thank your Señor Rosenthal for pursuing me."

Stefan had listened carefully. He was not yet certain. It could have been another clever ruse of inculpation, a stratagem to snare him into the *noblesse oblige* of confession, obliging him to transcend the meager Inspector with a more grand and eloquent declaration of conscience. He was not yet persuaded. He temporized, however, for there was a sad and tarnished ring of truth in what the Inspector had said. A minor crime, a terribly minor crime, and yet the Inspector had been near tears in his admission and was now positively flushed with the cleansing of his new vows. Stefan continued to hold back, although he knew their confrontation was no longer the unmasking of thieves and the catching of criminals. In the afternoon it had passed beyond the contest of lies, feints, and dissimulations. The Inspector had met the artist and, as he acknowledged, obsessions had coalesced. Quite a different matter. The Inspector repeated again, more slowly than before, saying the words that he might hear them, "Yes, I do thank your Señor Rosenthal with all my heart for pursuing me." Inspector Mariposa rubbed his eyes, the knuckles of his hand grinding about his sockets, removing one vision, pressing forth the blue stars of another. He no longer seemed the formidable Inspector of the Special Branch.

"Not you alone, Inspector," Stefan began tentatively.

"What?"

"It was not for you alone that my Clemens spoke. I had told him why you had come. He roared at me with no less contempt than he directed at you. Dying men are indiscriminate. No time left to be moderate. The idea that I might steal was as grotesque as the notion of your betrayals. He savaged us both, but we deserved it, don't you think? I'm as efficient as you at corrupting my world and although I can imagine the world I would make, I've lost the conviction along the way. More than conviction, the energy. One becomes tired, you know. But there has to be a balance. In the north they restore equities by fire. In ours, Jonah to the sea. Something? A kind of ransom to be paid. Something?"

Stefan Mauger walked about the room, his arms cutting the air, words like a tide; the associations, most of the associations upon which he drew, were lost upon the Inspector who watched him from the fireplace, his back to the warmth, invested now with his own sadness.

"Something? There has to be something, Inspector." He

came to rest before the Jaina maiden. He looked at her, his lips parted, his eyes narrowing to examine her own, reddish like almonds, their clay indifference muted in the firelight. They told him nothing. It was then that Stefan remembered among the assembly of women that crowded the colonial table from which the Inspector had earlier plucked the Olmec figurine, a small carving, affixed by thin metal dowels to a stone base. He had placed it there some hours earlier when he returned from the studio after the Inspector's first visit. Stefan had received the fossil eye from the Inspector's hands and after the thrust and parry of their first encounter had determined that when the moment came, the moment that deserved his triumph, he would—as a parting gesture—give the Inspector his trophy, the only trophy he might garner for his treasury, a modern sculpture, the only modern sculpture in the Inspector's collection.

It was different now. The moment had come, but it was a different moment from the one he had fantasied, the right moment, but no longer a moment of triumph. "Here, Inspector," Stefan said softly. "You wanted this. Please take it. It's yours now. Something for the sea." Stefan Mauger laid gently upon the Inspector's hands the fossil carving of the human eye. The Inspector grasped the piece, his fingers pinching its rim, the sightless eye unobscured. He lifted it up and a smile of distracted pleasure appeared on his lips, a smile without cynicism or suspicion. He looked at the eye intently, observing its uncanny simplicity and grace, its deep-etched clarity, its smooth retina, barely indented iris and pupil dot, floating upon the sandstone as though millennia ago a dogmatic devotee of Horus had carved an essential eye for the god's celebration, knowing all the while, however, that its sculptor stood before him watching the carving rise in his hands.

The hand of the Inspector raised the fossil eye like an

icon, raised it slowly, in slow ascents raised it before the upturned face of Stefan Mauger, higher still until he could no longer see it clearly in the shadows of the room. Finally, at the last, the smile of recognition still upon his face, the Inspector hesitated for an instant and then brought his hand down forcefully. The carving shattered upon the floor, little remaining of the original eye but slivers of soft stone.

As the Inspector's hand had risen, Stefan Mauger had traveled with his fossil eye, bidding it farewell. He saw the crash before he heard it and shuddered before the eye splintered. Stefan turned away, his shoulders sagging with exhaustion and grief. It is not certain whether he wept, but he began to speak after some minutes of choked silence in that wet speech that follows the torrents of remorse: "Inspector. My friend, Inspector. Break more. All of them. There's a whole storehouse for breaking. Everything. This whole room of your past and my own. Leave only the Jaina. Only her. Let her await the return of her companions. They will all come home. I swear it to you. I have no further need of them. Only the sculpture garden. That's all I need now. Only the sculpture garden."

The fire danced. It caught another log and flashed upward. Stefan became quiet. He blew his nose. The Inspector said nothing more. There was nothing that needed to be said. After some time in silence, Stefan stood up, smiled with gratitude, and put his arm around the Inspector and led him out into the night. Before he left the room he drew from the fire a branch of wood, an ancient arm that burned brightly and without effort, and took it with him as a torch to light their way. The Inspector believed that he was leading him to the studio, but Stefan Mauger determined to conduct Inspector Mariposa through the field he had passed through at dawn. By the time they had come to the other side, near the jungle beyond the studio, the high grass was alight in flames.